Olivier Bernard

Crossing Lines
Gay Love in the Shadows of War

Olivier Bernard

Crossing Lines

Gay Love in the Shadows of War

Historical Romance and War Fiction

Bibliografische Information der Deutschen Nationalbibliothek: Die Deutsche Nationalbibliothek verzeichnet diese Publikation in der Deutschen Nationalbibliografie; detaillierte bibliografische Daten sind im Internet über http://dnb.dnb.de abrufbar.

Verlag: BoD · Books on Demand GmbH,
In de Tarpen 42, 22848 Norderstedt

Druck: Libri Plureos GmbH, Friedensallee 273, 22763 Hamburg

ISBN: 978-3-7693-1345-1

ONE
« THEY ARE HERE ...»

Paul De Brion had been waiting all morning for his turn to be interrogated, sitting in a waiting-room somewhere in Paris. When he had gotten there, he had been with many other Frenchmen that had been arrested, just like him, because they didn't have their papers with them when checked by German soldiers. Paul had not known about that new German regulation that required everyone to carry his ID with him at all time. Hell, how could he have known: The Germans had got into Paris just the day before, and since then, he had not left his home except for this morning ... He had not listened to the radio either. Now, he wished he had!

Now Paul was sitting all alone in the waiting-room: One by one, the others had gone to another room, where they had been interrogated, Paul figured out. He had not seen any of them since and so now, he was nervously waiting for his turn. A door suddenly oopened, and a German officer politely said to Paul: „Please young man, do come in. Have a seat." – Paul entered the room. It was not a very large room. There was a table right in front of him where two German officers were sitting. To his left, he saw a secretary sitting at a small table with a type-writer in front of her. Paul became very nervous seeing all that: He had heard so many bad stories about the Germans, he was just sure his life would soon be coming to a very abrupt end.

Paul looked at the two officers sitting at the table. The elder of the two showed him a chair and said: „Please, please, do sit down. Don't be so agitated ... Do you understand what I say to you?" – Since the officer had shown him a chair, Paul had guessed he was requested to sit down ... but he wasn't sure. The officer had spoken to him in German, and Paul didn't understand a single word in that language. And so, he didn't move and kept staring at the officer, not wanting to do anything wrong ...

That's when the youngest officer asked him: „Tu n'as rien compris de ce qu'il t'a dit, n'est-ce pas?" (you didn't understand a word of what he said to you, did you?) – „Non" – „That's what I thought," the young officer said. His French was excellent, except for the light touch of his German accent ... The young officer was kindly smiling at Paul now ... – „Please, sit down," he said. „I'm a translator, and I will translate everything for you. You don't have to be afraid. Please, do sit ...“

Paul sat while the young officer explained something to the other officer. Again, Paul didn't understand a word of what they were saying, but it didn't seem menacing though. Paul tought the young officer had a very pleasant tone of voice. That surprised him a bit since he had always thought Germans were always barking at one another. But then again, what did he really knew about Germans? Not much, except for the stories and the propaganda he had heard about them, which of course were not favourable, to say the least ...

He was lost into his thoughts when he heard the young officer say to him: „We have not been properly introduced yet ... Please, do excuse us ... I'm Unterfeldwebel Whilhelm von Rundstedt. The officer next to me is Oberstleutnant Heinz Koch. He's my superior ...“ – Hearing his name, the older officer just kindly nodded to Paul ... Seeing the very puzzled look on Paul's face, the young officer grinned as he said: „I mean, I'm a Staff Sergeant ... and my superior officer here is a Lieutenant-colonel. I assure you he's a kind man although he doesn't speak French. No need for you to be afraid of him ... Now, he's going to ask you a few questions, and I will translate them for you to answer. Are you okay?" – „Oui, merci.“

Paul kept looking at the young officer as he was talking to him. Certainly, this guy was not much older than he was. Perhaps 20 or 21 ... Although the young officer was sitting beind the table, Paul could guess he was about 1.80 m tall. He had golden blond hair, and perfect blue eyes. When smiling, the young officer showed perfect bright white teeth. Since he was not wearing his service dress tunic due to the heat in the room, Paul could see the young officer had well defined muscles under his damped light beige army shirt. Indeed, this was a very good-looking guy, Paul thought.

Then the young officer said to him: „Are you ready?" – „Yes ...“ – The golden blond officer turned to his superior and nodded to him, letting him know he could start questionning the young man sitting in front of them. As the questions were asked in German, they were translated by the young officer for Paul to answer them, and then his answers were translated to German for the older officer and the secretary to understand them ... This long process kept going for a while. Paul could see his answers were typed down on a form by the secretary, and that the older officer was taking notes:

„Name?" – „De Brion" – „Vorname?" – „Paul" – „Geburtsdatum?" – „I was born on August 15, 1921 ..." – „Größe?" – „I'm 1.80 meter tall ..." – „Augenfarbe?" Paul didn't know exactly how to describe the colour of his eyes ... He looked at the young officer for some help. The young officer said to him: „Hmm ... I'd say you have emerald green eyes ..." – „Yes ... that's it ... emerald green eyes ... thank you," Paul said. The older officer looked at Paul with a grin on his face and asked the next question: „Haarfarbe?" Again, Paul looked to the young officer for the correct answer, which came quickly: „I would answer „dirty blond" if I were you ..." – „Yes, yes," Paul said, smiling ... „Dirty blond". „Wohnort?" – „I live at 120, Avenue Foch, 16e arrondissement, Paris, France". „What's an „arrondissement," the young officer asked Paul, looking a bit puzzled by that unknown expression ... – „ ... Well ... it's ... you know ... a Ward ... I live in the 16th Ward, here in Paris," Paul explained, a bit surprised by such a question ... It was so obvious to him ... – „Oh, I see ... it's just I had never heard that expression before and didn't know how to translate it ... sorry about that," the young officer said with a twinkle in his eye. „I guess I'll get used to it after a while ..." – „I guess so ...," Paul said lightly blushing. The young officer translated Paul's address to his superior, who then asked: „Beruf?" – „I'm a student ..." Setting aside his papers, the older officer turned to his subordinate and got into a conversation with him. Of course Paul didn't understand a word of it. Then, the young officer said to him: „How come you didn't have your papers with you then you got checked?" – „I didn't know I had to carry them with me all the time. I had not heard about that directive until I got arrested ..." – „Didn't you listen to the radio?" – „No. Sorry ... I guess I was too absorbed by other urgent matters ..." – „What was so urgent you didn't have time to listen to the radio?" the young officer asked. „You were probably the only one not listenning to the radio ... you know ... with us marching into Paris ..." – „Oh, yeah ... but you see ... my grandmother is sick at the

13

moment, and I had to visit her at the hospital. In fact, that's were I was going when I was arrested ..."

„Do you have your ID at home?" – „Sure," Paul answered. – „We need to have the identification number on your papers. Could you call home and get it for us?" – „I can call ... If the phone works ... but I'll get no answer. There's no one at home ... They have all fled a few days ago when we heard the German army was going to ... invade the city ... you know ..." – „How come you haven't fled with the rest of your family?" – „ ... Oh, I was supposed to ... believe me ... That was the subject of a much debated discussion with my father ... but in the end, it was obvious one of us had to stay in Paris with my grandmother ... since she was too sick to travel ... My sister and my brother being much younger than me, we couldn't leave them behind ... So I volunteered to stay. My Mumand Dad didn't like the idea at all but ... you know ... what choice did we have: It was that, or leave my grandmother all alone in Paris ... So here I am ..." The young officer opened his mouth as to say something, but then closed it and said nothing. He knew Paris was almost empty of its population ... it was as if most people had fled in fear of the German invasion ... the story Paul was telling made perfect sense to him ... He turned to his superior officer and explained everything Paul had said to him. Then he stopped talking. A long moment of silence followed. It looked like the young officer was lost in his thoughts, Paul thought ... What would they do with him? What would they do to him?

Again, the young officer turned to his superior and both of them got into a new conversation. The fact Paul was not able to understand what they were saying made him angry: Were they planning his death with him not knowing anything about it, stupidly sitting on a stupid chair in that stupid office ... If those Germans were going to stay in Paris for a while, though that seemed very unlikely to him, he would have to learn how to speak German, Paul decided. Unless they just killed him ... then there would be no need for that, would there? As stupid as it may be, Paul grinned at that thought ... He looked at the two German officers. They were still calmly talking ... What the hell were they saying?

„(Sir, may I speak my mind ...)", the young officer said to his superior ... „(Yes Wilhelm, please, feel free to do so ...)" – „(...Well, Sir ... What we have here is a very frightened kid ... I don't think he's a spy ...)" – „(We don't know about that for sure Wilhelm, do we?)" – „(Sir ... he's an

14

eighteen year old kid ... does he look like a spy to you ... just look at him ... and tell me ...)" The older officer looked at Paul and grinned ... „(I guess not, Wilhelm ... he doesn't seem very dangerous to me ... but nevertheless ... we've got to check his papers, don't we?)" – „(Yes, Sir. I think I have an idea, Sir ...)" – „(Oh, and what that might be?)"

„(Sir, we could call the hospital to check his story about his grandmother and if it's true, I could drive him to his home and check his papers there ... If they are in good order as he says, then I could let him go free ... Besides, he's the last one we have to interrogate today and as you know, in a few minutes, I'll be on leave up until next Thursday ... so that would give me a chance to discover Paris a bit ... If his papers are not in good order, we'll be right back before you know it ...)" – „(I don't know about that" the older officer answered pensively. Then he looked again at Paul and, after a few seconds, he said „Ask him where his grandmother has been admitted, then call there ... we'll see ...)" – „(Yes, Sir)"

Turning to Paul, the young officer asked him: „What's the name of the hospital where your grandmother is supposed to be?" Paul looked at him, not knowing why the young officer was asking him that question ... But he knew he had to give an answer ... „She's at the Hotel-Dieu Hospital ... it's on the Ile de la cité ... you know ... very near to the Notre-Dame Cathedral ..." – „I see ... and what's her name please?" – „Jeanne De Brion ..." – The young officer picked the phone he had on the table and waited for the operator to get on line ... „Oui ... Hello ..." he said „Oui ... passez-moi l'Hopital Hotel-Dieu, je vous prie ... Merci ..." Click, click, click „Hotel-Dieu Hospital, how can I help you?" came the answer at the other end of the line ... „Yes, Madame ... This is Unterfeldwebel Wilhelm von Rundstedt calling you from the German Kommandantur, here in Paris ..." – „ ..." – The young officer could sense his interlocutor was a bit stunned ... „Hello ... are you still there?" – „ ... Yes, Sir ...," answered a trembling voice „What can I do for you, Sir?" – „Yes ... I would like to know if you have a patient by the name of Jeanne De Brion in your hospital ..." – „Please Sir, wait for a moment so I can check ..." – „Yes ... I'm waiting ..." – „Sir ..." – „Yes ..." – „Yes, we do have a patient by that name. Would you like me to transfer your call to the section where she has been admitted?" – „Yes please, thank you for your help Madame ..." Click, click, click „Nurse Giroux speaking ... How can I help you?" – „Yes ..." The young officer explained to the nurse who he was and the reason

15

why he was calling. „Yes Sir ... we do have a patient by the name of De Brion ... she answered. The young officer had noticed that, contrary to the phone operator, the nurse had remained very calm ... – „Do you know her?" the nurse asked. – „No, not really ... but I'm with her grandson ..." – „Oh, young Monsieur Paul? We were expecting his visit ... is he alright?" asked the nurse. – „Yes, yes ... don't worry about him. He's going to visit his grandmother later today ..." – „ ... Well ... Tell him to come as soon as possible ... Madame De Brion is not well at all ... Her condition is worsening and ... quite frankly ... well ... I don't think she will be able to last very long ... if you see what I mean ..." – „Yes ... count on me Mademoiselle, I will tell Paul ... Thank you Mademoiselle ..." – „You're most welcome, Sir." Click.

The young officer did not even have time to hang up the phone when Paul was nervously asking him: „What is it you have to tell me?" Since the young officer had spoken in French with the nurse, Paul had been able to follow his part of the conversation ... – „ ...Oh, yes" answered the young officer „ ... your grandmother is really there ..." – „ ...I told you so ..." – „ ...Yes, and they are expecting your visit," the young officer calmly said. Then the young officer leaned to his superior and explained all he had learned from the nurse. Hearing the old lady was dying, the older officer said to the younger one: „(I'm sorry to hear that ... Does he know?)" – „(No, not yet ...)" – „(... Well ... since his story is true ... Do as you said Wilhelm ... Take a jeep and drive him to his home ... check his papers and if everything is in good order, let him go ... But until you have checked his papers, don't loose sight of him, you understand? Give me a call when you can, to let me know ...)" – „(Yes, Sir ... I understand he's under my responsibility ... Can I take my bag now, Sir?)" – „(... Your bag?)" – „(Yes, Sir ... Since I knew I was going on leave at the end of the day, I've packed some civilian clothes into my bag this morning ... you know ... to be ready to go ...)" – „(Oh, sure ... take it and go now Wilhelm, before I change my mind ...)"

The young officer explained everything to Paul, whom was simply dumbfounded by the sudden turn of events. He just couldn't believe it ... The young officer was brightly smiling at him now ... – „Shall we go now?" the young officer asked Paul. – „Oh, yes, yes" Paul answered as he rose from his chair. He turned to the older officer and warmly said to him: „Merci beaucoup Monsieur. Merci. Vous etes un type bien ..."

16

(Thanks a lot, Sir. Thanks. You're a good man ...) Guessing what Paul had just said to him, the German officer started smiling and said: „Wir sind keine Barbaren ..." – Paul looked at the young officer for the translation ... „ ...He said „We are not barbarians" – „ ...Oh ..." Paul said „I guess not ... I mean ..." – „See what you mean ..." the young officer said, smiling again ...

Looking at the young officer smiling at him, Paul couldn't refrain from thinking that that guy was indeed very good-looking ... and now that the young officer was standing behind the table ... he could see the German guy was taller than he had thought at first ... probably about 1.90 meters ...

Paul extended his hand to the older officer and said: „Encore une fois Monsieur: Merci" (Once again, Sir: Thanks) „Ja, Ja ..." the older officer said ... and they briefly shook hands. The young officer put his service dress tunic back on him ... took his officer's cap ... then his bag ... and, looking at his superior, he said to him: „(Don't worry, Sir, everything will be alright. I'll keep you informed ...)" – „(Yes ... and Wilhelm ... if his papers are in good order, why don't you give this poor lad a ride to the hospital ...)" – „(That's exactly what I was going to do, Sir ...)" – „(Fine. Have fun during your leave ... And never forget Wilhelm ... You're not in Berlin here ... Be very careful ...)" – „(Yes, Sir. I will ...)"

With that, both Paul and the young German officer left the room. They went to an underground parking where the young officer had to fill a form; they both got into a jeep, then drove out of the underground parking. For the first time, Paul realized where they had been: At Hotel Meurice, on rue de Rivoli. Right in front of them were the Tuileries garden and the Louvre Museum.

„Now you're going to have to tell me where to go, if we want to find that hospital ..." the young officer said to Paul. – „Um ..." Paul answered „Aren't we supposed to go to my house to get my papers?" – „No time for that now ... We'll see to that later. Let's go to the hospital first ..." And the the young officer explained everything to Paul, concerning his grandmother ... „I'm sorry Paul ..." and while saying that, the young officer placed a hand supportively on Paul's arm ... At that, Paul managed a small smile of gratitude. But tears stood in his eyes. – „Thanks Sir" Paul said ... – „Oh, please, call me Wilhelm ..." – „Can I call you „Will" instead ... that would be easier for me you know ... German names are a bit difficult for me to pronounce," said Paul, sensing the young officer was an easy-going guy. – „Sure ... so „Will" it shall be ..." – „Thanks." – „Now, tell me where to go, please ..." – „Oh, sure ... The hospital is not very far from here ..."

A few minutes later, they were parked in front of the Hotel-Dieu Hospital. Will knew no one would object to a German army jeep being parked right in front of the Hospital. Oh, no ... They got out of the jeep and ran into the Hospital. Looking at the door-keeper, Paul said to him: „Bonjour, I'm here to see my grandmother, Madame De Brion ..." The door-keeper just kept fearfully looking at the young German officer facing him ... Seeing the guy was scared as hell, Paul said: „Don't worry, I know where my grandmother is admitted ..." – „Oh ... then go ahead ..." the door-keeper said, too scared to say anything else ... At that, Will grinned at Paul, removed his officer's cap ad followed Paul into the hospital corridors. They rapidly got to where Paul's grandmother was admitted, and seeing nurse Giroux, Paul said to her: „Bonjour, garde, I hope we're not too late ..." – Nurse Giroux kindly smiled at Paul, then looked at the young German officer, not at all impressed by the fact she had an enemy officer right in front of her. She raised an eyebrow though, looking straight into Will's blue eyes ... Slightly bowing to her, Will very politely said: „Bonjour, Mademoiselle ... I'm Unterfeldwebel Wilhelm von Rundstedt ... We spoke over the phone earlier today ..." – „Yes ... I do remember" the nurse politely answered ... She then eyed the young German officer from head to foot and in the end, she had to admit to herself this young officer was very handsome, very polite and not at all threatening, as she would have expected a German officer to be. He had a very pleasant voice and was speaking French very well. Nurse Giroux was surprised and puzzled by that fact. She smiled at the officer, and told him: „You certainly understand we are not used to having a German officer in this hospital" ... Will gave her his most charming smile and replied: „Oh, yes, Mademoiselle, I do understand ... I assure you I would have preferred meeting you under more ... pleasant ...circumstances. But things being what they are ..." – „Yes ... but rest assured Sir I have no ill-feeling for you personally ... You're not personally responsable for the mess we're in now ..." the nurse said. Will nodded to her, letting her know he was perfectly aware of that. At this point Paul chose to make his presence known again ... „Sorry, Monsieur Paul" nurse Giroux said to him „ ... No, you are not too late ... but I'm sorry to tell you your grandmother is not well at all. The doctor saw her earlier today and ... well ... I'm very much afraid there is nothing we can do to save her now ... you know her condition ... and at her age ...“ – „I understand“ Paul answered to her „It was to be expected, I guess ... Could I see her now?“ – „Of course ... She's still conscious ... We gave her a strong pain killer to relieve her pain. She's resting now. So you can see her ... but please Monsieur Paul, do not alarm her with the ... recent news ...“ – „I won't, rest assured I won't ...“ – „Gentlemen please, follow me.“ Nurse Giroux lead them to the room where Paul's grandmother was and before entering the room, Will said to Paul: „ ... Better for me to stay outside ... you know ... with my uniform and all ...“ – „Thanks Will. I appreciate that,“ Paul replied. Again nurse Giroux gently smiled at Will. Obviously, she was growing very fond of him, and that made her feel a bit uncomfortable ... He was German, after all ... Nevertheless, she found it was very tactful of him to decide not to enter the room with Paul. With that in mind, she left.

Paul went to his grandmother's bed, put her hands into his and said to her: „Grandma ... it's me ... Paul ...“ She slowly opened her eyes and looked at Paul ... „Oh, you're here ... I was hopeless ... I thought you would never come ...“ – „How could you think such a thing Grandma. You know I would never leave you like that ...“ – „I know ...,“ she answered ... „I'm just an silly old lady ... How are you Paul? ... How is everything? ...“ – „I'm just fine Grandma ... everything is okay ...“ – „Are we still fighting them?“ – „I beg you pardon?“ – „You know ... the Germans ... have we been able to stop them and ride them back to where they came from, like we did last time?“ – Knowing perfectly well Will would be able to hear him outside the room, Paul nevertheless answered: „Oh, yes Grandma, they are no longer threatening Paris ... they have been stopped by General Weygand and now, he's driving them out of France. I've even heard ... but you know ... those are just gossips ...“ – “What, what ... tell me ...“ – „Well, I heard that when the news of his total defeat reached Hitler, he just killed himself ...“ – „Aaaaah ... How wonderful ... I hope it's true ...“ – Of course, outside the room, Will had heard everything ... and he was now grinning ... „Now Grandma you've got to get some rest ... You've become all agitated ... That's not good for you, you know ...,“ Paul said to her. – „Yes, you're right Paul ... I do need to rest. ... Paul?“ – „Yes, Grandma?“ – „I love you so much, Paul ... and I love all the rest of the

19

family ... Will you tell them, Paul?" – „Yes, Gradma, I will. But don't worry, soon you will be able to tell them yourself ..." At that, she smiled to Paul and slowly closed her eyes. She was peacefully resting now. Paul brought a chair to her bed and sat down, holding her hand, looking at her ... Then, he got lost in his thoughts. His grandmother had just told him she loved him. All along, deep in his heart, he knew his grandmother did love him. It's just that in the past, she never said it .... It runs in the family, Paul thought to himself: All of them always had problems expressing their feelings ... How come it's so hard to say „I love you" to the people you love? Do you have to be dying before telling some one you love him? That's stupid, Paul thought. He knew he was not much better at it than his Grandma but, having realized that, from now on, he would be working on that ... Paul looked again at his Grandma. She seemed to be resting very calmly. Thinking about her, Paul went back to his thoughts. Of course, he had known the old lady since the day he was born. They had never been very close to one another, though. She had always been kind of a „Grand lady", he thought. Very aristocratic. A bit distant. She kept to herself. She had always been a pillar to the family and had to keep the facade crackless ... She was playing her role. That was so silly, Paul thought. Would he have loved her less if she had showed her feelings to him? Not at all. Was he like her? If so, he would have to change that too. Life was too short to spend it playing roles ... Paul realized that for the first time since the last four or five days, he had time to relax, to think. Now, he had time to reflect over all the events he had been through recently.

Up until a day or two, his life had always been very easy. His family had money ... and so he had always been spoiled. Not that money was a problem now, or would be in the future. No. He had lots of money. His Dad had seen to that. No. It's just that up until recently, everything had been provided to him by others ... he never had to assume responsabilities ... he had been growing inside a golden cocoon. Nothing bad had ever happened to him in the past. He had always been very well protected ... As his thoughs wandered, Paul began to remember that, just five days ago, he had been sitting with friends at a cafe-terrasse on Champs Elysees Avenue, illegally drinking beers. That was fun! It was early summer. They were all laughing. To Paul and this friends, as to most people in Paris, war was a very distant threat. There was no danger at all, it seemed:

The Maginot Line was there to protect them and they all knew that line was so strong, the Germans could never cross it. Even his father had said so. Yeah. There was no threat at the time. Theatres were crowded ... as were the restaurants ... Everybody was having fun ... Then suddenly, everything had come to a halt. The German army was almost here, dangerously threatening Paris. Paul didn't know at the time the Germans had simply ignored the Maginot Line and had gone through Belgium instead, through deep woods, and that by doing so, they had successfully broken the Allieds' front. No, Paul didn't know that at the time, no more than he knew the meaning of the word „Blitzkrieg" ... With the Germans being so close to Paris, Prime Minister Reynaud as well as Monsieur Lebrun, the president of the Republic, had declared Paris „Ville ouverte", meaning the French capital would not be defended. How was that possible? Paul had then asked himself. He didn't know the answer to that and, for that matter, he didn't understand what was going on: The whole thing was too unbelievable. And what about the rest? Yeah. He remembered ...

Learning the whole government had fled Paris to try to find safety somewhere in the south of France, the rest of the population in Paris had suddenly decided to do the same and fled to the south. To Paul, Premier Reynaud and President Lebrun were just cowards and traitors. They should have stayed, and Paris should have been defended, he thought. Through their incompetence, they were responsible for the big mess France was in now, and instead of doing something about it, they had just fled like rats. Yeah, Paul thought, they were cowards. He just hoped that, someday, they would be held accountable for what they had done ... But to Paul, it was clear his father was not a coward, although he had also fled to the south, with the rest of the family. No. Paul's father was not a coward ... Being a Minister in the French Cabinet, he had had no choice but to leave Paris. He had not chosen to leave: He had been ordered to do so. Being part of the government, he had to go wherever the President had decided to go ...

Now Paul could remember the emptiness he had felt after everyone had gone. He could remember how he had felt last Thursday, June 13th, just two days ago, when he had gone through Place de la Concorde on his way to pay a visit to his Grandma at the hospital. He had felt miserable. Everything was so unreal. So aberrant. Everything was so quiet. He could remember that on Place de la Concorde he had seen no car ... no traffic ... Nothing. He had looked up Champs Elysees Avenue, and it was totally empty. Except for a few stranded dogs, he had seen no one. It was so strange. Oh, yes, he remembered now, he had seen a few men walking across Place de la Concorde, but they had not spoken to him. They were walking with emptiness in their eyes. He had not spoken to them either. Instead, he had crossed Place de la Concorde, then gone to the hospital. He had paid a visit to his Grandma and then, he had gone back home quickly ... That night, it had been hard to fall asleep ... Everything was too quiet in the house. For the first time in his life, he was all alone. His whole world was crumbling right before his eyes, and there was nothing he could do about it. What a way to loose your illusions, he had thought. Obviously, his golden childhood had come to an abrupt end! Sure, at eighteen, he was no longer a kid ... but nevertheless, all the recent events had come to him like a shock. He had not been prepared for that ... The moning after, he had woken up and had heard noises outside the house. Opening a window, he had heard something over there. Was it music? At the Arc de Triomphe? Nah. That was just not possible, was it? Wanting to find out what was going on, he had dressed and had decided to go see for himself.

He had walked his way to the Arc and then, he had seen it: THEY WERE HERE!!!! The Germans were here. He was stunned. He could remember all too well how he had felt ... what he had seen ... Yes, there was music alright ... the military kind. He didn't like it. He had seen a German army officer, riding on a splendid white horse, watching his victorious troops marching in front of him, down Champs Elysees Avenue. Looking at them, Paul had smiled to himself, seeing the Germans had not dared to march through the Arc. They were just going around it ... Now Paul could remember vividly the sound made by the German soldiers, goose-marching down Champs Elysees Avenue. It was awful. He hated that sound. He had seen enough! Walking back to his home, he remembered how everything had seemed so quiet on Avenue Foch ... Nevertheless, having seen what he had seen, he had decided he would not pay a visit to his Grandma that day. He had to admit to himself he was too frightened to go to the hospital, not knowing what was going on in the city ... Oh, he was not a coward ... No. It was prudence, he thought. He would wait a day or two before he would go out again, so things would have time to settle down a bit ... Yeah ... that's it, he had thought, let's wait a day or two ... But the day after, Saturday the 15th, he had felt too restless to stay home. He had to go to the hospital since the phone line was dead and he couldn't call nurse Giroux to inquire about his grandmother ... Yeah, he had to go. Besides, he wanted to see what was going on outside ... He wouldn't use his father's car though. He instinctively knew that wouldn't be a good idea. He would ride his bike instead. Now he could remember it was while riding his bike down the Champs Elysees Avenue he had been stopped by German soldiers at a check point. How could he ever forget about that? It had happened this very morning, but seemed to have happened so long ago ... He had not forgotten though!

The German soldiers were Feldgendarmen, but Paul had not known that at the time. Seeing he had not his ID with him, the soldiers had taken his bike away and put him into an army truck, where he had met with others. He had learned from them about the new decree from the Kommandantur, concerning the identification papers. All the others had been arrested for the same reason: Like him, they didn't have their papers with them. Later, they had been taken somewere, not very far though. But Paul didn't know then where they had been taken, since an awning had been drawn over the truck. Now the rest was history ...

That's when he had seen Will for the first time ... Ah, yeah, Will ... quite a guy, Paul was now thinking ... Very nice. Very friendly. Very handsome too. There was something special about that guy, Paul thought. He just didn't know what. Not yet.

Coming back to reality, Paul looked at his Grandma. She was peacefully resting. He decided he would leave her to rest for a while, and go back to Will, and have a chat with him ... Paul rose and quietly left the room to find Will. He found him right outside the room, sitting on a chair, peacefully dozing ... Paul took his time to look at him. Since Will was asleep, he could take all the time he wanted to look at the guy ... Indeed, Will was a very good-looking dude, Paul thought. Very handsome. Paul could see Will had broad shoulders. With his golden blond hair, he was just perfect. Will was quite a hunk, Paul thought. Women were probably chasing after him all the time ... Was he married? Paul looked at Will's fingers, but found no wedding-ring. Did he have a girlfriend? Paul would have to ask him ... But why the hell would he be asking such a question,

Paul suddenly thought. It was none of his business, was it? What the hell was he thinking about, Paul asked himself ... Why was he staring at Will like that? Yeah, the guy was nice and kind, but you know ... a guy is just a guy, and nothing else, no? What's wrong with me? Have I lost my mind? Paul asked himself.

Paul decided to brush away all those stupid thoughts and leaning to Will, slightly touching his shoulder to wake him up, Paul said: „Hey ... Look ... I'm running away now ..." – Will slowly opened his eyes to look at Paul, and with a smile on his face he then said: „Oh ... sure! I can see that ... running so fast I can't recapture you" he replied. – „Yeah, with that well toned body of yours, you would recapture me in no time at all ..." – Will burst out laughing at Paul's remark. Then, realizing where they were, he said: „Sorry about that". He stopped laughing and looked around to see if his burst of laughs had disturbed anyone. No. No problem with that. Everything was quiet. Looking back at Paul, he said: „Besides, pal, you're not my prisoner ... so why would I be running after you?" – „ ...Perhaps you don't consider me to be your prisoner, but that's what your superior officer thinks I am ..." – „Told you, Paul ... he's not a bad guy. Just doing his job, that's all. Heck ... he could have sent you to prison like the others, you know. Did he do that? No. He let me accompany you ... That should teach you something about him ..." – „I guess so ..." – „Anyway, how's your Grandma?" – „She's resting for now. I don't think she will last for very long though ..." – „I feel sorry for you, you know?" – „Don't. I saw it coming and had time to make my peace with the fact that she will soon die ..." – „Yeah ... I know what you mean ..." – „Think I will go back to her now, and see how she doing ..." – „Yeah" – So Paul went back to his Grandma and a few minutes later, came back to Will, asking him: „Could you go fetch nurse Giroux ... please? I think she's not well at all ..." – „Sure" – Paul went back into the room, and kept looking at the old lady ... He couldn't hear her breathing ... In a second, Will came back with nurse Giroux. She quickly leaned over the old lady, trying to feel her pulse. She couldn't find it. She tried again. She found nothing. She opened one of the old lady's eye, looked into it, then closed it again. She tried again to find a pulse, but to no avail. She waited for a few seconds before saying anything, then she turned to where Paul and Will were standing and, with tears in her eye, she said to Paul: „I'm sorry, Monsieur Paul ..." – „Is she dead?" Paul asked her. – „Yes, she is, I'm

24

afraid." – Hearing that, Paul started to shake like a leaf. Tears were now running down his cheeks ... Seeing that, and without any hesitation, Will took Paul into his strong arms, holding him tightly: „I'm so sorry, Paul. I don't know what to say" he told him. Seeing Will was taking care of Paul, nurse Giroux quietly left the room, closing the door behind her. Keeping his embrace tight around Paul, Will said: „Let go Paul, let it all go ..." A torrent of tears came down Paul's face, his head resting on Will's chest. It kept going for a while, then it stopped. And so did the shaking. Suddenly, Paul felt very secure in Will's strong arms and his embrace felt very soothing. They stayed like that for a while, not moving. Not talking. Then, Paul moved his head to look at Will and, finding his blue eyes, he smiled at him. „I'm okay now ... Thanks, I needed that ..." – Hearing that, Will let go of Paul. Paul turned to Will to say: „I apologize Will. I lost control over myself ..." – „No need to apologize Paul. It's not every day we loose some one we love ..." – „Oh, it's not just that. That was just the drop that caused the bucket to overflow. I guess I've been through too much the last few days, and I couldn't take it anymore. I had to explode I guess. Thanks for being with me when that happened ..." – „I'm glad I'm here with you ..." – Paul kept silent for a few minutes. He was lost in his deep thoughts. Too many things had happened too fast. For a while, he kept staring at the wall in front of him. Then, turning to Will, he said: „What else is going to happen to me now ... I mean ... what worse could happen. Guess I've hit the bottom of the barrel, haven't I?" – „Well, look at it the other way around: You've successfully been through being interrogated by German officers, you've made it on time to see and talk to your Grandma before she died ... It's not so bad, you know ... Now, I do realize it's no fun for you guy, me being here ... but ..." – „No, no Will" Paul said, interrupting Will „I'm so gratful to you for you being here with me. Thanks a lot for your support. I don't know how I would have managed without you, the last hours," he said to Will, very sincerely. Will could sense that sincerity in Paul's voice. It reassured him.

„Now, I've got no idea what I'm going to do. Now it's true ... you know ... I'm all alone in Paris. As long as Grandma was here, I didn't feel I was all alone. But now that she's gone ..." – „Hey, Paul, you're not all alone ... remember, I'm here for you. I'll do anything I can to help you. As for the rest, well, I guess we'll have to figure that out later. Now Paul, let's leave this hospital, and go to your home. There is nothing left to do here, is there?" – „Yeah ... you mean ... go to my home so you can finally check my papers, huh?" Paul coldly said to Will. Will was hurt by Paul's remark. He thought the blond guy had realized by now he was trying to be his friend ... „No, Paul. I don't give a shit about your papers. I know you've said the truth this afternoon, believe me ..." There was sadness in Will's voice, Paul realized, and now he felt guilty for having said what he had just said to him. Putting his hands on Will's arms, Paul said to him: „Look at me, Will ... Oh, my God, I'm so sorry for what I've just said to you. That was totally unwarranted. It was rude. And it's certainly not what I think. Please forgive me. I swear I didn't want to hurt your feelings. I wonder if I'm not loosing my marbles, now ..." Will felt Paul's hands were shaking while holding his arms. At this very minute, he knew he had to protect the blond youth. Looking straight at Paul, he said: „I know, Paul, you didn't mean what you said. I believe you. With all what you've been through recently, I guess it's only normal if you snap someone's head off from time to time. If you want to use me as a punching-bag, it's fine with me. And no, you're not loosing your marbles. I've watched you, going through all what you've been going through today, and you're a much stronger guy than you think, Paul. In your shoes, I don't think I would have fared so well ..." – „Thanks, Will. And don't worry, I won't be using you as my punching-bag ... And I'm sure you would have fared as well as I did ..." – „You're wrong about that, Paul. I may be physically strong but dealing with emotions ... Well ... I'm not too good at it ..." – „We're going to have to work on that, aren't we? Paul said, with a grin on his face. „Would you help me ... I mean ... working on that?" Will asked Paul. – „Count on me. I'm becoming quite an expert in that field, you know. Now, what should I do about my Grandma? We can't leave her here, can we?" – „I don't know about that. I don't know what you usually do in France ... you know ... with funerals and all those things. Do you want to take time to think about it?" – „Yeah. That would be best. Let's tell nurse Giroux and then, let's get the hell out of here ..."

With that, Paul gave his Grandma a last look, then started walking out of the room with Will, not knowing yet he was walking away from his past, not knowing a new chapter in his life was beginning. They found nurse Giroux sitting at her desk and, as she saw Paul, she said to him: „I assure you of my heartfelt sympathy, Monsieur Paul" – „Thank you very much" the blond young man replied. „Now, you're going to have to inform your father: Have you heard from your father, Monsieur le Min ..." She stopped right there in the middle of her sentence. She was going to say „Monsieur le Ministre" ... since she knew very well Monsieur De Brion was a Minister in the French Cabinet, and an important one at that ... Although she had grown found of the young German officer standing in front of her, it didn't change the fact he was German ... and she didn't know if Will knew how important Paul's father was. In doubt, she found it was better to abstain from saying anything about it ... It was not her role to reveal those things to a German officer, however good-loking he may be ... „Outch" she said, looking at one of her fingers, creating a diversion doing so. „I think I've got a splinter driven under my nail" ... Both young men looked at her finger. „Never mind that ... I'll take care of that later. And as I was saying, did you get news from your father?" – „No, not yet" Paul replied „In fact, I don't even know were my Dad and the rest of my family are at the present time. All the phone lines have been cut off with the rest of France. I guess we will have to wait a while before things settle down a bit, and we can communicate again. I'm sure that as soon as he can, my Dad will contact me ..." – „Yes, but don't you worry about your family and your Dad: He's a very fine man, you know that, and he'll find his way around, if you see what I mean ..." – „Yes, I know. It could take a few days before I can tell you what we do about my Grandma's funeral though. Do you have a problem with that?" – „No problem at all. We have what's needed here to keep her as long as need be ..." the nurse replied. – „Thanks a lot nurse Giroux. Thanks for all you did for my Grandma and my family. We are forever indebted towards you for all of that ..." – „Think nothing of it". Turning to Will, she said to him: „Can I take it you will safely get Monsieur Paul to his home?" – „It's my duty to do so, Mademoiselle, and I will gladly fulfill it" Will replied with a sincere smile on his face. „Bonsoir, Mademoiselle et merci pour tout." (good night, Miss, and thanks for everything). – „Bonsoir ... que Dieu vous protège ... tous les deux ..." (good night ... and may God bless you ... both of you ...) the nurse replied. Both young man nodded at her, then they left. The door-keeper saluted them as they left, and they went to the jeep, still parked where they had left it ... Will smiled at that ... He started the engine, and the door-keeper was very happy to see them leave ...

„So, where is your home?" Will asked Paul. „I gave you the address this afternoon, don't you remember?" Paul replied, with a smile on his

27

face. – „Sure, I remember your address, it's on Avenue Foch ... problem is, I don't have the slightest idea where the hell Avenue Foch is ...“ Will said, laughing ... Hearing that, Paul burst with laughs ... „It's good to hear you laugh, you know“ said Will. Paul kindly looked at Will, then he said: „Yeah, I didn't have too many occasions to laugh today ... It feels good nevertheless. Now, go down the street here, then turn to your right on De la Cite street, then take the „Notre-Dame“ bridge ... From there, I'll tell you where to go ... but so you have a general idea of where we are going, let's just say we're going to the Arc de Triomphe“. „You're kidding me, aren't you?“ Will asked. „No, no ... that's exactly where we're going ... You see ... past the Arc de Triomphe, the Avenue there is no longer called the „Champs Elysees“ ... but it's called „Avenue Foch“ ... simple as that“ Paul replied smiling ... – „Hmm ...“ Will said ... – „Come on dude, I'm not kidding you ... don't you trust me now?“ Paul exclaimed. – „Well ... sure I trust you.“ After a moment, Will said „Well then ... let's go ...“ – „On our way, I'll have a few questions for you, mister“ Paul joyfully said to Will. – „And what might that be“ Will replied, flashing a big smile at Paul ... – „Just drive, I'll be asking the questions ... It's my turn to conduct the interrogation, Herr von Rundstedt ...“ – „At least, you haven't forgotten my name ...“ – „I haven't forgotten anything about you, young man ...“ Paul said. – „Oooo ... getting personal now, aren't we?“ – „Drive, you, silly ... I'll do the talking ...“ – Will shifted, and they got on their way to Paul's home, with Will broadly smiling ...

„First question“, Paul started ... „Yeah ... I'm waiting“, Will lightly said.

TWO
«ARE YOU GAY?»

Now, Will and Paul were driving through Paris on their way to Paul's home on Avenue Foch. The night had fallen a while ago, and the streets were very quiet, except for a few German patrols they had met on their way. As Paul was guiding Will through the streets, he asked him: „I've been with you since this morning, we've met many German officers, and not once have I seen you give the Nazi salute to one of them. How come?" Will looked at Paul with a grin on his face, and replied: „You know, Paul, there's a big difference between us, German soldiers in general, and those Nazi guys. Most of us in the Wehrmacht, I mean... in the German army are not Nazis. We are just soldiers, doing our job... Of course, some soldiers are Nazis too, but they form a minority within the Wehrmacht. I'm not a Nazi, for sure. Like many others in the army, I don't like to give the Nazi salute... But if someone gives it to me, I have no choice, I must answer the same way and give the salute..." „I see. It's a bit complicated, though..." – „Yeah, I know. I will have to give you a crash-course on that later. But for the moment, just remember that if you see a soldier wearing a black uniform, that means he's not in the Wehrmacht, but part of the Schutzstaffel..." – „What's that", Paul asked. „The SS, if you prefer. You see, SS soldiers are not part of the regular German army, as I am. They form a second army... totally independent from the Wehrmacht. They are totally self-reliant and are controlled by Himmler, not by the generals of the Wehrmacht High Command..." „...So, why are you telling me that?" „Because the guys in black uniforms are very dangerous, Paul. That's why I'm telling you that. Be very, very careful with those guys. Never ever trust them. Never run from them, be polite to them, but don't trust them. Those SS men are Nazis from head to toes..." „... I'll try to remember

29

that..." – „No, Paul. Don't just try. Make sure you never forget it. Have you ever heard about the Gestapo?" – „... Oh, shit, yeah, I've heard stories about it..." „... Well, the Gestapo is controlled by the SS... If you see what I mean... And if you want to make sure a guy is part of the SS, not only will he be wearing a black uniform, but look at is black army cap: You'll see a deathshead cap badge on it. That's the best proof you can get..." „Don't worry, Will. I'll stay away from them. I swear." Seeing he had made his point, Will's face came back to its normal appeasing state. „... Here, on your left" Paul suddenly said to Will. „...What?" – „Take that street on your left..." – „Oh, yes. Sorry. You said you had a few questions to ask me. What's next?" Paul smiled, hearing Will say that. „Well, the next question is easier... I think". „Go ahead..." – „How come you speak French so well?" „Well, you see, when I was a kid in Berlin, we had a French family as our next-door neighbour. They had a kid my age, and eventually we became good friends, and I learned how to speak French playing with him. Later, I took school lessons, though. Because of that, I was able to get a fun job during the Berlin Olympic Games, you know..." „Weren't you a bit young to get a job at the time?" „I was 16 at that time, and it wasn't really a job, you know. For the duration of the Games, a group of young guys from the Hitler Youth were assigned to each team as errand boys and general dogsbodies... We were known as the „White Guides". Anyway, I was assigned to the French team, since I was fluent in French..." „That must have been fun, wasn't it?" Paul asked. „Yeah. It was great. The French athletes were terrific." „... Now, to your right" Paul indicated to Will. „Drive all around the arc, keep to your right until I tell you where to turn..." „...Ja, Ja, mein Herr. At your command! Und Sieg Heil to you..."

Now, both of them went hysterical, laughing so hard they could have awaken the dead. While driving around the Arc de Triomphe, Will gave it a look... He had to agree it was very beautiful... so imposing. Many times in the past, he had seen pictures of it, but had never realized how big it really was. Now, he was seeing it with his own eyes. As if he understood what Will was thinking, Paul said to him: „Pretty impressive, huh?" – „Shit, didn't think it was so big. I'm flabbergasted. Really..." „Yeah. Now turn to your right, and drive down that Avenue. That's my Avenue... That's Avenue Foch, just as I told you..." „Lots of trees", huh? Will said. „Yeah. Now, go slowly. It's not very far from here. See, it's right

30

there, on your right. Hey, it's here, I said..." „Yeah, yeah, I heard. Don't think it would be a good idea to park a German army jeep right in front of your home, though. What do you think?" „Whatever..." – „Here. That's better" Will said. „Come on. Let me show you where I live" Paul answered.

They got off the jeep, and started walking to Paul's home. There were so many trees on the Avenue that Will thought nobody could see them walking. When they reached Paul's home, will rose his head to look at the building in front of them. It was not a house, it was like a palace. He was stunned.

„That's where you live?" Will asked. „Yeah. You like it?" – „Hell. Do I like it... It's huge, and it's beautiful..." – „Lets go inside" Paul replied, smiling.

They walked up the stairs to the building, and Paul unlocked the big doors. They got inside an entrance-hall. Paul openedanother set of big doors, and they entered into another room. Although it was dark, Will could sense that room was much bigger. Paul searched for a switch and then, suddenly, the room was flooded by the lights of a very large chandelier, hanging way up from the ceiling.

„Wow! Is your father the King of France?" Will asked... „No way" Paul replied. „And you know, all the other buildings around here are like that. Nothing so special..." – „I tell you, your father must be a rich man, to live in a place like that. It's beautiful..." – „Thanks"

Paul examined Will while Will was looking around the great hall. Will was like a child unwrapping his Christmas gifts. He was so beautiful, and yet so strong. He wasn't wearing his army cap so Paul could see his golden blond hair shining under the chandelier's lights. What a gorgeous young hunk. He was so handsome...

„What?" Will asked Paul, with a smile on his face. „What do you mean „What"?" – „You're staring at me. What's wrong with me?" „Oh, nothing at all, I swear. You're just fine. How old are you, Will?" – „I got twenty last March..." – „That's what I thought, you're older than I am" – „Much older, you know" Will said, grinning. „Oh, sure. I'll be nineteen next August, so I guess that makes you much, much older than me..." They both laughed at that, and then Paul said: „Come on. Lets go to the drawing-room and relax. Want a beer? „You have beer?" – „Yeah. My Dad didn't have time to lock the cellar before he left so I can have all I

31

want. And it's full of beer... lots of bottles of wine too..." – „I'll have a beer, sure" Will replied. „Be right back. The drawing-room is to your left. You'll find the switch on the wall, to your right..."

While Paul was fetching the beers, Will entered the drawing-room, found the switch and put on the lights. The room was dimly lit, but Will could see it was a very large room. A beautiful room. On the opposite side of the room was a large fireplace and lots of furniture. Everything had been covered with sheets, to protect it against the dust. He sat on a sofa, not removing the sheet from it. Then he heard Paul, coming back...

„Hey, why didn't you remove the sheet?" Paul asked... „I just didn't dare, you know..." – „Well, you should have. Give me a hand with it, will you?" – „Wow. Everything is so beautiful in here..." Will stated. „Feel right at home. Since my family left, I haven't been in this room... you know... I don't like to be here all alone by myself. But with you here, it's okay." They sat on the sofa, and Paul gave Will his beer. „Cheers", Will said. „Yeah. Cheers" „Ah, that feels food, doesn't it?", Will asked. „God! I needed that..." „Eh, is that a grand piano you've got there, under the sheet?", Will asked. „Yeah"... „Do you play?", Will asked Paul... „Nah. My Mumdoes, though. She plays very well. Do you play?" „Yes. I learned to play when I was younger... Haven't played for a while, though. You know... with the war... not too many occasions to play when you're in the army..." Will replied. „I guess not. Hope you'll play for me sometime. What kind of music do you like?" – „Oh, all kinds... you know... I also like to play classical music like, I don't know... Mozart, Bach, Liszt, Schubert..." „Oh, Schubert... that's one of my favorites... my mother loved to play Schubert... I would sit here for hours, listening to her play Schubert..." „That's funny... He's my favorite too. All those composers were Germans, you know..." „I know. And you seem to be very proud to be German also, aren't you Will?" „I am. As much as you, being a Frenchman. Most of us in Germany are not Nazis, I told you... I've already told you I'm not a Nazi... never been a member of the Nazi party, and never will. I didn't choose to be part of the Hitler Youth: It was compulsory for kids my age... and I didn't choose to enter the army either. That too, was compulsory..." „I know that... I believe you, when you say you're not a Nazi. But you know... It doesn't change the fact we are almost defeated now... From what I've seen, it won't take long before we beg for mercy. And England will follow suit not long afterward, I guess. Whether we like it or not, you now have the most powerful army in the world, and your leader is none other than Hitler. The war will soon be over Will, and that's scares me... What's going to happen tu us after the war, Will?" „I don't know, Paul... but we're not there yet. The war is far from being over... England is not defeated yet..." – „Well, I guess they must be as demoralized as we are here, in France..." „That's possible... maybe... I don't know about that. What I know for sure, it's that the war is just not over yet. So in the meantime, as I've already said to you Paul, be very careful... stay away from the SS... keep your feelings to yourself. If you ever get arrested again, I may not be able to help you then..." „And why would you try to help me... We don't know each other really that well, you know..." „Yeah, you're right. We don't know each other that well, yet. But I sure would like to know you better... All I know is that I like you, and I wouldn't like to see you into troubles..."

Saying that, Will blushed, which was quite apparent due to his fair-complexion. Paul noticed it and found Will to be... well... kind of cute. Paul had never even conceived he could be attracted to another man before. Until that day that was. Since the first moment he had seen Will, he had known there was something special about that guy. In a way, he felt attracted to him. Now, having heard what Will had just said to him, he was feeling something in his stomach... a feeling he had never felt before. He didn't know what it was, though. And he could not explain it either. All he knew was he had felt secure at the hospital, pressed into Will's strong arms. He would have stayed just like that for hours, if that had been possible. Suddenly, his deep thoughts were interrupted by Will, saying to him: „Besides Paul, whatever I said before, you and I are almost the same age and, you know, it's not easy being in the army. Sometimes, I feel home-sick. I miss my family. I have a few friends in my unit but, you see, I guess they would not do very much to help me save my skin, should I need help. The only one I could count on is Lutz... he's a good friend of mine. We live on the same street in Berlin, and I've known him since we were kids... Thanks God, he's in my unit..." „Is he here, in Paris?" Paul asked... „Yeah. He is." „I guess your lucky to have him here in Paris, with you. At least, you're not all alone here. All my friends fled Paris before you guys got into the capital. There is no one left..." And Paul continued: „As for my family, I don't even know where they are... so I know how you feel, being home-sick sometimes... to say the truth... I miss my family... a lot. At first, when they left, I thought being on my own in Paris would be fun... Besides I had to visit my Grandma at the hospital, and so I was not really all alone in Paris. But now she's dead. I don't even know what to do. Now I realize I'm all alone. I don't even know how to reach my father to let him know my Grandma has died, and..." Paul eyes were full of tears... „... Wait... Wait... Wait Paul for a second", Will interrupted, „First, you're not all alone. I told you... or at least that's what I tried to tell you: If you wish... we could be friends... I'm not too good with words... I told you that... and sometimes I just don't know how to express my feelings... you know... but I would really like to be friends with you. Now, perhaps I can try to locate your family through our services... and get in touch with him... first to let him know you're okay... and then to let him know about your Grandma..." „Would you do that for me?", Paul asked... „Well I can try...", Will answered. „But you will have to tell me more about your father... Where was he the last time you heard from him? You know... that kind of stuff so I can initiate some research... Where do you think we should be looking for him?"

„Yeah... that would help, wouldn't it?" Now, it was late at night; he was sitting with a German soldier next to him, right there in his own home, having to decide whether or not he could trust that guy. Although very attractive and good-looking that guy next to him may be, nevertheless, he was a German soldier. He was the avowed enemy! Could an avowed enemy be trusted. The first answer that came into Paul's mind was NO! But something was telling Paul he could trust Will. He had been very helpful up to now and had driven Paul directly to the hospital, instead of going first to Paul's home to check his ID. By doing so, Will had violated the direct orders given to him by a superior officer. And thanks to Will, Paul had been able to see his Grandma for a last time before she died... By doing what he had done, Will had shown Paul he trusted him... that was a good sign. Could Paul in turn trust Will? Paul got quite agitated doing all that thinking, and Will, sitting next to him, could only guess what his new friend was going through in his mind...

„Paul... Hey, Paul... are you still there?" Will asked... „Oh, sorry. I was just thinking... you know..." – „What were you thinking about that got you so agitated?" – „Well, Will... I don't know. So many things have happened in such a short period of time that I no longer know where I stand", Paul replied. „What do you mean, Paul?" „Listen Will: You have asked me to give you a lot of details... information concerning my father and my family... and... I just don't know if I can trust you with this information. You could be working for... say... the Gestapo for God's sake... and if so, I could get my father and the rest of my family into big troubles and dangers..."

Will got troubled by what Paul had just said to him. It had not occured to him that Paul could be frightened... Obviously Paul was scared to death! Will was now looking at Paul and deep in his heart he felt that he would do anything to help him. Never would he betray Paul. Never. He was feeling something for Paul he could not identify yet, but there was something there. Will could perceive that very well. Paul was so handsome and so young... Yet Paul's physical appearances were that of a man. Paul was no longer a child, that's for sure. He was tall... had broad shoulders and Will could see at a glance that Paul's body was well toned. Quite a specimen! How could he think such things about another guy? Will didn't know. He had never looked at another guy that way before. But Will didn't have time now to reflect on that... He would later. For now, Paul was sitting next to him, and he was frightened. Will would have liked to take Paul into his strong arms and press him to his body, so he could hold him and make him feel more secure... to protect him against the whole world, if need be. In fact Will had to refrain himself from jumping onto Paul and start kissing him passionately. Will got shocked by his own reaction... Was he going mad? Was he totally insane? Will had never been into such a situation before. This was all new territory for him. Up until now, he had never questioned his sexuality. He had never been „in love" with a woman, and surely not with a man for that matter. That had never occured to him before. But again, Will decided it was not the time to reflect on that and not the time to ponder those questions. He would have time later. For now, Will had a very desirable but terrorized guy sitting next to him, and now he could imagine as well as understand the reasons why Paul was so terrorized. Will decided not to jump on Paul and start kissing him, as he would have liked to do, but instead let his heart speak so Paul could be assured... Will slowly took Paul's hands into his own, and started saying: „... Now that I come to think of it, I understand, Paul, you're not sure about trusting me. You've been through a lot lately... and I realize my asking about your father and your family must have scared you a bit... It's just that I really want to help you. Sorry

35

for asking though. But Paul, please, just look into my eyes: Do you see anything bad within me? Do you think for a minute that I could be as wicked as to trick you into something as dreadful as selling to me your father and your family, so I can send them I don't know where... to a prison maybe... Do you see that in my eyes, Paul? Do you?" „... NO. No I don't", Paul answered. „But..." – „...Let me finish, Paul, please?" „... Paul, I'm really who I told you I am. A simple guy from Berlin... like you... A simple guy... I've been dragged into this bloody war against my will... Most of us in Germany didn't want that goddam war, you know... I've told you, we're not all Nazis... It's not my fault if we have a crazy guy as Chancellor! Yes Paul, in my view, the Führer is totally insane! Have you ever listened to him on the radio? Have you ever listened to one of his speeches, where he screams and shouts like a mad man? Many times I was forced to listen to him during my time in the Hitler Youth, and I can tell you, it's no fun... Yes, Paul, that's what I think: Hitler is mad as hell and so are all the others... you know... Goering, Himmler and Hess and Dr. Goebbels... Oh, that one... a lunatic! I tell you. A very dangerous guy... and an impostor... Very deceitful with that. That's what I think Paul. It doesn't mean I'm not proud of being German. I am. But that's quite another story... and it has nothing to do with the Nazis... You know, Paul, I could be shot by a firing squad should the wrong person in the army learn about what I just said to you. Now you may choose not to believe me. That's your choice. But I'm telling you the truth. I swear to you..." „... I believe you, Will... I don't know why... But I do", Paul answered. „... And there are two more reasons why you should believe me" Will added. „The first one is that not only I'm not a member of the Gestapo but in fact, the Gestapo has not yet arrived in Paris. Oh, It won't take long before they get here, believe me... And when they do, you will notice... The party will be over! I tell you! Most of us guys in the Wehrmacht are correct... but those guys from the Gestapo, it's quiteanother ball game. Even we Germans fear the Gestapo, and you wouldn't want to have any business with them..." – „... You scare me, you know, Will..." – „Well, you should be scared of them, trust me Paul. When they get into Paris, stay away from those guys..." – „... Count on me, Will, that's what I'm going to do... and I sure hope you will teach me how I can identify those guys... but Will, you said there were two reasons why I should believe you: What about the second reason?" – „... Well, Paul, until this morning, I didn't know you at all. Until the moment you entered our office, you were totally unknown to us, and to me... I don't even know who your father is... So why would I try to locate him unless it was to help you get in touch with your family? Hum? You know we've got into Paris only yesterday... and according to what I've heard, almost two million people fled Paris before we got here... So it's no surprise that your family fled... Do you think we're searching those two million people? Get serious! Furthermore, do you remember when you entered our office this morning?" – „... What do you think, you silly... It's not every day I get arrested by German soldiers, you know... How could I forget..." – „... I guess so, Paul... but anyway, from the moment you entered our office, I never left you, did I?" – „...No..." – „... So, when do you think it would have been possible for me to receive instructions concerning your father and your family? I know about our efficiency in the German army, but, come on man, there are limits you know..."

„... When the war is over, what do you plan to do, Will?" – „I don't know yet. Why?" – „Well, you should become a lawyer: You've presented your case very well to me. And you know what? I do believe you. Something inside me tells me I should trust you. What you just said just makes good sense... But why Will, why for God's sake would you want to help me? As you said, up until this morning, you didn't even know that I existed..." – „I don't know for sure Paul... I guess no one can escape his destiny. And I guess it was destiny that placed you on my path... I think destiny wanted us to meet... Besides, I'm as lost as you are... We are about the same, as I've said. Just like you, I'm all alone here, in Paris, except for my friend Lutz... but he has his girlfriend in Berlin to write to... I have no one except my family... And most of all, I like you. You're a good guy, that I can tell... I feel it inside me. That's all I can say, Paul..."

Now, Paul was just staring at Will, still holding his hands. He could feel Will's warmth through his hands. That German guy was something! Suddenly, Paul felt very secure with Will. That's the way it was... simple as that!

„You're doing it again: You're staring at me again... Why", Will asked. „Sorry again, Will, I didn't mean to stare at you like that. Don't be offended..." – „I'm not..." – „It's just that I and you... Well... I don't know... You're quite a specimen, you know, even in your German uniform... I like you, and no, I don't think all Germans are barbarians... and I certainly don't believe you are a barbarian, Will..." – „Thanks, Paul, what you just said means a lot to me... I'm touched, you know. And you already know I'm not too good with words, so..." – „Yeah..."

„Hey! I have to leave before the curfew if I don't want to be arrested by the Feldgendarmen... What time is it?" Will asked. „It's a quater past midnight..." – „WHAT? SHIT! With all our talking I lost track of time... I can't drive through Paris at this time of night, because of the curfew. And I didn't even report to Oberstleutnant Koch... Shit. Shit. Shit. I'm dead meat now!" – „Wait. Wait. Wait for a second, Will: Aren't you on leave for a week?" – „Yeah. But I had to report to Herr Koch... Otherwise they will be searching for me..." – „Well, couldn't you just give him a call from here, and let him know you're okay?" – „I guess so... but where will I go at this time of night? It doesn't solve my problem..." – „You just could stay here for the night, you know. I have no problem with that. And as you can see, it's quite a large place I have here, and I'm all alone... No one will bother you here... and it's the least thing in the world I can do for you, after all you did for me..." – „You owe me nothing, Paul. I don't want to impose myself..." – „You're not, Will. Believe me..." – „Okay then. Do you have a phone?" – „Sure. But I'm not sure if it works... Yesterday it didn't work..." – „Paul, give us some credit: Even if we got in here yesterday, I'm sure our services have already solved such a minor problem... Where's your phone?" – „Right there, to your left..." – „Thanks"

Will took the phone and Paul asked: „Is it working?" – „Yes, Will answered. Just as I said. Let me get to the operator... Hello? Yes. Would you please connect me with the Hotel Meurice, please?" – „... You stay at hotel Meurice" Paul exclaimed... „Well, just for now... I'm sure I won't be staying there for long you know... it's too chique for soldiers like me... I suspect we will soon be moved to a barrack somewhere... As soon as they are done... Hello? Hotel Meurice? Yes. Would you please connect me with Oberstleutnant Koch. Tell him Wilhelm von Rundstedt is on the line for him... What? No, „that" von Rundstedt is not my father... So, please, will you connect me to Oberstleutnant Koch, please, he knows me, and I need to speak to him..." Click. Click. Click. „Hello? Oberstleutnant Heinz Koch speaking. Is that you, Wilhelm? Where the hell are you? Do you know it's past midnight?" „Sorry Oberstleutnant Koch... I'm okay... don't worry..." – „Well I was worried about you, you know. Have you forgotten we're at war? Have you forgotten where we are?" – „Sorry about that

38

Oberstleutnant Koch... It's just that I got lost in Paris, and I couldn't find a phone..." – „Well... Where the hell are you?" – „.... I'm with a friend I met... nothing to worry about, Sir" – „I hope she's good-looking..." Mr Koch asked, chuckling. „What, Sir?" – „I said I hope your friend is good-looking..." – „Oh. Yes Sir. Very much..." – „Well, are you having fun, Will?" – „Yes, Sir..." – „Well Wilhelm, I will cover for you, don't worry. You're on leave for a few days, aren't you?" „Yes Sir. Up until Thursday the 18th..." „Good. You've earned it Wilhelm... Now listen to me kid: Keep the jeep... I will file the proper papers to cover for you... don't worry about that... you're young... you're not married... so have fun kid... but never forget you're not in Berlin here... Be very careful... if you see what I mean... never forget you're a German soldier in a foreign land... Many people don't like us being here..." „I know, Sir. I won't forget..." – „Now, Wilhelm, while you're on leave, keep in touch with me, so I know where to find you, should I need to..." – „Sure, Sir. I will call you every day..." – „Oh, Wilhelm, what about the kid we arrested and you offered to accompany to check his ID? Any problems with him?" „No, Sir. Everything he had said was true. I've checked his papers, and everything was regular... so I freed him. Did I do the right thing, Sir?" „Yes Wilhelm, you did. That poor kid was scared to death..." – „I know, Sir." „So have fun, Wilhelm... My only regret is that I'm too old to join you... and besides, my wife would not like that, would she?" „I don't think she would, Sir..." – „Ah! Youth" Don't do anything I wouldn't do kid, if you see what I mean..." „Yes, Sir. And thanks for taking my call, and thanks for covering for me: I really do appreciate it... Don't worry for me... I'll take good care... May I say something to you, Sir?" „Yes, Wilhelm. Feel free to speak" – „Well Sir, since we left Germany, you've been like a father to me. I just wanted to tell you that I appreciate it..." – „Yes Wilhelm. Please, don't make me regret it... will you?" – „I won't, Sir..." – „Night, Wilhelm, and have fun now..." – „Night, Sir. I will..." Click.

„So, Will, what did he say", Paul asked. „Well he thinks I'm spending the night with a girl I just met... He thinks I'm having fun with her... you know..." – „Yeah! I see! Bet you would prefer being with such a girl right now, instead of being with me..." „You're wrong, Paul. I'm very happy to be here with you tonight... Well... I mean..." „I know what you mean... don't worry... I'm not offended... if that's you were afraid of. But nevertheless, I'm not a pretty girl you just met... And I'm not that easy, you know..." Paul said with a grin on his face.

They just burst out laughing at that... But then, Will had a more urgent problem to solve... „Paul, I've got to go back to the jeep to get my bag... and I must park the jeep away from your place..." – „Why?" – „How naïve you are, Paul! I just can't believe that..." – „What the hell do you mean?" – „Well Paul, let's just say you don't want to be seen with a guy wearing a German uniform and have a German jeep parked near your home..." – „I don't understand, Will" „I can see that. I don't have time now to explain, but what do you think your neighbours would think, seeing you with a German soldier?" „I don't know. I just never thought about it..." „Well, they would think that you're a traitor... That's what they would think..." „But anyway, Will, there're all gone... They have all fled Paris..." „Poor Paul. That's what you think... But you don't know that for sure. Anyway, I'm taking no risk... I will move the jeep somewhere else... and get my bag. I will be back in ten minutes..." „Sure... as you like..."

So Will went back to the jeep, made as much noises as possible so all the neighbours would hear him leaving... and drove the jeep to a nearby street. He took his bag and quickly but quietly changed into civilian clothes inside the jeep, and ran back to Paul's home. When Paul opened the door to him, he said:

„Eh, Will: What the hell happened to your uniform?" – „I just changed into civilian clothes, and left my uniform with the jeep..." – „I must say I'm flabbergasted: You look even more handsome with civilian clothes... I mean... you know..." – „Yeah, yeah. I know... I mean I know it's better... isn't it?" – „Well yeah. But where did you buy those clothes?" „In Berlin, why?" „I can see the „good" German taste... No offence intended... But really... Tomorrow we'll have to take care of it... you know... You may have the most powerful army in the world... but concerning fashion, well, I'd say you're not too good at it... trust me" „I told you, Paul. I trust you completely... totally..." „As much as I do?" „Yes, have no doubt about it. Do you still have doubt about me, Paul?" „No" „So, where do I sleep?" „I'm afraid that when my mother left, the only room that was left „organized", if I can use that word... is my own room... So for tonight, I guess we will have to share my bed.. Do you mind?" „No problem with me, Paul" – „Fine. Come upstairs, so I can show you where my room is..." – „Sure..."

40

So they went upstairs, and Paul showed Will his room... It was quite breath-taking. Not only was it very large, but it was just beautiful! A bedroom with it's own fireplace... and what about the rest of the furniture... everything was so nice and very expensive. Will had not seen very much of the rest of the house, but what he saw now in Paul's bedroom was just stunning... He asked Paul: „Eh, buddy... Can I take a shower before I go to bed... you know... it was a very long day, and I feel like I need to take a shower...“ „Oh, sure Will. I'm sorry. Where are my good manners... I have a shower-bath next to my beedroom“ – „I don't want to take a bath... just a quick shower... you know...“ – „Yeah. No problem. I'll take one right after you. The door to the shower is right there, to your left...“ – „Thanks“

And so, without any inhibition at all, Will started to undress right there in front of Paul. Paul was quite shocked, but very interested by what he was seeing. In fact he was quite aroused by what he was watching, and was totally thrown back by it all...

„What“, Will asked. „Haven't you seen a naked guy before? You've never been in the army, haven't you?“ – „No. I mean... you know... here in France... we are a lot more... prude... about that, at least, I know I am...“ – „I'm sorry if you feel uncomfortable with me being stark naked in front of you...“ – „No. no... no problem... I'm not uncomfortable at all... it's just that...“ – „What? Do I look like a monster to you?“ – „Oh“ God. No. You're so...“ – „So what?“ Will asked. „Well, so... I don't know... how can I say... so... well...“ – „Well, what?“ – „You know... so... I don't know how to say it, but, you are so... beautiful...“ – „So you like what you see?“ – „Well... yes... I mean...“ – „Nah! Don't be ashamed, Paul. What's wrong with it? You say you find me beautiful... no one ever told me that before... it's quite a compliment! I'm flattered...“ „Will, you are beautiful. It's just that I feel... you know, I feel it's not „normal“ for a guy to say to another guy that he finds him beautiful...“ „Nah, Paul. You're silly! I'm not offended one bit. Don't worry... If we have to become friends... you know... you're going to have to learn to see me naked sometimes...“ „I look forward to that... I mean... to be your friend, of course...“ „Yeah. I know what you mean... Now, let's hit the shower. It won't take long, and you're next. It's going to be my turn to see you stark naked! „Oh, no you won't... I'm too shy for that...“ „I swear... if you're not undressed when I get back, I will undress you myself...“ Will said, laughing... „You would never do that, would

41

you?" „Just watch me..." Will replied... Although Paul was laughing too, nevertheless, he was blushing also... „Why do you giggle, Paul?" „I don't know... it feels a bit awkward... you know... having a gorgeous young hunk like you, standing naked in front of me... in my bedroom... It's just that I'm a bit confused..."

Will grinned as Paul said that. It's true it was a bit awkward. But what the hell. Those were awkward times. Nothing was normal anymore... So Will just walked to Paul and started hugging him. Will's strong arms were holding him tight and Paul could smell Will's sensuous scent. He quivered. He could feel his dick stiffening inside his pants. How the hell was that possible? Paul had never felt something like that before. All he hoped for was that Will would not notice his swollen crotch... it didn't help that he was now blushing scarlet red... He turned his face to look at Will. The guy had such an angelic face... He was just perfect... Paul looked into Will's perfect blue eyes... they were so beautiful. Paul felt so secure in Will's arms... Now it was clear Paul had gotten a boner... Could Will feel it? And then Paul realized that something hard was pressing against his crotch. Was Will having a hardon, too? Paul couldn't look... for Will was still holding him tightly... but he could feel Will was hard... Oh! My God! What was going on?

„It feels so good, Paul, hugging you like that..." Will said. „Yeah!" – „I needed that" – „Me too" – „Thanks, Paul. Now buddy, I've got to hit that shower... May I have a bath towel, please?" – „Huh?... Oh, sure... sorry..."

Will released Paul, so he could get the towel. Now Paul could see that indeed, Will had gotten a boner too. And what a boner! Paul had never seen such a big dick... it was beautiful. About 23 cm, he would say... and then, Paul took a glance at Will's low hangers... WOW... they were big... But what surprised Paul most was the fact Will had no hair at all around his dick... and the rest of his whole body was smooth like a baby's. He was gorgeous. No trace of hair on Will's abs, pecs and chest either... For a minute, Paul just kept staring at Will's well tanned body... at his six pack... and most of all, at his hard dick... Will was grinning... „„...What? I'm just normal, you know", Will said. „Holding tight a handsome guy like you Paul... you know... it just had to happen... and besides, my dick has its own mind... sometimes I've no control over it... But you know what Paul? I think you have your own problems with your dick... you have quite a hardon, I believe..." Now Will was all smiles, looking directly at the sizeable bulge Paul had in his pants. Paul started looking at his crotch, where his boner was quite obvious. But what was worst was that his dick was oozing so much, he had a large wet spot on his pants. He blushed again, and started giggling. „Oops! Sorry about that, Will...“ – „Hey! Don't be sorry... and don't be ashamed. It's only natural, you know. So, what about that towel?“ – „Yeah...“ Paul went to fetch two bath towels and came back into the bedroom. He gave one to Will, and kept the other for himself. „Thanks. Now while I'm in the shower, do your homework and get undressed... You better be as stark naked as I am when I come back... Otherwise, like I said, I will have to take care of it myself: You've had the pleasure of seeing me naked... so I now have the right to see you naked too... It's only fair!“ Paul giggled at that and replied: „...Well... I'm not too sure about that...“ „You've got five minutes to make up your mind about that... and as Herr Koch likes to say: „...I better see results when I'm back...“

Will turned around with his towel, laughing his way to the bathroom. He didn't close the bathroom door behind him though. He left it open, so Paul had a good view at Will taking his shower... The hot water running all over his naked body made it glisten. Looking at Will, Paul got so hot. His prick was throbbing and stretching so much that he felt as if his balls were ready to burst. He got undressed very quickly, hoping that by the time Will came back, his dick would have lost its hardness... He took his towel and wrapped it around his lean waist. Then, the water stopped running in the bathroom and after a few seconds, Will was back into the bedroom, his towel draped around his broad shoulders... Paul could see that Will was still sporting a big hardon and that he was looking straight at him...

„Oh no, you don't“, Will stated. „What...“ Paul answered. „Oh no, you won't play that game on me“, Will said, laughing... „Get that towel off... It's my turn to have some pleasure...“ „Nah! You don't want to see me naked. Who would like to see an eighteen year old body like mine... Don't be silly...“ – „Don't be silly yourself: I'm more than eager to see my prize! Take that off...“ – „.... Your prize? I'm your prize now? Am I your slave, too?“, Paul said, laughing... „.... Yeah. You're my prize, now that I've found you, I'll never let you go... But you're no slave to me, Paul. Come on Paul, make me happy... take that towel off...“ „Okay then. But only because I like you...“

43

Paul took the towel off and Will was stunned. For an eighteen year old guy, Paul had a well muscled body. Like Will, he had broad shoulders, nice abs and pecs... no six pack though... but a nice smooth chest... Will had a grin on his face... Paul was just perfect. His dirty blond hair... his emerald green eyes... a light blond patch of hair going down to his blond pubes... and there... Oh! God. What a beautiful dick... probably 20 cm long... rock hard and throbbing... and nice balls... as smooth as his own... Will was just mesmerized by what he was looking at... He looked at Paul's soft pink lips and thought of how much he wanted to kiss that guy. But Will didn't want to scare Paul. So he just kept staring at him with a smile on his face... „I knew it", Paul said... „You knew what?" „.... That you would start laughing at my body... it's obvious I'm not as well... as well endowed as you are!", Paul said. „Shit, Paul... stop kidding... you are just gorgeous... And I'm not laughing at you, I swear... You are the most handsome guy I've ever seen!" „Nah!", Paul replied, laughing, showing his perfect bright white teeth... „You just say that to make me feel good..." „If you think that, you're crazy. You're a gorgeous hunk, Paul. I've never said that to anyother guy before... To be honest, I'm quite puzzled by this whole situation... I don't know..." „I know how you feel... same thing here... Will, may I ask you a question? You don't have to answer me, you know..." „Go ahead..." „Will... Are you gay?" „Sure... do I look like I'm sad?" „No. no. That's not what I meant. Here in Paris, the term „gay" also means... well... what I want to ask you is..." „Come on Paul... what is it?" „Well I just want to know if you are... are you a homosexual?" „Shit, Paul! What a question! Do I look like I'm a fag?" „No. NO... That's not what I meant at all... I didn't want to insult you..." „Gee, Paul, until today, I've never even considered that I could be... gay... as you said. I've always thought I was a very straight guy, you know... I've never ever been attracted to a man before..." „Have you ever been attracted to a woman?" – „....No... it seems... like... you know... I never had time for that..." „Have you ever kissed a woman before?" „No. And I've never kissed a man either! To tell you the truth Paul, what you have in front of you is... a virgin... I've never done anything sexual..." „It's the same for me..." Paul said. „Now that you've asked me Paul, may I ask you if you're gay?" „Same as you... I don't know... I've never asked myself that question... But since I met you... I don't know Will... All I know is that I like you a lot... and... and... that I'm attracted to you. And it felt good when you hugged

44

me the way you did..." „Yeah! I loved it, too... don't know what it means though... But I sure would like to do it again..." „Yeah, me too. But for now, I think it's better that I go take a quick shower... let things cool down a bit... and then let's have something to eat. I'm just starving. What do you think?" „Great idea... I'm starving too..." Will replied.

Paul took his shower. By now, their hardons had subsided and so they could wrap a towel around their waist without their dicks making tents... Paul took Will's hand. Will quivered under his touch... They went to the kitchen, Paul guiding Will... and Paul started making sandwichs for both of them... „Wow! What a kitchen you have... it's almost as if we were standing in the kitchen of the Adlon Hotel in Berlin...", Will commented. „Yeah... but I'm not too familiar about the things around here... I rarely come into this kitchen, you know. We have a chef... Well, I mean... we used to have a chef... He fled with all the others... So I guess from now on, we will have to manage without him „around here..." „No problem. Let me help you..."

A lunch was quickly fixed as both boys were hungry like hell... Food was placed on the table as well as a bottle of good red wine... „Hey, mate! I'm not used to drinking wine, so go slowly with that..." Will said. „You don't drink wine in Germany", Paul asked... „Well in Germany, it's not like here in France. We do have wine of course... but we drink wine only at special occasions... you know... but I drink beer quite often..." Will answered. „I see. Well this is a very special occasion... So let's drink wine..." – „.... What do you mean, a very special occasion?" „Well, I met you... and I like you a lot... As crazy as it may sound, I think I'm falling in love with you guy... and to my astonishment, I don't feel ashamed saying that..." „Please Paul, never be ashamed for saying what you said... for I feel the same for you, and I'm not ashamed of it. So you're right: Lets celebrate... I'm so happy we got acquainted..." „I'll drink to that: Cheers!"

Both boys were so hungry that they just kept eagerly devouring all the food on the table. The wine kept flowing and in the end, both young men were a bit dizzy. Now that their cravings had been sated, both of them started to realize they were just exhausted from the long day and all the emotions they had been through the last few hours... For now, they were just relaxing as Will kept gazing at Paul... „Hey, why do you gaze at me like that", Paul asked... „Um, sorry Paul, I didn't realize I was gazing at you. Does it bother you?" – „No, not really..." Paul answered, feeling a

45

little uneasy... an uneasiness Will perceived at once... „Sorry again Paul... I didn't want to make you uneasy... it's just that I find you so... cute...“ – „Cute? Hey dude, I'm not a baby you know... Babies are cute... not grown men...“ „I sure don't think you're a baby Paul... look at you... I mean... You're a grown man for sure, and a fine one. You know... sometimes... I have problems finding the right words in French to say something or express how I feel. It's easy for me to translate what someone else says... but to convey my own thoughts in French words... well... sometimes, it's difficult. When I said you're cute, I certainly didn't mean cute as a baby... Um... I should have said I find you're a gorgeous, beautiful, stunning, handsome young hunk. What else could I think of... Um... let's see now...“ „Cut it out...“ Paul said, chuckling but blushing as well... „How come you have such a well toned body? Do you exercise? You have a swimmers body...“ Will asked out of nowhere... „Not really... but you're right...“ – „Right about what...“ „I'm on my college swimming team. Or at least, I used to be... Now the college is closed, everybody has left... I don't even know where the other members of the team are: They could all be dead by now, for what I know...“ „Don't worry Paul, I'm sure they're all fine...“ „Except for those who are in the army...“ Paul ventured to say. But he didn't want to go into such a discussion for now, so Paul added: „So are you...“ – „What?“ Will asked, looking a bit puzzled... „... You know... a gorgeous, beautiful, stunning, handsome young hunk. I would also add he word attractive to that list... as well as the word lovely...“ Now it was Will's turn to start blushing under his beautiful golden blond hair... „I could also think of other words, you know...“ – „Not necessary“, Will answered. „I get the picture...“ – „... Just trying to add new words to your French vocabulary...“ – „Yeah, yeah, how thoughtful of you...“ – „Yeah... I'm like that...“ Paul said with a grin on his face. „But you know Will, each and everyone of those words apply to you perfectly...“ – „Thanks. No one has ever told me that before...“ Hearing that, Paul frowned doubtfully... „No. No, Paul, I swear... Well I guess I know I'm not bad-looking... Sometimes, I can see women looking at me with longing eyes... you know... but that's about it. Like... I can't imagine my friend Lutz saying to me he finds me gorgeous, handsome... attractive... or things like that...“ „Do you find your friend Lutz to be gorgeous, handsome and attractive?“ „What? I don't know. I suppose he is. But I just never thought of him that way... In Lutz, what I see is a very good friend... not a gorgeous guy, you

46

see?" „But you say you find me to be an attractive guy..." „Yeah, Paul. That's quite different with you. Don't embarrass me, please. Don't ask me to explain how I feel about you... Hell, I don't even know what it is. It's all too new to me and to say the truth, I'm all mixed-up. I've told you: All my life, I've always thought I was a very straight guy... and now I look at you, and find you very attractive. All I know is I'm very attracted to you Paul. I don't know what it means, but I hope I can find out..." „Yeah. That's exactly how I feel about you, Will. I think we need time to sort out our emotions... Lets give time a chance, and let's see where it all leads to. What do you think?" „You know, Paul, for a young dude your age, you're quite a shrewd guy... What you've said makes good sense to me..." „Being a shrewd guy, I suggest we go to bed now. I don't know about you, but I'm totally exhausted." – „Yes, me too. I'm dead-beat... Enough for today..."

Paul shut the lights off, made sure all the doors were well locked and then lead Will upstairs to his bedroom, holding Will's hand into his, in a very tenderly way. Once they got there, Paul looked into Will's eyes and asked him: „Do you think we need pyjamas?" Will burst out laughing and replied: „I never wear pyjamas... do you?" – „Sometimes..." – „If it makes you more at ease, just put your pyjama on... but please, Paul, don't ask me to put one on me... I just can't sleep wearing a pyjama..." Paul grinned. „I just asked cause I didn't know what you're used to... I don't know you that well you know... For my part, I don't wear pyjamas at this time of the year... that's all. Besides, you've already seen me naked, haven't you... so I have nothing to hide from you..." – „Not only have I seen you in your naked glory, but if I remember correctly, you had quite a nice hardon at the time..." Now Paul was slowly turning a lovely shade of scarlet... „Yeah, speak for yourself, mate... if my memory serves me well, you also had quite a boner...", Paul replied. „No. I didn't" Will said, laughing all his way to Paul's bed... „Not only were you hard as hell, but your dick was throbbing... I saw you, you know..." – „That may be so, Paul, but it was all your fault." – „My fault? No way... look at me... I'm totally innocent here... a poor angel fallen from the sky... as pure as snow... in other words... a Saint!" – „... Yeah... sure... Don't know about that holiness shit of yours... but I sure see the tent your dick is making now in your towel: Until now, I didn't know angels could have hardons..." Paul looked down to the tent in question, then he looked back at Will, saying: „It's all your fault again... You'll go to hell for that... trying to corrupt an innocent angel like me..." – „Yes... I'm bad, am I not? Now may I ask my angel to come and join me in bed or does the poor fallen angel prefer to sleep on the floor?"

Although Will had been lying on the bed for some time while talking to Paul, he had not yet removed his towel from around his waist... „Now boy, remove that towel and come to bed", Will said, longingly looking at Paul. „... And I suppose you're going to keep yours?", Paul said frowning... That drew a chuckle from Will, and he took off his towel immediately, revealing his own hardon to Paul. „Well, well, well... what would you know. The devil is harder than the angel!", Paul exclaimed. „Come on Paul, join me now... and don't you worry: I won't rape you... remember... we've decided we would take our time... knowing each other... sorting things out..." „Yes, you're right, Will. We'll do that. But I can't hide I'm quite aroused by you nonetheless. You know, you make quite a sight, lying like that on my bed. I would never have thought such a thing possible last morning when I woke up..." „Do you think last morning I could have forseen I would be sleeping tonight with a naked hunk like you?" – „I guess not, uh?", Paul replied. Paul took off his towel and, no longer hidding his throbbing hard dick, joined Will in the bed. „Now, are you satisfied?", Paul asked. „Very much, thank you, my angel", Will answered with a grin on his beautiful face. „Now turn off the light, pull the sheet over us and let's go to sleep..." „That suits me well", Paul said. The lights were turned off, the sheet was pulled over their stiff pricks... Two young hunks, lying side by side, stark naked... not knowing what the future was holding for them. They stayed still like that for a while... no noise... only their breathing could be heard... then Paul turned to Will, and asked: „Will... may I ask you something?" „Sure..." „Well, it's just that it puzzles me a bit..." „What is it?" „Well... and please don't get me wrong, I like it a lot..." „Come on, Paul, what is it that puzzles you, but you like a lot?" „You know... the fact that... that you're hairless down there..." Will couldn't hold it and just burst laughing. He turned to Paul, and replied: „Hell, I like it that way... that's why... I don't know... I just find its..." „...Sexy?" „Yeah, could say that... You find it sexy?", Will asked. „A lot", Paul answered... „It must take you a lot of time each morning to shave though..." „No. First, I don't have to shave every morning down there as you say, and then, I'm so used to it by now, shaving my pubes, that when I need a shave there, it doesn't take much

48

time. It takes more time shaving my beard..." „Do you also shave your chest?" „No need... I've got no hair growing there for the moment... and if I consider my father... I don't think I'll ever have... I guess it comes with my light complexion... at least I think it has something to do with it... You know Paul, you have the same light complexion as I do, so I guess you will never grow much hair on your chest either..." „I hope you're right. I wouldn't like to have a hairy body. And Will, will you teach me?" – „Teach you what?" – „Will you teach me how to shave my pubes? I wouldn't like to cut myself everywhere down there..." – „You'd like to shave your pubes? If you do that just so I find you more attractive, you're dead wrong, Paul. I find you very attractive just the way you are..." – „No. NO. Will... I'd really like that... it's just I never thought of it before..." – „Sure. I'll teach you..." – „Will you help me doing it, the first time?" – „Sure, I will... I'll be glad to..." – „Tomorrow?" – „If that's what you want, yes then, tomorrow..." – „Thanks" – „Now, Paul, unless you still have pressing questions to ask, could we just go to sleep now?" – „Um-huh"... Oh, but yes, I have another pressing question for you..." – „Rrrrrrr... What is it that is so pressing now?" – „Will, would you please hold me tight... I need it... I'm not asking for anything more... Just you holding me in your arms... just that"

Paul turned to his right side so Will could cuddle him... and Will, with his strong arms, took hold of paul's well toned body and stated holding him tightly... yet so tenderly. Paul sighed, and said: „Yeah... feels so good... Night, Will" – „... Night, Paul." Making himself comfortable, while still holding Paul into his arms, Will just gave him a light kiss on the neck, and closed his eyes. Paul sighed once more. Paul felt so secure in Will's arms... It felt all so natural to him... as if he had been waiting all his life for Will to come into his life... and now, he had found him. Whatever the future, he knew he would not let go of Will. That, he knew from the bottom of his heart. So for the time being, he just cuddled into Paul's warm smooth body and then fell asleep.

Later during that night, Paul woke up, Will's arms still holding him tenderly, his stiff rod pressed in his arse crack. Paul loved it. He smiled. He realized that not only was his dick as hard as Will's... but that he was also leaking precum. God, was he horny. He had never felt like that before. It felt so good. He just loved being wrapped by Will's arms... his body curled against him... Paul had taken his decision. He knew now he

49

was madly in love with that hot guy sleeping next to him. Yes. He was in love with that guy. There was nothing to be ashamed about it. No. Paul was now content. He had found his path. He had found what he had always been looking for: True love. He realized he would have to have a serious talk with Will about all that... Will had to know the truth. Now, it was almost dawn. He had to go back to sleep. He closed his eyes, and waited for sleep to come. It didn't take long.

Will was dreaming. So many things had happened just the day before. He was dreaming, but it was not a very restful dream. Not a bad dream though. He was dreaming of Paul. His embrace around Paul tightened for a moment. He didn't want to lose him. What was he feeling for him? What he felt was like... as if a tide of emotions was threatening to drown him. No. It wasn't threatening to drown him. Not at all. And those emotions were good. His dream lead him to realize he was in love with Paul. It was as simple as that! To hell with the rest. It was as simple as that! He could stop searching now. He had found the answer. He just didn't consciously know it yet, but his heart and mind had made their decision. Obviously, he would have to have a serious talk with Paul about all that... Then he felt a very pleasant feeling of peace invade him. He went into deep sleep. He needed all the good sleep he could get: Tomorrow, no doubt, would be a very stirring day for him. And for Paul, too. Thinking about Paul made his sleep soothingly good. He got lost into it. Tomorrow would be another day!

THREE
«I THINK, I'VE FOUND LOVE.»

When he awoke the morning after, Paul slowly opened his eyes and realized he was still cuddled into Will's smooth body. It felt so good. Will was still sleeping, still sporting a boner. Paul could feel it, hard pressed against his butt. He smiled to himself. Will was not alone in that situation: Paul had a hardon that only the sheet could hide from view... He could feel it though, and it felt good. Although the window-shutters were closed and the widow-curtains were drawn, Paul could sense the sun was shining outside. What time was it? He turned to look at a clock on a small table beside the bed: He couldn't believe it: It was almost eleven o'clock. He wasn't used to sleep so late in the morning. With all the emotions he had been through the day before, he needed that rest, he thought. Slowly, he shifted his body, so he could lay on his back. Now of course, his hardon was clearly visible under the sheet, and his movement caused Will to awaken. Paul looked at him and, with a smile on his face, he said: „Eh, sleephead, wake up..." Will sighed and, looking back at Paul he asked: „What time is it?" „It's almost eleven..." „Huh?" „Yeah, I guess we needed some rest, didn't we?" „I guess so" Will replied, with the cutest smile on his face. „What's what I feel, pressed against my thigh?", Paul asked... „Don't grin like that, dude, from what I see, you're not much better than I am..." Paul looked down to see his own hardon stretching the sheet... „Oh, my God. I'm shocked. How can that be...", he replied, unrepentantly. Then he burst out laughing, and added: „I told you last night, it's all your fault..." „Yeah, Yeah, sure... I'm the bad guy here, huh?" „Yes, that's right. Did you sleep well?" „Like a God. And you?" „Same for me..."

Then, silence fell, as the two beautiful young men suddenly felt a bit uncomfortable... You could hear an angel go through the room... After a while, Paul looked into Will's blue eyes, and told him: „You know what, Will?" „No..." „We're going to have to have a good talk, you and me..." – „Yeah, I guess so... Are you mad at me, Paul?" „Hell, why would I be mad at you? I've never felt better in my whole life, and that's because of you, Will. But I think we need to talk about that... We shouldn't leave things unexplained, that's what I mean. You know Will, when my Grandma died last evening, I promised myself that I wouldn't be like her... that I would express my feelings, not hide them, as she did all her life. So, I want to tell you how I feel about you... It's important to me..." „And to me too, Paul. I need to know. And I also need to tell you how I feel about you..." „So it's agreed then... We'll do that. But first, I need to take a shower, then I'll go downstairs to start breakfast, what do you think?" „Fine with me. Take your shower first, then I'll take mine, and after that, I'll join you downstairs..." Paul rose from the bed, put the sheet back, went to a closet and took two bath-robes; he got into one and, coming back to the bed, placed the other one on it, saying: „It should fit you... You're a bit taller than I am, but I think it will fit... It's going to be a bit shorter on you, that's all..."

Paul went to the bathroom and then, started to shower. A few minutes later, he came back into the bedroom and, seeing Will was still lying in bed, he said: „Hey, buddy, don't fall back to sleep... I'll be waiting for you down stairs..." „Don't worry. Hope you didn't make a mess in the bathroom? Did you? ... with you... rich guys, we never know. You're used to always having someone clean up after you..." Will replied, laughing his way out of bed... „Nah, I didn't leave a mess behind me... I swear. But you make a good point, you know... I guess I'll have to solve a few problems over the next few days... This house can't be run and kept in good order without the assistance from at least two or three people, you know... not counting a chef... Without someone competent in the kitchen, I'll starve to death before long!" „Hooooo, I do understand... Without servants and a chef, I don't know how I would survive myself, my dear", Will answered, with a big smile... „Oh, but you forgot, Paul..." „...What..." You gorgot to mention a chauffeur... You just can't drive your car yourself... That would be so «basse classe»... You have to have a chauffeur... That's a must! But there is worse..." „Oh, what now...", Paul answered... „Can you imagine you, having to take the tube?" „The what?" „The tube..., you know, the subway..." „Oh. Now first, learn that here in

Paris it's called «Metro». And second, go to hell, you silly. I'm leaving. You're just an insensitive bastard. That's what you are..." „Oooooooo.... That's a good reply... Did you learn it from Sarah Bernhardt?", Will said, laughing... „That's it. I'm gone!" „Yeah. And don't forget... I like my coffee strong..."

Paul could hear Will laughing in the bathroom. That guy was something. Laughing to himself, he left and went downstairs. First, he went to the drawing-room. He pulled all the window-curtains open, then opened the windows and then the window-shutters. Ah! Yeah. It was a beautiful morning. Everything was so quiet. He could feel it was already warm outside. It would be a very beautiful day today, he thought. Then, he went to the kitchen. He opened all the windows and window-shutters too. He heard a cat miaow at the kitchen door, and went to see. There was a cat there alright... He unlocked and opened the door, and the cat didn't wait being invited before he got inside the kitchen... „You seem to be hungry you, big fellow..." More miaows were heard through the kitchen... „Well, I don't know what I can find for you, but I'll find something..." Indeed, Paul found something for the cat to eat... and the poor cat just devoured it without asking for its rest. Then, he went near the table, stretched himself at full length and started to lick its paws. Yes, he had found a home!... Then Paul went to make coffee and breakfast. When Will entered the kitchen a while later, he found croissants heating in an oven as well as scrambled eggs slowly frying in a pan. Then he saw butter and all kinds of jam-pots on the table. He just couldn't believe it... „Wow! It smells so good in here...", he said, with a very large smile on his face. „Where did you get all those things?" „Huh?" „I mean... eggs, butter and jam..." „Oh, from there" answered Paul, showing Will the door to a very large larder. „It's very well supplied. My Dad made sure it was full before my family fled, you know... Just in case..." „And what's that door over there?" Will asked. „That's the door to the freezer-room..." „The freezer-room? You're kidding..." „NO. No. The freezer-room... Open it if you want to see..." So Will opened the door, and what he saw just stunned him: There was enough food and meat inside that room to feed a whole army... „I can't believe it. I just can't. There's enough food in there to last for a year or two..." „Yeah, that's unless we loose power! If we do, I'll be in big trouble, and I'll have to throw a big party so that everything isn't lost..." Will closed the door, not knowing what to think... and went back to the table... „Have a seat", Paut said to him. „Thanks. Is that your cat?", Will asked Paul... „No. My sister took our cat with her when my family fled. I found that cat at the door this morning when I got in here, and I let him in, and gave him something to eat..." „Well, I guess you've got yourself a new tenant here. What are you going to call him?" „I don't know. Didn't have time to think about that... What about... let's see... Boussole?" „Compass?" that's not a name for a cat, is it?" „Well, it seems he lost his compass, so, I guess that name would fit him... don't you think?" „So, Boussole it shall be", Will said, laughing. „Yeah. You're a funny guy, Paul, do you know that?" „And much more beside it...", Paul answered. „Yeah. But that, I can only guess..." „Are you hungry", Paul asked Will. „Like a bear"...

Paul took plates and cups from a cupboard, then served Will with scrambled eggs, croissants and coffee... „Help yourself, for as you know, I have no servants to do so", Paul said, with a grin on his face.

„Dunno if I should drink that coffee of yours... could be poisoned, you know... With all I said to you upstairs... You could be trying to kill me, from what I know..." „I'll drink first, to make you sure nothing is poisoned...", Paul said, heartily laughing. At that, the two young studs went for it, and started eating like wolves. „It's good, Paul, God, it's good. I haven't eaten like that for years... You are very marriageable, you know, don't you?" – „Well, I'm all free, you know..." Both burst laughing at that, and finished their breakfast. „Another coffee?", Paul asked Will, „I'm afraid we don't have cream though. The milkman must have fled with the rest, you know. Another problem I'll have to solve... but later. Lets go to the drawing-room, and have our coffee over there, what do you think?" „Sure. Let's go"

So they went to the drawing-room, and sat on the same sofa they had sat the night before. „Nice painting you've got there over the fireplace?", Will stated. „Thanks. That's my Mumand dad", Paul replied. „Now I see from where you got your good look..." At that, Paul put his cup of coffee on the table in front of them, and looked straight into Will's blue eyes. „Will, I want to say something to you. It's important. Now, please, don't interrupt me before I've finished, do you promise?" „...I do..."

„Now, Will, I don't know how to say that... It's not easy for me to say because I can't explain it to myself... But last night, I made a lot of thinking, you know... And I went to sleep... and while I slept, my mind made some thinking of its own... you know... Anyway, all that to say that now, I know in my heart how I feel for you, Will, and as... offensive or improper as it may sound to you... I know, Will, that I'm in love with you. No. No. Don't say a word... you promised... Let me finish, please... So, Will, as I was saying, I know deep in my heart that I'm in love with you. Now, you can decide to punch me in the face... You can decide you leave, and we don't see each other again... Yeah, you can decide to walk through that door, and we never see each other again... It's your choice. But at least, I'm being honest with you, and I'm telling you how I feel, and I feel great just doing that..."

„Are you finished?", Will asked... „Yeah" Will slowly put his coffee cup on the table and then, turned to Paul. Leaning on him, he slowly moved his head towards Paul's and then, their full lips touched. „Kiss me, Will... Please, kiss me" The tip of Will's tongue poked Paul's lips until he parted them. The tip of Will's hot tongue circled Paul's and then, Will stuck his tongue inside Paul's mouth. Paul could feel Will's tongue swirling around his. He shuddered and groaned. Will started grinding his crotch into Paul's, teasing him. Through the thin fabric of their bath-robes, both studs could feel their respective hardon. Their cocks throbbed. Paul locked his arms around Will's strong shoulders and then, their kiss intensified. It was so good. So erotic. They didn't want it to come to a close, so they kept kissing like that for a while, moaning and gasping. Paul lowered his arms to encompass Will's ass globes, squeezing his buns. Opening his eyes, he looked into Will's deep blue eyes, and he saw so much love into them. Like all great things, their kiss had to end. „I love you so much, Will. I need you. I want you. Kiss me again, Will". „What are we doing Paul? Are you sure that's what you want?" „Shut up, Will, just kiss me", Paul demanded, staring into Will's eyes, „Just kiss me...". And they went into a second round of kissing, loving each and every second of it.

„Lets go to my room, Will" Will blushed, and asked: „Are we going to have..." „Yes, Will, unless that's not what you want..." „Oh, God! Paul, I want it so much. I want you so much, Paul", Will replied. They rose from the sofa and Paul, taking Will's hand into his, looking at him, intensively said: „Lets go then..." They went upstairs to Paul's room and as soon as they got in, Paul took off his bath-robe. For a guy still a bit shy only the night before, now, he no longer felt any inhibition. Will looked at him.

55

His eyes were glued to Paul's well toned body. He looked down, and he stared at Paul's gorgeous throbbing hard dick. „You're so beautiful, Paul. Do you know that?" Paul grinned and started walking to Will, slowly pushing him towards the bed, forcing him to lay down on it. Then, Paul laid down on Will, and started kissing him violently and passionately. Their breathing became heavier. Both young men were in heaven. Paul started nibbling the side of Will's neck, sending shivers up and down Will's spine. „Oh, Paul, what are you doing to me?" Will asked, shuddering. „Do you like that?" „Do I like that?... I love it..." „Well, get ready, for there's lots of other things I have in mind for you..." „Ooooo, that's naughty, you're a bad boy... I just can't wait..." At that, Paul rose himself a bit from Will and threw open Will's bath-robe, exposing his firm body as well as his throbbing hardon. Both youth were leaking precum by now. Paul sat over Will's crotch, straddling him. He could feel Will's hot stiff rod pressed hard against his arse crack. He loved it. Will sighed, and his sigh drew a chuckle from Paul. „Feels good, huh?" Paul asked, looking at the golden blond hunk shivering under him... „If you keep grinding your arse like that, I warn you, I'm going to shoot..." „Oh no, you don't. Not yet. I've just begun..."

That drew a hard laugh from Will and Paul kept trying not to break into a fit of giggles. Instead, he lowered his lips, and started nibbling Will's left ear lobe. Will sighed again. He was no longer laughing, but a sensuous smile was now gracing his beautiful face. Paul lowered his lips under Will's chin, then went down until his lips reached Will's smooth left nipple. Feeling Paul's hot lips pinching then sucking his tender nipple, Will quivered under the gentle touch. After a while, Paul went to Will's right nipple, where he continued his sensuous ministrations. Will was in paradise. He could feel Paul's hot tongue licking his erect nipple... Paul left Will's nipple and started slowly kissing and licking his way down Will's smooth pecs and abs. He took his time, exploring each and every part of Will's chest with his tongue. Paul pressed his lips into Will's navel, before he kissed Will's crotch, lowering his head. The golden blond hunk was panting and gasping. Paul licked and kissed Will's very smooth skin surronding his cock shaft, and then took his time looking at Will's cock's head. It was beautiful. Will was firing torrents of precum by now. Paul opened his mouth and tasted it, with the tip of his tongue. It was delicious. Then Paul decided to go for it. He wrapped his right hand around Will's very thick dick, and squeezed his oozing knob. He kissed it, then licked Will's swollen mushroom cap. He opened his mouth, and started sucking it all the way to his throat. Not being experienced, Paul gagged a little. He pulled his head off a bit, and swirled his tongue around Will's cock. He suck his cock shaft and tasted Will's precum, flowing out of him like a river. Paul greedily gulped all of it. Then he started stroking up and down the full lenght of Will's dick with his mouth. Will went wild and cried out in ecstasy. Now his breathing was made of short, sharp gasps. Paul could hear Will's shouts of pleasure. He looked at him and grinned. They both stared into one another's eye. Paul let go of Will's dick, and started kissing his way to his smooth balls. He began sucking his nut sack, and Will groaned. „Oh, Paul... it's so good. You're so good. Are you sure you've never done that before?" „I'm sure. How am I doing?" „You're the best. I've never felt so good in my whole life. It's incredible. You're a fast learner..." – „Thanks. You taste so good. I love your sensuous scent... could do that for hours..."

„I want to do you, too, Paul. Lets do it at one another at the same time..." „How can we do that?", Paul asked. Although he had nil experience at it, Will instinctively knew what to do. He instructed Paul: „Lets lay on our sides, and do as I do, okay?" Will turned up side down on the bed, resting his head on Paul's thigh. Paul did the same in reverse. A second later, they were sucking one another's hot hard pricks. Will took Paul's balls into his right hand, caressing them very tenderly, giving them gentle squeezes. Paul rammed his boner deep into Will's warm mouth, not believing how good it felt. For the first time in his life, he was experiencing pleasures he didn't know even existed before. Obviously, Will was loving it as much as he was, for he was now groaning and moaning non stop...

After a while, Will felt his dick stiffening inside Paul's hot mouth and his balls felt ready to burst. Letting go of Paul's dick for a second, he suddenly said: „Stop, Paul. Stop, or I'm going to cum. Let go of it, or I'll cum into your mouth"... „Huh, Huh...", Paul said, sealing his lips on Will's dick inside his hot mouth... „Oh my God... Oh my God, Paul..." Will grunted, and he only had time to take back Paul's prick inside his mouth before he felt it coming. Will's cock gulped, then erupted, firing torrents of cum inside Paul's mouth. His pulsing prick kept pumping his spunk, as Paul kept sucking it. Paul quickly swallowed every drop of the sweet nectar, loosing nothing of it. He loved the taste of Will's hot jizz and even though most of it went deep down to his gut, he let the rest of it fill his mouth so he could taste it better. Will just couldn't believe how good it felt. He had known all about wanking since his early teens, but the pleasure he was now experiencing was much more intense and much more satisfying... Now, it was Paul's turn to let go of Will's dick, just in time to say: „I'm going to cum... I'm going to cum..." Will did exactly what Paul had done to him. He sealed his lips around Paul's dick and started pumping it faster and faster until Paul erupted into his hot mouth... He quickly gulped every time the blond stud shot another load of his delicious warm juice, not loosing one single drop. He loved it. Paul was ecstatic and cried out in ecstasy, his eighteen year old body shaking with pleasure. His dick glided deep into Will's mouth and stayed there until his last cum squirt, as Will kept sucking it. Paul was shocked. How was it possible to feel so much pleasure...

Slowly, Paul moved his dick away from Will's mouth, then shifted his body so he could cuddle into Will's smooth body. Will lay on his back so he could gather his trembling lover into his strong arms. As Will looked into Paul's emerald green eyes, he tenderly smiled to him. His pearly whites dazzled. Paul moved gently on top of Will and started kissing him. Will's arms were holding Paul tight, as they cum kissed for long minutes. After their lips parted, Paul laid his head to rest onto Will's muscular chest. He sighed, and looked back at Will: „You're simply the best, Will..." „Yeah, like you could compare me with others, huh?" „No. Don't need to... I have you, and I know what's best for me", Paul replied, smiling... „Well, you're the best for me too, Paul, and I want you to know something else: I love you, Paul. I didn't know before, but now, I do." Paul rose his head, and they started to kiss again. „Wow, that was fantastic, Will. Best kiss I ever got. Not that I've got so many... I mean... and those I've got were all from you..." „You're a very good kisser too, Paul. In fact, you're good at everything you do. Thanks to you, I've seen heaven..."

„Will?" „What?" „Do you think we will rot in hell for the rest of eternity, for what we just did? I'm serious..."Will raised an eyebrow at that, and took his time, thinking about the answer he was about to give Paul... „You know Paul, I'm not even sure God exists... But if He does, well, then He made us the way we are. I haven't choosen to come into this world, and neither have you. I haven't choosen the way I am. Neither have you, huh? And from what I've heard, this God of yours is all about love, so, how could He be mad with us, loving each other? If He's angry against us for what we just did, then, I don't want to have anything to do with that God. But I'm sure He's not angry, if He really exists... that is." „Guess you're right. He can't be mad at us. Loving someone can't be a sin..." „Surely not" Having said that, Will tenderly laid a kiss on Paul's head, inhaling the sweet fragrance from his lover's blond hair, holding him into his arms. Both of them were now drinking in the calm and quiet. Slowly, without them noticing it, they both fell asleep.

FOUR
« A N E W D A W N »

„Hey, how long have we slept?", Will asked, having awaken from what he thought had been a very long nap... „I don't know", Paul replied, turning to his right side to look at his clock. „It's almost four o'clock..." Will smiled, slowly stretching his well toned body, giving a sweet kiss to Paul's left cheek. Paul smiled in return... „I love you guy. I don't want you to leave me. Ever!", Paul said to Will, looking straight into his lover's blue eyes. „Oh, I'm not planning on leaving you... For best or worst, you're stuck with me now... At least for the next few days, that is... since I'm on leave until next Tuesday, and unless you want to get rid of me, of course...", Will replied, with a grin on his face. „Don't you dare think about leaving me, you silly. I'll chain you to the bedpost, if I need to..." „Oooooo... I might like that, you know...", Will answered, laughing out loud. „Now I recognize the German in you, you creepy, silly ass..." „Me? A poor angel, fallen from the sky... as pure as snow?" „Hey! That's my line! Not yours...", Paul said, laughing his heart out. „Oh, it's true, I'm the devil here, huh?", Will answered, not being able to control his laughters. „Yeah, I told you so last night..." „Yeah, but that's before you did what you did to me this morning...", Will added. „Hell, as if you were not a very willing participant..." „No. No. No. I was raped, that's what it was: A rape! I'm the innocent victim here...", Will answered. At that, Paul jumped on Will and started tickling his beautiful lover. They were both laughing. Then they started kissing. They could feel their respective dick stiffening...

„Hey buddy... we've got to stop that, at least for now...", Will said, „I've got to report to Oberstleutnant Koch... to let him know I'm alright, you know. I must call him..." „Yeah, you're right..." „What day is it, today?"

61

Will asked. „Um... Sunday, the 16th...“ „Right. I'm going to call him first, then I think I'll drive back the jeep to Hôtel Meurice, you know... I just don't think it's useful for me to keep it, and I don't want to get Herr Koch into troubles, because I kept it, although he said he would cover for me...“ „You're right. That's a good idea. I could follow you with my dad's car, and then bring you back here. The thank is full, so no problem with gas. At least for now... And besides, Hôtel Meurice is not that far away from here...“, Paul replied. „Good idea. But once at Hôtel Meurice, I don't want you to wait for me there... Too many soldiers there... We'll have to find another place where you can pick me up...“ „Easy. You bring back the jeep, and in the meantime, I'll keep driving nearby. When you're finished, just walk to where I'll show you, and I'll pick you up there. What do you think?“ „Perfect... I'll have to go and get my uniform in the jeep, though. But first, I'll call Herr Koch ro report to him, and tell him I'm going to bring back the jeep...“ „Fine with me!“, Paul replied. Will called Oberstleutnant Koch, letting him know he was fine, telling him he would bring the jeep back within the next hour... Will gave him Paul's phone number, so he could be reached at all time, while he was on leave. Will was glad Oberstleutnant Koch didn't ask questions as to where he was staying... But then, Will knew Herr Koch was not an intrusive guy. After his phone call, Will went back to Paul.

„Everything is fine. Now, I'll go get my uniform, and change...“ „Okay“, Paul replied. After a few minutes, Will was back and, in the meantime, Paul had dressed. „Didn't see anyone outside. Everything is quiet. That doesn't mean people are not watching behind their curtains, though. And I've moved the jeep, so now it's parked not too far from here...“ – „You're getting a bit paranoid with that, you know, Will...“ „No, I'm just careful, that's all. And it's for your own security. You might think everybody is gone, but I don't believe that. I don't want you to be seen in public with a German officer in uniform...“ „You may be right. So now, hear my plan: You get dressed, and then go get your jeep. I'll get my father's car, and then drive slowly up on Avenue Foch. You'll see me, since I'll be driving a big black Citroën... Then follow me. When we get to Place de la Concorde, I'll show you where I want us to meet later, okay?“, Paul explained. „Is that okay with you?“. „Lets do it... and Paul?“ „... What?“ „This time, don't forget your ID, please?“, Will said, with a large smile on his face. „Nah...“. Both of them started to chuckle. Will changed, then left, and Paul went to the underground garage, where his dad's car was parked. He opened the doors, started the engine, drove out of the garage, then went back to close and lock the doors. Seconds later, he was slowly driving up on Avenue Foch, and a few seconds later, he saw Will, sitting in his jeep. He passed him and kept slowly driving up on the Avenue. After a while, Paul looked into the side-mirror, and saw that the jeep was following him at a good distance. They reached the rond point de l'Étoile, in the middle of which stood the Arc de triomphe, circled it, and then drove down the Champs Élysées Avenue. There was not much traffic on the large Avenue, mainly German army trucks and jeeps... Paul saw that Will was closing in on him, to make sure to everyone both car and jeep were together. That played well, and Paul's car wasn't stopped. They eventually reached Place de la Concorde, where Paul made a sign to Will, indicating to him a statue. Paul looked at Will, and saw him nodding, meaning he had understood that would be their meeting place. Then Will turned on rue de Rivoli, and went to Hôtel Meurice. Paul turned on rue Royale, and slowly kept driving, giving Will all the time he needed to bring back the jeep. After a long run, he went back to Place de la Concorde, where he saw Will waiting near the statue he had indicated to him. He stopped, and Will quickly got into the car. They immediately left, turning on the Champs Élysées, on their way back to Paul's home.

„Everything's fine", Will said. „I had time to hear some news, though. It seems things are going from bad to worse for the French army. They have been completely routed, and the Wehrmacht is now running through France, and there's nothing left to stop them. Unbelievable. I never thought I'd see that day..." „Neither did I..." „They said the French Government is in Bordeaux now..." „... If so, we don't have to search for my father anymore: He's in Bordeaux for sure...", Paul stated. „Why do you say that?"

While driving, Paul gave Will a glance, then said: „He's a Minister in the French Cabinet. So if the Government is in Bordeaux, he's there too, no doubt." „Oh shit... I didn't know that. Sorry Paul. Really... I mean..." „Yes... But it's not you're fault, Will, you know..." „Well at least, you know now where your family is...", Will replied. „Yes.... Hey... do you see that big building right there, to your right?", Paul asked Will. „Which one?" „The white one, right there..." „Yes... I see it now..." „Well, that's where our offices are. I mean, our company's head office..." – „What do you mean", Will asked. „Well, my father is a member of the Cabinet, as I said... but he's also a businessman... We own a large building society, with real properties scattered all over Paris, as well as some in Switzerland and even some in New York...", Paul answered. „Now, that explains a lot...", Will said. „What?" „Well, you know... your house... where you live..." Paul grinned, then added: „You know, here, in Paris, it's not called a house. It's called a «Hôtel particulier»..." „Yeah... I've heard about those... Now, I've seen one... I've even slept in one last night", Will replied, with a grin on his face, as he said that.

Since Paul had turned to drive down on Avenue Foch, Will suddenly ducked under the dashboard, so no one could see him... „... My uniform... you know...", he said. Paul smiled. He drove past his home, then turned to a lane to his right. He slowly drove for a while, then stopped. „Wait in the car", he said to Will. Paul went to the underground garage, unlocked the doors, opened them, then came back to the car. He drove into the underground garage, stopped the engine, went back to close and lock the doors, and came back to the car. „You can come out from your hiding place, you gorgeous...", he said to Will, smiling. At that, Will smiled and got out of the car. He could see now that they were standing in a spacious garage, where two other cars were also parked. „Where are we?", Will asked."Under our Hôtel particulier", Paul replied. „Under our house..." – „Unbelievable", Will exclaimed. „Yeah, isn't it? It's very useful. Follow me.", Paul said to Will. Will followed Paul. They went up a back-staircase and found themself in a small service room. Paul opened a door, and Will realized they were back into the main kitchen where they had had breakfast earlier that day. Boussole, the cat, was there, looking very happy to see them again...

„You, little rat, don't tell me you're hungry again?, Paul asked the cat. Miaows were heard all through the kitchen, and Paul smiled. „Yeah... you're hungry... and I'm starving too. What about you, Will?" „Hell, I'm starving." „Lets get this little fellow here something to eat, then let's make a lunch... What do you think?" „Fine with me", Will replied. „I'd like to change into something more comfortable, though...", he added, looking at his uniform. „Okay. Let me give Boussole something to eat, and then let's go to my room. I'll find something for you to wear, and then, we'll have lunch" „Fine." So Paul took care of the cat, and minutes later, both of them were back into Paul's bedroom, looking at so many clothes Will thought they were in a garment store.

„Unbelievable", Will exclaimed... „Stop saying that... It's not as if I was the Prince of Wales, you know..." „Even the Prince of Wales... you know... I don't think he has so many clothes to wear... I'm pretty sure of that...", Will answered, laughing. „Nah... So, what would you like to wear? What about that blue shirt, there... It would go well with your golden blond hair and your beautiful and sexy blue eyes. Besides, we're almost the same size... except you're a bit taller than me..." „Yeah. That shirt is perfect...", Will answered. „And those light beige troussers... What do you think... Im sure they will fit you perfectly, since they are too long for me..." Will started to get undressed. He took off his uniform under Paul's very watchful eyes. Now that he was only wearing his underwear, Paul said to him: „God! You're so beautiful, Will. I'll never tire looking at your gorgeous body. Just can't keep my eyes off you... you make me so horny..." Will could see Paul now had a sizeable bulge in his pants. He didn't fare better either, since he could feel his dick stiffening... „Stop that, will you? Remember... we're starving", Will said to Paul. „If you expect me to... you now... perform... later, I've got to eat something..." „Yeah. I'm starving too... but for you, that is", Paul replied, bursting out laughing. „Get the hell out of here, if you can't resist your temptation. I've got to try those clothes, you know..." „Sure Will, I'll wait. I mean, I'll wait before I rape you again, and abuse your sexy body once more. Go ahead..." – „Yeah... poor me..." „But wait until tonight, though. I've got something in store for you, mister...", Paul said. „Yeah? And what might that be?", Will asked, smiling... „Just wait and see. I won't say anything else for now", Paul replied, with a very sexy grin on his face. „Shit, Paul... you're driving me mad with your sexy talk... I wonder if you haven't become a sex maniac. Yeah!. I've created a sex animal, that's what I've done!" „Grrrrrr... Just wait for tonight, you'll see what a sex beast I've become..."

Even though he was still laughing, Will nevertheless started to get dressed, trying his new clothes. Everything was fitting perfectly. He looked at Paul: „Wow! You look perfect. So handsome. Look at yourself in the mirror", Paul said to Will. Will took a look at himself in the mirror, and found that indeed, he looked very handsome in those clothes. He had to admit it, the French had their way with fashion. The way the shirt fitted him... the cut... and those trousers... WOW... Much, much better than

65

what he had ever bought in Berlin. Everything seemed so out of fashion in Berlin, he thought for himself. Now, he just loved his new look... „So... What do you think? Like what you see?" Paul asked. „WOW... It's perfect Paul. Thanks..." „Now Will, everything you see there, in the wardrobes, belongs to you, too, from now on. So just feel free to wear whatever you want. Don't ask. Take it. If you don't, I swear, I'll get mad at you, and I tell you... you won't like it, if I get mad at you..." „Are you sure, Paul... I mean..." „Look at me, Will: Do I look like an idiot to you? I'm dead serious. I intend to share with you all I have. So get used to it. Now, let's go and have something to eat, shall we?"

„Be my guide. Oh, Paul, wait a second..." Will went to Paul and took him into his arms. He looked straight into Paul's beautiful emerald green eyes and started kissing him very passionately. „Wow...", Paul said, after they had parted... „That was something: It's getting better and better every time... I wonder if it will ever stop getting better... There must be a limit to perfection, you know..." „Dunno. We'll take all our time finding out, won't we... Guess we'll need lots and lots of practice..." „I like that idea..." They went downstairs to the main kitchen, where they prepared a real feast. Paul opened a bottle of very good wine, and then another one... They had fun, eating and drinking. Even Boussole seemed to be very happy... „Sorry if we have to eat in here, you know... The dining-room is all clad under protecting sheets..." – „I don't mind. Aren't you used to eating in here?" „Are you kidding? Monsieur Michel... that's our chef... would never allow me to eat in here... no one is allowed in here, except him and his helpers... When he's in the kitchen, he's the king in here, you know, and he doesn't tolerate us very long in HIS kitchen. I think he believes that when we come in here, it's to spy on him, to get our hands on his secret recipes... as if we gave a damn about them..."

„That's funny, you know. It's not like that at my house, back in Berlin..." „How is it? What does your Dad do for a living?", Paul asked. „Well, he's a doctor. He has his own private practice in Berlin, and I guess he does very well. But we're not as rich as you are, far from that. We live quite well, though. And even though things have not been always easy in Germany over the past few years, we've always managed quite well." Will took a sip from his glass of wine, and then continued explaining: „I was born in Berlin, and we've always lived there. We have a house in Charlottenburg that's a borough of Berlin... like an arrondissement here in Paris... you know... Anyway... So that's where we live. It's very nice, lots of trees... The Olympic Stadium is located in Charlottenburg, to give you an idea... We also have the Charlottenburg Palace... It's not too far from where I live... My friend Lutz and I, we both live on the same street. But I've already told you that, I think..." „Yeah, you did...", Paul replied. „At home, things are not as formal as they are here. We don't have a chef... and my Mumdoes all the cooking... and she's a very good cook, I tell you." „Do you have brothers and sisters?" „Like you, I have a younger brother and a younger sister. My sister is sixteen, and my brother is twelve. I tell you... I miss them..." „Don't you receive letters from your family?" „Yes, I do. But it's on a very irregular basis... you know... me, being in the army... Until now, we were constantly on the move... And of course, all our letters are censured... so we can't write all we would like..." „Can't you call them, sometimes..." „Are you kidding, Paul? First, in the army, all the phone lines are reserved for army purposes and second, even if I had access to a phone, long-distance calls are very, very expensive. I don't make a lot of money in the army, you know..." „Sorry Will, I never thought about that. Hey, you should try using our phone here and see if you can reach your family in Berlin... You know, we could charge the call on our business phone account, so it would not cost us anything... My Dad has a phone in is study, and he uses it very often to call our director in Geneva. If my Dad can reach him in Geneva, using that phone, why couldn't we use it to try to reach Berlin?" „It could work, you know... But I'm not sure if the phone lines have been re-establish with the outside world...", Will stated. „Lets give it a try, shall we?" „Do you think it's a good idea?", Will asked. „Just follow me...", Paul replied. They went to the study, opened the doors and once inside, Paul went to where he knew his father's desk was. „Will you help me fold this sheet, please?" „Sure." Once the sheet had been removed, Will saw the desk as well as the phone. „Now Will, try to get the operator on line, and asked her if she can get a line for you to talk with Berlin... go ahead... do as I say" Will took the phone, and after a few moments, he got the operator on line. He talked to her in French. Yes, the lines to Berlin had been re-established, but not with the rest of the outside world, and certainly not with the rest of France, she said. She would look if she could get a line for him to Berlin. He was waiting. She came back on line, and told him a line was available, but she warned Will that the line could be cut at any time, should it be needed for more pressing calls. He told her he understood. Click. Click. Click... Now he had a German operator on line. Of course, he began speaking to her in German... Yes, she was in Berlin, and yes, she could connect him with the phone number he was about to give her... Will looked at Paul and nodded to him, giving him a very nervous smile. Indeed, Will was very nervous now... He gave the operator the phone number he wanted to reach, then waited.

„Hello? Is that you, mum? It's Wilhelm speaking...“ The line was not very good... with lots of parasites on it... „Wilhelm? Is that really you?“, his Mumasked. „Yes, mum, it's me... Can you hear me?“ „Yes Wilhelm... I hear you...“ Now, Will could hear his Mumcalling, for his father and the rest of his family to come and join with her, near the phone... „How are you Wilhelm? Are you alright? Are you wounded?“ „I'm fine, mum, and no, I'm not wounded at all. Now mum, we could loose the line at any time, and if we do, don't you worry...“ „Yes, I understand. Where are you? Can you tell?“ „Yes, Yes... I'm in Paris, Mum...“ „....In Paris?... It's unbelievable... so it's all true, what we hear, here in Berlin?“ „Yes Mum. We got in the capital city the day before yesterday. How are you in Berlin? How's Dad, and what about the others?“ „We're all fine, Wilhelm. Your father wants to talk to you... hold on...“ „Dad? Is that you?“ „Yes, it's me, Wilhelm...“ Paul could see tears rolling down Will's face. He had not spoken with his family for over a year... Those tears on his face were good tears, though. Tears of joy... „Yes father, we're in Paris. Lutz is here with me too... Will you tell his Mumand dad? No. We're not wounded. We're just fine. I'll send you my address here, in Paris, as soon as we know where we'll be staying... Yes, father, I love you too. Very much. I miss you all. I don't know if I will be able to call you again... but I'll try. I'll send you a letter as soon as I can. No father, there is no danger here, in Paris... everybody has fled... It's very quiet... How is...“ CLICK!

„I've lost the line“, Will said to Paul. „That was to be expected, I guess... At least, I've been able to talk to my Mumand Dad... and I know they're okay. How can I thank you for that, Paul... I owe you big for what you just did...“ „You owe me nothing, Will. Nothing. If you're happy, I'm happy. If you're sad, I'm sad. That's the way I see it. Now, are you happy, Will?“ „Shit... Yeah Paul. You've made me the happiest guy in the world...“ „Well, that calls for a celebration“. Go to the drawing-room, and wait for me there... I'll meet you there in a few minutes...“ True enough, a few minutes later, Paul was back with a big bottle of champagne in one hand, and two beautiful crystal champagne glasses in the other. He twisted the cork, and it went dying across the drawing-room. The both laughed at it. Paul filled the glasses with champagne, and presented a glass to Will, who took it gladly. „To us, and to our families", Paul said. „To us, and to our families", Will replied, taking a sip... „And to France!" „To France!", Paul answered, with tears in his eyes. „Thank you Will, that was very thoughtful of you..." „Hey Paul, as you said: If you're happy, I'm happy. If you're sad, I'm sad. That's the way I see it, too. We're together in that shit, you know. I'm here with you, and for you. You can count on me! I told you Paul, I love you, and I'm not saying that lightly... I love you!" „Oh, Will... I love you too so much... it hurts..." At that, Will walked to Paul, took him into his strong arms and started kissing him passionately. „I'm telling you again, Will, each time, it's getting better and better..." „Yeah, I've noticed too", Will replied with a laugh.

„Come on Will, let's take a sip, then help me with those sheets... I want this drawing-room to look alive again..." So they went to each and every piece of furniture, and removed all the sheets... Then Paul turned on all the lights in the room. Will looked at the furniture, and all in there seemed hideously expensive to him. All so beautiful. „Will, would you do me a favour?" „Anything you want... Just ask!" „Would you play for me?" Paul was looking at the grand piano. He walked to it, and opened the cover over the keyboard. „Where are your mother's music-books?" Will asked... „Right there", Paul answered, showing Will where he would find them. Will went through several music-books, and chose some. Then he sat on the music-stool, and tried the piano. „Wow...", Will said, „That's a very good grand piano... A Pleycl... Wow..." Then Will opened a music-book, looked at it for a while, slowly turning the pages... „You know, I haven't played in a while... but I'll do my best for you", he said to Paul. Then the music started flowing through the room. It was so beautiful, so romantic, so appealing. Paul knew that music well. His mother used to play it all the time. He loved it. Always had... „Schubert", Paul said... „He's my favorite..." – „You like it?", Will asked. „I love it. Please, Will, keep playing...", Paul answered. As he was saying that, Paul took the two crystal glasses and walked to the grand piano. He went back for the bottle of champagne, came back, and filled the glasses. He brought Will's glass to his lips, so he could have a sip, while playing... Will took a few sips, and continued. He turned the pages one after the other. When the last note was played, Will looked at Paul, and he saw tears in Paul's eye. „That was so beautiful, Will. Will you playanother one for me, please?" „Yes, sure... Which one?" Paul went through the music-books and chose one... „This one..." „Ohhhhhh, you have good taste, my love. Chopin!. Did you know, Paul, we're not allowed to play Chopin in Germany anymore? „But why?", Paul asked. „Just because Chopin was Polish... That stupid! Like if music knew about borders..." „Music is like love, Will... it knows nothing about borders... and I will spend the rest of my life fighting, to make sure it stays that way, if need be...", Paul replied. „You're so right, Paul. And I'll be at your side all the way, fighting for that..." Again, Will opened the music-book, turned the pages very slowly, looked at each and every one of them... then, he began to play... Oh, boy... This was fantastic... Will's long fingers were flying so fast over the keyboard, Paul couldn't believe it. The music kept flowing like a river... and Paul kept drinking at it. Then, Will played a Polonaise... „It feels so good, playing that...", Will said, with a broad smile on his face... Then after that, both young men took several sips of champagne, and Will starded playing something Paul had never heard before. „What's that?" he asked... „It's beautiful", he said. „It's nothing, really. I just improvise...", Will replied, looking at Paul. „It's from my heart. It's a love song for you. It tells you how I feel about you..." After a while, Paul said: „It's so romantic, Will. I didn't know you loved me so much..." „That's how I feel about you, Paul. It's hard for me, sometimes, to find the right words... you know... but now, you can hear my words through my music... my heart is speaking to you now..."

„And I love what I hear..." That kept going for quite a while, two young handsome guys, looking into one another's eyes, drinking champagne, listening to the music Will kept playing...

Later, Will stopped playing, and, looking at Paul, he said: „...Lets go to bed now... I'm tired, aren't you? It's getting late..." „Sure. Good idea. Help me close the shutters and the windows, and then, let's go to bed", Paul answered, with a grin on his face. „Ohhhhh, you... I know what you have on your mind! You're naughty. Are you going to rape me again? Against my will? Like the last time?", Will asked, with a very big smile on his face. „Ohhhhh,, Much worse than that. I've told you... I've something in store for you... And you're going to like it, I can tell...", Paul replied. „What's that?", Will asked... „I've told you, just wait and see... But first, we've got

70

to take a shower... together... Remember? You've got a shaving job ahead of you...", Paul stated, with a sexy grin on his face. „Oh, shit, Paul! My dick is already starting to swell..." „Yeah... We'll take care of that upstairs..."

They went through the room and closed all the shutters and windows. Paul turned the lights off, then they went upstairs. Paul was holding Will's hand tighly, quivering all the way to his bedroom. Once there, they both got undressed with the speed of light, and they began laughing, seeing both of them had boners... Paul took Will's hand and led him to the bathroom. „What will you need?", Paul asked Will... „We'll need some scissors... a razor and some shaving cream...", Will replied. „Wait for me... I'll be back...", Paul said. After a short while, Paul was back and had all what Will had asked for... They got into the shower and soon after, hot water started running down their perfect young bodies. Will's arms were firmly wrapped around Paul's upper back. His full lips touched Paul's, and they started tenderly kissing. They both moaned, feeling their hard dicks pressed against one another... It feld so good... Their cocks throbbed... They were oozing so much... Will let go of Paul, and went down on his knees, facing Paul's massive boner. He opened his mouth, and slowly started to give Paul's dick a good tongue bath. What a blowjob! Paul was gasping with lust by now...

Then, Will let go of Paul's dick; He took the scissors, and began to cut the hair away from Paul's dick and balls. Paul moaned quietly... Then, Will took the shaving cream. He covered Paul's privates with foam, took the razor, and began to shave Paul's dick and balls. He was so gentle, and Paul could see Will was getting off on this just as much as he was... Will had a massive boner, too, and his dick was throbbing... Will began shaving Paul's pubes, shaving round the root of Paul's dick and up the sides. When he had shaved one side clean, he did the same to the other side. After that, he handled Paul's balls, squeezing them and stretching them as he shaved off the hair well... Paul looked down at Will, then looked at his shaved dick: The sight of his cock without hair took a bit of getting use to, but it felt so wonderful... Paul felt his body was as smooth as silk... as smooth as the day he was born... Paul ran his hand around his dick: The sensation was incredible. He loved it! Will finally threw down the razor and stepped back to admire his work: His abundant practice had made him a master with the razor, and so he was pleased with the result of his work... Paul looked so gorgeous...

Will just couldn't resist, and he started sucking Paul's beautiful cock shaft. Paul was gasping and shuddering by now... After a while, Paul exclaimed: „Stop, Will... Please stop... I don't want to cum, not just yet...“ Will sighed, and looked back at Paul. They both stared into another's eye. Paul smiled. Will let go of Paul's dick and rose to his feet, then wrapped his muscular arms around Paul's lean waist, holding him tight... „You're right... let's take our time... We're in no hurry... Lets go to your bed... what do you think?“, Will asked. „Um-huh“, Paul replied, with a grin on his face... They got out of the shower, took the towels Paul had brought and dried their hairless bodies... They looked fantastic! Then Paul led Will to his bed, where Will lay down on his back. He was lying still, admiring Paul's superb body... „God! You're so beautiful Paul... just look at you...“ „Thanks... You're so beautiful too...“, Paul replied.

Paul joined Will into bed, and began slowly caressing Will's throbbing dick. Then, Paul lowered his body, and took Will's dick into his warm mouth: It was his turn to give his lover's dick a good tongue bath... Now Paul was deep throuting Will's dick in his mouth, driving Will wild... Then he stopped, and suddenly he straddled Will, placing his arse crack over Will's very stiff prick... Paul extended a hand and took a small bottle of baby lotion he had placed on his night-table, without Will knowing about it... Will looked at Paul and, with a worried frown, he said: „What are you doing, Paul?“ „I told you I had a surprise for you tonight... so just close your eyes, and enjoy!“, Paul replied. Will smiled at Paul, then closed his eyes... Paul opened the bottle of baby lotion and, after he had poured a gob on his fingers, he poked his index finger in his ass, and slowly began fingering himself. Once he was sure he had fully prepped his hole, he sat up on Will's knees and moved back just a little. Then, he poured some lotion on the palm of his hand and smeared it all over Will's beautiful dick. „Ohhhhhh... God! That feels good...“, Will exclaimed. „Just wait... You have seen nothing yet“, Paul replied, grinning... Paul then leaned up slightly and moved until his ass hovered directly over Will's dick, pointed it upward, and slowly lowered himself on it... He felt Will's dick touch his rosy spot, and then lowered his body until Will's dickhead slowly penetrated through his sphincter. Pain shot through him for a moment, so he stopped, and waited for he pain to subside... „Hey! What are you doing, Paul?", Will suddenly asked, opening his eyes... „Don't move, Will... give me some time to get used to you being inside of me... I want you to make love to me, Will... I want to have you inside me... I want you so much...", Paul replied. As the ache inside him dimmed, Paul felt it turn into pleasure... He took his time... He then lowered himself ever so slowly, until Will's dick worked its way into his sweet hole. Once Will's dick was all the way in, Paul paused, to give his hole time to adjust... „Are you okay?", Will asked... „Does it hurt?"... „At first, it did hurt... but now, I'm getting adjusted... and I don't feel pain anymore... How do you feel?" „WOW", Will replied „It feels so good... you can't believe how good it feels... I mean... you're so tight... I'm in heaven..." With the pain all gone, Paul began to enjoy the awesome feeling Will's dick was giving to him... Now, all Paul was wanting was too pump that beautiful dick with his tight ass.

Slowly, he began working his body up and down on Will's very hard and slippery dick. Oh, God! It felt so good... Paul got a little faster... Will couldn't believe how good it felt, and after a while, looking at Paul, he pumped his body upward, driving the full thrust of his dick deep inside Paul, while Paul continued to ride him like crazy... They looked at each other. Will was groaning and moaning... Now, Paul was looking directly into Will's deep blue eyes. They could see the looks of pleasurable bliss on each other's faces... „I love you, Will... How can I tell you how much I love you?" „You don't have to tell me, Paul... You're proving your love fo me, just doing what you're doing to me now... I feel so good... And I love you so much, Paul, for all the pleasures you're giving to me..." As Paul began riding up and down Will's oozing dick, faster and faster, Will sreamed, as he felt so much pleasure. Paul was passionately making love to him, and their passions were beyond their control. Both of them were panting and sweating, gasping and shuddering. Will wrapped his hand around Paul's hairless dick, and began jacking him off... He kept looking at Paul's perfectly sculpted body, at his well defined muscles. God! Was he in love with that blond guy... Paul's dick was so hot in his hand, so stiff... With his skilled hand, Will bobbed faster on Paul's prick... Paul could feel Will's dick stiffening inside him. He squeezed the base of Will's cock, using his ass ring... Now, Will couldn't take it no more: He just had to cum... He was gasping with lust... He just had to get off soon... He had

73

gotten so hot... He was oozing so much inside Paul's hot and very thigh ass chute... Now, his balls felt ready to burst...

„Oh! Shit, Paul... Oh! Shit... I'm going to cum... I'm going to cum..." Saying that, Will started beating Paul's dick faster and faster. „I'm going to cum too... Oh! My God!", Paul replied. As Will suddenly cried out in ecstasy, he started firing torrents of cum inside Paul's tight fuckhole. As he rammed his boner deep inside Paul's fuckhole, he hit Paul's prostate several times, and that did it: Paul's dick exploded and shot his load all over Will's smooth chest and stomach, while Will's dick remained deep inside his body. He was in the seventh heaven of delight and pleasure.

After their orgasms subsided, Paul looked at Will and, with the most satisfied smile on his face, he said:

„God! Will... I don't know what you've hit down there... but I can't believe it... It felt so good... I didn't know such pleasure existed... I love you so much, Will... so much..." „I love you too, Paul... and it felt incredibly good for me too. I can't explain it... it was just too good!", Will replied, his blue eyes sparkling... As their dicks started to deflate, Will's dick slowly got out of Paul's love chute; Paul leaned over Will, and they passionately kissed. As their lips parted, Paul said: „Now, you belong to me, mister... and I'll never let you go... never... you hear that?" „Hey, handsome, you belong to me too now... and I sure don't plan leaving you...", Will replied.

From that moment, Paul knew he had to make plans... make decisions... to make sure Will would never be forced to leave him. He had the means to protect Will... He had to protect him, whatever the costs... No, that crazy dictator in Berlin would never take Will away from him! Paul didn't know yet what he would, or even could do to make sure no one could ever threaten his new found happiness or his gorgeous lover... He just knew he was madly in love with him... Now, Paul had a reason in life to fight for... And he was going to fight... He felt invincible! What would he do, in order to attain his goal? He would have to think about that... but he knew deep down in his heart he would do anything to protect Will. Knowing there was not much Will could do on his own to protect their happiness, Paul realized the responsibility lay heavily on his own shoulders. He had to take things into his own hands, and count on no one but himself. Paul went on thinking that just a few days ago, he was still a very unconcerned and thoughtless eighteen year old guy... He smiled to himself, thinking how his Dad used to tell him he had to grow up and start acting like an adult... Well, Paul thought, in just a few days, he had grown up, indeed... He said to himself: Just watch me Dad... just watch me... I'll make you proud... As Paul was grinning, thinking about all that, Will looked at him, and said: „Hey, dude... What are you thinking about?" „Ahhhhh... You occupy all my thoughts, you big handsome boy... And I love you... And I would like the whole world to know just how much I'm in love with you", Paul answered, with a loving smile on his face. „Don't think that would be such a great idea, though... You know... If my superiors knew about what we just did... If they learned how much we're in love, you and me... they would send me to prison so fast...", Will replied. Hearing that, Paul stopped smiling. Will was right! He had to make sure no one would find out the truth about them. He would never be the one to provoke Will's downfall... or worse... He would have to figure something to make sure Will was perfectly and totally protected in that regard. That too, was his sole responsibility... Yeah! He would figure that out... „Don't worry, Will. I'll never do anything that could put you in jeopardy... Our secret is safe with me", Paul stated. „Trust me..." „I know..."

At that, Paul cuddled into Will's smooth body, and sighed... „You know, Paul... I never thought I could love someone so much..." „Neither did I", Paul replied... „I guess that's what we call a «coup de foudre»... „A what?", Will asked. „A coup de foudre... you know... as if we had been struck by a thunderbolt..." „I love that expression... I didn't know it... My French is getting better and better, thanks to you..." „Yeah... But you know what, Will?" „What..." „You're going to have to teach me how to speak German... I want to be able to tell you in German how much I love you... I want to be able to tell you how I feel about you, in your own tongue... Do you know what we should do? I should speak to you in French, and you should speak to me in German... Sure, at first, it's going to be hard for me... but you'll see... I'm a fast learner..." „Yeah... I've seen how fast a learner you are..." Will replied, with a large smile on his face... And I think you've got a great idea. Lets do that... And I'll bring you some books in German, to help you learn..." „Instead of learning English at school, I should have learned German... it would be more useful now, wouldn't it?", Paul said. „You speak English?", Will asked... „Yes... I'm pretty fluent in English", Paul replied. „Well, that's going to help you learn German..." „I hope you're right... but anyway, I count on you to teach me..." – „When do we start?", Will inquired... „Right now, mein Herr...", Paul answered, laughing... And so, from then on, Will spoke German to Paul, whom at first didn't understand a thing... He asked a lot of questions to Will... who answered, very patiently. As he had said, Will later brought Paul a few German books and a German dictionary... and gradually, Paul started to understand more and more of what Will was saying to him. He loved it! He was a fast learner, indeed. Very often, over the next few months, he would listen to the German radio, and thanks to Will, after a while, he became quite fluent in German. He didn't know it, yet... but that would serve him well in a not so distant future...

„Now, what about a good shower?", Paul asked... „Yeah... with that mess you made on my poor body... again... I've been abused...", Will replied, laughing his heart out. „Ah... but if I remember correctly, you're the one that kept jacking me off... If I pumped my spunk on you're poor body, it's because your hand kept riding up and down my poor oozing prick... It's all your fault again..." They both stared into each other's eyes, and then burst out laughing... „Yeah... And I loved each an every second of it...", Will replied. „So did I..." „Und schon rief der Posten, sie blasen Zapfenstreich...", Will added... „Ja", Paul replied, „Wie einst..." „Now, let's hit the shower, shall we?" „Oui, mon amour!", Paul said, grinning... After a quick shower, they came back into the bedroom, tucked into bed, for a good night's sleep. Paul turned off he lights, and again, he cuddled into Will's warm and smooth body... „You've made me feel so good tonight, Paul... That will be a night to remember... Thanks... I love you Paul... I'm yours for ever, if that's what you want..." „I told you, Will: You're mine... I'll never let you go... And I shall remember tonight for the rest of my life... And don't you worry about the future, Will, I will shield our love from all dangers... And I will shield you, my love... Trust me..." „I trust you Paul, for I don't see what I could do in that regard... In fact, there's nothing I can do..." „I know... Just watch me, Will... and count on me... There's nothing I can't do..." „I love you Paul..." „I love you too, Will..." „Night, Paul!" „Night Will, have sweet dreams..." „You too, my love..."

Will was so exhausted, it didn't take long before he fell asleep... Paul was exhausted too... but it took a long time before he fell asleep: His mind was working hard to find solutions to his problems... to Will's problems...

He had to find ways... As his mind got organized, and things started to slowly fall into place... as he began sorting out everything... Paul began to see light at the end of the tunnel. Slowly, he made his plans... After a while, he got the general idea about what he would do... He smiled to himself... Now he could rest! Later, he would have time to work over the details... He hadn't known before that he could be so wicked... But to protect and shield Will, there would be nothing to stop him! Without him noticing it, he fell asleep... The days ahead would be quite exhausting, and he needed all his energy to face them... But in the end, he knew he would succeed!

FIVE
« A PLAN »

„Good morning, my love", Paul said to Will, as he saw Will had awaken... „Did you sleep well?" „Hi, handsome..." Will replied to his young blond lover... „Yeah... I did sleep very well, thanks to you... I've dreamed about you all night, and I didn't want to awake, for fear you wouldn't be there anymore..." „Nah... I've told you... you will not get rid of me that easily" Paul replied with a grin on his face. „And you... did you sleep well?" Will asked. „Of course, and I've dreamed about you too..." „Oh! And did you enjoy your dreams?" „A lot! But I prefer to see you here, alive, beside me... than in my dreams...", Paul said, as he leaned over Will to give him a sweet kiss. „That's nice, thanks... It's Monday today, isn't it?" "Yes, June 17th..." Paul answered. „Time flew so fast, yesterday... I just can't believe it's already Monday... Do you have plans for today?" Will ventured to ask, tenderly smiling to Paul... „Oh... Yes... big plans... and you fit right into them, you gorgeous, good-looking and so handsome dude...", Paul answered, with a very big smile. „Ah, and what are your plans, may I ask?" „First, we'll have breakfast... and after that, I'll need your help" – „What for?" „I need you to go into Paris... meet with some of your German friends... I need you to collect each and every bit of information you can get your hands on... We must know about the most recent news... We must know where we stand... What's going to happen, you know... so we can get organized", Paul answered. „Sure... no problem." „You'll take my father's car... you'll find the registrations inside... And don't forget your ID... Driving a French car like that one, you could be stopped and get checked, you know..." „That would be fun... getting check by my own brothers in arms...", Will said, with a big smile on his face. „Well, if that happens, don't fall in love with the guy checking

79

you..." Paul answered, frowning... „Oh, that could never happen since you occupy all the place in my heart... so don't worry", Will said, flashing a big smile to Paul. „Hey, you, sexy... cut it out..." Paul replied, grinning. „And while you're collecting news, I'll be in my father's study... I must go over some documents and papers he left for me... just in case, as he then said..." „In case of what?", Will asked. „Well, before he left, I had a long talk with my Dad... I must say I was not too interested at the time... Anyway, my Dad wanted me to know how he runs his business... What I should do, should something happen to him... Who I should contact... He explained everything to me... showed me documents... He even had a document, written by Maître Langlois, our attorney, so I would be authorized to take every decisions in his place, should need be..." „Oh yeah... It's called a «Power of attorney», I think", Will said. „That's it... and my Dad also told me about all the different bank accounts we have, not only here in Paris, but in Geneva and in New York as well... I'm authorized to draw whatever I want from those accounts..." „Shit Paul... that's unbelievable..." „Yeah! My Dad is a very wise man, you know... I guess he saw how things were going... and I think he saw it coming... you know... so he made his plans, and now, it's my turn to make mine..." „What do you intend to do?", Will asked. „I'm not too sure, yet... that depends on what I'll find in my dad's study... It also depends on the news you will bring back... and most of all, it depends on what my father will decide to do, from now on... But as I know him, he will never come back to Paris as long as you guys are in here... That's for sure..." – „Well.. I find my life is very simple compared to yours, Paul. With all those decisions you'll have to take... For my part, all the decisions are taken by the army, you know... They tell me what to do, and I do it, that's all..." „Yeah... but as you told me last night Will, you're with me in that boat... You're very much concerned by all the decisions I'll be taking... My decisions will have an impact on your own life, you know... If you still want to be with me, that is... But don't worry, I will never take a decision that could have an influence on your life without consulting you first..." „I'm with you all the way, Paul. You can count on that... As I have already told you, I trust you... and I know deep in my heart you wouldn't do anything that could hurt me... at least, not knowingly..." „No, I would never do anything that could hurt you Will. I swear... All I want is for us to be happy... That's all. But I'll do everything I can to make sure that happens..." „I know Paul.

And I love you for that!" „I love you too, Will", Paul replied... „Now, what about breakfast? Huh?" „Yeah. Let's have a quick shower first, then let's go to eat...", Will said, with a big smile.

It was a quick shower alright, for both young guys were starving. They ate breakfast so fast... but Paul didn't forget to give their new cat, Boussole... something to eat. Then, he said to Will: „Now, take the car's key and go fetch the news... And don't worry Will, I'm not asking you to tell me secrets you wouldn't tell to your enemy..." „You're not the enemy to me, Paul..." „I know... but nevertheless, I want you to feel at ease with that..." „Anyway Paul, I'm not in a position to know about great secrets, you know. I haven't talked to Hitler recently..." Will said, grinning... „Yeah... Well, if you do talk to him, would you tell him something for me?" – „What?" „Tell him to go to hell..." Hearing what Paul had said, Will burst out laughing... Then he said: „Well Paul, I guess he's already burning in hell by now..." – „Huh?" „Sure... he's already dead, you know... as you told your Grandma the other night... He killed himself, according to what you said..." „I wish that was true..." „Don't even dream about that... Hitler would never kill himself..." „Whatever... Now, get going, gorgeous... get going..." Will looked at his lover's very green eyes, he smiled, then said: „I'm on my way, mein Herr... at your service... after all, I'm your Kriegsgefangener..." – „My what?" „Your prisoner of war... a new German word for you to learn..." Will replied, laughing... „Yeah... You're my Kriegsgefangener... and as I can see, you're a very willing one at that..."

So Will left, and then Paul went to his father's study. He opened each and every file... Studied each document... took notes... The hours went by without him noticing... In the end, he had taken several very important decisions. The first one concerned the family business: Should his father decide not to come back to Paris, he would take his place, and go on with their business... With the help of their attorney, Maître Langlois, he would manage... But of course, he had to wait for their company's employees to come back to Paris... That should not take long, he thought... they are not rich people... and they can't last very long without their jobs... His second decision concerned Will. As soon as possible, he would have to get in touch with their director in Geneva so a bank account was opened there for Will. Paul would transfer a sizable amount on that new account, so Will would feel financially independent from him... That was important for Paul... He wanted Will to be his own man... Then, Will made a list of all the other problems he would have to solve over the next few days... When he finished, he looked at the list, and smiled. He wished his father could see him now... He would be proud of his son... Yes, Paul was a „De Brion" alright. He was as shrewd as his father was... It's probably running in my blood, he said to himself, smiling... Later on, he heard someone coming... It was probably Will, Paul thought. He went to the kitchen, and waited... Minutes later, the door to the underground garage opened, and Will came in...

„I'm glad you're back... I missed you..." Paul said with a big smile. „I missed you, too... Did you have time to go through all you wanted to see and read? Will asked. „Yup! I'm done..." „And?" „I've made a list of all what I'll have to do, as soon as we know what's going to happen around here... How about the

news?" Will looked at the door and remained silent for a while. Then he walked over to Paul, took him into his arms, and kissed him. After their lips parted, Paul said: „That was good... but looking at you, I guess you don't have good news for me, do you?" „Come and sit, please Paul..." So they sat at the table, and Will started saying: „You're right Paul. I don't have good news for you..." „Go ahead..." „Well... it seems France is indeed totally defeated... They say that tonight, Marshal Pétain will make a speech on the radio..." „Marshal Pétain? ...You must be wrong... He is an old guy... you know... He retired from the army a long time ago... and besides, he's not a member of the Cabinet..." „Well Paul, I tell you what I've heard..." − „What else?" „Well, since the evacuation at Dunkerque, the british have left... as well as a good chunk of your own soldiers... furthermore, I've heard we've made a lot of prisoners of war... Well over a million, they say... I've also heard that a few days ago, your President as well as your Prime Minister have asked for President Roosevelt's help..." „And?" „According to documents we have seized, President Roosevelt said France could count on America's sincere sympathy... but that no help would come from America..." „..." „I've been to Hôtel Meurice this morning... and I've heard one of our generals laughing his heart out, saying Hitler knew about that all along... That America would do nothing... He said that was obvious, since there will soon be an election in America, and Roosevelt is running for re-election... and that his slogan is: „Peace at all cost..." „Shit! ...So, Will... We really stand all alone, now, don't we?" „Yes..." „It seems there's nothing left to be save... Hitler will do whatever he wants..." „ I don't think so, Paul. At Hôtel Meurice, I've heard army officers say Hitler is scared like hell France will continue fighting, after having transferred the rest of your army to your vast colonial empire... They said Hitler fears your navy could join with the Royal navy... And as you know Paul, France has one of the most powerful navies in the world... much more powerful than our own Kriegsmarine... So I guess Hitler will have to refrain his ambitions if he wants to avoid that from happening..." „I hope you're right Will... We do not have may other cards in our hand, do we?" – „(...)" „Let's go to the drawing-room, Will, and let's turn on the radio..." „Good idea..."

They went to the drawing-room and turned the radio on... They heard mournful music on each station Paul checked... Then a speaker came on the air... Saying that later Maréchal Pétain would give a very important speech to the Nation... Paul looked at Will, and said: „You were right..." „I guess so... Now Paul, stay near the radio while I go to the kitchen to make some lunch for the both of us... I'm starving, aren't you?" „Just do that, Will... but I'm not very hungry... you know... with all what's going on... Will you manage in the kitchen?" – „Just watch me...", Will replied with a smile... Paul remained glued to the radio, while Will got busy in the kitchen, making lunch... From time to time, the speaker would come back on the air... telling again about the speech Pétain would give later... While in the kitchen making lunch, Will felt sad for Paul and for France... Sure, Germany was victorious... but nevertheless, he felt sad. Let's pray that such a thing never happens to Germany, Will tought to himself... But he also thought about the fact that if, indeed, France had lost a major battle, the war was not over yet. The British were still fighting... and by now, they probably had very well fortified themselves on their island... He stopped working for a while, and started thinking about that... England! That island would not be easy to take, Will thought... It was not as if the Wehrmacht could just walk to London... The Channel was there... and the Royal navy was the most powerful in the world... Every German ship trying to carry troops over there, would be sunk so fast... Hitler was not crazy enough to try that, Will said to himself. Yeah... England was well protected by the Channel... Hitler would have to take care of the Royal navy first, before trying anything else... That explained why Hitler didn't want to see the French navy join the Royal navy... Will smiled at that... Yeah, he thought... the French had a few good cards on their hand... Hitler will have to refrain himself... Will finshed preparing lunch, then joined Paul in the drawing-room.

„Here, my love... that will be sustaining... you have to eat if you want to survive... so I can make love to you again..." Will said to Paul, smiling while giving him a large plate full of food... „Thanks, Will. I guess your right... as always... I should eat a little, because I sure intend to have you making love to me in a very near future...", Paul replied, smiling... „So... what's new? Have you heard anything?" Will asked. „No. Nothing. Always the same speaker... you know..." „We'll have to wait..." „Yeah!" So they slowly ate their lunch... listening to the music on the radio... Not much was said... Later on, they heard someone at the front door. Paul looked at Will, a bit puzzled... „Are you expecting someone?" „No!"

Paul rose and started walking to the entrance hall, Will following right behind him. He went to the door and, through the large panes, he saw two people standing outside. He smiled. He knew them... so he opened one of the large doors: „Bonsoir, madame et monsieur Bloomfield... comment allez-vous? Mais entrez, je vous prie..." „Oh, good evening, monsieur Paul... How are you?" madame Bloomfield asked. „Very well, thank you" Then Paul noticed Mrs & Mr Bloomfield were looking at Will, standing right behind him... „Please, come in, and join us... Do you remember my cousin Guillaume, from Strasbourg?", Paul asked them... „I'm not sure we've ever met", Mr Bloomfield replied, with a smile on his face... „And if we did... you were probably very young at the time..." „At any rate, Guillaume, this is Mrs & Mr Bloomfield, our neighbours...", Paul said. They shook hands and Will, thinking fast, said to them: „Oh!... yes... I remember having seen you in the past... but that's a long time ago... So, you're right Mrs Bloomfield, I was very young at the time... I guess I've grown up since then..." „You're right, Guillaume... You've certainly grown up... look at you... What a fine young man you are now..." Mrs Bloomfield said. „Please, Mrs & Mr Bloomfield, call me Will... that's my nickname..." Will replied, smiling to them.... „Please, do join us into the drawing-room", Paul said... As they were walking towards the drawing-room, Mrs Bloomfield kept searching her memory to remember when they could have met with Will in the past... Did she even knew that the De Brion had family in Strasbourg? She wasn't sure... But anyway, she concluded, sometimes, I have bad memory... so... On his side, her husband had come to the same conclusion... "Ah! Old age...", he thought... "Bad memory..." While walking towards the drawing-room, Paul gave a look to Will, with a grin on his face... Will returned the look with a frown... „Please... do sit down. We were just waiting to listen to the speech Maréchal Pétain will give to the Nation, later... I hope you will stay with us to hear it...", Paul said. „Oh, yes... We've heard about that speech... That's the reason why we came...“ Mr Bloomfield said „... „So we can talk with your father, after the speech...“ „Well Mr Bloomfield, I'm afraid you won't be able to talk with my father... for my family isn't back yet...", Paul replied. „Oh", Mrs Bloomfield said... „We thought they were back... The other night, we thought we heard your mother play the piano... And this morning, we saw your father's car, going and coming back... so we thought...“ Will smiled at Mrs & Mr Bloomfield, and said: „It's me, you heard playing the piano the other night... and it's me you saw this morning, driving my uncle's car... I just couldn't stay put... I had to go out... and get some fresh news...“ „Oh, you play so well...“ Mrs Bloomfield replied. „Thank you very much... I guess I've inherited that talent from my aunt, Paul's mother...“ Will said, giving a big smile to Paul... Paul smiled back to Will, thinking about what a good liar Will was! He had some guts! And Will had been right about everything else: The neighbours, not being all gone; people watching everything of what was going on outside, on the street... Yeah. Will had a very good judgment, Paul thought. He was always right about all those things... On his side, Will was crossing his fingers in the hope that Mrs & Mr Bloomfield would not start questioning him about Strasbourg, for he knew nothing about that place... and he hoped they wouldn't question him about his new «aunt» ... Shit... He didn't even know what her first name was... He had to do something to change the subject... „Cousin Paul...", Will said, grinning... „Do you think we could serve coffee to our guest?" „Oh, but of course... Where are my good manners...", Paul answered. Will rose: „Keep company to our guests, Paul... I'll go make coffee... you know... I've been around here so often, that I know very well where to find everything I need...“ Will stated, trying not to break into a fit of giggles, saying that... „Yes, cousin Will... You're so right...“ Paul replied, thinking that if that was possible, he would strangle Will for what he had said... and the way he had said that... "Oh, you, devil! You'll pay for that", he said to himself...

85

Will began walking out of the drawing-room, and Paul could see his lover was glowing... Will was too happy to leave Paul and later see how he had swam out of the mess he had created... A few minutes later, Will was back, carrying a large tray with coffee, sugar, cups and saucers on it... As he laid the tray on the coffee table, Paul said to him: „Oh, cousin Will... I see you did find all you needed...“ Will sat and, looking at Mrs & Mr Bloomfield, he said to them: „Yes... but you know... it's not easy... poor cousin Paul... now that my uncle's chef is gone... He no longer even has a maid, you know! All gone!!! All of them!!! Gone!!! Ahhhhhh! I tell you... Life is so dreadful, nowadays...“ Keeping his serious face, Will turned to Paul, a twinkle in his eye... "Oh shit!" Paul thought... "That does it! You're going to pay dearly for that, mister!" Nonetheless, he had to refrain himself because, otherwise, he would have burst out laughing... He didn't know Will could be such a clown... He looked at Will and, being as serious as Will had been, Paul replied: „Oh dear cousin... you're so right... And you can understand our situation so well... since you were all forced to evacuate Strasbourg last year... It must have been so hard...“ „Yes“, Will said... „You know... it's been so hard... I prefer not to talk about that...“ „Oh... We do understand...“ Mrs Bloomfield stated... „Poor you...“ „Yes“, Will answered, giving a malicious smile to Paul, without their guest noticing... But their little game was cut short, when the speaker came back on the air to say that in five minutes, Maréchal Pétain would start to give his speech... The mood changed inside the drawing-room, as everyone nervously waited...

„Chers auditeurs, Monsieur le Maréchal Pétain s'adresse à vous maintenant.“ There was a pause, then they began hearing the voice of the old Maréchal: „.... Français! À la demande de Monsieur le Président de la République, j'assume à partir d'aujourd'hui la direction du Gouvernement de la France!“ And the old Maréchal went on, saying he knew he could count on the support of the army, on the support of the ex-servicemen he had had the privilege to command in the past, as he knew he could count on the unbounded faith the whole of France had in him... And then, he got to the main part of his speech: „C'est le coeur brisé que je vous dis aujourd'hui qu'il faut cesser le combat!“ ... And the old Maréchal went on, explaining that the night before, he had contacted the opposite side, to inquire as if they had the will to explore, along with France, and with honour, ways to end the hostilities... Hearing that, Mr

„Bloomfield"... you know..." – „Yes... they are..." „Well Paul, if you're still making plans to shield you and me from troubles, you may as well include them into your plans..." „Why do you say that, Will?" „From what we've heard tonight on the radio, things are going to change here, in France... Yes Paul, whether we like it or not, things are going to change... As the Gestapo will get in here, they will start looking for the Jews... I'm sure of that... That's what they did in Berlin... Back in Berlin, Lutz and I, we had good friends who were Jews. They were living on our street... And one by one, they all disappeared into the night... We never saw them again, and never heard from them again..." „Do you know where they were taken to?" „No. We don't. It's too dangerous to ask such a question in Germany, nowadays... But wherever they were taken to, I just can't explain why they haven't written to us... you know... That's a sign they are no longer free to do so... otherwise, I'm sure our friends would have written to us...", Will answered. „Shit, Will... it's awful, what you just said..." „I know... I don't want to be a scare-monger, you know, but I think you should be aware of what could happen here... since it happened in Germany... and it's still going on there ..." „Obviously, I will have to take Mrs and Mr Bloomfield into account, in my plans... for I do not intend to see them disappear like that...That won't happen... I swear... Trust me!" „I've already told you Paul: I trust you with everything..." „... Yeah... You know what, Will? You make a pretty good liar..." Paul stated, out of nowhere...

„Huh?", Will replied... „Yeah... We'll make a very good pair... You've got along very fast, with my story... you know... you being my cousin Guillaume from Strasbourg..." „Shit Paul, I didn't see that one coming... I've never even seen Strasbourg in my life... But why Strasbourg?" „Well, in Alsace... not only do they speak French... but they also speak a German dialect... So I thought that would explain your slight accent..." „WOW... You're good, Paul! I'm amazed... Good thing they didn't start asking me questions about Strasbourg or Alsace, though... I know nothing about those places..." „Well you'll have to learn Will... Cause from now on, you're from there... and you shall be able to answer any questions, so our story sticks... I'll give you books to read about Alsace and Strasbourg... And I'm sure very soon,

you'll be able to lie unblushingly about your false city of origin..." „How wicked you are, Paul De Brion... I think you're as wicked as Hitler

89

and Goebbels are..." „Worse! ... Will... Worse...to protect you, I'll do anything... and if I have to sell my soul to the devil to do that, I will gladly do it..." „You love me that much, Paul?" „Much more than you can think, Will... I would gladly give my life to save yours, Will... I swear!" „Come here, Paul De Brion... come here, and kiss me!" Paul went to Will, and they began to kiss passionately. After a while, Will said: „Guess it's time to go to bed, don't you think?" „Yeah. I guess it's enough for today... What about a good bath, before we go to bed... relax a bit... What do you think?" Paul asked Will. „That's a good idea... let's go..." So they went upstairs, got undressed and then, took a very hot and relaxing bath together. Will wanted to make love to Paul... to kiss him everywhere... but he knew Paul had been through many emotions today. All Paul wanted for now, was to be hold by Will's strong arms... to feel he was there for him... with him... Will sensed that, and respected that. He loved Paul so much. His sexual needs would have to wait...

Will was lying on his back in the bathtub, as Paul laid between his legs, his back hard pressed against Will's chest... Will knew Paul could feel his boner, but having check, Paul wasn't sporting one. Paul was resting... Will kissed Paul on the back of his neck, very tenderly, telling him how much he was in love with him... „You're horny, huh?", Paul asked Will... „I can't deny it... as you see and feel... but not tonight. I want you to get some rest. It's not a good time for you, you know... And I understand that... Tonight, we're going to take it easy. Besides, we've got a lot of time before us... We've got the whole future...", Will answered. „I could give you a hell of a good blowjob right now", Paul replied, smiling to Will... „I know..." Will answered, smiling. „And I'm sure I would love it. But, Paul, you will give me a good blowjob when you really feel you want to, not only because you want to make me feel good... So now, what I suggest is we go to bed, and get a very good night's sleep... There will be many other nights, Paul... but for tonight, let's just go to sleep, what do you think?" „...You're right... as always...", Paul answered. So they went to bed, and Paul cuddled into Will's warm and smooth body. He felt so secure there... He could feel Will's hardon press against his arse crack. He knew Will was horny... but not him... He loved Will so much because Will respected that. Yeah, Paul thought, he had found the love of his life!

SIX
«WHAT A BEAUTIFUL DAY»

Tuesday, June 18, Paul woke up in a very good mood, although he knew Will's leave would end later that day. Paul wanted this last day to be special, so he decided to brush away the bad news they had heard the night before, on the radio: There was nothing he could do to change the situation, so why lose precious time dwelling on the past? Full steam ahead to the future, he thought to himself, grinning! „You look so lovely when you're smiling like that", Will said to Paul. „Oh... I didn't realize you were awake... did I wake you up?", Paul replied, smiling to Will... „No... but I'm glad I am... What were you thinking about, that made you smile like that?" „I was just thinking how lucky I am having found you... and how much I love you... you, handsome hunk...", Paul replied. „Come here... and kiss me", Will answered, with a sexy smile on his face, lying on his back... So Paul went to Will, stretching his firm body over Will's and, looking into his lover's perfect blue eyes, Paul started kissing him.

It didn't take long for their cocks to get hard as steel, as Paul kept grinding his big hard dick into Will's groins... Since both of them were hairless and oozing so much, Will's crotch soon became very slippery, and it felt so good having their dicks rubbing against one another... They kept kissing like that for a while and, suddenly, Will couldn't hold it anymore. He felt his dick stiffening and his balls ready to shoot. "I'm going to shoot Paul... Oh shit... I'm going to shoot...", Will shouted. Paul quickly went for Will's dick, and took it deep inside his warm mouth, bobbing fast on his lover's throbbing prick. As Will gasped and moaned, he started shooting his sweet young cum deep down Paul's gut, the rest filling his mouth. Paul gulped all of it, as he gave Will a smile of gratitude... „GOD! You taste so good, Will... so good...", Paul said.

„Thanks", Will answered, with a big smile on his face... „That was sooooooo good Paul... I whish it could last for ever... But, you haven't cum yet, have you?" „No.." „Ahhhhh... Now, I have something for you... Come here and lay on your back..." Will said. Paul did as asked, and grinned as he figured Will would give him a good blowjob...

But that's not what Will had in mind... Instead, he took the bottle of lotion Paul had left on the small table next to the bed, opened it, and smeared some all over Paul's dick. With one hand, he bobbed slowly on Paul's slippery prick and, with his other hand, he smeared some oil over his arse crack and onto his rosy spot. Then, he straddled Paul's crotch and guided Paul's very hard dick to his hole... „Are you doing what I'm thinking you're doing?, Paul asked Will, with a worried smile... „Yeah! It's your turn to be inside me... I want to feel you, deep inside... I want to feel you belong to me... and I want you to know the pleasure it gives, having your dick deep inside me...", Will answered, grinning. Will then started to impale himself on Paul's very slippery hard dick, and he felt a bolt of pain shoot through his body, when Paul's large mushroom cap penetrated his hole. Paul could see the pain on Will's handsome face, and said to his blond lover: „Take your time my love. Give yourself time to adjust... the pain won't last, I swear..." „Yeah!"

Will went down a little further on Paul's big dick, and when he felt Paul's mushroom cap was all inside him, he paused for a while... and as the pain subsided, he went all the way down on Paul's hot cock. „Oh shit!", Will said... as he took a long pause, and as Paul began playing with Will's balls and hardening dick. In no time, Will's cock was rock hard again, and oozing into paul's slippery hand... „How does it feel now?", Paul asked... „Better. The pain is almost gone..." A while later, Will began to go up and down on Paul's hard prick, now that his hole was loosening up... It began to feel good, and Will started to groan... Paul was groaning and moaning like hell, feeling his big hard dick being massage by Will's ass muscles... „Ahhhhh", Paul shouted... „I can't believe how good it feels... How about you?" „It's getting better and better", Will answered, giving Paul his biggest smile... „I love you, Paul..." „I love you too, Will."

Then, Will increased his speed on Paul's shaft and began shuddering as Paul's dick kept hitting his love spot. „Shit! Shit! Shit!", Will said... „Now, I know what you were talking about... It's fantastic! Can't believe it..." Now Will's breathing was heavy, as Paul, gasping with lust, got faster, wanking Will's dick and squeezing his big smooth balls... „I can't hold it anymore...", Will said, as he squeezed Paul's hot dick, using his ass ring. Seconds later, he began shooting his spunk all over Paul's face, lips, abs and smooth chest... „I'm going to shoot too...", Paul cried out, his eighteen year old body quivering as he began firing torrents of cum deep inside Will's love chute. Will, still gasping, leaned to Paul and started kissing him, tasting his own cum on Paul's hot lips... Their naked bodies glistened with sweat as their passions went beyond their control... Paul hold Will in his arms, until Will stopped shaking...

„That was Oh so good..." Will exclaimed, moments later... „...I know... Do you still remember the pain?", Paul asked Will... „Are you kidding? What pain? But I remember the pleasure: That, I remember!", Will answered, as he burst out, laughing... „Yeah... isn't it incredible?", Paul replied. „Sure is... I could keep doing that all day long and all night long..." „Oh no, you won't!", Paul said, laughing... „You've got to fuck me too, not just me fucking you..." „Don't worry", Will answered, laughing. „Next time, I'm going to shag you senseless..." „Oh yeah?... And why don't you do it right now, mister?" „Right now?", Will asked, a bit surprised... „Yeah... right now! I can feel your stiff cock hard pressed on my stomach... Why don't you use it to «shag» me, as you say..." „You ask for it, mister... Now, get on to a new position... Kneel before me, and rest on your elbows... I'm going to fuck you doggie style...", Will replied, with a very sexy grin on his face. „Ohhhhhh... I like that", Paul replied, assuming his position... „Now, go right for it... please..." „... It's going to hurt, if I do that... I should put some lotion first..." „NO. Your dick is so slippery, we don't need lotion. I'm telling you, go for it... all the way in... That's what I want", Paul stated. „As you wish... but don't blame me if it hurts...", Will replied, grinning. As he said that, Will put his dick head over Paul's rosy spot, then ram is big dick all the way in, up to the hilt... Paul shouted, then said: „Come on now, shag me... Fuck me good and hard..." Will didn't wait and began to fuck Paul's love chute hard, going all the way out, then all the way in... Knowing Paul was jacking off his hard prick, Will took hold of Paul's smooth balls, and squeezed them hard... „Oh shit... That feels good, Will"... Will began ramming his big dick faster and faster into Paul's tight but slippery asshole, then deep inside his love chute, hitting his love spot each time... „WOW...", Paul exclaimed... „Faster"... Will was now stretching and squeezing Paul's

93

balls, as he kept going in and out of Paul's hot ass, faster and faster. With his other hand, he even put one finger inside Paul's ass ring, beside his slippery dick... „Ahhhhhh...", Paul shouted.... „That feels sooooo good..." Hearing that, Will added a second finger, then a third, as Paul was panting non-stop. Then, Will got a fourth finger inside... still fucking Paul with his big dick... but after a while, he couldn't hold it anymore, and he started to cum so hard inside Paul's hot chute, he couldn't believe it... „Faster Will... faster", Paul asked... „But I can't, Paul... I've just cum...", Will replied...

So Will took his dick out of Paul's very hot ass and started to rotate his four fingers inside and out of Paul's love chute... then, he added his tumb... „Yeah"... Paul said... „That's it..." Without Will noticing it, his fist started to enter Paul's arse..." „Oh shit...", Paul said, still jacking off his hard and oozing dick... „That feels so good... How many fingers do you have inside my hole?" „It's not only my fingers, Paul... it's my fist also...", Will replied... Paul was as much stunned as Will was, hearing that... but it felt so good... „Whatever... Keep doing that... I love it...", he replied. So Will slowly pushed his fist deeper inside Paul... who was now shaking non-stop, panting and sweating... When Will's fist hit Paul's love spot, Paul said: „That's it... stay there... it feels so good..." Paul couldn't keep it anymore, and he let the floodgate open, as wave after wave of cum squirts started to come out of his very hard dick... He cried out in ecstasy, as Will kept swirling around his fist inside Paul's ass... After Paul's orgasm subsided, Will started to slowly take his fist out of Paul's love chute. Paul gasped, then, looking at Will, he said: „I never, ever thought it was possible to attain such level of pleasure, Will... I swear..." „You liked what I did?" „Shit Will, I loooooooved it!" Paul answered, laughing his heart out... „Come here, and kiss me..." Paul laid on his back, and Will cuddled into Paul's smooth body, then they kissed... „I love you so much, Paul... I didn't want to hurt you..." „Don't worry, you didn't hurt me at all, Will. I loved it... and I love you, too..." „I guess you're going to feel some pain for a day or two, walking...", Will replied, grinning... „I don't care... I loved it", Paul answered, kissing Will deeply...

After that hot sex, they went for a good shower... and they relaxed, taking care of each other's body... „Hey, what about breakfast...? I'm starving", Will said... „Me too..." So they got breakfast, then Paul said to Will: „Let's get dressed and go for a walk... to see what's going on... what do you think?" „Yeah... I haven't seen much, yet...", Will replied, grinning... „So, let's go!" So they went, walking through Paris... It was such a beautiful day... on the Champs Élysées Avenue, they met a few people... as if the population was slowly coming back to the city of Lights... They walked down on Kléber Avenue, and reached the Trocadéro Place. There, they took a break... looking at the Eiffel Tower, on the other side of the Seine River... What a sight! „It's beautiful..." Will said... „Everything is so beautiful here in Paris... including you..." „Thanks", Paul replied, with a sincere smile on his face... „Everything is beautiful here, except for that big flag on top of the Tower... That makes me sick..." Will looked up to the top of the Eiffel Tower, where he could see a very large Nazi flag, with it's black Svastika, flying in the wind... He looked at Paul, then started kissing him wih his full lips... „That's better...", Paul said, after a while... I guess if it was not for that damn flag, you wouldn't be here now, with me..." „Forget about that flag, Paul, I'm here, and I love you... To hell with the rest...", Will answered. „You're right again, Will... To hell with the rest...", Paul sincerely said. „Come, follow me..."...

They went down to the Trocadéro gardens, then crossed the Iéna bridge and went right under the Eiffel Tower. They saw German soldiers there, having their picture taken by other soldiers... They smiled... They kept walking and, after quite a while, they reached the Quartier latin, where Paul showed to Will the Panthéon... „It's beautiful...", Will said. After that, they walked back to the Jardin du Luxembourg, where Will couldn't believe his eyes... „My God! It's so beautiful, here..." „Yeah", Paul answered... „When I was young, I used to come here with my father... so I could play, and make my ship sail across the pond, there... (...) All of that seems so far away, now..." Will took hold of Paul's hand, and squeezed it. „I know what you mean...", Will said. Paul managed a small smile of gratitude, then said: „Let's try to find out if there is a place open, so we can eat something..." „Do you have money on you?", Will asked Paul... „Sure... Don't worry about that... I've got plenty... and let's spend it entirely, for I don't know what it will be worth tomorrow...", Paul said, with a grin on his face... Seing Will had frowned at what he had just said, Paul added: „Oh, don't worry about me... I don't give a damn about what the Nazis will do to the French Franc... As long as they keep their hands off Switzerland, I'll be fine... since most of our money is there, and

95

a large chunk of our income comes from there... as well as from the United-States... So, as long as the Nazis don't put their hands on the Swiss Franc, I'll be alright..." Will grinned, hearing that, and then said: „You know... We're not at war with Switzerland and we're not at war with America either... I don't know about America, but I'm certain we won't touch Switzerland... It's too useful to Hitler... and beside that, it's not threatening... you know..." „Yeah... I know... But since they speak German in parts of Switzerland, I wonder if Hitler will not try to incorporate them into the Reich...", Paul said. Will started laughing, hearing that, and then he replied: „True, Paul... a lot of people speak German in Switzerland... but it's not the same German we speak in Berlin... In fact, the way the Swiss speak German makes us laugh... It's as if they were backward people... you know... But they are also very proud and very strong... it wouldn't be easy for us to take Switzerland... they would fight us to the end... in the mountains... everywhere... Why spend so much, taking Switzerland, when we do not need to? I've told you... it's useful to keep Switzerland as it is... trust me on that..." „I do trust you Will, and I hope you're right... Now, let's find some place to eat, if that's possible..."

After a long walk, finding nothing open... they finally found a small place that was open... They got inside, and sat at a small table. Rapidly, a young waiter came to them and asked, smiling: „Enfin! des clients... Que puis-je vous servir?" „Anything you have... We're starving... But first, do you have beer", Paul asked... „Ah! Monsieur... we have plenty! Two large beers?" „Yeah!", Paul answered, smiling... „Two large beers"... A bit later, the young waiter came back to their table with the largest beers Paul and Will had ever seen... „There you are!", the young waiter said... „Enjoy!" „Why don't you join us...", Will asked... „Well... I guess I could... since you're our only clients, and I don't think we'll have many today...", the waiter answered. So the young waiter sat at the table, and they started talking... having fun... Suddenly, the young waiter asked Will: „Are you German?" „Hell, no..." Will replied... „I'm from Strasbourg... why do you ask?" „Oh! That explains your accent..." Paul grinned at Will... „Yeah... Yeah... I know", Will said... „No offence intended...", the waiter said... „And none taken", Will replied, with a grin... So eventually, they ordered and ate a very good lunch. Then they left, Paul leaving a very large tip to the young waiter... „Thanks, dude..." The waiter said... „It's been fun, having you here today..."

„It's my pleasure", Paul answered, giving the young waiter a big and sincere smile...

Now they went back into the street, and Paul was very satisfied... „Why do you smile like that?", Will asked Paul... „Now I know it works... my plan works... you see... that waiter back there believed you when you said you were from Alsace..." „Well, as you said... you will have to teach me about Alsace and Strasbourg... I'm lucky he didn't start questioning me... you know..." „Count on me for that... All I wanted to know was if it would work... and it does...", Paul said, laughing all the way to the sidewalk... „Yeah... but now it's getting dark... and we have to get back to your place, so I can change and report to my unit...", Will answered... „Oh! You...! What a way to break my party...", Paul replied. „I know Paul... And I'm sorry... but I've got to report to my unit, as much as I would prefer staying with you... You know that, don't you? „Yes Will... I know... (...) I wonder if the Métro is working... If it's working, then we could go home much faster..." „Let's find out", Will answered.

So they walked to the nearest subway station, which was the Odéon Station... and were pleasingly surprised by the fact the Métro was working... They went to the teller, where they bought two first class tickets... But the guy at the teller told them: „Yeah... It's working... but I don't know where you're going... all the lines are not working..." „I live on Foch Avenue...", Paul answered... „You're going to have to get off at the Kléber station... that's as far as that line goes tonight... You're going to have to walk the distance... „No problem", Paul answered with a smile on his face. So they got off at the Kléber station, then walked the distance from there to Paul's home, on Foch Avenue.

While they walked, Will took Paul's hand into his... They were all alone on the sidewalk... and Will didn't give a damn if they met someone... It felt so good, walking in Paris... holding hands... Was he dreaming? The night was warm, and for the first time in his life, Will felt totally happy... „I love you, Paul... I want you to know just how much I love you...", Will suddenly said... „I love you, too, Will". As they stopped walking, they started kissing very tenderly... An old lady walked by and, as she passed near them she said: „What a shame!" „Va chier, vieille folle! It's better being in love than being killed at the front for you, old bitch...", Paul

97

shouted... „Stop it Paul... She isn't worth it...", Will said, laughing his heart out... Eventually, they reached Paul's home, and got inside. They went to Paul's bedroom and Will got changed... Now, Paul looked at Will, with tears in his eye... „When will I see you again, Will... I can't go on without you...", Paul cried out... „Now Paul... it's hard for me too, you know... But I'll find a way... I swear... I'll find a way to get in touch with you as soon as I can... I swear... I love you, Paul..." They kissed again, very tenderly... „You know Will, without you, it's not worth it... If I'm going to fight, it's because I'm sure you'll be by my side... I'm ready to fight... but for the both of us, not just for me..." „I've told you Paul, I love you... I'll be at your side all the way... it's hard enough as it is... Be strong Paul, for the both of us... cause I'm not that strong... I need you to be strong..." „I will, my love... for you... I will. I swear... Now, I'm going to drive you to Hôtel Meurice..." „Are you sure it's safe for you?" „Don't worry... I have my ID..." Paul answered, smiling at Will. „Yeah...", Will replied, smiling back at Paul... So Paul drove Will back to Hôtel Meurice... and as Will got off the car, Paul said to him: „I'll be waiting for your call... You've got my number... I love you Will..." „...Love you too... I'll call you as soon as I can..." Will left, as Paul drove back to Foch Avenue, crying all he way. Later, when he got all alone into his bed, he took the shirt Will had worn that day, and started crying into it like a baby... After a long time, he went to sleep.

„Hey... did you have fun, during your leave?", Lutz asked his good friend Will, as Will got to the room they shared at Hôtel Meurice. Will looked at Lutz with tears in his eye... „Yeah... but it's not what you think... I'm in love...", Will answered. „Oh shit! That bad?", Lutz asked... „Yeah, that bad! But again, it's not what you think...", Will replied. What do you mean, it's not what I think?", Lutz asked, a bit puzzled... Will sat on his bed and looked at Lutz, who was also sitting on his own bed... then Will said:

„Lutz, we've known each other since... since we were kids, right? Are you really my friend? For what I'm about to tell you will stun you... really..." Lutz looked at his friend, not knowing what Will was about to tell him... But he knew Will was like a brother to him... So whatever Will was about to say to him, he knew he could take it... „You can speak your heart out, Will... You're my best friend, and I love you... Tell me what's on your heart... I will understand, please, trust me...", Lutz said. So Will took a pause... then started to tell Lutz the whole story... and how much he was in love with Paul... After a while and a long pause, after Will had stopped speaking... Lutz looked straight into Will's blue eyes and started saying: „...Well Will, I'm not sure I understand, you know... It comes to me as a shock... I mean...".

Lutz paused for a while, then continued: „You know Will, I love you... I love you as I love my own brother... You've always been a brother to me... Now, it's your life... If you really love that guy as you say you do... then, I'm happy for you... Who am I to judge? I will not judge you, Will... I love you too much for that. I've always been your friend, and I'll always be... Count on me! But please, Will, be careful... you know what they would do to you, if they find out..." „Yeah, I know... Thanks Lutz for not punching me in the face... And Lutz... don't worry... I won't rape you, you know", Will said, laughing... Hearing that, Lutz rose from his bed, went to Will, and took him into his strong arms... „I know Will... you're my brother... and you know I'm not „gay", as you said. Nevertheless, I love you Will, and if I can do anything to help you... you know... With you being in love with... what's his name again?" „Paul..." „Yeah... Paul... Well if I can help you, count on me. I'll be there for you..." „Thanks Lutz... you don't know how much it means to me..." „I'm here for you dude... and I want you to be happy, that's all..." Then Lutz went to his bed, and turned the light off... „Have sweet dreams, Will... and if you jack off, thinking about Paul... please... don't cum over me!", Lutz said laughing his heart out... „Don't worry, Lutz... although I'd like to jack off, thinking about Paul... I won't. I'm keeping all of my spunk for him..." – „The hell with you..." Lutz replied, laughing... „Good night, Will" „Yeah, good night Lutz... and thanks for you being so comprehensive... I dreaded telling you all I told you... It wasn't easy, you know..." „Yeah... I know... and I love you for being so honest with me... Now, go to sleep, and keep your hands off your dick..." Lutz answered, with a big laugh... „Oh... Lutz... would you help me with this... „hard" problem I have here?", Will asked, chuckling... „Fuck you, man! Don't ever count on me for that...", Lutz replied, laughing so hard he could have been heard all across the Hôtel... „Nah!... That's what I thought..." Will answered, „And that's the way I want it..." „Now, go to sleep, you bastard... and again... have sweet dreams", Lutz finally said... „I will... thanks... ,,, Will answered, before he fell to sleep... And he slept well that night, dreaming about Paul...

SEVEN
«HI, LUTZ, NICE TO MEET YOU...»

Wednesday morning, when Paul woke up, all alone in his bed, he felt miserable. Will wasn't there anymore, and there was an empty space in the bed where he had slept not so long ago... Paul knew he had to shake himself and stop turning over in his mind how much he missed Will... He knew he would see him again, but he didn't know when. But in the meantime, Will would call... and that was better than nothing. Paul took a quick shower, got dressed and went downstairs to make breakfast. Boussole, the cat, was there, very happy to see him... Paul smiled at the cat and gave him food... the poor little fellow was so hungry... After breakfast, Paul was slowly drinking his coffee when he heard someone ring at the front door. He went to answer the door and saw madame Louise and her husband, monsieur Pierre, standing there, outside the door... Madame Louise was their governess and monsieur Pierre, their gardener. They had been at his family's service for... well... as long as he could remember, and they used to live in a small annex, behind the big mansion. Paul quickly opened the door, thinking that maybe the day wouldn't be so bad, after all... With a big smile, Paul greeted madame Louise and her husband, saying to them: „Ah! You're back... Since you fled Paris, I missed you so much... Come in... and join me... I'm having coffee in the kitchen..." They all went to the kitchen, where madame Louise made fresh coffee... Then the couple explained with much details what they had been through, after they had fled Paris, and for his part, Paul explained his Grandma had died, that he had not heard from his father yet, but that life had to go on... and that he was taking charge of everything from now on... The couple was very please to hear they still had their jobs, and that they were most welcome... Madame Louise was put in charge of trying to get in touch with the rest of the staff, including

101

monsieur Michel, the chef... as Paul wanted to have him back as soon as he was back in Paris... Madame Louise smiled, saying she understood... and that in the meantime, she would take charge of the kitchen... As all the subjects had been covered, including Boussole the new cat, Paul left for his father's study, saying to the couple: „Heureux que vous soyez de retour à la maison!

In his father's study, Paul went through some papers, and tried to call Maître Langlois, the attorney... but to no avail. Obviously, he wasn't back yet. Paul then decided to go to his father's office, to see for himself if he could do something or learn something there... Paul drove to the company's head office, and found nobody there. He went to his father's office, and went through some papers there. Then he decided to make a big poster sign, saying:

TO ALL PERSONNEL: PLEASE, TAKE NOTE THAT WE WILL RE-OPEN FOR BUSINESS AS USUAL STARTING MONDAY, JUNE 24, AT 9H00. WE COUNT ON YOUR USUAL CO-OPERATION TO BE AT YOUR POST. THANK YOU ALL.

And he signed „Paul De Brion"... Since both his father and he were bearing the same name, nobody would know before next Monday that from now on, they would have to deal with the young son, and not his father... He took the poster sign and placed it on the company's front door. Then, he went back home, satisfied he had done what he wanted to do...

Later, madame Louise told him there was a call for him from a person named Will... Paul got excited and told madame Louise he would take the call in his father's study. Of course, Will wasn't free to speak as he whished, but told Paul he was fine, and that he had had a good «talk» with Lutz... and that everything was okay... Paul told Will that madame Louise and monsieur Pierre were back; that he had been to the company's head office, and what he had done there... Will explained that Lutz and he, as well as a few other translators from their unit, had been told they would be on special assignment outside Paris, next Friday and Saturday, but would be back on Sunday the 23rd and would have two days off, on the 26th and 27th... Yes, Will explained, he would be able to come and spend some time with Paul... but he would also have to spend some time with Lutz, since his friend was all alone in Paris... Hearing that, Paul said to Will: „Well... bring him along with you... He's your friend and I'm eager to meet him... He'll stay here, and I'll have a room prepared for him... at the other end of the corridor..." Will could sense Paul was smiling... „Are you sure?" „Yeah! Tell Lutz he's most welcome... and that I'll be glad to have him here during your leave...", Paul answered. „Okay then. As soon as we're back in Paris, I'll give you a call..." „Will? ... you know..." „Yes... I know... Same for me...", Will replied. „Yeah. Take good care..." „You too..."

Later that night, Will met with Lutz in the bedroom they were sharing at Hôtel Meurice and Will told Lutz about Paul's invitation... At first, Lutz remained silent... Will could see he didn't feel too comfortable about the invitation... Suddenly, it hit Will: Was Lutz thinking that he would be forced to witness things he didn't want to know about... or worse...? „Hey, you..." Will said to Lutz... „I know what you're thinking... and you're wrong! Do you think we're going to rape you? Paul and I are not like that, you know... I've always respected you, and you've always respected me... things haven't changed, just because I'm in love with Paul... And don't worry... I assure you we'll do nothing... nothing at all that could make you feel uncomfortable. Besides, you'll have your own room and your own bathroom, far from our room... So you've got no reason to worry..." Lutz smiled at Will, and replied: „I'm sorry Will... I didn't want to offend you... it's just... you know... I don't know how to react... how to behave with Paul... This situation is all too new for me, and... I guess I'm a bit scared... This is unknown territory for me..." „I know Lutz. But don't worry... You'll do just fine... And I'm sure you're going to like Paul... He's just a guy like you and me. And he's not a maniac, just because he loves me. Do you think I'm a maniac?" „Of course not", Lutz replied. „And did you feel uncomfortable last night, sharing the room with me?" „Don't be silly Will... of course not..." „And did you feel uncomfortable, getting undressed in front of me... knowing that I'm gay?" – „No. It didn't even cross my mind..." „So you see... I'm still the same Will you've always known... I haven't changed... and you know Lutz: Sure, you're a good-looking dude... but I'm not attracted to you, and I've never been... And I'm glad you're in love with your girlfriend Klara... and you can continue jacking off at night, thinking about her... I don't care... and I won't jump on you when you're busy taking care of your needs..." „Huh?... you know about that... each time, I thought you were asleep... I mean... We've been sharing a room for a year now, and I never thought you knew that I was...", Lutz replied, a bit stunned by the fact Will knew he was jacking

103

off at night... „Oh, come on, Lutz! Cut it out... do you think I'm deaf?", Will asked, grinning.... „Guess not, huh..." Lutz answered, with an uneasy smile on his face... „It's just that I never heard you doing it..." „Ah! But don't worry... I take good care of my needs... it's just that I prefer jacking off in the shower... that's all...", Will answered, laughing. „To tell the truth... I guess I envy you... you know... you and Paul... Not that I would like to do things with another guy... no... It's just that I whish Klara would be more... open, you know..." „Do you mean that you and Klara have never..." „Noooo! Never! She says we have to wait until we get married..." „Oh!" „So I guess the only thing I have, to take care of my needs as you say, is my right hand here", Lutz said, laughing his heart out, looking at his right hand... „Well, while in Paris, I guess we will have to find you a nice girl to take care of you and of your needs...", Will replied, laughing. „Shit Will! Klara would never forgive me..." „To hell with that! First, you're not married to her yet. Second, she doesn't have to know... Third, you're a young and healthy guy... so she probably thinks you've already done something... And last, it's her decision, not having sex with you before you marry... it doesn't mean you can't make your own decision, you know... Have you sworn to her you wouldn't have sex until you marry her?" „No!" „You see! Besides, with that damn war going on, we could all be dead in a month or two... so don't waste your time, waiting for something that, perhaps, will never happen..." „...Perhaps you're right... I'll have to think about that...", Lutz answered. „So... Are you going to come?" „Huh?" „I didn't say 'cum'... I said 'come'... you know... to Paul's home?", will said, laughing... „Oh!"... Lutz exclaimed... „Sure, I'll go... Tell Paul I'm glad he invited me... and that I'm eager to meet him..." „Thanks, Lutz... I do appreciate... Now, let's pack a few things for that damn assignment..." „Do you know where we're going?", Lutz asked. „I've got no idea. They wouldn't say. But I think it's going to be big, from what I've heard...", Will answered. „Probably a big swine from Berlin, on a visit to France... you know...", Lutz said, with a grin on his face. They started laughing at that, and began packing...

Soon, they found themselves at Rethondes, a small village in Picardie, where they acted as translators to some French officers who were there to sign the Armistice with the Reich... They didn't get into the Pullman car, where the Armistice was signed... since Herr Schmidt, Hitler's personal translator was there, as well as Hitler himself... When Hitler went down

104

the railway car, after his conditions had been dictated to the French officers, and as he walked not too far from where Will and Lutz were standing, they could see how triumphant the Führer looked. They stood at attention, while the 'Deutschland über alles' and the 'Horst-Wessel-Lied' were played by an army band... Then, they saw him leave... „Shit", Will later said... „I knew it would be big... but not that big..." „I know... Now, let's go, cause the French officers and their own translators may need our help...", Lutz replied.

Not knowing what was going at Rethondes, Paul was busy taking a call from the Swiss embassy, where his presence was requested because, it seemed, they had an important message for him there... Later that day, monsieur Pierre drove Paul to the embassy, where he was greeted by the ambassador himself... The ambassador explained that they had received a very long message from the Swiss embassy in Lisbon. Because the message was coded, it took some time before the text had been established, the ambassador explained. The message was from monsieur le Ministre De Brion, Paul's father... Paul was stunned... "Why Lisbon, of all places?" „Because Portugal is not at war with Germany...", the ambassador explained... Then, the ambassador introduced Paul to a young guy who was part of the ambassador's staff. His name was Franz, and Paul should have complete confidence in him, the ambassador explained. Franz would assist Paul writing his reply to his father, since the reply had to be coded before it was sent... But first, Paul could take all his time, reading his father's message, as they would be at his disposal when need be... The ambassador gave Paul the dispatch, and showed him to a private room. Paul started reading it, as his hands were shaking. He was glad he was alone... In the long message, Paul's father explained that all the family had fled to Lisbon, where they intended to leave for America. As a member of the French Cabinet, Paul's father had refused to be associated with the most recent decisions made by the Government, and had preferred to give his resignation! Paul's father didn't intend to come back to Paris... and he would not come back until the Germans had left... His father had heard his own mother had died, and he wanted Paul to join them in Lisbon so, as soon as possible, they could all leave for America. All would be arranged by the Swiss embassy, and Paul didn't have to worry about a thing, the message said. A quick reply from Paul was expected. Paul took his time, reading the message twice. Then he informed the ambassador he was ready to reply...

„You don't have to worry, young man, there will be no danger for you to travel to Lisbon... You will travel there in an official car from the embassy, with Swiss papers...", the ambassador kindly said to Paul. „Thank you very much, Sir, but I'm not going anywhere. I'm staying right here, in Paris... and I have my own plans...", Paul replied. „Oh but...", the ambassador replied... „Yes, Sir... I'm ready to write my reply to my father..." – „Of course..., Please follow me..." They went to Franz's office, where Paul sat. Franz smiled to him, and Paul found he was a very good-looking guy... In fact, Franz looked a lot like Paul... same hair colour, same green eyes... except he was a bit smaller than Paul... about 1.78, Paul would say... „Now my young friend, I leave you with Franz here... He will help you in any way he can with your reply... And should you need my assistance, please, just ask for me... Your father and I are good friends, and we will help you the best we can..." the ambassador explained, with a very kind smile on his face. „Thank you very much, monsieur l'Ambassadeur..." Paul replied. After the ambassador had left, Franz looked at Paul and said: „Now, Sir, what is your reply?" „Call me Paul, please... no „Sir" with me, please..." „Okay Paul... you can call me Franz... it's going to be easier..." – „Yeah!", Paul answered... „Now, let's work on that reply..."

So Paul explained to his father he was glad they were all safe in Lisbon, that he understood his father's motivations, not wanting to come back to Paris, but that for his part, he didn't want to leave Paris. He went on explaining that everything was alright here in Paris... and that he was alright. He further explained all about his plans... that he could manage the family business, here in Paris, with the help of Maître Langlois, their attorney, and that his father could supervise the whole thing from New York... Paul added he had already gone through all the important papers, and that he knew what he was doing. He also added: „I'm growing up, Dad... and I've grown a lot since you have left. Let me live my life... I'll make you proud!" Paul also said that he was very resolute with his decisions, and that he would not go to Lisbon. The reply ended with Paul saying he loved them all... He missed them... and that in the future, they could communicate through the Swiss embassy, or even through the US embassy here, in Paris... Franz was stunned by the reply...

106

„Are you sure you want me to send that reply?, he asked Paul... „Yep! That's it. I had time to think, you know... over the last few days... I know what I'm doing! And I'm going to do it!", Paul replied. „Okay then...", Franz answered, grinning... Now, I'm going to type your message on that machine over there... The machine will code it, then we can send it to our embassy in Lisbon... Don't worry, the Germans can't decipher our code... and we change it quite often... „Take your time... I'm in no hurry..." Paul replied, smiling at Franz. After a while, the whole message was coded and sent to Lisbon. „Now, I'm sure that, later, we'll receive a reply from your father", Franz said... „That's to be expected, I guess... But in the meantime, why don't we go out and have something to eat... I'm starving... Are you free for lunch? You're my guest..." Paul asked Franz... „Thanks... There's no obligation, you know..." „I insist...", Paul replied, smiling at Franz... „Give me five minutes... I'll check with the ambassador, to make sure he doesn't need me..." „Sure..."

Later on, Franz was back with a big smile on his face, saying he was free to go, but didn't know where they would find something open, not too far from the embassy... „We'll find something...", Paul replied... „Come on..." So they walked for a while and, true enough, they found a small place opened for business, where they could order a decent meal. While they were eating, Paul could sense Franz was checking him out... Taking glances at Paul, when he thought Paul was not looking... It was obvious to Paul that Franz felt attracted to him... „He must be gay...", Paul thought. Although he's very attractive, Paul thought, he's in for a big disappointment... After their lunch, they walked back to the embassy, and Paul had no doubt by now that Franz was indeed checking him all over... They went back to Franz's office, and waited for a reply to come in... making small talk in the meantime... „How old are you Paul", Franz asked... „Eighteen. I'll be nineteen next August... And you?"„Twenty", Franz answered. „Same age as my friend Will..." „Oh... and who is Will, may I ask?" „Look, Franz... I won't play cat and mouse with you... I'm gay, and Will is my boyfriend. And I'm madly in love with him. That's the reason why I want to stay in Paris. I'm not leaving him..." „WOW! You're a direct and honest guy, Paul", Franz answered.... „Well I feel that to you, I can tell the thruth..." „Why?" „Because I saw how you were checking me out, earlier... and, unless I'm mistaken, I think you're gay too, Franz... And if so, I want you to know I'm already taken... you

107

know..." Now Franz was blushing scarlet red, hearing Paul say that... „Is it so obvious?", Franz asked, looking at the carpet... „No. No... That's not what I mean Franz... You don't look like a fag at all... You're very masculin... Very good-looking... and I swear if I was not so much in love with Will, I could fall for a guy like you...", Paul answered. „Thanks Paul... You see... it's not easy to find a nice decent guy... And as you know, I can't go around, saying I'm gay and that I'm looking for someone to love... If they new I was gay, here at the embassy, I would loose my job..." „I understand", Paul replied... „But I'm sure you'll find someone... Somewhere, there's a nice guy waiting for you... You'll find him. Don't worry..." „I hope so... When I saw you earlier... I thought you were that guy... you know... I even experienced shortness of breath, seeing you... You're so..." „Gorgeous?", Paul said, laughing... „Yeah!... That's what..." „I know... Will says that all the time to me... But then, that's what I say to him too... cause he's really gorgeous..." – „You're so lucky, Paul..." „So Franz, I sure can't be your boyfriend... but we could be friends... you know... if you're okay with that, that is..." – „I would love to be friend with you Paul... Sure... (...) Hey: Something is coming in... look..."

Indeed, a reply from the Swiss embassy in Lisbon was coming in... Franz took a pen and started to write it down... Paul looked, but the message didn't make sense to him... He kept silent, as Franz kept writing it down, pages after page... Then, Franz stop writing. Franz took all the pages and began typing the text on the machine. As Paul watched, he could see that, on the other side of the special machine, a new text was appearing... „How does it work?", Paul asked... „Oh, it's very simple... as simple as ABC... the coded message is sent over the air waves... „But then, anybody can hear it?", Paul said... „Yeah... but what they would hear would mean nothing to them... You've got to have this machine here to decipher the message... No machine... no message... And do I need to tell you those machines are highly secret... and closely kept... You've seen the guards outside, at the door?" „Yes..." „Well, they would shoot anyone trying to get in here without proper clearance... Now Paul, take the message and read it. Do you want to go to a more private place to read it?" „No need Franz... you're my friend and I can trust you, as the ambassador said...", Paul answered, smiling.

Paul read the message. His father understood. He was glad Paul was growing up, and he was proud of him. His mother was not too happy with the whole idea... but would respect Paul's decision: She had to, because there was no way they could force Paul to come to Lisbon... Yes, Paul was requested to make contact with Maître Langlois, who would be very helpful... Through the Swiss embassy, Paul's father would make all the necessary arrangements so that Paul could take charge, not only of their business in Paris, but also in Switzerland... And from New York, Paul's father would take charge of their business in America. Once a week they would communicate through the Swiss embassy... Paul's father would tell the ambassador how to proceed... Paul didn't need to worry about that, since the ambassador was a good friend of his, and the Swiss knew that the De Brion had large investments in Switzerland: That would help a lot... A few other details were also examined by Paul's father, then the message ended with a short note from his mother... telling him how much she loved him... How much they all loved him..."

„YEAH!!!" Paul shouted, jumping to his feet! Franz stared at him, not knowing what to say or do... „YEAH!!!, I'm staying in Paris... and I'm in charge! YEAH!!! Now, I guess I must speak to the ambassador...", Paul said. „Yes... Maybe we could call his office and see if he's available...", Franz answered with a smile... A moment later, Paul and Franz were sitting with the ambassador, in his office... and Paul was showing him the message they had just received from Lisbon... The ambassador read it, then said: „Well, I think your father is right, being proud of you young man... And I'll always be there for you... to help you and assist you... You can count on me as well as on the embassy's staff...", The ambassador said, looking at Paul, then at Franz... „Absolutely...", Franz answered, smiling at Paul. „Thank you, Sir... And thank you Franz for your help...", Paul replied. As Paul was leaving the embassy, he looked at Franz and said to him: „Hey, give me your phone number... you already have mine, don't you? So, we can call each other... you know..." – „My pleasure", Franz replied with a very big smile, as he gave Paul his phone number.

Paul left the Swiss embassy and went back home, where he held a small meeting with madame Louise and her husband, to let them know about his father, and tell them he was now in charge... Everything went smooth, and Paul was very satisfied with their reactions... On Friday, Paul finally got in touch with Maître Langlois, who was back and had already received a long message from Paul's father, through the Swiss embassy... On that day, Paul met with the attorney and they agreed that on Monday,

June 24th, they would call a meeting of all the company's employees present, and that, first, Maître Langlois would explain the situation to them and then, Paul would make a small speech. He would tell the employees that, from now on, he was the boss here in Paris, and that they were all expected to fulfil their duties with the same efficiency as they had in the past, under his father's management. To those who could resent his new management, due to his young age, Paul would make it very clear he was expecting their resignation, and that a severance pay would be paid to them. But anyone who would decide to stay now, and later challenge his leadership would then be fired on the spot without pay. Furthermore, Paul gave Maître Langlois a list of things he would need and, among them were direct phone lines to Geneva, New York and... Berlin! „Berlin?", the attorney asked... „But you don't do business in Germany, as far as I know..." „We will...", Paul replied. „I intend to make some investments in Berlin, in order to make some contacts over there, and get to know as many important businessmen in Berlin as I can... I know that, in the end, if they loose the war, our investments over there will be lost... but I don't care... In the meantime, I'm buying an insurance policy: If we know and do business with people in high places in Berlin, well... things are going to be much easier, here in Paris... In other words, I'm going to buy protection..." „I see you're a lot like your father... quite a shrewd person, for a young man your age...", the attorney answered, grinning... „And later next week, we'll have to meet again to discuss your grandmother's estate: I am the executor of her last will, as you may know, and you're the only heir to your grandma's estate..." „Does my father know about that?", Paul asked... „Oh yes, he does. When your grandfather died, your father inherited the company and the rest of his estate... Your grandmother had money of her own, you know, and she was quite a wealthy person... As you are her oldest grandson, you inherit everything... Among other things, she had some inversments here, in France, but most of her money is invested in America... Perhaps, you will want to repatriate those investments... You also inherit her small Château, near Paris..." „Yes... But concerning her investments in America, I will repatriate nothing. That's another insurance policy I'll keep... and I'll ask my father to manage those investments... as for the rest, we'll see later... I presume you'll give me a full report concerning her estate...", Paul answered. „Yes. You'll have it next week...", the attorney replied, smiling... „Fine... And thank you very much for your help, Maître... It's a pleasure, working with you, and I count on you...“ – „You can count on me, do not worry...“, the attorney said, before he left.

On Sunday, Will called: They were back... and he would tell everything to Paul, where they had been... as soon as they would meet... Both Lutz and him would be on leave for two days, as he had said, starting at 18h00, Monday night. Yes, Lutz had agreed to come along, and was eager to meet Paul... Paul told Will they could meet at the company's headoffice on the Champs Elysées Avenue... Paul would bring civilian clothes for Will as well as for Lutz... so they could change, leave their uniforms there, and get them back next Wednesday night... Will had told Paul Lutz was about the same size as Paul was, so there would be no problem with the clothes... Now Paul was so excited: Soon, he would see Will again, and they would spend some good time together!

Monday morning came fast and, as agreed with Maître Langlois, there was a meeting at the head office, with the employees that had returned to Paris... Some were still missing, but most of them were there... The meeting went well, as most employees were too happy just having their jobs back. No one resigned. Later, Paul had a long meeting with his father's personal secretary, madame Mercier. Paul needed her help, as she was very competent and knew everything concerning the company's business... But she wasn't an easy person... Very stiff... and very susceptible... Paul gave her is most charming smile and told her how much she was important to him... How much he was reliant on her... Hearing what Paul had said to her, she went as red as the Nazi flag, and assured Paul he could count on her... Paul told her she was promoted to the rank of general manager, and he gave her a very big raise... She was ecstatic when she left Paul's office, and Paul smiled to himself, knowing that now, he had her inside his pocket. At the end of the day, as usual, everybody left the office and, before leaving the office, madame Mercier asked if he needed anything else... No, Paul replied... He told her that Tuesday and Wednesday, he wouldn't be at the office, so she would be in charge. She was beaming... He also told her he was expecting two gentlemen, and asked her to make sure the door-keeper knew about that... After she had left, Paul took time to go through some papers and later, he received a call from the door-keeper, telling him two German officers were standing in the entrance hall, asking for him... Paul went

111

downstairs and met with Will and Lutz... He smiled at them and, looking at the door-keeper, he said: „That will be all for today... Thank you... and don't forget to lock the doors when you leave..." „Yes, Sir! Have a good evening, Sir!", the door-keeper respectfully replied. Looking at Will and Lutz, Paul said: „Please, follow me gentlemen..." They took the elevator and went to Paul's office.

As soon as they got there, Paul turned to Will and said: „God, Will... I missed you so much..." „So did I...", Will answered, with a big smile on his face... They refrained from kissing because of Lutz, of course... „And you must be Lutz... Will told me so much about you... I'm so glad to meet you...", Paul said, giving Lutz his most sincere smile... „I heard a lot about you too, Paul... and I'm glad I finally get to know you", Lutz answered, smiling at Paul... „Now I have civilian clothes here for you, so you can change... We'll put your uniforms here, as my office will be locked, and I'm the only one to have a key... So, no problem... Get changed, and then we'll go to our mansion and have supper and have some fun...", Paul said. Just to make sure Lutz didn't feel uncomfortable, Paul left the room and closed the door behind him, so that Will and Lutz could change...

„Now I see why you like him...", Lutz said to Will... „He's very good-looking... and he's cool too"... „Yeah... told you so...", Will replied, grinning... While they were changing, Paul thought to himself how good-looking Lutz was... 1.83 tall... Very well built, with blond curly hair and the most beautiful blue eyes he had ever seen... Yeah... his girlfriend Klara was very lucky to have a guy like that, Paul thought. After a few minutes, the door opened, and Paul looked at Will and Lutz, now dressed in civilian clothes... „WOW", Paul exclaimed... „You look stunning... both of you..." „Thanks", they both replied, with big smiles on their faces... „Now, before we leave, I'd like to say something to you Lutz...", Paul said. „... Yes...", Lutz answered, with a worried frown... „First, you'll realize I have a lot of money, but that's not my fault. I didn't earn that money... it's just that I was born into a wealthy family... but as you'll discover, I'm a very simple guy... and I'm just like you two guys... so there is no need of silly ceremony among friends, if you see what I mean..." „Yeah... Thanks, Paul....", Lutz replied, smiling... „And there's another thing I want to say... Now, I understand Will already told you about the two of us..." – „Yes, he did", Lutz answered... „So I want you to know that I do love Will... and that I have no interest in other men... Not at all... you included... So

112

feel at ease with that... I know you have a girlfriend back in Berlin, and I'm glad you do. I just wanted to make things perfectly clear between us, so you don't go thinking that I could try to make a pass at you... That will never happen... I respect you, as I know you respect Will and I..." „Thanks a lot Paul... Will told me you were an honest and sincere guy... Now I see that it's true, and I appreciate that. Although I'm not gay, I don't care about what the two of you do together... it's none of my business, and I want you to know I don't pass judgment on that... Now that things are clear between us, I feel much more comfortable with the two of you... This matter is now settled in my mind, and I don't think it needs further discussions, does it?", Lutz said... „No, Lutz... things are clear...", Paul replied... „Now, let's get the hell out of here, and have some fun..." – „Before we leave, can I use your bathroom?", Lutz asked Paul... „Sure... at the end of the corridor, to your left...", Paul replied.

While Lutz went to the bathroom, Paul went to Will and they began kissing... „Thanks Paul for what you just said to Lutz..." „I'm sincere, you know that...", Paul answered... „I know Paul, that's one of the reasons why I love you so much... Of course... there are other reasons... you know...", Will said, with the most beautiful sexy grin on his face. „... You, sexy guy... wait until tonight...", Paul answered, grinning. „Ohhhhh... I'm already getting hard, just thinking about that...", Will answered, grinning too... „Yeah! I can feel that... Now, get it down, before Lutz comes back..." Lutz took all his time in the bathroom... He didn't need to go to the bathroom... He just wanted to give Will and Paul a chance to... you know... When he came back, he looked at Will and Paul, and said, smiling: „Sorry I wasn't gone much longer..." They all burst out laughing, then they left and went to Paul's mansion.

„Shit! Paul... I've never seen a place like that before... Will told me your family was rich, but I mean... that's something... I can't believe I'm in here... in such a beautiful place...", Lutz exclaimed, as they went inside Paul's mansion... „Feel right at home... Now come, I'll show you your room... and then we'll have supper...", Paul replied, smiling to Lutz... Paul showed Lutz his room... at the end of the corridor... far from his own room... Lutz left his belongings there, and after, they all went to the drawing-room for a drink... „What about a cold beer, guys?, Paul asked... „Hell yeah!", Will and Lutz said. They all had a beer, then a second one, then a third... „So your governess and your gardner are back?", Will asked... „Yeah... You'll see them tomorrow... Madame Louise prepared the supper for us and then, I gave her the night off", Paul answered... Then Paul explained to Will and Lutz all that had happened the last few days... The messages he had exchanged with his father, through the Swiss embassy... The meeting with the employees... everything... He even told them about Franz, from the Swiss embassy... „Poor guy...", Will said... „I hope we'll have a chance to meet him... you know... he must be pretty lonely, all alone here, in Paris" „Yeah"... Lutz said... „...I know how he must be feeling... It would be fun meeting him... as long as he knows I'm not 'available'... you know..." They all started laughing, then went to the dining-room madame Louise had reopened, and ate the supper she had prepared... They drank wine, and had some fun...

After supper, they went back to the drawing-room and Will told Paul about where they had been and what they had seen at Rethondes... „He forgot to mention that we also saw the devil himself, there...", Lutz said. „Huh?", Paul replied... „Yeah... We saw Hitler...", Lutz answered... „And I heard that he even visited Paris, last Sunday..." – „Yeah... I've heard that too", Will said. „And I've heard the big swine will also be in town soon, to plunder... as usual...", Lutz added... „Who?", Paul asked... „The big swine", Lutz replied, with a grin on his face „... you know... Göring..." Paul burst out laughing, hearing how Lutz was calling Reichsmarschall Göring... „I would laugh, too", Will said... „If it wasn't so saddening..."

„You're cool Lutz... I like that", Paul said... laughing... „Hey... I'm just trying to go through this damn war without a scratch, you know...", Lutz answered... „Yeah...", Paul replied, still laughing... „Oh... and I forgot to tell you..." Will said to Paul... „They will move us from Hôtel Meurice to a barrack, somewhere in Paris..." „Yeah", Lutz added... „And I've been told that, as officers, we're not under the obligation to go there... We're allowed to have our own place, and be on our own, here in Paris... but you know... with our small allowance... besides, it's free at the barrack..." „Do you know when you'll be moving?", Paul asked... „No. Not yet...", Will replied. „Now, I don't know about you, guys, but I'm exhausted... What do you think we hit the sack?", Lutz asked... „Yeah", Will replied, grinning at Paul... „Oh, yes... yes..." Paul replied, a little uncomfortable... „Come on, Paul..." Lutz said to him... „Do you think I have no clue as to what you two guys are going to do tonight... Hell! I even envy you... All I have is my right hand, here... I would prefer to have a pretty girl

114

though... you know..." „Told you Lutz... Sometime or another, we're going to have to find one for you", Will answered, laughing... „Yeah... I'm sure that could be arranged", Paul added, with his usual big smile... „Go to hell, both of you", Lutz replied, laughing all the way to his bedroom...

Will and Paul were left alone in the drawing-room, and it didn't take long before Will began passionately kissing Paul... „Oh... it's been so long since you've kissed me like that", Paul said. „Yeah... Let's go to your room, shall we?", Will said, grinning... „OUR room...", Paul said... „Yes... OUR room", Will replied... As soon as they got to their room, both of them got undressed and they began kissing again... their pulsing dicks hard pressed one against the other... In no time, they were in bed, as Will pressed his lips into Paul's navel, before kissing his crotch, lowering his head. As Will's lips touched Paul's balls, he cried in ecstasy... Then, Will's tongue traced the underside of Paul's hard oozing dick. Will wrapped his right fist around it, squeezed it then guided it to his mouth... Paul was groaning and moaning and he shuddered when Will took his hard cock into his warm mouth... „Ah... Shit, Will... It feels so good...", Paul said. „Un-huh"... Will replied... „Hey Will, let's do a 69..." Paul suggested... „Let's lay on our sides..." In no time, they had assumed the right position, and were sucking one another's dicks... Paul softly moaned, tasting Will's sweet precum, and in no time, he had the head of Will's big hard cock in his throat... Will gasped, as Paul was driving him wild... Paul kept driving his dick in and out of Will's hot mouth, his precum flowing out of him like a river... Then, his dick glided deep inside Will's mouth... where he began shooting his young jizz... Paul pulled his head off Will's cock, then said: „Take it all, Will..." „Um-huh..." Then Paul resumed his position on Will's hard prick and began deep throuting him... Just a few seconds later, Will quivered, then exploded into Paul's mouth, Paul eagerly swallowing every drop... Without a word, Will turned and went to Paul, and he started cum kissing him... As their lips finally parted, Paul said: „God... I've missed you so much..." „I've missed you too, gorgeous...", Will replied...

As he loved so much to do, Paul cuddled into Will's smooth body and Will's embrace tightened for a moment... „I'll never tell you enough how much I love you, Paul..." „I love to hear you saying that Will... Without you, I wouldn't have the courage nor the strength to go on..." „I don't know why you say that... because sometimes, I feel so weak...", Will answered... „Don't say that, Will... I don't like it when you say that... Without you, I would be nothing... I would be in Lisbon... on my way to America, still dependent on my father... the same immature guy I was before I met you. You've made me grow up, Will... and fast... That's what you did! And thanks to you, I know now what true love means..." „You had it all inside you, Paul...It's just that now, you've discovered your strenght... You've discovered yourself..." „That maybe so, Will, but you're the one who made me discover myself... and I need you, to keep going on... (...) Will?" „What?" „Promise me you'll never get tired of me..." „I swear to you Paul that I'll never do. And I swear I'll always be faithful to you..." „And I swear I will always be faithful to you too, Will. I swear to that..." „You know what, Paul... It's almost as if, tonight, we were getting married, you and me..." „We are, Will! That's how I feel about you..." „Me too..." Paul turned to Will, and looking straight into his lover's sparkling blue eyes, he said: „You may think I'm silly and way too romantic, but tonight Will, in my heart, I marry you, Whilhelm von Rundstedt... I'll always be with you, for the best and for the worst, for as long as you will want me to be with you..." „No... You're not silly Paul... and I'm as romantic as you are... And I marry you, too, Paul De Brion, and I will always be with you, for the best and for the worst... for as long as you will want me to be with you... (...) I will never break that vow, and only you could release me from it..." „I make the same vow to you, Will... so only you can release me from it too... and from the bottom of my heart, I pray you never will..." „I will not, Paul!"

After a long and tender kiss, Paul turned the light off, and they went to sleep, Paul tightly cuddled into Will's strong arms... „I wonder...", Paul asked, smiling... „What?" „I wonder if Lutz is wanking in his bed..." Will chuckled, and answered: „Don't laugh... that's what I would be doing if I had not met you..." „Me too... I'll help you finding him a good-looking girl... you know... But we'll have to ask her first if she's good at giving blowjobs..." „That's gross, Paul De Brion!" „Yeah... I know... but you love that, don't you?" „YES!" Will replied... „I love that... and I like the idea, trying to find a girl for Lutz..." Now, go to sleep, you scum..." – „Um-huh... Good night my love...", Paul said. „Night Paul... sweet dreams..." „I will, dreaming about you..."

EIGHT
«I NEED YOUR HELP, GUYS...»

„Hey.... sleephead... get up!", Paul said to Will... „Huh?"... „Come on, good-looking... We won't spend our day sleeping, are we?" „No...", Will replied, stretching his arm and nice body, tossing his arms around Paul's chest... „Kiss me, gorgeous, then go fetch Lutz... We have something to talk about, before we go downstairs...", Paul said. „What?" „Go get him... you'll see...", Paul simply answered.

A bit later, Will and Lutz were back, Will wearing his boxers, while Lutz had a towel wrapped around his lean waist, having already taken a shower... As Lutz stood near the bedroom door, Paul could see he had a perfectly sculpted body... He looked at Lutz's broad shoulders and very nice pecs... at his six pack, and at the trail of blond hair going down somewhere under the towel. Paul didn't fail to notice Lutz had very firm legs also... Quite a sight, Paul thought to himself... „Come in, Lutz, we've got to talk for a second...", Paul said to him. Lutz came in and sat at the end of the bed. Paul was sitting on the bed, not too far from Lutz, his crotch covered by the sheet. Nevertheless, Lutz could see that, for an eighteen year old guy, Paul had a well toned body... and he could understand why Will was so attracted to this blond guy...

„In a few minutes, we'll go down for breakfast...", Paul started to say. „Yeah... and I'm starving...", Will said, smiling... „Yes", Paul continued... „and you'll meet madame Louise and chances are you'll also meet her husband, monsieur Pierre, our gardner... Now, I've already told our next-door neighbours Will was my cousin Guillaume from Strasbourg... That's how I intend to introduce both of you to madame Louise and her husband... both of you are my cousins from Strasbourg..." „But why Strasbourg? I've never been there...", Lutz replied... „I've never been there

117

either..." Will said to Lutz, before saying to him: „... but listen to Paul... it's a good idea..." „Yes... as I was saying, you're my two cousins from Strasbourg. That will explain your slight accent... Besides, I really had an uncle living there, with his large family... He's on my mother's side of the family and he has many children... some my age, or a bit older... That's why they didn't come to visit us very often: There are too many of them... So madame Louise knows about them, but hasn't seen them for many years... She will find you have grown since the last time she saw you, that's all..." „Now, you must understand I have complete confidence in madame Louise and her husband... But should neighbours or other people question them about you two, I don't want them to lie... Not knowing the truth, they will convincingly answer you're my two cousins from Strasbourg... see?" „Oh... I see... And what's my name?", Lutz asked, grinning... „You're Luc Harbourg...", Paul answered... „but your nickname is Lutz..." „How convenient", Lutz replied, laughing. „And may I introduce you to your new brother here... Guillaume Harbourg... and as you may have guess, his nickname is Will..." „Hi! Bro...", Will said to Lutz, laughing too... „Nice to know you, bro!", Lutz answered... „Now both of you fled Strasbourg when the city was evacuated last year... The rest of your family is in the South... Nice... Yeah! Nice... that's it... they live in Nice! Now you're in Paris because both of you are students...", Paul explained to Will and Lutz. „But it's true", Will said... „Both of us were students before the war..." „...See... Keep your story as close to reality as possible, so you won't get all mixed up in your lies! Execpt now, you study at La Sorbonne... We don't know when the university will re-open, but you want to be here, in Paris, when it does..." „Fine with me", Lutz said, smiling. „With me too...", Will answered. „Good! Now I'll take a quick shower, then let's go and have breakfast...", Paul said. At that, Paul tossed the sheet and walked to the shower... „Hey, dude... nice body you have...", Lutz said, grinning... „Thanks..." Paul answered, laughing... „but then again, you're not interested, and me neither..." – „You're right... Now I'll get dress, and meet you in here in a few minutes", Lutz replied, still laughing... „Fine...", both Will and Paul answered. Paul and Will took a quick shower together, but they didn't have time to fool around. They got dress, and when Lutz came back, they were ready.

The three of them went downstairs where they met with madame Louise and her husband. Paul introduced the two young men to them, and both madame Louise and her husband believed the story Paul was telling them... „Oh yes, I do remember you...", madame Louise said, „but it's such a long time ago... and you were so young... besides, you had so many brothers and sisters, I could never tell you apart..." „I hope your parents are well?", monsieur Pierre asked the two young men. „Yeah" Lutz prelied... „they are safe... the rest of the family is in Nice..." „Good for them" monsieur Pierre said, and as he was leaving, Paul said him: „Wait monsieur Pierre... I have a special assignment for you..."

„Yes, sure, what might that be?" I want you to drive to our company's head office building. In the underground parking, you'll and a truck containing a large tank..." „Yes... I know... I've used that truck once in the past...", monsieur Pierre replied... „Good. Now, drive wherever you want, fill in as much gas as you can buy... buy everything you can... Pay five times the price, I don't care! I'll give you all the money you need... Now, do you know about the five big gas tanks we have under the head office building?", Paul asked him... „Yes... Your father showed them to me once..." „I want you to fill them up... Do your best... And I want you to find a locksmith, and make sure nobody has access to those tanks, except you and me..." „Sure... but monsieur Paul... the war is over now, so I don't see why you worry about gas...", monsieur Pierre said. „Yeah... I know", Paul answered with a grin... „And I hope the people you'll buy gas from will think the same way you do... But you see monsieur Pierre, Germany is still at war... and they will need all the gas they can and do you really think they will let France go without asking for certain „contributions" to their war effort?" „I can't believe...", monsieur Pierre started to reply... „Yeah, yeah... in the meantime, make sure our tanks are full... Wait for me, I'll get you the money you need..." Paul went to his father's study, and later came back with a big stack of French Francs. „Here, take it..." Paul said, as he gave monsieur Pierre the money... „And please, spend as much as you can... buy as much gas as you can... don't try to save money... Anyway, I figure that soon, that money will not be worth much..." „As you wish, monsieur Paul... as you wish...", monsieur Pierre answered.

Monsieur Pierre left, and then Paul said to madame Louise: „Now... we're starving! Let's have breakfast..." The three of them ate all madame Louise had prepared... and asked for more. After they had eaten everything, Paul asked madame Louise: „Do you think you could prepare

119

us a picnic for this afternoon... I'd like to take my two cousins here for a ride... go to Versailles perhaps... and don't forget to put some beers and two or three bottles of wine... no... four bottles...", Paul said to her, grinning... „Sure, monsieur Paul... My pleasure!", madame Louise answered, smiling. „Oh, and I wanted to tell you that I've given the green bedroom to my cousin Lutz... as Will didn't mind sharing mine..." „Do you want me to re-open another bedroom for monsieur Will?", madame Louise asked... „Nah... Don't bother... I don't mind sharing Paul's room...", Will quickly replied... „Besides, I don't want you to re-open all the other rooms... You have enough work as it is... and we still have to do with a reduced staff...", Paul added. „That's very considerate of you, Sir...", madame Louise answered. „So that's settled! When Lutz is here to visit, he'll stay in the green bedroom... You can leave all you want in there... it's your room now... And when Will is here, he'll share my bedroom... I'll make some space there for your stuff...", Paul said. Hearing that, they all smiled... as madame Louise was too happy not to have to re-open another bedroom: Maintenance was not among her favourite chores...

In the afternoon, the three young men drove to Versailles and went to see the Palace... Of course, it was closed, but there was no one to stop them from strolling around the vast and majestic park surrounding the Palace... They decided to have their picnic there... While they were resting, drinking wine and making small talk, Paul asked Will: „Hey, you said you were moving out of Hôtel Meurice... does it mean you will no longer work there either?" „Oberstleutnant Koch told me that, starting next Monday, our services will be transferred to the Palais Bourbon... where much of the administration offices will be located. The Komandantur will stay at Hôtel Meurice, though. It seems von Stütnitz, the military governor, has requisitioned Hôtel Crillon, and that's where his services will be." – „I've heard our big swine has requisitioned the Palais du Luxembourg, and that's where the Luftwaffe's headquaters in Paris will go...", Lutz added. „Well", Paul replied... „If both of you go to work at the Palais Bourbon, it's an easy drive from there to my home... You're going to need cars, though... I know what we'll do: Will, I will sell to you the white car you saw in the underground garage at my place... for one Reichsmark! What do you think, Will?" „Are you kidding me or what?", Will replied, stunned... „Not at all"... Paul answered, smiling.

120

„And you, Lutz, I will sell to you the green car we have there... For one Reichsmark too! Would it be too much for you?", Paul asked, giggling... „I'm not sure I can make such an extravagant expense... you know... one Reichsmark for a car... that's a lot of money...", Lutz answered, laughing... „Go to hell...", Paul replied, laughing too. „But why would you sell those two cars to us, at such a ridiculous price?", Will asked... „First, I don't need those cars... Second, they will be useful to both of you and third, I'm sure it won't take long before the Komandantur starts to seize every car available... So I prefer to sell those cars to you than see them go to people I know nothing about...", Paul answered. „But what about you father's car?", Will asked.

„Don't worry! I need it... And I'll make sure they can't put their hands on it... Count on me...", Paul replied, smiling... „Hey guys... I guess it's time for us to go back to Paris, what do you think?", Lutz asked. „Yeah... Let's go...", the other two answered. As they drove back to Paris, they could see there was a lot of traffic on the road... „I guess many of those who had fled are coming back now...", Will said. „That's good news! I sure hope our chef is among them...", Paul said. „Yeah... Poor you... No chef... I told you: I don't know how you can manage without him...", Will answered, bursting out with laughs... „And I've already told you to go to hell...", Paul replied, laughing too...

Once they were back at the mansion, Paul suggested they invite Franz for supper... and everyone agreed. Paul called the Swiss embassy and Franz said he could make it, and would meet them at around seven that night. Paul took the occasion to diplomatically explain to Franz Lutz wasn't gay.... Franz said he understood and so, everything was settled... Indeed, at around seven, madame Louise answered the door, and Franz joined the three others in the drawing-room. „Thanks Paul for inviting me... You know, I've been in Paris for more than a year, and I haven't been invited too many times to private homes..." Franz said... „And you have a great place here. I've never seen anything like that before..." „Thanks, Franz", Paul answered... „Feel right at home... we're among friends here, so have fun with us... Want a beer?" „Sure..." As Franz was introduced to Will and Lutz, he was stunned to see how good-looking they were. He knew Will was deeply in love with Paul, and he thought of how lucky the both of them were. As for Lutz, he felt sorry the guy was straight, for it would have been very easy for him to fall in love with such a gorgeous young hunk!

They all sat and had a few beers... making small talk and having fun. They mostly spoke in German, since Franz, being Swiss, was fluent both in French and German, and Paul had said he wanted to become fluent in German as fast as possible... He didn't reveal he had hired a private teacher to give him private lessons in German, three hours a day... He wanted to keep it a secret... After supper, Will played the piano, and the fun continued... Paul noticed how Franz kept looking at Lutz and obviously, Lutz had not realized their Swiss friend was very much attracted to him... As long as it didn't bother Lutz, Paul thought, who would care about that! And Lutz didn't seem bothered at all, since he was not even aware he was the object of Franz desires... So the evening went on very pleasantly and later, Franz said: „Hey... I'm sorry to say that, but I have to leave soon... cause I'm working tomorrow... I'm not a rich guy like Paul, here! I do have to work...", he said grinning... „Yeah, yeah!", Paul replied, laughing... „And don't worry Franz", Will added... „Lutz and I are not rich either... so the three of us are in the same boat..." „Anyway, thanks for having me here tonight. I had a lot of fun, and I sure hope we'll have other occasions to party again... Thanks Paul!", Franz said. „Hey, it's been fun having you here, and count on us... We'll party again soon... Besides, I'll call you very soon cause I'd like to discuss a few things with the ambassador...", Paul said. „Good! Maybe we can have lunch then...", Franz replied with a broad smile on his face... „Okay... I'll give you a call...", Paul answered.

„See you soon", Will and Lutz said to Franz, as he was leaving... After Franz had left, Will said: „He's a nice guy... don't you think? And a good-looking one too... Too bad you're straight, Lutz...", Will said, with a grin on his face. „True... He's a nice guy", Lutz replied... „But you know, I'm a lost cause for him... He doesn't have the slightest chance with me... it's hopeless..." „Yeah. Yeah. They all say that...", Will answered... laughing his heart out. „Perhaps, at our contact, you'll become gay, you never know!" „Nah!", Lutz exclaimed... „Besides, you don't become gay: You're gay from the day you were born... it's just that, sometimes, it takes a while before you discover what you really are...", Paul added... „Like you and Will?" Lutz asked... „Yeah", Paul answered. „And how do I know that I'm not gay... I mean... Could it be that I am and haven't discovered it just yet?", Lutz seriously asked... „If you want to know for sure, just answer my questions as honestly as you can. Do you want to try?", Paul asked him... „Sure... go ahead", Lutz answered, laughing... „How long have you known your girlfriend Klara?" „About three years..." „Would you like to have sex with her?" „Hell, yes... it's just she refuses to have sex with me before we get married..." „Do you like to kiss her, or does she always have to ask you to kiss her?" „I love kissing her... And I tell you, she never has to ask me to kiss her... I'm always all over her..." – „Now, like us, do you wank?" „I've already told you my best friend is my right hand here..." „When you wank, do you think about guys?" „Never..." „Have you ever wanked thinking about a guy in particular?" „Never... when I'm jacking off, I think about Klara... Oh, well... maybe sometimes, I also think about other girls... you know... but never about guys!" „Well", Paul said, smiling... „No doubt, you're as straight as an arrow... and you're right: Poor Franz has no chance with you..." „Told you so...", Lutz said, laughing... „Back to square one then...", Will said, laughing... Indeed, we'll have to find you a nice girl while we're here in Paris... Otherwise, your right hand will get tired with so much exercise..." „Hey you two... Don't laugh at me like that... The way I see it, you two do the same as I do, except you do it together, that's all", Lutz answered. „Is that what you really think?", Will asked, as he turned to look at Paul, grinning... „What's so funny?", Lutz asked...

„It's just that there is a lot more we do than just jerk off, you know...", Paul said, as he burst out laughing... „Huh?", Lutz said, „... what do you mean „a lot more"... What else could there be?" „Never mind! You just don't want to know about that... remember: You're straight!", Will answered, laughing... „Hey you... just because I'm straight doesn't mean I don't like sex!", Lutz exclaimed... „Come on guys... tell me.... I want to know... Pleasssssssse" „Well... We won't tell you everything... you know... some things are rather private...", Will answered grinning... „Here's an easy one though", Paul said... „Have you ever used a finger or two to massage your love spot while wanking?" „(...)" „I'll bet he knows nothing about his love spot... and I'll bet he doesn't even know where to find it...", Will said, with a loud laugh... „I told you... stop laughing at me... it's not fun", Lutz seriously answered. „And no... I don't know about what you're talking about, Will... Are you happy now?" „Sorry Lutz... really, I'm sorry... I didn't want to offend you...", Will said. „Okay. But then,

123

explain... Go ahead!", Lutz replied. „You see Lutz", Paul started explaining... „There are two ways that I know of that can make a man cum, if I exclude wet dreams... The first you know all about it, and it's when you make love... let's say with a woman... or when you wank! The second, is when you get something up your ass... a finger or a dick... or something else, and you... How could I say... When you excite your ass chute and keep touching your prostate... That's your love spot! When that happens, a man can shoot without even touching his dick... Of course, if you wank at the same time, or if someone gives you a blowjob at the same time, it's even more satisfying..." „Shit: That's gross", Lutz replied... „That may be so to you... but nevertheless, it's a lot of fun! Besides, you're the one who wanted to know about some of the things we do... so don't be so virtuous!", Paul answered, laughing... „Sorry... that's not what I meant", Lutz answered... „Best way to try it is when you take a shower... use some baby oil... Never do it dry... First, play with your hole... you know... your rosy spot... and give your ass ring a chance to relax a bit. Then, slowly get one finger inside... make sure your finger is slippery... and later, you can put a second finger in... even a third... it's as you like... Then find your love spot and play with it with the tip of your finger: You'll see... but I'm sure you'll never try that... it's too gross, isn't it?, Paul said, laughing his heart out... „No, no... I'm sure he'll never try that... Just looking at the sizeable bulge he has in his pants, I'd say he's already hard as hell and he's horny as a forteen year old...", Will said, laughing and looking at Lutz... „Hey, I told you... It's true I love sex, don't you? It's not my fault if I get a hardon..." Lutz answered, grinning... „At least, now I know why Will spends so much time in the shower...", he said, trying not to break into a fit of giggles... „Yeah... I love to do that in the shower... but I tell you: With Paul, it's much, much better...", Will replied, laughing. „You mean he...", Lutz asked... „... Puts his dick deep inside my ass, and fucks me... yeah!", Will answered... „That must hurt like hell?", Lutz asked, stunned... „At first, it does... yes. But then, the pain turns into a lot of pleasure... I swear! It's incredible... I've never cum so much...", Will answered. „Oh my God! I never thought that was possible...", Lutz said, looking at Will and Paul... „What else do you do together?" „We 69...", Paul answered... and then explained to Lutz... „WOW... That's too much... What else?" „Now, that's enough...", Will intervened... „The rest is private... And you will never do it with Klara or with any other woman for that matter... So you don't need to know about the rest! And if you really want to know, you'll have to ask some other gay guys..." „Okay, okay... no problem... but from what I've heard, you're really having fun guys... I don't even think Klara will ever agree to give me a blowjob, you know..." „Most women don't... They find it gross, like you said..." Paul answered, grinning... „Besides, in my view, only a man can really know how to please another man... at least, that's what I think!" „Okay guys, anough talking... time to go to bed", Will said, giving Paul a very sexy grin... So they turned off the lights and went upstairs.

As they were walking near Lutz's bedroom, he said to Will and Paul: „Um... guys... I think I'll need to shower before going to bed... and I was wondering if, by any chance... you know... you wouldn't have some baby oil left?" They all burst out laughing... „You'll find a bottle in your bathroom... look inside the cabinet there..." Paul answered. „Do you have a rash or something Lutz?", Will asked laughing... „Yeah... A big one... And I'm going to take care of it right now...", he answered with a big smile... „Have fun!", Will and Paul said, as they walked to their own room. As soon as they got there, they started kissing, and quickly got undressed... „Shit Paul, all that talk made me so horny... I think my dick is going to explode!" „Yeah! Just look at my own dick... It hurts!" Will took Paul into his arms and Paul started to swivel his hips and press his swollen prick agains Will's hard dick... They kissed for a while, then Paul said: „Hey... We could take a shower too... you know..." „Do you have something in mind?", Will asked, grinning... „Yeah... I have lots of ideas..." As they were walking to their bathroom, they heard Lutz asking for something. His voice was very faint voice due to the distance between their rooms... „What does he need? I didn't understand...", Will asked Paul... „I don't know... I didn't understand it either." They wrapped a towel around their waist, and went to Lutz's bedroom. They knocked on the door and heard Lutz say: „Get in here, you bastards! I can't find it!"

„It's in the cabinet... I told you..." Paul answered, as both he and Will were walking to Lutz's bathroom. Since the door wasn't totally closed, they could see Lutz was in the shower...

„No, you silly... I found the bottle... but I can't find my love spot, as you call it... get in here and help me find it...", Lutz answered. Both Paul and Will entered the bathroom and started laughing... „Ohhhhh no, you're going to have to find it by yourself!... We ain't getting in there...",

125

Will replied. „Shit guys... You're my friends... You can't leave me like that... I really need help! Besides, you know I'm not gay, so no problem with that, is there? I just want to find it... unless what you told me was just a big lie...", Lutz said... As he turned to look at Paul and Will, they saw he was very hard, and had a very thick dick. Not too long, but very thick... He also had nice big balls, and a nice blond bush... „Join me guys... and no kissing, okay? Just help me!" „What do you think Will? I don't mind, really... as long as I'm in here with you...", Paul asked. „Okay... but just for once...", Will replied. So they both took their towels off and got into the shower with Lutz, where Paul turned off the water. „Hey Lutz... nice dick you have there... very nice body too... Klara doesn't know what she's missing", Paul said laughing... „Nice butt too", Will added... „You're pretty well hung too, both of you, as I can see...", Lutz replied, laughing... „I guess Franz would love to be in here with you", Paul said to Lutz, chuckling... „Yeah... Well I'm not in love with you guys, and will never be... That makes a big difference, doesn't it? I just need you to teach me a few tricks, that's all!, Lutz answered. „Okay, okay..." Paul answered... „Where's the baby oil?" – „There", Lutz replied. „Now put your hands to rest on the wall, and spread your legs apart... Yeah... just like that...", Will told Lutz. "Now, while I'm teaching you how to do it, you can wank... I'm telling you: You'll love that!" „Yeah... Well I won't wank in front of Paul, if he just keeps looking at me..." „No problem", Paul answered, laughing... „I'll wank, watching Will do his job on your cute bubble butt..." So Will took the baby oil, lubed his index finger then Lutz's glory hole, doing a very fine job. Lutz started to wank and soon, he was moaning... Then Will took his index finger and slowly inserted it inside Lutz's ass. Lutz grunted... „Does it hurt?" „Just a bit..." „Let's give your ass time to loosen up...", Will replied. „... Now it's okay... it feels good...", Lutz answered. So as Will began to slowly fuck Lutz with his index finger, Lutz began pumping his dick faster... and he quivered as Will's finger hit his love spot. „Oh shit! Will! That feels good..." Lutz said. Both Will and Paul grinned as Will said: „Told you... that's where it is...I've found it for you." „Ohhhhhh... Keep doing that...", Lutz answered, groaning and moaning... „Hey Lutz... what about a blowjob?, Paul asked, grinning... „Thought you'd never ask..." Lutz replied, his pearly whites dazzling... „Sure! But don't cum in my mouth... Only Will is allowed to do that...", Paul answered, giggling. „No problem!" Paul knelt in front of Lutz and

126

took his thick oozing dick in his hand, as his tongue started to stroke up and down the full length of Lutz's very hard prick. Then, Lutz shuddered and gasped as Paul began giving his dick a very good tongue bath... „Ohhhhhhh... My God!!! Shit Paul! I can't believe it... Oh shit!!!" Lutz said, gasping, also feeling Will's finger going in and out of his fuckhole... It didn't take long before Will added a second finger in there, then a third... From his vantage point, Paul could see Lutz's well defined muscles flex under the intense pleasure he was experiencing... Lutz was panting and sweating non-stop by now... When Paul began deepthroating Lutz's throbbing dick, Lutz shuddered, trusting his prick deep inside Paul's very hot mouth.

„I want your dick in my ass", Lutz said to Will... „I want to know how it feels... I want it now!" „You're kidding...", Will replied... „It's big, you know... and your ass is still a bit tight..." Lutz looked down at Paul and asked him: „Do you take his dick up your ass?" Rather then replying verbally, Paul just nodded, grinning... „If Paul can take it up his ass, so can I! But go slowly, okay?" „If that's what you want... okay then!", Will answered. Will took the baby lotion and lubed his massive dick. When he began playing around Lutz's pink fuckhole with the tip of his dick, Lutz moaned. He stopped moaning though when he felt Will's big mushroom cap enter his sphincter: Pain shot through him and he shouted! Knowing that was causing him some pain, Will asked Lutz: „Do you want me to take it out? ... But I suggest you wait... The pain will turn into pleasure before long, I swear!" – „No, don't take it out... just take it easy..." Lutz answered. „Do as if you needed crapping... I mean... Push as you do when you take a dump... you'll see... it's going to help a lot", Will explained. Lutz did as he was told and in no time, a few centimeters of Will's big dick were right inside his tight ass chute. Will moaned as it felt so good in there, and it felt even better after Lutz's ass lips squeezed his very hard cock. „Does it hurt?", Will asked. „It stings a bit... but now, it's not so bad..." „Good! I'll take my time!", Will replied. But as Paul began sucking on Lutz's smooth balls, Lutz groaned and forgot all about Will's dick inside his ass chute. Then Paul went back to Lutz's oozing dick and he tightened his lips around his hard prick... With his lips he bobbed faster and faster on Lutz's cock. Lutz couldn't stop groaning and moaning, and when Paul perceived his blond friend was about to cum, he stopped and paused... „Hey... Why the hell did you stop?", Lutz asked... „Are you in

127

a hurry, mein Herr? Let's make it last for a while... You have seen nothing yet...", Paul answered, grinning. Then, as Will started to trust his dick in and out of Lutz's love chute, Paul resumed his good work on his hard dick... „Oh Shit!... That feels good... I love it... go faster Will...", Lutz said.

Paul gave Will a wink, took the bottle of baby oil and spread some all over his own rosebud; then he rose between Lutz and the wall, turned, and placed Lutz's thick dick right on his hole... „What are you doing?", Lutz asked Paul... „Now your going to know first hand how it feels to fuck a tight ass...", Paul answered, grinning. Then Paul quickly impaled himself on Lutz's thick dick and they both quivered. Paul paused for a minute then told Lutz: „Now, start fucking my ass dude! Go for it!" Will remained motionless, his dick deep inside Lutz's ass, as Lutz began fucking Paul's tight warm ass... „That's too much guys... I can't believe it...", Lutz exclaimed. With his right fist, Lutz took Paul's dick and began to masturbate his young friend who sighed, feeling Lutz's warm and slippery hand go up and down his hard shaft. „Thanks buddy... I needed that...", Paul said to Lutz. Lutz's dick glided deep inside Paul, where he hit his love spot... „That feels so good Lutz...", Paul said, panting and sweating... „I know... Will is doing the same to me... I just don't believe it...", Lutz replied. As Lutz began working his hips back and forth, going faster and faster, they all cried in ecstasy. Feeling Will's big dick fucking him as he was fucking Paul, Lutz just couldn't stop! In and out, he went, in and out... faster and faster... As Paul felt Lutz thick dick stiffening inside him and his own balls ready to shoot, he cried out: „Oh, God! I'm going to cum! I can't stop it..." Paul's ass ring squeezed Lutz's hard dick and that started a chain reaction, as Lutz ass ring also squeezed Will's dick deep inside him. Both Will and Lutz cried out at the same time they were about to cum... and at that, the three friends began to shoot cum so hard, they couldn't believe it... Lutz kept his hand going up and down Paul's very hard dick as it erupted, shooting squirt after squirt of hot young jizz all over the wall. Seconds later, Paul felt Lutz warm cum deep inside his ass chute, and Lutz felt the same, as Will's pulsing prick began shooting torrents of cum deep inside his blond friend... „Ahhhhhhhh... I'm in heaven! I'm shooting again... Come on Paul, take it! Keep shooting Will... I love it... it's so hot inside my ass... I can feel it... Come on... shoot! Shoot!", Lutz cried out...

Of course, like all good things, their orgasms slowly subsided and, after a few minutes, Lutz took his softening dick out of Paul's tight ass... „That was soooooooooo good, dudes... I don't know how to thank both of you, making me feel so good...", Lutz said, still shaking... „Now, do you still think we only wank when we make love, Will and I?", Paul asked, giggling... „Shit no! How could I be so stupid...", Lutz answered. „So you liked it?", Will asked, taking his softening dick out of Lutz's ass... „It felt so good Will, having your big dick deep inside me... I swear... I loved it, though it did hurt a lot at first... but just like you had said, it turned into a kind of pleasure I knew nothing about before tonight", Lutz replied, smiling at Will... „And, turning to Paul, Lutz said: „And fucking your tight ass felt so good... God! I swear, I could keep doing that for the rest of my life!", he said, laughing... „So now you know where it is?", Paul asked Lutz, laughing too... „Huh?" „Your love spot, idiot..." „Oh shit... do I know now...", Lutz answered. „Now that the lesson is over, I suggest to you guys we go to sleep... And Lutz, I suggest you give your right hand a break for tonight... don't exaggerate, you know", Will said, laughing... „Anyway, I feel totally exhausted, so I think I won't need my right hand tonight", Lutz answered, grinning... „Yeah, let's go to sleep", Paul added.

Will and Paul left Lutz, and went back to their room, where they got into bed fast, for they were exhausted too. „That was fun", Paul told Will... „But only because you were there with me..." „Yeah!" Will replied, grinning... „But I've told him this was a once in a life time shot... And I intended that! We've helped him, now he has to make it on his own... We did our part... that's how I see it, and I don't intend to share you... even with Lutz! I love you Paul, and in my mind, that's the end of the story with Lutz!" „Yeah", Paul answered... „And I don't want to share you either... But I wonder... Since he had a taste of that kind of pleasure... Will he just return to his old habits, you know..." „I don't know... but he's straight... so...", Will said. „I know he's straight... or he could be bi for what I know... but most of all, he loves sex!!! The way he fucked me, I think he would fuck anything with two legs..." „He's that good?", Will asked Paul... „Sure, he's good... but not as good as you... cause I love you, and that makes a big difference..." „I know what you mean... I felt the same when I fucked him", Will said. „Now, let's go to sleep... You're still on leave tomorrow, and I want us to have fun, so let's get some rest", Paul said. „Right!.... Paul? I love you!!!", Will said, kissing his lover very tenderly. „And I love you, too... Night!" „Night, Paul."

NINE
« MOVING IN... »

When Paul woke up that morning, Will was still sound asleep... Paul looked at his handsome lover, at his blond hair and his sensuous lips and thought that many women would love to be at his place to contemplate such a gorgeous hunk... He smiled to himself and, very slowly, he went out of bed, not wanting to wake up Will. He went to the bathroom, took a quick shower, then went downstairs for a coffee. „Hi", Paul said to madame Louise and her husband... „How are you today?" „Fine monsieur Paul... did you sleep Well?", monsieur Pierre asked... „Yes... yes... my two cousins are still sleeping... but I wanted a coffee... I see you got a newspaper, monsieur Pierre... What's the news?" „I've got a copy of the Petit-Parisien... They say almost 700 000 people have come back to Paris as of now... That's good, and do you know what, monsieur Paul?" „No..." „Well... you did the right thing reopening for business... Look here: It says the Militärbefehlshaber has ordered all business, all stores and all banks to reopen... And look here... it says Sacha Guitry will soon star in a new play at La Madeleine... and here: Harry Baur will perform at the Gymnase... And look at the title here: It says „Paris has turned on all its lights, again...".. „Yeah.. but that maybe just an illusion", Paul answered, smiling at monsieur Pierre... „I guess the Germans want the world to believe that nothing has changed in Paris... but you'll see... things will change... (...) By the way monsieur Pierre, how are you doing with the gas tanks?" „Oh fine... I've done more than twenty trips to the Head office, and so far, two of the tanks are full. And the locksmith came... so now, nobody has access to the tanks without the key here. But I'll need you to give me more money, if you want me to continue, and fill all the other tanks..." „No problem... I told you monsieur Pierre: Buy as much gas as you can, that's what I want..."

131

Then, Lutz came in and said: „Hey... Good morning to you all... Where's Will?" „Good morning Lutz..." Paul answered, smiling at Lutz... „Will is still sleeping... Care for a coffee?" „Ah, sure!", Lutz answered, as he sat at the table... Paul went to his father's study and came back with another big stack of French Francs... He gave the money to monsieur Pierre, who took it and said, while leaving: „Well, I'm going now... I hope today I'll be able to fill up one of the big tanks, at least... When all the big tanks are full... you'll be able to satisfy the needs of a whole army, you know?" „That's not my goal", Paul answered, laughing... „Do you want to wait for monsieur Will to join you before I serve you breakfast?", madame Louise asked? „... Yes... He should be up soon... we will wait for him...", Paul answered. „Oh... I forgot to tell you..." madame Louise said to Paul... „Last evening, I got a call from monsieur Michel... our chef... and he's back... I told him you were expecting him to resume is job, and he was very happy to hear that... He said he will be back on the job tomorrow, and that he'll bring along two of our maids, since they live in the same building he does and has seen them coming back too..." „Ahhhhh, that's good news madame Louise... We're starting to get organized now...", Paul answered with a big smile as Will came in... „What good news are you talking about?", Will asked, smiling at Paul, then at Lutz... „Our chef is back...", Paul answered, giggling... „Oh, I see... now, I will no longer be able to tease you with that... It's so sad!", Will answered, laughing... „Sit down, you silly... so we can have breakfast", Paul replied, laughing too. So they ate breakfast, as madame Louise was so happy to see those three young stud eat with appetite all she had prepared...

„So, what do we do today?", Will asked. „I don't know... What would you like to do... only thing, I have to make a quick stop to the Swiss embassy since I have a message I want to send to our director in Geneva... But it will only take five minutes... I'll give the message to Franz there, and he's going to send it for me...", Paul answered. „I'd like to visit Paris... you know... there's so much I want to see...", Lutz replied. „Good idea...", Will answered. „We'll take my father's car, and I'll show you around...", Paul replied. So they first drove to the Swiss embassy, then went for a visit through Paris where Paul showed Lutz and Will the Opéra Garnier, the Louvre museum, Notre-Dame, then the Sacré-Coeur in Montmartre... the even visited the Père Lachaise Cemetery, where Paul showed Will

Chopin's burial-place... When Paul saw a nice restaurant he knew well was opened, he invided his two friends for a good dinner... As they sat at a table, they quickly realized a young waitress was looking at them with lust in her eyes... „Poor girl... She doesn't know we're hopeless... at least, the two of us...", Paul said, grinning... „But I'm not...", Lutz answered, laughing... Then Lutz looked around to make sure no one could hear him... and then he said: „Hey guys... I wanted to thank you both for last night... you know... that was fastastic... You gave me the best night I've ever had, up until now... Thanks again... I owe you!" „No sweat, Lutz... it was fun for us too", Will said, smiling... „But you know... now that we've helped you with your 'proble', you're going to have to find yourself a nice girl... to help you, you know... We did help you once, but that's it!" „Yeah... I know. Only problem is, if I find a nice girl, as you say, she won't fuck me... And I loved that...", Lutz answered, looking at the table to avoid Will's stare... „Ahhhhhh", Paul said, laughing... „Then, not only will you have to find a nice girl, but a fuck buddy too..." „A what?", Lutz asked... „A fuck buddy... A guy who would fuck you, and that you could fuck...", Paul answered, grinning. „Shit... I never thought about that...", Lutz replied. „And don't look at me, dude... I've got Paul here, and I love him... and he's my only partner...", Will said, laughing. „Yeah, I know. It's sad though... you did such a great job last night...", Lutz answered, grinning... „At least, for the moment, I still have my right hand..." They all burst out laughing at that, as the young waitress came back with what they had ordered.

They took their time, eating and drinking wine... laughing and having fun. When the dinner was over, the young waitress brought the bill, as well as a note where she had put her phone number, saying to them she was 'available'... Paul took the bill and paid it... while Lutz looked at the waitress and said:

„You know mademoiselle, I may call you... I'm all alone here in Paris, and if you're free, we could go out sometime..." – „I would love that...", she answered, with a very sexy smile... As the three of them left, Lutz turned to her and said: „May I ask what's your name?" „I'm Jeannine... And what's yours?" „I'm Luc from Strasbourg... And I will call you..." „I sure hope you will, Luc...", she answered, smiling at him... Back in the car, Paul and Will began laughing and they said to Lutz: „It seems you won't need your right hand after all..." „Oh sure, I'll need it... you know...

a good fuck once in a while is not enough for me anymore, now that, thanks to you, I've dicovered the pleasures of sex", Lutz answered, laughing too... „And I'm going to buy some baby oil too... Thank God, I have ten fingers..." They all laughed as Paul drove them back to his company's Head office, where they had left their uniforms... Everybody had left the office when they got there... and so Lutz and Will had no problem to put back their uniforms... „You know guys", Lutz said... „You don't have to hide from me... you can kiss all you want... I don't mind..." Both Paul and Will smiled, hearing that, and indeed, they began to kiss vey tenderly.

„Now tomorrow, I must meet with the two of you", Paul later said. „Why?", Lutz asked. „You must find time to come to the registrar... so I can sell to you the two cars..." „Oh shit", Will said... „When can we do that?" „I don't know... but I'll wait for your call...", Paul answered. „Yeah... I'll call you" Will replied, then kissing Paul again... „Now let's go... you don't want to be late, do you?, Paul asked them... „Oh no", Lutz answered... „And again Paul, thanks for everything... Thanks a lot... You're a great pal..." „It's been my pleasure Lutz. We're building a strong friendship here, and it's important to me...", Paul answered. „To me too", Lutz said, leaving the two lovers alone for a minute. Paul and Will started kissing again and, after their lips had parted, Will said to Paul: „You know how much I love you... And I love you even more for what you did for Lutz... You're my lover, but he's my

best friend from childhood... and he's important to me..." „I know Will... and now, he's my friend too... and I'm very happy about that!" – „I love you, Paul de Brion..." „And I love you too..." Paul drove them to Hôtel Meurice and, as they parted, Paul said to Will: „I love you... I'll be waiting for your call..." „I love you too... I'll call as soon as I can...", Will answered, smiling at Paul.

The day after, Paul was back at the Head office, where he had a call from Maître Langlois, the attorney... Yes, Paul said to him, he could meet with him on Friday, to go through the list of his Grandma's estate... and discuss her funerals... Then Paul asked madame Mercier to bring him the list of all the empty flats the company had on rent at the moment in Paris. Later, madame Mercier came back with the list, and Paul went through it... „Um... madame Mercier... What about this flat, on Avenue d'Iéna?" „Oh! That flat is located in a very nice building, Sir. It's very expensive..."

134

„I see... And what about that flat on rue Lapérouse?" „Nice building too... But it's less expensive..." The flat has five rooms... two bedrooms... and as it says there on your list, it's furnished..." „Yes, I see... Please madame Mercier, take that flat off the list. We'll rent it to two of my cousins that are in Paris for a while... I'll give you the details, so you can prepare the lease... Do you think it could be ready by the end of the day?" „Absolutely Sir!" „Thank you, madame Mercier... You are so helpful...".

Later, Paul received another call from Maître Langlois... The attorney told Paul he had made all the necessary arrangements so that he would have access to direct phone lines to Berlin as well as Geneva... It would take longer to obtain a line to New York, but they would get one as soon as possible. The direct lines would also be accessible from Paul's study at the mansion on Avenue Foch, the attorney said... The attorney had something else he wanted to tell Paul... The attorney explained the new German ambassador in Paris, Herr Abetz, was trowing a big party at the German embassy next week, to entertain some French businessmen... and Paul had been invited... The attorney explained Herr Abetz had heard about Paul, being so young and being at the head of such a big company... and wanted to meet with him... That would also be a good occasion for Paul to make some contacts, should he still want to make some investments in Germany, the attorney explained... Yes, Paul would attend the party, he told Maître Langlois... but he was not too happy about that. The attorney answered that, anyway, the Germans were here, and there was nothing Paul could do to change that! If Paul wanted to stay in business, there was no way he could avoid them... Paul had to agree to that, but nevertheless, he was less than happy having to go to that damn party... After his talk with Maître Langlois, Paul was eager to see if the direct phone line to Geneva was working... So he tried it and indeed, it was working since a few seconds later, he had the company's director in Geneva at the end of the line... „Bonjour monsieur de Chartrand... comment allez-vous?" „Oh, I'm fine, and you? I've received a long message from your father, yesterday... I understand that, from now on, I shall report to you..." „I'm fine monsieur de Chartrand... and yes, I now assume control over the company's business, not only in France, but also in Switzerland..." „Yes, I know... I'm glad to see the company is back to business... you know..." – „Yes...", Paul replied. Both Paul and Mr de Chartrand were wise enough not to say too much over the phone,

135

knowing the Germans were probably listening... „As soon as I can, I'll go to Geneva, to meet with you, monsieur de Chartrand, so we can discuss business..." „Oh, I would like that very much..." „Yes... But in the meantime, I would ask you to open two new bank accounts in Geneva. I'll give you the details..." Paul gave Mr de Chartrand Will's name as well as Lutz's name. On Will's new account, Paul transferred a sizable amount of Swiss Francs, and a smaller amount on Lutz's new account... „That's quite a lot of money, Sir..." the director in Geneva said... „Yes, I know... Do we have a problem with that?" „Not at all... but..." „Good! monsieur de Chartrand... Good!", Paul answered... „I understand you will send me a telegram to confirm the transfers... as soon as possible..." „Of course, monsieur de Brion... It will be done today...". „Good... Thank you monsieur de Chartrand... I'm sure it's going to be a pleasure doing business with you... I look forward meeting you..." „Yes Sir... Have a good day Sir!". „Thank you... and have a good day too..." Paul hung up the phone and smiled to himself... Yeah! He would give a good raise to his director in Geneva... to make sure he had that man inside his pocket too, just like he had done with madame Mercier... Later on, madame Mercier told him he had a call from a gentleman named Guillaume Harbourg... Paul smiled, then took the call... „Hi! I was thinking about you...", Paul said. „Me too", Will replied... „I can't talk to you very long... but Lutz and I could meet you tomorrow afternoon, at the registrar..." „Fine with me... at what time?" „At two... would it be okay?" „No problem... I'll meet you there...", Paul answered. „Fine... L.Y. ..." „Yeah, L.Y., and L.O.K.", Paul replied, grinning... Paul hung up the phone. He had agreed with Will that on the phone, or elsewhere for that matter, „L.Y." would mean „Love You"... and „L.O.K." would mean „Lots Of Kisses"...

Now Paul was satisfied with his day: The pieces of his plans were starting to fall into place, and he smiled thinking about the surprises he had for Will and Lutz... Later, madame Mercier came back with the new lease, and with a note they had received from the Kommandantur... „I'm not sure you'll be happy with that note", madame Mercier told Paul... Paul took the note and read it. „SHIT" !!!!, Paul exclaimed... „Oh... I'm sorry madame Mercier..." „No problem... I understand... Will that be all for today Sir... I'm about to leave now, so if..." „Yes... That will be all for today madame Mercier... Thank you, and have a good evening...", Paul answered.

As madame Mercier left, Paul read the note for the second time. It said the Germans had unilaterally decided that, from now on, the Reichsmark would be worth twenty French Francs... so it would take only five Pfennigs to buy one French Franc! Paul couldn't believe it! That was catastrophic... It meant the Germans would be able to buy all they wanted in France, at a very, very low price... Paul suddenly smiled, thinking about a joke he had heard that morning, concerning the plates on the German army vehicles, which bore the letters „WH" meaning „Wehrmacht Heer", to indicate they were with the German army... As the joke went, when those vehicles were coming into France, the letters „WH" meant „Wir Holen", and when those vehicles were going back to Germany, they meant „Wir Haben". Yes, Paul thought, the Reich will take all it can take from France... It's going to be a real plunder, Paul thought. Thank God all of this didn't affect the value of the Swiss Franc... Fuck with Das Dritte Reich, Paul said to himself in German: At least, thanks to my German lessons, I can swear in German now! Paul left the office, and went back to his home on Avenue Foch. He had supper all alone in the vast dining-room, and again, he felt miserable... He missed Will so much... So he decided to go through the list of new words his German teacher had given to him, and after that, he went to his father's study... HIS STUDY, from now on, he thought! There, he listen to Radio Berlin, so that his ear could get used to the new language he was quickly learning... After that, he went to bed, thinking about Will...

When he woke up on Friday morning, he rushed through a quick shower and a small breakfast, then went to the Head office, where he had a meeting with Maître Langlois... The attorney gave him a list of all his Grandma's assets and, as Paul went through the list, his eyes became as wide as two big saucers... He looked at the attorney and said: „I didn't know she was that rich..." „Yes... She was... Now, please sign all the papers here, so I can make all the necessary transfers... Oh, and here are the keys to your new Château... I've made sure that the staff there will keep it in good condition... But you may decide to sell it...", the attorney said... „No Maître Langlois... I'm going to keep it... I'm sure that's what my Grandma would have wanted me to do..." – „Yes... That's what she hoped... She told me so at the time..." After that, they talked about madame de Brion's funerals... and agreed that, under the circumstances, the ceremony would be very simple and very private. Maître Langlois

137

would make all the necessary arrangements, and Paul thanked him for that... After the attorney had left, Paul went through the list of assets his Grandma had bestowed upon him... Again, he couldn't believe it! He would have to go to the Château as soon as possible... to make sure the staff there was okay, and he would have to get in touch with his father, to let him know about the investments he now had in the United States, so his father could manage them from New York...

Paul had a quick dinner, then went to the registrar's office, to meet with Will and Lutz, as they had agreed to... Indeed, at two o'clock, he met them and all the papers were signed. Paul gave the keys to Will and Lutz, then said: „So, each of you is the new owner of a car, waiting for you in our underground garage..." „Again Paul... I don't know how to thank you", Will said, as Lutz agreed. „Oh... but that's not all... Here: Sign this document", Paul said, as he gave Will and Lutz the new lease... „What's that?", Will asked... „You are now my new tenants: You got yourself a new flat, not too far from where I live... It's located on rue Lapérouse... Now of course, only Lutz will live there... since you, Will, will move in with me on Avenue Foch! But each day, you'll have to go to the flat to get changed, you know... and the flat will also be your permanent address here in Paris, although you won't really live there... I guess Lutz will be very happy to have that flat all to himself"!, Paul said, laughing... „Are you kidding?", both Will and Lutz said... „But I can't afford such a flat, you know...", Lutz added... „Don't worry, it won't cost you one single Reichsmark... I took care of everything... Oh, but Lutz? You do owe me one Reichsmark... and you too, Will...", Paul said, grinning... „Huh?", they both replied... „For the cars!!!", Paul answered, laughing his heart out... „Shit!", Will exclaimed... „I just can't believe it... Are you sure about that... me, moving in with you... on Avenue Foch? ... I mean..." „That's what I want, Will... Don't you trust me?", Paul asked... „Yes... I do... but I mean..." „Unless you don't want to move in with me... of course... After all, you're a free man Will...", Paul said. „No! I'm your Kriegsgefangener... I told you so...", Will answered, laughing... „His prisoner of war?", Lutz asked, laughing... „Yeah...", Will replied, laughing too... „And I love it!" „Well guys... when can you move?", Paul asked... „We could move next Sunday... That's the day we were suppose to move out of Hôtel Meurice to our new barrack...", Will answered. „Can you come over to my place, Saturday night, and take the cars?", Paul asked Will and Lutz... „That would make your moving easier, for both of you..." „Yeah, that could be arranged...", Will answered... „Don't you think Lutz?" – „Sure... no problem!" „Now we've got to go back Lutz...", Will said to him. And, looking at Paul, Will said: I'll call you tomorrow, and in the meantime, I'll try to find a way to thank you for all what you did..." „Me too", Lutz said, smiling... „But I'm sure it's going to be different from what I think Will has in mind...", he added, laughing... They all laughed at that, then they parted, since Lutz and Will really had to go back to the Palais Bourbon, where their services had just been transferred... As he left, Will said to Paul: „L.Y. and L.O.K...". "L.Y.", Paul replied... "and L.O.K. too..." „What does that mean?", Lutz asked... „It's not for you to know...", Will told him, laughing... „I see...", Lutz replied, grinning...

True enough, Saturday afternoon Will called, telling Paul they would meet on Avenue Foch at around 5 p.m., later that night, to get the cars... Then they would go back to Hôtel Meurice to pack the few things they had there... For his part, Paul explained to Will that after they had parted the day before, he had paid a visit to the Swiss embassy, since he wanted to send a message to his father. He had told Franz about the moving that would take place on Sunday, and Franz had offered to give a hand... Paul explained to his lover that it would be helpful having Franz with them, since he wanted to give a few things to Lutz, to help him better furnish the flat on rue Lapérouse, and all those things would have to be moved... „Yeah, that's a great idea", Will said... „And Franz will help, I'm sure... he's a strong guy..." Indeed at around 5 p.m., Lutz and Will arrived at Paul's mansion and were very excited to take delivery of their new cars... „Now", Paul began to explain... „Both tanks are full... It's my gift to you... but from now on, you'll have to get your gas from the Wehrmacht... „No problem, Paul... though we are rationed, we're allowed to buy some gas from the Wehrmacht... And we won't need much, you know...", Will answered... „Yes, I agree..." Paul replied with a smile... „So, at what time do you plan to be here tomorrow?" „Well, we'll pack our cars early tomorrow morning and I should be here at around 10 a.m.", Will explained... „Lutz will go directly to the flat on rue Lapérouse, to put his things there... and after that, he will join us here, so we can move to the flat the things you want to give to him..." „I'll go to the head office and get a truck... cause some of the furniture I want to give Lutz can't fit into a car... Only problem is, I don't know how to drive such a big truck", Paul said... „Wait for me then... and I'll go with you: I know how to drive big trucks, you know... I'm in the Wehrmacht, don't forget...", Will replied, laughing... „Fine... I'll wait for you then, and I'll tell Franz to be here at around 9.30, tomorrow morning...", Paul answered. „Good." Will and Paul kissed in front of Lutz, who didn't seem to be bothered at all... „Thanks so much Paul... I love you...", Will said to him. Then Lutz came to Paul and hugged him. „Thanks Paul... you're quite a pal... sorry though, if I don't kiss you the way Will did...", Lutz said, laughing... „Go to hell!", Paul answered to Lutz, with a broad smile on his face.

Both young dudes went to their new cars and, beaming, they left. A few minutes later, they were both driving up on Avenue Foch. They were ravished, having a car of their own for the first time in their life... Such a thing would not have been possible in Germany... and they both recognized Paul's generosity, for without him, all of this would not have been possible... While driving his new car down on the Champs Elysées, Lutz thought that Will was very lucky to have met such a great guy like Paul... and how he, himself, was lucky to have Paul as a good friend... At the same time, Will was driving down the Champs Elysées too, and just couldn't believe how happy he was, moving in with Paul in that great mansion on Avenue Foch! Paul was brilliant, he thought... And he loved him so much... Will didn't care about Paul's money... It was Paul he loved not his money... Will thought that tonight would be his last night as a bachelor... He smiled to himself, thinking about that...

Sunday morning came very fast, and Franz got to Paul's mansion at 9.30... A bit later, Will got there too, and they unpacked his car... Paul was a bit troubled, seing Will didn't own much... He had a heavy heart, thinking about that... Will was all smiles, taking off the car the few things he had and, looking at Paul, he said to him: „Don't worry... Lutz has all my uniforms with him..." They both started laughing... „Now, let's go to the head office and get the truck", Will said. Paul drove his father's car - HIS CAR- now, to the head office, where Will got into the truck along with Franz, and they all drove back to Avenue Foch. Later, Lutz joined them, and Paul showed him the furniture he wanted to give to him. „Are you kidding me?", Lutz exclaimed... „Hey... I'm not the Kaiser, you know..." They all burst out laughing, hearing that... „Hey... you're my friend Lutz... so take all you want...", Paul answered... „And tell me Lutz: Did you plug in the refrigerator, back at the flat?" „Sure did!.. I've even put a few beers in it..." „Good... Follow me guys... We're going to make some grocery shopping for Lutz...", Paul replied. So the four young men went upstairs to the main kitchen where Paul had a very big cardboard box ready... And he said to Lutz: „Now Lutz... open all the doors you see there, and choose all you want... go on... and if you don't take enough, I'll do it myself... except that if I do it, there's a possibility you won't like what I will choose for you..." „I can't do that, Paul... I just can't... and I haven't seen so much food in a single place in my whole life...", Lutz answered, stunned. „I'm telling you Lutz: If you don't serve yourself, I'm going to do it for you...", Paul replied, laughing... Lutz was so stunned... He didn't know what to do... „Come on Lutz, I'll help you", Franz said... And both Franz and Lutz began taking all Lutz wanted... putting all the stuff in the big cardboard box... „I'm dreaming...", Lutz said... „Do you have an idea how much it would cost to buy all those things in Germany? ... And anyway, most of those things are not available..." Lutz said to Paul. „My pleasure..." Paul answered, laughing... „After all, you've got to eat... if you want to keep your sexy body in good shape..." They all started laughing, except for Franz, who slowly turned a lovely shade of scarlet... Of course, Paul was the only one to notice that...

„Now, let's pack the furniture... and let's go to your new flat", Paul said to Lutz... So they all went back to the basement, and started loading the furniture into the truck... But after a while, and since it was a very hot day, they were all sweating... and decided to take off their shirts. As they went back to work, Paul noticed Franz was checking out Lutz... Paul looked at Lutz, and he had to admit to himself the hunk was very gorgeous... His naked torso glistened, and his very well toned body was quite a sight! His blond hair complemented his stunning features, and Paul thought any gay guy would easily fall for a dude like Lutz... But Paul felt sorry for Franz, for he knew Lutz was straight... „Okay guys... That's it! Now, let's move on", Paul said... So Paul and Will got into Paul's car, and Lutz got into the truck with... Franz since Lutz also knew how to drive such big truck... and Franz didn't want to „leave poor Lutz all alone" in the truck, as he said... Yeah, sure!, Paul thought to himself! They went to Lutz's new flat on rue Lapérouse, where they unloaded the truck, then Will drove back the truck to the head office, followed by Paul. Both of them went back to Lutz's flat, to help him get organized and eat

141

something... Of course, Paul had brought a few bottles of wine... and so the four of them drank and had lots of fun!

Much later, Will said to Paul: „Time to leave... I've got to be at the office tomorrow morning..." „Well, it's my turn to be on leave for a few days", Lutz said... „So I'm not going to bed so soon..." „I'm off tomorrow... so I'm in no hurry to go home either...", Franz said, smiling... „So buddy... you're going to stay, after those two leave... and we're going to celebrate my new flat.. what do you say?", Lutz asked Franz... „It's a deal", Franz answered, beaming... „Well you two... have fun, but please, don't disturb the neighbours... I don't want to receive complaints from them, you know...", Paul said, grinning... „Don't worry Paul... We'll keep quiet...", Lutz replied, grinning too... „And Paul: Thanks again for all you did for me... I love you!", Lutz said to Paul, as he hugged him... „Hey you...", Will said, laughing... „He's my lover... not yours! Let him go..." „Calm down, dude... I hugged him like a friend would, not like a lover", Lutz answered, laughing his heart out... „Yeah, well, cut it out anyway...", Will answered, grinning... „Do you think Franz, it's safe to leave you here with this maniac...", Paul asked, laughing... „No problem, I'll tame the beast, should I need to...", Franz replied laughing. „Well, good night to you two, and have fun...", Will said to Lutz and Franz, as both he and Paul were leaving the flat... „You too, have a good night...", Lutz and Franz answered. Will and Paul went back to Paul's car and drove back to Avenue Foch... Later on, as they got to their bedroom, Paul asked Will: „Do you think it was a good idea to leave those two together?" „Why do you ask?" „Well... I'm not sure... I wonder if Lutz has not found his new fuck buddy..." „Good for them...", Will replied, smiling... „I'm not sure that would be good for Franz, Will... I think he's really in love with Lutz..." „Well, if so, he's in for a big disappointment..." „Yeah... and that's the problem!" Paul replied. „Well, there's nothing we can do about that my love... So come to bed... I want to celebrate my moving in with you... if you see what I mean...", Will answered... „Ahhhhhh... you... gorgeous... I'm going to eat you alive!", Paul replied, with a very sexy grin on his face... „Come, and eat me my love! I'm all yours...", Will answered, grinning... „Grrrrrrr", Paul answered!

TEN
«I CAN'T BELIEVE I'M MOVING IN...»

„I can't believe I'm living here now... it's like a dream come true...", Will said, looking into Paul's green eyes... „Yes... but don't forget your official address in on rue Lapérouse... you wouldn't like to receive letters here from your family... with German stamps on them... That would be hard to explain to madame Louise...", Paul answered, smiling... „Yeah...", Will replied, grinning... „And many of our stamps have Hitler's face on them... that wouldn't be a good idea indeed..." „Come here, you... and let me kiss you all over...", Paul said. „Ohhhh, but don't forget I'm working tomorrow...", Will replied, with a sexy grin... „You're young... you'll survive to what I'm about to do to you...", Paul answered, laughing.

Will was lying on his back, in the center of the bed... Paul crawled to him and in no time, his lips covered Will's left nipple... Will moaned... Paul started to kiss it, lick it and suck on it, while his right hand began working on Will's right nipple: His fingertips locked onto it, stretching the hard nipple, twisting, tugging and pinching it... After a while, Paul went down on Will's smooth body, his tongue licking it's way to his nice pecs and his six pack... „You're so beautiful Will... I can't believe you are here with me... stark naked... in our bed... You have the most beautiful body I've ever seen..." „You have such a beautiful body, too, my love... besides, others have nice bodies too... take Lutz... and Franz...", Will answered, grinning... „I'm not the only one..." „Yeah, maybe... but of them all, you're the most gorgeous my love! And you belong to me...", Paul answered. Then he started to go further down on Will's body and reached his crotch, where he kept licking and kissing... He licked his way all around Will's hairless dick and as Will sighed, he took his hard dick in his hand and began kissing his oozing knob, licking it very tenderly... „Ohhhh that feels good", Will shouted... Paul loved tasting Will's clear nectar, and he moaned, taking Will's big hard prick into his warm mouth. Will quivered as Paul began deep throating his dick... After a while, Paul let go of Will's hard shaft and went lower to his smooth nut sack, tenderly licking his nice balls... Paul took his time smelling Will's very sensuous scent, giving his nuts a long and hot tongue bath. Will's was groaning and moaning non-stop under Paul's fantastic ministrations, and he loved it when Paul took his balls into his mouth to play with them with his tongue... Then, leaving Will's smooth balls, Paul went further down, kissing and lightly licking Will's miracle inch with the tip of his tongue. Before long, Paul began to lick all around Will's pink fuck hole, kissing his rosebud and playing with it with the tip of his hot tongue. Will cried out in ecstasy as he felt Paul's hot lips and tongue all over his rosy spot... As Paul began to tongue fuck his lover, Will moaned and took his hard oozing dick in his hand, slowly pumping it... „Ohhhh... Paul, fuck me... please, fuck me...", Will pleaded, gripping his heels and spreading his legs so Paul would have easy access to his hot ass... „I love you Will... I love you so much..." „I want to feel you inside me Paul... Please...", Will answered, panting... Paul hooked Will's knees over his strong shoulders, dragging Will's ass into his oozing prick. Then, Paul gripped Will's legs and trusted his hips forward... As Will grabbed his ass cheeks to make sure they were separated, Paul thrusted his hips a little further, and his big mushroom cap slowly started to enter Will's well lubricated hot asshole... „Oh, God...", Will shouted... Paul paused for a few seconds, giving Will time to adjust... „You're so tight Will... it feels so good... you tell me when you're ready...", Paul said, looking into his lover's beautiful blue eyes... As Will's ass began relaxing, Will nodded to Paul, who began to slowly penetrate his lover's love chute. His hard dick was oozing so much, it didn't take long before it was stuck up Will's ass, down to the base of his prick trunk. Then, Paul paused again. He leaned over Will's rippled stomach and began to kiss him very tenderly... „Shit Paul... I love feeling your hard dick deep inside me... it feels incredibly pleasurable... I can't believe it... It's so hot... Please, fuck me now Paul... fuck me hard", Will said, looking deep into his lover's green eyes... Paul began to slowly work his hips back and forth, taking his slippery dick almost all the way out, then trusting it back, deep inside Will's tight ass chute... As he kept ramming his hard boner in and out, Paul hit Will's walnut several times, and Will began groaning and moaning... „Ahhhh... that's it Paul... that's it... right there... Yeah! You've got it... Keep doing that right there... Paul swivelled his hips several times, keeping his dick at a certain distance inside Will's fuck hole, slowly massaging Will's love spot with the tip of his oozing dick. Paul looked at his lover's perfectly sculpted body and said: „You're so beautiful Will... I love you so much... I wish I could keep fucking you like that for the rest of my life...“ „I love you, too, Paul... and I feel we're not just having sex together, we're really making love to each other... It's quite another feeling...“ Will squeezed the base of Paul's cock trunk, using his ass ring, and saw the looks of pleasurable bliss on his young lover's face... With his hand, Will started to bob faster on his slippery prick... As Paul began working his dick faster and faster in and out of Will's tight arse, he started to groan and moan, feeling his dick stiffening inside Will's hot and slippery ass chute... „Oh shit Will... I can't keep it any longer... I'm going to cum... I'm going to cum Will...“ He went faster and faster, driving his dick in and out of Will's tight ass... then he exploded, as his prick slid deep inside his lover, where he began shooting his young hot spunk. His breathing was made of short, sharp gasps by now, and he couldn't believe he was enjoying such intense pleasures, as his cock kept shooting torrents of cum... Looking into his blue-eyed lover, he shouted: „Ahhhhh.... This is so good Will.... so good....“ „I'm about to cum, too...“, Will answered, panting and sweating... Paul lowered his body and took Will's big throbbing dick into his warm mouth, deep throating it... It didn't take long before Will's very hard dick started to swell even more and seconds later, he began firing torrents of cum deep inside his gorgeous lover's mouth, gasping and shouting with lust... „Oh shit... Oh shit Paul... keep doing that...“ Paul lips sealed tight Will's dick inside his hot mouth as his head kept moving back and forth... As Will started shooting, he quickly gulped, making sure he wouldn't lose any of his lover's hot and sweet jizz... and he got it all just fine, loving it so much... „That's fantastic... you're fantastic...“, Will shouted... Pulling his spent cock out of Will's love chute, Paul went for his lover's hot lips and started cum kissing him very passionately... After their lips parted, Paul looked into Will's sparkling blue eyes and said to him, smiling: „That was sooooooo good... Hell.... How can it get any better...“ „I know“, Will answered, smiling too... They resumed kissing, Paul's body wrapped by Will's strong arms in a close embrace...

145

After that hot session, Paul tenderly whispered to Will: „I wish you were not working tomorrow...I could keep going like that for hours...“ „Me too...“, Will answered, grinning... „Yeah... Guess we have to be reasonable though... After all... you need some rest... I'm already thinking about tomorrow night...“, Paul replied, grinning too... Will started laughing, and answered: „Well... before we get to tomorrow night... I guess we must first go to sleep, and go through the day tomorrow, don't we?“ „Do we?“ „Hey, I'm only human you know...“ „Okay, okay... I'll let you go to sleep... but only because I love you, and because I want you to be in shape tomorrow night, so you can fuck me long and hard...“, Paul answered... „How considerate of you“, Will replied, laughing... „I know... I'm like that... very considerate...“, Paul answered, chuckling... Will took Paul into his arms again, and very tenderly kissed him. „I love to cuddle into your smooth, strong body“, Paul said. „Yeah... And I love to hold you like that...“ Paul sighed and, before long, the two young lovers were sleeping, Will's arms still wrapped around Paul's eighteen years old body...

Meanwhile on rue Lapérouse: „Hey pal... want another beer?“, Lutz asked Franz... „Sure...“ As Lutz rose from the couch where he was sitting right next to Franz, and started walking to the kitchen to get the beers, Franz looked at him... Since it was still very hot inside the flat, both young men had remained shirtless... Franz looked at Lutz strong shoulders, at his strong back and at his very firm and cute bubble butt... Franz also noticed Lutz's very strong thighs, since both of them were only wearing shorts... It had been too hot during the day to wear anything else... and they had sweat so much, moving in all the furniture... When Lutz came back with the beers, he realized Franz was staring at him... „What's wrong with me?“, Lutz asked... „Oh... nothing... nothing at all... sorry“, Franz replied, smiling... Franz could feel his dick twitching inside his shorts, and he only hoped Lutz wouldn't notice it... Lutz went back to the couch and, as he sat by Franz, he gave him his beer, saying: „Here you are, pal... take a sip... that's going to cool you down...“ „.... what do you mean?“, Franz nervously asked. „You know... it's so hot in here...“, Lutz replied, grinning. „...Oh...“, Franz answered, a bit relieved. Lutz laughed and, looking at Franz, he added: „...No... I wasn't talking about your dick... but I sure can see the bulge in your shorts...“ For the second time that day, Franz was now blushing scarlet red under his blond hair... Lutz was now trying not to break into a fit of giggles, seeing Franz was so embarrassed... „Nah, dude... Don't worry... I don't care, you know... do you think I didn't realize how you were checking me out all day long? I'm not blind you know...", Lutz said, with a big laugh..."Only problem is... I'm not gay... and that's your problem, not mine..." „Yeah, I know you're not gay... Paul told me that...", Franz replied, looking at his feet. „I guess you like what you see though...", Lutz asked, grinning... „Hell! You're the most beautiful stud I've ever seen in my life... and I'm sitting here right next to you... I can smell your sensuous scent from where I am... just a glance at your well toned body makes my dick twist... What can I say, except that I'm sorry if I make you uncomfortable...", Franz answered. „Hell Franz, you don't have to feel sorry... I mean... you're honest with me, and I appreciate that... Do you want me to put back on my shirt?" „Noooooo", Franz exclaimed.... „If I can't have you, at least I can look at you..." „Why do you say you can't have me? I didn't say that... I just said that I'm not gay, that's all", Lutz replied, laughing. „I don't understand", Franz replied with a puzzled look on his face.

Lutz brought his beer to his very sensuous lips, took a sip as his left leg touched Franz's smooth thigh... Franz quivered at the touch, and felt his blood rush through his whole body... „Look Franz...", Lutz began to explain, with a grin on his face, „I'm not gay... but I love sex... just like you do, I'm sure... My girlfriend Klara is in Berlin and I'm here, all alone... Will and Paul taught me a few things the other night... and I loved it... but that doesn't mean I'm gay... only that I love sex..." „You mean.. you made love with Will and Paul?" „No... not really... You see... That's the difference... I didn't make love with them... I don't love them and they don't love me... at least, not that way... No... We had some sex, that's all... They gave me a hand... you see... Making love to someone you love is one thing... but it's totally different from simply having sex with someone.. When you're having sex with someone, it's only to satisfy your sexual needs... At least, that's the way I see it..." „I see what you mean... and Lutz... may I ask you something?" – „Sure... go ahead, pal..." „Would you have sex with me?"

Lutz burst out laughing! „You really want to have sex with a guy like me?", Lutz asked Franz... „Shit Lutz... I would give anything just to have sex with you..." „Yeah... well... But you know, I want it to be very clear between you and me, you know: I will never fall in love with you... And

147

I will never make love to you: Just sex.. just plain sex...And please, don't fall in love with me either... And no kissing... Good sex...that's all. Do we agree on that?", Lutz replied, smiling at Franz. „Agreed!", Franz replied, beaming...

Lutz took his beer and put it down on the floor, then did the same with Franz's beer... He then turned to Franz and put his right hand on Franz's sizeable bulge, feeling his hardening dick... „Um... you seem to have a nice dick here...", Lutz said, grinning... „God... I can't believe you're groping me... it feels so good...", Franz replied as he sighed... „Take off your shorts Franz..." Franz rose and took off his shorts, revealing his now very stiff rod, his nice smooth balls and his well trimmed blond bush... „Nice", Lutz said... „Come here..." As Franz went to Lutz who was still sitting on the couch, his hard dick was only inches from Lutz's hot lips... Lutz took Franz's throbbing dick and guided it to his warm mouth. Opening his mouth, he took it right inside and started giving it a very good tongue bath... Franz almost fainted and started panting, feeling his stiff rod being massaged by Lutz's hot tongue... He put his hands on Lutz's head, then started caressing his face, looking at Lutz's curly blond hair, he smelled it... „Ahhhhh", Franz exclaimed... Lutz looked up to his blue-eyed blond friend and grinned... He knew he was driving Franz wild... Then, wanting the pleasure to last longer, Lutz let go of Lutz hardon and began kissing and licking Franz's smooth balls, giving them a gentle squeeze... „Ah shit Lutz... you're going to drive me mad...", Franz said, panting... „You like that?", Lutz asked... „It's the best thing that ever happened to me... I've never felt like that..." „First time?", Lutz asked, grinning... „Yeah!" „Ever done anything else before?" „I've been wanking, of course... but no... nothing else. Do you have much experience?", Franz asked... „Not much... except for what Will and Paul taught me the other night...", Lutz answered... „Have you..." „If I've fucked?... Yes... And Will fucked me... I loved it..." „Oh shit, how come I wasn't there?" „You had left... you said you had to go, because you were working the day after... remember?" „Oh shit!... Now I want to see you naked Lutz, take off those shorts...", Franz said. In no time, Lutz was stark naked, showing Franz his very thick dick and his big balls... „Oh my God Lutz, you're so beautiful... even better than I had imagined in my dreams..." „You've dreamt about me?", Lutz asked... „Since the first night I saw you, I've been dreaming about you non-stop! And I've been jerking

148

off, thinking about you..." „You like me that much?", Lutz asked, a bit surprised... „Don't make me blush again...", Franz answered. Then Franz knelt in front of Lutz, opened his mouth and took his thick prick inside his warm mouth... „Watch your teeth, Franz...", Lutz said to him, smiling... Franz grinned and made sure his teeth would remain as far away from Lutz dick as possible... „Now... you're doing a great job Franz... I love it... that's a good blowjob dude..." That drew a chuckle from Franz, who started to bob faster on Lutz's cock with his mouth, his lips tightly sealed around his shaft... „Ohhhh... that's good Franz... that's good", Lutz exclaimed, looking down at his blond friend, seeing he was wanking his own oozing dick... After a while, Lutz said: „Let's go to the shower Franz... I want to show you another trick Will and Paul taught me..." „And what's that?" „You'll see", Lutz answered, grinning... They went to the bathroom and took a quick shower together... Then Lutz shot the water off...

„Put your hands on the wall Franz, and spread your legs.. Yeah.. that's it... Now, stand still..." Seeing Lutz was taking something from the cabinet, Franz asked: „What's that?" „A gift Will and Paul gave me... it's only a bottle of baby oil... but you'll see... it's a very helpful gift..." Lutz opened the bottle and smeared some oil all over Franz's arse crack and fuckhole... Then he smeared some all over his hard dick and all over Franz's cock... „Ohhhh... that feels good", Franz replied, feeling Lutz index finger play with his slippery rosebud... Then, Lutz's right arm slipped around Franz's waist and he took hold of his stiff rod with his hand, slowly wanking it... „Oh shit Lutz..." „Yeah... I know...", Lutz answered, laughing... With his other hand, Lutz kept playing with Franz's arse, his index finger massaging his very tender rosy spot. Then Lutz slowly began to press his finger inside Franz's sphincter... „Ohhhhhhh...." Franz exclaimed... „I love that..." Lutz played for a while with his finger deep inside Franz's love chute, then he added a second finger... Now Franz was gasping with lust, and he didn't say a word when Lutz inserted a third finger inside his warm and tight chute... After a while, Lutz said: "Now, I think you're ready... As he said that, Lutz removed his fingers from Franz's ass. "Are you going to..." "Yeah", Lutz answered, grinning ... "And you're going to love it... but first, I warn you, it's going to hurt like hell... then, pain will turn into pleasure... I swear... I've been through that when Will fucked me, and I loved it..."

149

Franz didn't care about pain: He wanted to lose his virginity, and he wanted to lose it with Lutz making love to him... He was so much in love with the guy... He would do anything for him... to make him feel good... He wanted to satisfy Lutz... even if it meant he was going to suffer like hell. That didn't count, he thought, as long as Lutz sexual needs were satisfied... His only problem was that he couldn't tell that to Lutz... He had agreed: Only sex... no love... While Franz was thinking about that, Lutz pressed his thick dick slowly through his sphincter... Franz screamed, as it felt like his ass had been pierced by a giant sword... Lutz kept jacking him off with his right hand, and put his left hand over one of Franz's hard nipples, twisting and pinching it hard... Lutz then started to nibble on Franz left ear lobe, whispering to his blond friend the pain would go soon... The diversion worked, for seconds later Franz stopped shaking... "Are you okay?", Lutz whispered to Franz... "I guess I am... it's less painful now... but your dick is so thick..." "I know...", Lutz answered, giggling... As he giggled, his big dick went deeper inside Franz's love chute... "Go easy, dude... Go easy with your weapon...", Franz said... „Do you want me to take it out?", Lutz asked... „Nooooooo", Franz shouted... „No fucking way... I want you inside me... all of your monster prick... just go easy..." − „Hey, don't insult my Jerry here... He's not a monster... he's just a little fat, that's all", Lutz answered, laughing... „Yeah... Well, ask your Jerry to stay still for a few minutes, so I get used to him inside me..." „You're so tight Franz... My Jerry likes it... a lot... I can feel it..." Now Franz burst out laughing hearing that, and doing so, he relaxed his ass muscles enough so that Lutz's big slippery dick went all the way inside him... „Oh my God!... Oh my God", Franz exclaimed... „No, it's not your God... it's my big dick", Lutz replied, chuckling... That drew a chuckle from Franz and he really started to relax... „Is your Jerry all the way inside me?" „Yup!", Lutz answered. „Hello Jerry", Franz replied, chuckling... Lutz burst out laughing and, without knowing it, he swivelled his hips and screwed Franz love chute good... Franz could feel Lutz's very hard prick all inside him, and Lutz's firm muscled chest hard pressed against his back... Lutz swivelled his hips again, and felt the pleasure Franz's tight ass was giving to him... He moaned, nibbling the side of Franz's neck, sending shivers up and down his blond friend's spine... Franz was a bit surprised when he feld Lutz kissing him between his shoulder blades... and he loved that! „Now Lutz... fuck me... go ahead... fuck me... I want you.. Please!" Lutz began working his hips back and forth, and before long, Franz was panting and gasping... With his right hand, Lutz grabbed again Franz's oozing dick and started to bob faster and faster on his hard slippery dick. „Oh hell Lutz... that's too much... I'm in paradise..." As Lutz kept driving his thick dick in and out of Franz's love chute, each time hitting his walnut, his Swiss lover began panting and sweating like hell, loving every thrust Lutz's dick made deep inside him... „Told you, you would love it...", Lutz said, grinning... „I love it Lutz..." Franz wanted to add „And I love you Lutz...", but he refrained from saying that, knowing Lutz wouldn't like hearing about that... "I'm going to cum, Franz... I'm going to cum deep inside you..." „I want you to... I want you so much, Lutz..." Lutz pumped his hard dick deep inside Franz ass and started shooting wad after wad of his hot young spunk inside Franz hot and very tight love chute... „Oh Lutz, keep wanking me... please... I'm about to cum too... Oh God! Oh God..." Franz's breathing was so heavy, Lutz thought he was about to have a seizure... „Here I cum, Lutz... Ahhhhhhhhhh" Franz gasped and started to pump his hot juzz into the air... firing torrents of cum... „Shit! Shit! Shit!... I can't believe it... did you see that? I've never cum like that before", Franz cried out... „I love fucking your tight ass Franz... it feels soooooooo god...", Lutz replied. „Thanks... I love being fucked by your Jerry... and thank God he's so big... He did a very good job. You're going to have to thank him for me", Franz replied, chuckling... Of course, Lutz burst out laughing, and that caused his spent cock to come out of Franz's hot ass... „Now, let's take a good shower... guess we need it...", Lutz said, smiling at Franz...

After their shower, they dried themselves and went back to sit on the couch, stark naked, their towels draped around their strong shoulders. „... Care for a beer?...", Lutz asked... „Yeah! ... I need it!", Franz replied, grinning... Two minutes later, Lutz was back with two cold beers... „Hey pal... you're sleeping here tonight, aren't you?", Lutz asked, with a grin on his face... „... Well... I didn't...", Franz started to answer... „Come on dude... You're not working tomorrow... and neither am I... so, what's the problem... Besides, you owe me...", Lutz said... „Oh?"..., Franz answered... „Sure... The way it works, I fuck you... and then, you fuck me... And as far as I know...I haven't been fucked by your big long dick yet!", Lutz answered, laughing... „Are you kidding? You want me to fuck you... really?", Franz asked, beaming... „Hell yeah! I'm longing for a good

151

fuck...", Lutz replied, laughing... „Really?... But you're not gay..." „What the fuck does it has to do with that? It has nothing to do with the fact that I'm straight... I just love a good fuck, and I love having my love spot massaged... that's all!", Lutz answered, looking at Franz with a big grin on his face. „You'll find it hard, when you're going back to your girlfriend in Berlin, you know..." – „Well... I'm not leaving tomorrow, am I? So I'll think about that later...", Lutz replied. „You're right... And yes... I'll spend the night with you... and I'll fuck you as many times as you wish... you're so gorgeous..." „Hey dude... don't fall in love with me... I told you... no strings attached... That's the deal you've agreed to...", Lutz warned Franz... „No problem... but that doesn't change the fact that you're gorgeous... In fact, you're perfect! Simply perfect! You're drop dead gorgeous... that's what you are", Franz answered, giggling... „You know... for a guy... you're not bad either...", Lutz answered, laughing... „You really think so?" „Hell, look at you Franz... You have a very well toned body... nice abs... gorgeous blue eyes... I mean... if you weren't gay, all the women in town would be running after you..." „No, they wouldn't... cause they would all be running after you instead..." „Ah Franz... Cut it out... you know you're good-looking... I'm telling you... You really are a gorgeous hunk. Really!" – „Thanks Lutz... coming from you, I take it as a compliment..." „Hey... I told you... don't fall in love with me... that's a warning, you know..." „Don't worry about that... I like good sex just as much as you do... No strings attached...", Franz answered. „That's it dude... Now, let's go to bed... I'm exhausted... But I'm happy you're here with me tonight... so I won't spend my first night here all alone..." „I'm glad I'm here with you, Lutz... But prepare yourself: Tomorrow morning, you'll get fucked hard... very hard..." „Ohhhhhhh... and I'm sure I'll love it... a lot..."

So they went to bed... but there was no cuddling... and no kissing... Lutz went to sleep fast, just like a real jock... not spending one second thinking about how Franz really felt... He was satisfied... That was all! It took a lot of time before Franz fell asleep though... He was thinking about how much he was lucky to have met Lutz... To be able to make love to him... because that's how Franz felt about it: He had made love to Lutz! That was not just sex... He knew that. But he also knew he had to hide his feelings... He didn't want to lose Lutz, now that he had found him... But Franz wanted more that that... He wanted Lutz to love him... and he knew that was just not possible... Franz looked at his curly blond lover sleeping right next to him... He looked at Lutz perfectly sculpted naked body... at his sensuous lips... Oh!... He wished he could passionately kiss him... Then he thought about Will and Paul: How lucky they were to be deeply in love with each other... Again, Franz looked at the sleeping form of his lover next to him, then closed his eyes... As he was exhausted, too, and as he was overcome with sleep, he fell asleep without knowing it...

ELEVEN
«AN UNEXPECTED TURN OF EVENTS»

„Wake up sleephead... you're working today... Have you forgotten?", Paul said to Will, giving him a sweet kiss on his tender lips... „Huh? ... What time is it?" „Six o'clock... and you've got to take your shower, then have breakfast... then drive to rue Lapérouse to get your uniform..." „Okay... okay..." Will answered, smiling at Paul... „You're worse than my mother..." „I take that as a compliment", Paul replied, grinning... „It was meant as a compliment, you know..." „Now, go on... run to the shower... I'll take mine after you..." „Why don't we take it together?", Will asked, grinning... „... Okay... But no fooling around... We have no time for that this morning", Paul answered, giving Will a big wet kiss... „Okay... okay..." They took a quick shower, then they had breakfast and soon after, Will left... „See you tonight... at around six...", Will shouted... „Yeah... Have a good day Will... L.Y.... and L.O.K.", Paul answered. „Same for me"... Will said, leaving...

Paul went to his study and sat at his desk. He was worried about the invitation he had received to attend a party later that week at the German embassy... He could not refuse the invitation... but he didn't like the idea of having to go to the German embassy and meet with „those people"... He called Maître Langlois, and the attorney confirmed the party would take place next Wednesday, on June 26th... Maître Langlois also said he had almost completed the list of his Grandma's assets... and that he could give it to Paul the next day. That was fine with Paul... Then Paul drove to the Head office, where madame Mercier gave him a telegram from monsieur De Chartrand in Geneva, confirming the two new bank accounts had been opened and the transfers made. Paul grinned. Paul gave a call to Will... asking him to invite Lutz for supper... since he had something for him... Will reminded Paul that Lutz was on leave today...

Paul answered that he had forgotten, but said he would call Lutz at his new flat... to invite him. Paul could perceive Will was grinning... but he didn't know why: He asked Will, but Will said nothing, except that he would tell Paul later that night... So Paul called Lutz at his new flat and he was surprised to hear Franz answer the phone... „... Franz?", Paul asked.... „Yeah!" „... I don't know how that's possible... I asked for Lutz's phone number... not the Swiss embassy..." – „Well... you've got what you've asked for... They didn't connect you with the embassy... I'm with Lutz at his flat... He's in the shower..." „Oh... (...) well... I'd like to talk to him, if that's possible..." „Sure... stay on the line Paul", Franz answered, grinning... (...) „Sorry Paul... I was in the shower", Lutz answered a while later... „Yeah... Well... I just wanted to invite you for supper tonight... Are you free?" „...Well... Franz is here..." „... Yes... I can see that... Well... Why don't you invite him to come along with you? We would be expecting you at around seven, would that be fine with you?" „... Yes...Fine... Thanks, We'll be there...", Lutz answered.

Paul didn't know what to think about the fact Franz was still at Lutz's flat... Maybe he drank too much last night and had decided to sleep over there, he said to himself... Anyway... Paul had many other things to think about that day, and time kew so fast that before he knew it, he realized it was already five o'clock. He left the office and drove back home, where Will met him a bit later... „You will never believe what I saw this morning...", Will said to Paul, grinning... „What?" „When I went to rue Lapérouse to get changed, I saw Franz's car parked nearby... I went to the flat, to get changed, and when I got there... I heard noises coming from Lutz's bedroom... I looked... and I saw... You won't believe what I saw! I saw Franz fucking Lutz doggystyle..." „Oh my God! (...) But that explains why Franz answered the phone when I called Lutz this morning...", Paul answered... „Yeah! I can't believe it... Lutz and Franz..." „Well... I'm not really surprised, you know! Lutz is in love with sex... and I think Franz is in love with Lutz, as I told you last night... So...", Paul replied. „Shit!" „Well Will, it's none of our business, is it? Although I'm not sure..." – „No... you're right" „So we'll act as if we knew nothing about that... no question... nothing... No wise jokes, Will!!! Okay? If they want to tell us, they will... If not, it's their business...", Paul said, looking at Will... „Okay, okay... no wise cracks, I swear", Will answered, laughing...

„Now, before Lutz and Franz get here... I have something for you...",
Paul said. „What's that?" „It's a gift..." Will opened the envelope Paul was
giving to him; he opened it, and started to read the note that confirmed a
new bank account had been opened for him in Switzerland, and that a
sizable amount had been deposited on that account... He looked at Paul
and asked: „I don't understand..." „It's a gift to you...", Paul answered,
smiling... „Are you kidding... I can't accept that... NO, I can't! You've
already done enough for me Paul! You let me stay here with you... you
gave me a car... That's enough Paul! I will not accept your money..."
„Please Will, hear me before you make a decision..." – „... I don't see..."
„Please! Will you hear me just for a second? Please?" – „(...)" „Thanks! ...
Now you see Will, I've got a lot of money... and I've inherited a lot from
my Grandma... What I'm giving you here is just a very very small part of
what I own... And as you see, the money I'm giving you is in Swiss Franc...
so whatever happens to the French Franc, or to the Reichsmark for that
matter... is not important... Now, you're safe from want: That's what I
want! And there's another reason why I want you to have that money... I
want you to be totally independent from me, financially speaking I
mean...", Paul said, with a grin on his face... „I see your point Paul... but
how do you think I'm feeling about that... I mean... I'll never be able to
ever give you a gift like that..." „You've already given me much more than
that Will... much more... You've given me happiness... That's something
money can't buy..." Paul leaned to Will and began kissing him, caressing
his beautiful face, running his fingers through his lover's golden blond
hair... „I love you so much Will... so much... and the only thing that scares
me like hell is that I could loose you, because of that goddamn war!" „I
love you too Paul ... You know that... And you won't loose me... First,
we've made a vow to each other, remember? I'll be with you for as long
as you want me to... And second... the war... well the war... Don't worry
about it..." „... Yes...If you say so... But anyway, Will: Pleeeeeease accept
my gift..." – „... Do I have a choice?" „NO!, Paul replied, laughing... „So,
in that case... I accept... with all my love...", Will answered, before kissing
Paul very tenderly... „I also have an envelope for Lutz!, Paul later said...
„Huh?" „...Yes... I'm going to give him some money, too... not as much as
I gave to you... no... but nevertheless, what I'll give to him will make him
safe from want for quite a while..." – „... But why do you do that Paul?"
„He's your best friend Will... and he's my friend now... I guess he'll be

157

spending a lot of time with us... going out... having fun... and I don't see how he could afford that with his meagre allowance! And I don't want to have to pay for him each time we go out... that would make him feel bad... So with the money I'm going to give him, he'll be independent from you and me..." „... Good luck!... I'm not sure Lutz will accept..." – „We'll see...", Paul answered, grinning... Later, Lutz and Franz arrived and joined Will and Paul in the drawing-room. They had a few beers and had fun... but Paul could perceive Lutz and Franz felt a bit uncomfortable... and Paul knew why! But he didn't say anything... Instead, he spoke about the party he would have to attend at the German embassy, and explained he felt very uneasy about that... „...Perhaps you'll meet with Herr Funk... He's the Reich Minister of Economic Affairs, and I've heard he's in town...", Lutz said... „That's probably why they are throwing that party, you know... So Herr Funk can meet with French businessmen...", Will said... „... I also heard Herr Funk is a notorius homosexual...", Lutz added... „How's that possible... I mean... Do you think the Führer knows?", Paul asked... „I'm sure he does! But he needs Funk... that guy is very well connected with the big financial brass in Germany... and the Führer needs their money! So Herr Funk is untouchable... Even the Gestapo can't do anything against him! At least, that's what my father said...", Lutz answered... „Maybe he'll fall in love with you Paul...", Franz said, laughing... „OH! KNOCK IT OFF, Franz... I really don't want to go to that damn party...", Paul answered, not laughing at all... „But you must go Paul", Franz replied, no longer laughing... „Now, I can understand that you're not happy with the fact that you've been invited to that party... but you know... that comes with the territory! If you want your business to stay open, you'll have to deal with the Nazis... they are here Paul, whether you like it or not. And they make the rules now... it doesn't mean you have to like them... but that's the way things are..." „Maybe I should stop doing business... close the company... I don't like the idea of having to do business with the Reich... Doing so, we only help the Nazis... Maître Langlois told me about a radio speech a French general gave from London a few days ago... I think his name is de Gaulle... He said he intends to continue fighting... Perhaps that's what we should do...", Paul answered... „...I've never heard about that de Gaulle guy...", Franz answered..." But it's easy for him to say whatever he wants, he's in London! Not here in Paris! Now if you shut down your company... if everyone in France does

158

the same... say goodbye to France! That would mean the end of your country... And if you shut it down Paul, what do you think will happen to all your employees? They need their jobs, you know! Being Swiss, I can give you an independent opinion Paul... Look! In Switzerland, we have no choice but to do business with the Nazis! Do you think we like that? NO! But we're caught right in the middle... just like you are... It's very easy for President Roosevelt to say he won't do business with the Nazis: He's in America, far, far away from here... and America doesn't need to do business with the Reich to survive. We do! That may be sad... but that's the truth!" „... You may be right, Franz... But that doesn't mean I like that...", Paul answered... „We all know that Paul...", Franz replied...

As madame Louise told Paul supper was ready to be served, they all went to the diningroom, where a delicous meal was served to them... „It's obvious your chef is back Paul... It's really delicious...", Lutz said, smiling... „You didn't like madame Louise's cooking?", Paul replied, laughing... „Sure... I liked it... but that's something else...", Lutz answered, laughing too... „Now... I have something for you Lutz!", Paul said to him... Paul gave Lutz an envelope, saying: „...Open it..." Lutz took the envelope then opened it and read the note concerning his new bank account in Switzerland... „... That doesn't belong to me...", Lutz exclaimed, looking at Paul... „Now it does!", Paul answered, grinning... And he went on to explain to Lutz the reasons he wanted him to have that money... Lutz listened... with his characteristic frown... „... I hear you Paul... But I can't accept..." „Oh shut up, Lutz! It's no use to argue with him... It's lost in advance... believe me: I've tried...", Will said, laughing... „YUP!!, Paul answered, laughing... „... But...", Lutz tried to say... „... I told you Lutz: Shut up and take it", Will replied... „... But... How can I thank you?... I mean..." „You've already thanked me Lutz... Now I don't want to hear anything about that anymore. It's settled... That's it! Over with!", Paul answered. „(...)" „Good!", Paul said!... „Now Will, let's talk about your new work schedule you told me about..." „OH! Yes! Well... starting next week, Lutz and I will be working from Monday trough Friday... and we'll have the weekends off... That's unless there's an urgent matter that requires us to work on a Saturday or a Sunday..." „...HEY! That's cool..." Paul answered... „and you know what? When my Grandma died, I've inherited her small château near Chartres... The château is called 'Bagatelle', cause it's not very big... But it's beautiful, and the estate is quite

159

large... it includes a small farm as well as a small lake... I will have to go there soon to make sure everything is okay... and meet with the staff, you know... So, we could all go and spend the next weekend there... That would be fun... what do you think?" „Hey! that would be great...", Will replied... „Do you think you could come?", Paul asked Franz... „Sure... no problem! I'd like that...", Franz replied, smiling... „...And you Lutz?"... „Don't ask me man! My suitcase is already packed"... Lutz answered, laughing... „Tomorrow, I'll call Bagatelle to let the staff know we'll be there, so they can prepare the place and the bedrooms..." „... Yeah... well... about that, Paul... Franz and I won't need... I mean... We'll share the same bedroom, if you don't mind...", Lutz said, looking into his empty plate, a bit embarrassed... Will grinned... „Shut up!", Paul said, looking at Will... Then, looking at Lutz and Franz he said: „That's okay... no problem" „...You don't ask why?", Lutz asked Paul, looking him straight in the eyes... „No. It's your business... If you want to tell, fine... If you don't... fine...", Paul answered. „And you... stop grinning like that", Paul said to Will, looking at him... Lutz looked at Franz, who nodded... then at Will and at Paul... „...Well... Anyway, I'm sure you've already guessed...", Lutz said. „...From what I've seen this morning on rue Lapérouse, I mean... I didn't have to guess, you know: I saw it...", Will answered, laughing... „OH YOU!", Paul shouted... „...You mean... You mean you came to the flat this morning?", Lutz asked... „Hell Lutz... from where do you think I've got my uniform? And when I saw what I saw... and heard what I heard... well... you know... I just changed, and left the flat as quietly as possible...", Will answered, grinning... „Oh"... Lutz replied, as Franz was turning red... „Hey guys, it's your business... Not ours! Besides, it would be hard for me and Will to pass judgment on what you're doing...", Paul said. „... Yeah! But that's different... you are gay... I'm not...", Lutz answered. „You know Lutz, that's too complicated for me to understand... but as long as both of you feel comfortable with that, well, I don't give a shit...", Paul replied. „Thanks Paul...", Franz said, looking at Paul... „Now it's agreed? We'll all spend next weekend at Bagatelle?", Paul asked them, smiling... „YES!", they all answered. "I would suggest you two come to sleep here on Friday night, so we can all leave early, Saturday morning..." „Fine with me...", Lutz answered... „What about you Franz?" „Fine with me too", Franz answered, smiling...

160

Later that evening, while Will and Lutz were captivated by a discussion they were having concerning a certain person both of them knew in Berlin, Franz went to Paul and asked him if he could have a private chat with him... „Sure...", Paul answered... „Hey you guys, we're going to my study for a few minutes... I have some papers I want Franz to bring back to the embassy..." „Go ahead...", Will and Lutz answered... Both Paul and Franz walked over to Paul's study, and as soon as they were there, Franz said to Paul: „Thanks a lot for what you said... you know... about Lutz and me..." „...Sure... But you didn't asked me to come in here just to tell me that, did you Franz? You have something else on your mind, I can tell..." „Yes... I'd like to have your opinion on that...", Franz answered. „Can I be honest with you Franz?" „I want you to..." „Well, I understand perfectly well that you find Lutz to be very, very attractive... He's a real hunk! But I'm looking at you... and I'm afraid you're falling in love with him... and I worry about that, you see... Lutz isn't gay, and he's not in love with you... he has his girlfriend in Berlin and one day, he'll go back to her... Lutz has no problem with that... all he wants is good sex! And I'm sure he's getting it from you... You're a nice and good-looking guy Franz, and I sure hope you won't get hurt in this whole affair..." „You know Paul, Lutz has been very honest with me about all that... He told me he wasn't gay, and that he wasn't in love with me! He told me all he wants is a good fuck buddy, that's all! He doesn't want me to kiss him... and he warned me not to fall in love with him! As he said: „We fuck... no strings attached..." „And how do you feel about that?" „I know I'm in love with him... you just don't know how much I love him Paul... And I know that in the end, I may be the only one to suffer... but in the meantime, I'll take all I can... At least, when I grow old, I'll have good memories to think about, not regrets..." „You're in for some hard time, you know that?" „.... Perhaps... But for now, I have him... and that's enough for me! I know... I know... I will suffer... and I suffer already when we make love and I can't kiss him... and I suffer when I would like to tell him how much I love him... and I can't! I don't want to loose him Paul... Last night, after he went to sleep, I kept looking at him... He's so beautiful! I felt so happy... I just couldn't believe I was in the same bed with him... What can I say... I know Paul... he doesn't really care about me... Oh, not that he's not kind with me... no... He's very nice... And when we made love, he was very attentive and very kind to me... Shit! If you

161

only knew how much I hate that Klara in Berlin... and I don't even know her!!! I wish I was Klara! I wish Lutz was in love with me... I wish... Why the hell did God made me like I am? Why can't I be that Klara? Why? (...) Now you see... I'm crying... Shit! Sorry! ... I feel so bad... (...) Thank God Paul you're listening to me... (...) At least for now... I have him..." Paul took Franz's face into is hands and gave his friend a kiss on the head... „... I feel so sorry for you Franz... But you must realize... you don't 'have him...' as you say... you're only having sex with him... you realize that, don't you? Tell me you do! Tell me... Oh shit Franz... You're such a nice guy... And you deserve so much more..." „... Well... That's all I have for now... And I'll live each and every moment with Lutz to the fullest..." „... I suppose you know what you're doing Franz... And I respect that... I want you to know I'll always be there for you, should you need help..." „... Thanks Paul... I know you're my friend... you're a good guy Paul! And I think Will is very lucky to have you..." „Well, I'm very lucky to have him... And Franz... some day... I'm sure you'll find a guy that really loves you... You will Franz! I swear... Now... we have to go back to Will and Lutz... Are you okay?" „... Yes... Let's go back... Paul?" – „yes?" „Thanks again... If you were not there... no one would be there to listen to me... I don't know what I would do... You're my best friend..." „Hey pal... I told you... I'm here for you... anytime..." Paul hugged Franz... and as he was about to let go of him, Franz said: „You know Paul... I'll always be there for you, too... should you need me... If you ever think there's something I can do for you... Just ask! And I'll do it..." „You're a pal!", Paul answered, smiling at Franz as they began walking out of his study to join Will and Lutz... „Now, put a smile on that face!", Paul said to Franz, grinning... „Yeah... How do I look now?" „... You would fool the devil himself...", Paul answered, laughing... „...As long as I can fool Lutz..."

After their chat, Franz and Paul returned to the drawing-room, and Paul said: „Hey guys... why don't we meet here tomorrow night for supper... then after supper, I'd like to ask you some questions about a few German words I have some problems with... And I'd like you to explain to me a few things: I'm not too good with verbs..." „Sure! Lutz answered... And you know Paul, you seem to understand more and more of our language... you're really learning fast... but don't learn from Franz, you know... The way they speak German in Switzerland..." Both Will and Lutz burst out laughing, but not Franz of course, nor Paul... „... Go to Hell you two..." Franz answered. „Perhaps we don't speak like you, but at least, we're not invading neighbouring countries... and besides... not only do I speak German and French, but I also speak English... so it's better than you two..." Will and Lutz were no longer laughing... „Sorry Franz... really... We didn't intend to insult you... really", Lutz said, looking very sorry... „... Well, it's not funny! I'm sick and tired, hearing you people from Berlin laughing about our accent. I've met people from all over Germany, and I can tell you there are many different accents in Germany, so..." „Okay, okay Franz... We got the message...!", Will replied. „You speak English Franz?", Paul asked... „Yeah..." „So do I... Maybe we could speak in English from time to time... and besides, the two clowns over there would not understand a word we say... So we would be able to laugh about them right under their nose, and they wouldn't even know...", Paul said, laughing. „Good idea!", Franz answered, grinning... „Hey! Cut it out you two... We said we were sorry", Lutz said. „Okay, okay..." Franz answered, laughing. „Now, sorry to have to say that, but I've got to go... I'm working tomorrow...", Lutz said. „And so am I...", Will replied. „Me too", Franz said. „Only our rich friend Paul doesn't have to work tomorrow...", Lutz said, grinning... „Oh yeah? Is that what you think? What the hell do you think I do when I'm at the Head office? Play pocker? And do you want to take my place next Wednesday, and go to that damn party at YOUR embassy?", Paul asked... „No... I don't think so... sorry!", Lutz answered. „Well, let's go big boy, before you say anything else you'll feel sorry for later...", Franz said, laughing... „So we'll see you here tomorrow evening?", Will asked. „Yup", both Lutz and Paul answered.... „That's if we're still welcome here...", Lutz added, grinning... „You are, bastard... you are... That's my problem: I like you!", Paul answered, laughing... „Thanks again Paul", Lutz said... „for all what you've done for me... you know... the flat... the car... and now this envelope... I can't believe it! Are you sure you're not in love with me? Cause I would marry you anytime...", Lutz said, laughing is heart out... „Sorry Lutz, I'm not in love with you... besides, I'm already married to that beautiful guy there, and I love him so much, you can't believe it...", Paul answered, grinning, and taking Will into his arms. „Oh well... too bad!", Lutz finally answered, still laughing... „But anyway... thanks again... that's what I wanted to say..." „Okay, you've thanked me enough! It's done!" Lutz and Franz left, and Will and Paul went back to the drawing-room where Paul pressed on a button Will had not noticed before... „What's that for?", he asked... „You'll see in a minute...", Paul answered, grinning. Seconds later, a maid came to the drawing-room and said: „Monsieur a appelé?" „Oui... We're going to bed... You can clean the place now... Good night!", Paul said to her... „Merci monsieur, bonne nuit à vous également monsieur..." Paul and Will went upstairs where Will said: „I think I will never get used to it... having all that staff around here..."

„Oh yes you will... It's very easy to get used to it... you'll see... But now mister, you're all mine... and I intend to take good care of your well toned body..." „Are you going to rape me again... are you going to tie me up and force me to have sex with you... against my will?", Will asked, laughing... „... That would be a great idea... I'm just sorry I didn't think of that before you did... but no... I have no rope with me tonight... so I guess I'll have to count on your willingness for tonight...", Paul answered, laughing too... „And what makes you think I'm willing?" Paul went to his lover and put his hand on the sizeable bulge in Will's pants... „Something tells me you're willing...", Paul answered, grinning and rubbing Will's big hardon through his pants... „Ohhhh... I like that...", Will said, grinning... „I know..." Paul started to undress Will, taking his shirt off... kissing his smooth arm pecs and licking his way to Will's nipples... kissing them with his hot full lips. Will moaned... Will's long fingers kept running through Paul's blond hair, his dick so hard it was hurting him! „I'm all yours Paul... And I want you to be mine..." Paul pressed his lips into Will's navel... tenderly kissing it...then he unsnapped the button at the top of Will's pants, unziped his fly, then rolled Will's pants down to his ankles... Will raised each foot so Paul could remove them... Will was not wearing any underwear, and Paul loved that!

Paul began licking Will's arm and strong smooth thighs, then slowly made his way up to Will's balls... Will was moaning... feeling Paul's hot tongue all over his lower body... Then Paul started licking Will's balls, ever so slowly... and one after the other... „Oh God Paul! You're so good..." Going a bit lower, Paul started licking Will's miracle inch as Will parted his legs... With his hot tongue, Paul started to play under Will's big balls, slowly kissing his way up to Will's asshole... But he didn't play with Will's asshole... no... he was keeping that for later... Instead, he slowly made his way back to his lover's smooth balls, and tried to take both of them into his hot mouth... but realized they were too big for that... so he took one, and gave it a very good mouth bath... Then he serviced the other one, as Will kept gasping... Paul then slowly licked his way to Will's hot throbbing dick, using his hot tongue to lick all around Will's hairless shaft. Will quivered as Paul's tongue started stroking up and down the full length of his big cock... Then Paul grabbed Will's dick in his hand and very delicately began to kiss and lick his mushroom cap, taking his time to enjoy the sweet taste of Will's precum... „Shit Paul! You torture me... Oh!... God! it feels so good..." Paul grinned. Indeed, he was taking his time... but after a while he couldn't wait any longer and he took Will's very hard and oozing prick in his mouth, and guided it right down his throat where he began deep throating it... Paul began groaning and the vibrations in his throat gave Will's dick a very pleasurable feeling... With his hot mouth, Paul began to bob faster on Will's dick: As he looked up at his blue-eyed lover, he saw Will was gasping with lust. He grinned, his mouth all the time riding up and down Will's oozing prick. His own dick was very hard under his pants, but Paul didn't touched it: He had other plans... and wanted to take all his time... Will began slowly pumping his dick in and out of Paul's hot mouth, then faster and harder... His rod was so stiff, and it felt so good... Paul started squeezing and twitching Will's balls and, with his other hand, he squeezed the base of Will's cock trunk, driving his dick deep down into his hot velvety throat... Will couldn't stand it anymore... He was gasping and shuddering so much by now, Paul knew he was about to shoot... Seconds later, Will shot his young sweet spunk down deep Paul's gut. Paul quickly took Will's dick out of his throat but kept it inside his hot mouth: He wanted to fully taste Will's jizz before gulping it... Will cried out in ecstasy as he kept driving his dick in and out of Paul's mouth, firing torrents of cum... squirt after squirt after squirt... „Ahhhhhhh take it Paul... take it..." Paul hungrily gulped it all, savourily tasting his lover's hot and delicious cum...

„I love you Will... and I love having your big dick in my mouth...", Paul later said, grinning... „... I want you to fuck me Paul... I want to feel you inside me... right now!" Seconds later, Paul was stark naked and smiling at Will... „Come to the bed, then lay on your back, you gorgeous...", Paul said, grinning... Paul looked at his lover's perfect body and admired it... Although he had just cum, Will's dick was still very hard and still throbbing... „You're so beautiful Will... I can't believe I have you

165

all to myself... How can a guy be so perfect?" Paul leaned over his lover and kissed him very tenderly, then shoved Will's legs apart as he stood on his knees in the middle of them... He took the baby lotion he kept handy and smeared some all over his dick. He smeared some lotion all over Will's dick and balls too, and started to play with them... After a while, his right hand went lower, and with his middle finger, he started rubbing Will's rosy pink and hairless asshole. Will moaned, loving the feeling... With the lotion, Paul took all his time to lubed Will's hole... Later... and knowing his lover's hot asshole was now very well lubed, Paul slowly inserted his finger into it... Will looked at him in the eyes, and whispered: „Ohhhhh... yeah... Aaaaaah.... that feels so good... I love you..." Paul got up on his knees and put Will's strong legs over his shoulders. Now that Will's ass was nicely elevated, Paul moved in closer and began playing with his big mushroom cap against Will's rosebud... „Take me now! I want you...", Will said in a sigh... Paul grinned and started to push his big cock against Will's asshole. His mushroom cap slowly penetrated his beautiful lover's ass lips, and he paused for a second... then pushed harder and his big slippery shaft went in slowly... „Oooooooooh... I love it! I can feel your veiny dick glide inside me... keep going in...", Will said, panting... „Aaaaaaah...YES!", Will shouted as he felt Paul's dick glide completely inside his ass chute...

With his right hand, Paul took hold of Will's very hard cook and started gently jacking it as he began thrusting his prick in and out of his lover's chute... „Shhhhit! Keep doing that... go faster..." Paul could feel his hard dick being squeezed by Will's ass muscle and it didn't take long before he felt his cum rise from his balls... He stood still for a while, since he didn't want to cum just yet... When he felt it was safe to resume fucking Will, he went back at it, gliding his very hard dick in and out of his lover's tight ass, taking good care of Will's dick with his hand... With his slippery fingers, he started to play with Will's mushroom cap, playing all around it... rubbing it... „Aaaaaah! You're teasing me Paul... come on... wank me good!" Paul grinned, then began jacking Will's oozing dick faster and faster... „... That's it... Yeah!... You're good Paul!!!" „... Shit Will... I won't last very long... I'm about to cum..." „I'm almost there, too... almost... Yeah..." Paul rammed his boner deep inside Will's hot ass and as he felt his dick squeezed by Will's ass muscle he stopped moving: Again, he felt his cum rise from his balls... then he climaxed and shuddered, as his cum

166

burst deep inside Will's tight ass: „Here I cum, Will.... Oh my God!.... Aaaaaaaaah!" Paul began jacking Will faster and faster, his big dick still shooting cum deep inside his lover... „Aaaaaaaah", Will shouted out, when his jizz burst all over his six pack and even on his abs... Paul grinned and kept masturbating his lover until he ejaculated his last squirt of hot young cum... Then Paul went down on Will's perfectly sculpted body and began kissing him gently, licking his lover's warm cum spread all over his smooth chest... Having cleaned Will's chest with his hot tongue, Paul went to Will's lips, and they started to cum kiss... They slowly shared Will's hot cum, and they both loved it! „...That was so gooooood Paul... You're becoming an expert, I tell you...", Will said later, tenderly smiling to his young lover... „It's because I'm a fast learner, thanks to you...", Paul replied, grinning... They kissed for what seemed like hours... Then Will closed his arms on Paul's warm body curled against him and wrapped him in a close embrace. Paul sighed. „I love you Paul...I would like to stay just like that for the rest of my life..." „I love you, too, Will... I love everything about you.. You're so beautiful... Hold me tight Will...Yeah! That's it...just like that" (...) „Are you asleep Will?" „Almost...", Will answered, grinning... „Did I forget to tell you how much I love you?" „... I'm not sure you did..." They began tenderly kissing again, and after their lips parted, Paul rested his head on his lover's strong shoulder. Before long, they were both sound asleep...

Tuesday morning came fast... much too fast for the two young hunks! Will ran to the shower, then had a quick breakfast, not wanting to be late... Since Paul was in no hurry, he took his time, enjoying the good breakfast his chef had made for him... As monsieur Pierre, the gardener, came in, Paul asked him: „So... How are you doing with the gas thanks?" „The last one is almost totally filled... but it's getting hard now to find people willing to sell me their gas... You were right, Sir, about the rationing..." Paul grinned, hearing that... „The Germans have decided not only to ration gas, but also food..." „Well at least, we won't have to worry about food... We have enought food here to feed an army...", Paul answered, smiling... „Yeah... But it won't be easy for the rest of the population you know! Most of them are not as lucky as you are...", monsieur Pierre answered. „I know... and I feel sorry for them... But there's nothing I can do about it...", Paul replied.

Later that morning, Paul drove to the Head office... went through some papers... then went to the basement to inspect the five big gas thanks. He was satisfied, seeing monsieur Pierre and the locksmith had done a good job, making sure no one could have access to the thanks. He wondered how long it would take before someone started trying to steal gas from those thanks... He smiled, looking at the strong iron bars protecting the thanks, and at the way the doors to the thanks were locked... Anyone trying to steal gas would find it almost impossible to get to those thanks... During the afternoon, Paul met with his private teacher for his usual German lesson, then drove back to Avenue Foch. He was in the drawing-room, reading, when Will came back from work...

„How was your day?", Paul asked his lover... „Oh... the usual... nothing special... I've heard Hitler is going to make a speech tonight on the radio...following his victory here...", Will answered... „Perhaps we should listen... We could learn something...", Paul said. „Yeah... maybe..." „...Have a beer and relax... Lutz and Franz should be here any minute now...", Paul said to Will, smiling... Indeed, moments later, Lutz and Franz arrived and Paul started asking some questions about a few German words he had problems with... He wanted to be able to say a few words in German at the party at the embassy... After a good supper, they went back to the drawing-room, where they listened to Hitler giving his speech on the radio... Of course, the Führer was ecstatic! „I have ordered the cities all over Germany to dress with our beautiful flags... Furthermore, the Führer said, everywhere in the Reich, the bells will toll for the next six days..." „Thank God your family and mine don't live near a church...", Will said to Lutz, grinning... „Yeah!", Lutz answered, laughing... But apart from that, they didn't learn much from Hitler's speech... And after the speech, when a band was starting to play the Horst-Wessel-Lied, Paul asked Will: „Can you turn the radio off, please? I just can't hear that song again! I'm fed up with it!" Will did as asked, grinning... Lutz and Franz left early that night, sensing Paul was a bit restive, thinking about the damn party at the German embassy... And Hitler's speech had not help either... nor that goddamn song! Will and Paul went to bed and, knowing Paul was not in a very good mood, Will just said: „Don't worry... everything will be just fine..." „I hope you're right! (...) Good night", Paul answered... „Good night, my love", Will replied.

168

The day after, Paul took his time choosing what he would wear for the party. The invitation said "tenue de ville"... He chose a dark blue suit, a white shirt and a red tie... the exact colours of the French flag! Realizing that, Paul smiled to himself... Nevertheless, he looked stunning in that suit, with his blond hair and his emerald green eyes... Monsieur Pierre drove Paul to the German embassy and, as he entered the large building, he realized there was a big crowd there... He gave his invitation to a footman, who announced: „Monsieur Paul de Brion!" Paul joined the crowd and, a few minutes later, he heard a voice behind him: „Ah... Monsieur de Brion..." Paul turned to a man standing there, with a broad smile on his face: „Please, allow me to introduce myself: I'm Otto Abetz, the German ambassador..." They shook hands, and Paul said: „Nice meeting you, Sir... Thank you for the invitation..." „Ah... but I've heard so much about you... I wanted to meet with you... I've been told your company was one of the first to re-open... You're such a young man: I'm impressed... I've also heard your father has decided not to come back?" „Yes... Your information is correct, Sir. As you certainly know, he's in New York now, with the rest of my family..." – „Oh?" „...He wanted to make sure my younger sister and brother were sheltered from danger... And he doesn't intend to come back to Paris until the war is over and France is no longer occupied. But I'm sure you already know about that, Herr Abetz", Paul answered, grinning... „You're a very honest and frank young man, monsieur de Brion... I like that! And you've decided not to leave Paris?" „I had my reasons... My life is here in Paris... and I intend to expand our business all over Europe... Actually, we do business in France and in Switzerland, but I'd like to make some investments in Germany, too..." „That's nice to hear about that... And I think I know a man that could give you a hand in that regard... Herr Funk, the Reich Minister of Economic Affairs will be here later... I shall introduce you to him! Now please, do excuse me... I must attend to our other guests..." „Please do Herr Abetz... please do", Paul answered, smiling at the ambassador...

Paul mingled with the other guests, making small talk with some... many of whom knew his father well... He answered their questions concerning his father and the fact he was in New York now... Later, a footman came to him, telling him the ambassador wanted to see him... Paul followed the footman and was introduced into a large study, where Herr Abetz was sitting with another man... „...Ah! Monsieur de Brion...

Glad we could find you", Herr Abetz said, as he rose to greet Paul. "Please, come... I would like to introduce you to Herr Funk... I've already told him about you..." „It's an honour meeting you, Herr Funk", Paul said, smiling, as the two men shook hands. Looking at Herr Abetz, Paul added: „But I'm afraid my German is not too good... I've just started learning..." „No problem young man... I will translate for you... So you're learning German?" „Yes... and I want to become fluent in German as soon as possible..." Paul answered, not telling the ambassador the only reason he wanted to speak German was that he wanted to be able to tell his lover, in his own tongue, how much he was in love with him... „That is very nice... We will need men like you to built Das Neue Europa the Führer is talking about...", Herr Abetz answered... While the ambassador was talking, Paul could sense Herr Funk was checking him all over... and by the way the Minister was checking him out, Paul had no doubt Herr Funk was very much gay... It was obvious! They all sat, and started talking about the investments Paul wanted to make in the Reich. The Minister was very interested, and said he wanted to help... "Of course, he would like to help himself into my pants", Paul thought for himself... The Minister gave Paul a short list of important people Paul should talk to in Berlin... And Paul took the opportunity to underline the fact that, as travels were strictly restricted, it was almost impossible for him and his associates to go to Germany to meet those people... and impossible for them to travel to Switzerland, to meet with his business partners over there... „Oh, but that can be arranged very easily", the Minister said. Turning to the ambassador, the Minister told him: „Herr Abetz, make sure this fine young man gets a permanent Ausweis to travel freely to the Reich as well as to Switzerland... for... How many people did you say?" Herr Funk asked Paul... „Four... That would be perfect, thank you so much... That will help immensely", Paul answered, with a big smile on his face... „It's our pleasure", the Minister replied... Oh... and when you come to Berlin, please, come to see me..." „I sure will, Sir", Paul answered, thinking he would make sure he would not be alone if he had to meet the old goat again... „And you should travel by air when you come to Berlin: It's much faster...", the Minister said, telling Herr Abetz to make sure Paul's Ausweis would authorize air travelling also... „I don't know how to thank you both...", Paul said as he was leaving... The ambassador called one of his assistants and gave him the necessary instructions pertaining to the Ausweis... Then, looking at Paul, he said: „My assistant will be here in a few seconds... Will you please go with him so he can take all the personal information he needs to issue the Ausweis and, of course, your picture will have to be taken too..." „Of course, Sir", Paul answered, smiling at the ambassador... Paul rose and shook hands with Herr Abetz and Herr Funk, thanking them profusely... Paul smiled to himself, seeing Herr Funk had kept Paul's hand into his much longer than he needed to... Then Paul followed the ambassador's assistant into a small office where his picture was taken, as well as all the personal information needed. The young assistant explained to Paul the Ausweis would allow him to travel to Germany or Switzerland as often as he whished, along with tree other people. Those people would be covered by the Ausweis as long as they would be travelling with Paul, and they would only have to show their passport to gain entry in Germany or in Switzerland... as long as Paul was with them, the young assistant stressed again... „Yes, I understand...", Paul answered, smiling... A few minutes later, Paul had his Ausweis in his pocket and was ecstatic, thinking that he would be able to take Will and Lutz to Berlin, so they could visit their families over there... „Wait till I tell them", he thought... They will be stunned...

Paul went back to Avenue Foch where Will was waiting for him... Paul told Will everything that had happened at the German embassy and indeed, Will was stunned... „You know Paul, it's a very rare privilege to obtain such an Ausweis... Obviously, the Minister likes you...", Will said. „Yeah! I noticed", Paul answered, grinning... „And he wants me to pay him a visit when I'll go to Berlin... Let me tell you he's gay alright... and I wouldn't like to be all alone with him...I don't know how old he is... but he's much older than my Dad...", Paul replied, laughing... „Well, as you can see, your good looks paid...", Will replied, laughing too... „Whatever... But anyway, I won't travel to Germany until I can speak German well... There's no sense meeting with people there, if I don't understand what they are saying... And you just can't do business through a translator..."

As things got organized on Avenue Foch, with Will living there now, time flew so fast that neither Will nor Paul had time to notice. Almost every night, Lutz and Franz were there for supper... From time to time, Will and Lutz would call their families in Berlin, and were very thankful to Paul for that. Of course, neither of them told their families about their

171

respective lovers, although Will's mother asked a lot of questions about Paul, since Will was talking so much about his new „friend"...

On Friday, July 5, Franz called Paul to tell him he was free next weekend to go to Bagatelle... and inquired as to whether or not Paul still intended to spend the weekend there... Paul confirmed all had been organized, and that he was expecting Franz to sleep over on Avenue Foch that night, so the four young men could leave early the next day. As planned, on Saturday morning they all left Paris and drove to Bagatelle...

It was a beautiful summer day, and they were almost all alone on the roads, since these days not many people had the means to travel by car, due to the gas restrictions... When they got to Bagatelle, Paul's three friends were stunned by the beauty of the estate... The château was not very big, but it was beautiful... and the staff was very friendly. Paul had a meeting with the staff and they were all told their jobs were safe... Later, Paul had a long meeting with the guy in charge of managing the estate on his behalf, and was surprised to learn the small farm on his new estate was producing so much... He received the manager's full report on that, and realized most of what was produced on the farm was sold at the local market... He visited the barn, the hen-house, the stables... After his inspection, Paul had a second meeting with his manager, to tell him about the decisions he Dad made: They would no longer sell their production at the local market, but would keep it for themselves. „But, monsieur... You will lose a good source of income...", the manager politely stressed, thinking his new boss was too young, and didn't have much experience in life... „Yes... That may be so... But you see... I don't need money: What we need is food... with the food rationing, many things are no longer available in Paris...", Paul answered. „It's that bad, Sir, in Paris?" „... And it will get worse...", Paul replied. „Oh... I see, Sir..." Paul then explained that from now on, once a week, he would send someone from Paris to get food like milk, cream, eggs, butter... things like that... and that he wanted the rest of the prodction to be shared among the staff personnel at Bagatelle... „And I want you and your employees to produce as much as possible on this farm... Should you need to hire new workers, don't hesitate: Do it! And next year, I want the farm to produce wheat and barley too...", Paul said. „But Sir, how are we going to do that... it's very hard nowadays to find gas to operate the machinery...", the manager answered. „I know... but in the old days, didn't you manage with horses?

172

In the shed, I saw we still have the old equipment... and you have seven horses in the stables... Can't we manage with that? As you know, we're going through hard times now, and we don't know how long it's going to last... So in the meantime, we'll have to be imaginative, won't we?", Paul replied. „Yes, Sir", the manager answered, thinking his new boss was not so inexperienced as he had first thought, and that what he had just said made good sense... „And every month, I will expect a full report from you, concerning all the activities on the estate..." „Yes, Sir!"

After the meeting with the manager, Paul went back to his friends. He found them lying on the terrace, where they were sun-bathing, wearing nothing else but trunks... „Ah! There you are...", Will said to Paul, smiling... „Where have you been?" Paul told him what he had been doing all morning and Will grinned, thinking his lover was indeed a very wise guy... Then Lutz said: „I tell you Paul... life is good in France! Do you know in Germany we often say, talking about someone who has a good life, that he 'lives like a king in France...'. Now I understand why we say that..." „Yeah... But I know I'm privileged... I don't think all our soldiers the Wehrmacht made prisoners are as lucky as I am...", Paul answered. „...No!", Franz replied. There was a long moment of silence, as each of them kept thinking that indeed, they were very privileged to be at Bagatelle, sun-bathing... while so many other guys their age were stationed all over Northern France, waiting for Hitler's orders to invade England...

„Enough guys!", Paul suddenly said... „Why don't we go try to find the small lake we have on the estate and have some fun over there?" „Do you know where to find it?", Will asked Paul... „Well... I vaguely remember, but I'm not sure. I've seen it years ago when we came to visit my Grandma... I only remember we have to walk in that direction over there..." Paul replied... „If you're willing guys, we could have a picnic at the lake..." „Good idea..." the three others replied. A while later, they were on their way to find the lake, walking through deep woods, Paul carrying the lunch, Will carring a few bottles of wine...

The day was so beautiful... a warm breeze was caressing their strong bodies as they followed an old path through the woods that, obviously, had not been used for a long time... They had been walking for about twenty minutes when they heard water cascading somewhere nearby. They walked in that direction and found a nice brook: They followed it for a while and then found the small lake... „WOW! That's nice...", Will exclaimed, touching the water to feel its temperature... „And the water is warm..." „It's so secluded here... so beautiful... It all belongs to you?", Franz asked Paul... „Yes... It's located on the estate, so it's private... and since the estate has ben fenced years ago, no one else but us has access to the lake...", Paul answered, smiling... They found a small clearing on the shore next to the lake and sat, looking at the deep woods all around the lake... Yes! This place was very secluded... very peaceful... „Hey! Let's go for a swim...", Will said to Paul... „Sure...", Paul answered, laughing... They took off their trunks, and Will started running into the lake, Paul running after him... Franz looked at the two young hunks, naked before his eyes... and looked at their very cute bubble butts... Shit!, he thought... Those two are really handsome... Watching his two friends running into the water, Lutz took off his trunk and ran after them, laughing and shouting to them that he was coming to drown them... The three of them were laughing hard, as Lutz began batteling with Paul, trying to force him under the water... Of course, Will came to Paul's rescue, and both of them turned against Lutz, who was trying to defend himself, laughing his heart out... The three of them were all laughing and shouting, fighting one against the other, like children... except that, as their strong bodies kept brushing, the three of them started getting hardons... Lutz looked at Franz who was still on the shore and said to him: „Hey... come to my rescue... it's not fair here... two against one... come on... don't be shy: Take it off and join us... you chicken..." „... I'd like to... but I don't know how to swim..." Franz shamefully admitted... „You mean you were born near Lac Léman... and you don't know how to swim?", Lutz sarcastically asked... „... Well... I wasn't born in that lake, you silly... do I look like I'm a fish?", Franz replied... „... I wish you were... I would catch you, and have you for dinner...", Lutz replied, chuckling... as Will and Paul burst out laughing...

Franz turned red, hearing that... But is ordeal was not over: As Will and Paul started to walk out of the water, Franz looked at their perfectly sculpted bodies and at their beautiful hairless very hard dicks... His own dick started to grow in his trunk, as Lutz shouted to him: „Come on Franz... join me... I'll teach you how to swim..." Although Franz was not too eager to learn how to swim, he found it was preferable to go in the water than stay on the shore with a big hardon in his trunk, right in front of Will and Paul... thus admitting he was aroused by their beautiful bodies... So in no time, Franz was out of his trunk and in the water... doing his best to hide his very hard dick... He joined Lutz, who took him into his strong arms and said: „Don't be afraid... I'm here... there's no danger..." Feeling Lutz's hard dick press against his groins, Franz chuckled and answered: „I'm not too sure about that..." Both Lutz and Franz started laughing and turned to look at Will and Paul, now sitting on the shore with very visible hard dicks... „You like their dicks, don't you?", Lutz asked Franz, grinning... Franz blushed, but didn't answer... Lutz began caressing Franz's rippling stomach, then his hand went down, finding Franz's throbbing dick, squeezing it... Franz sighed... „You don't have to answer my question"... Lutz said to Franz, still grinning... „Your dick says it all..." Turning to Will and Paul on the shore, Lutz shouted to them: „Hey guys... do you know what? I've got a very hard fish here in my arms..." „That's not true...", Franz replied, laughing... „Oh yeah?", Lutz answered... And with his strong arms, he pulled Franz out of the water enough for Will and Paul to see Franz's very hard cock... „See for yourself, guys...", Lutz shouted, laughing... „Hey Franz... nice dick you have there... hope Lutz appreciates it!", Will shouted back, laughing too... „Go to hell...", Franz replied, blushing scarlet red... Oh yes... Franz thought to himself... It's going to be a long day... What's going to happen next? „Hey Franz", Paul said to his Swiss friend, speaking to him in English... „Why don't you take Lutz for a walk into the woods... you know... to „explore" him a bit more..." „...Not a bad idea...", Franz answered in English, laughing... „What the hell did he say?", Lutz asked Franz... „Oh... nothing... (...) Why don't we get out of the water now... and maybe, we could go for a walk..." – „A walk?", Lutz replied, a bit puzzled.. „Un-Huh"... Franz answered, grinning... „A walk..." After all, Franz thought to himself... I think it's going to be a nice day, today... Yup! a nice day!

175

TWELVE
« QUITE A SURPRISE »

Lutz and Franz had played for a while in the water and, although Lutz had really tried to teach Franz how to swim, it didn't work: As soon as Franz would feel his feet had lost contact with the bottom of the lake, he would panic and throw his arms around Lutz's strong shoulders... When Lutz realized Franz was really scared, he quit trying to teach him anything and they just started fooling around in shallow water... That's when Paul suggested to Franz, in English, that he should take Lutz for „a walk" to „explore" the woods... Franz was laughing, and Lutz was wondering what the two friends were talking about, since he didn't understand a single word in English... A bit later, Lutz came out of the water and joined Will and Paul on the shore, while Franz continued playing in the lake in waist-deep water, making sure he was not going any deeper... Franz looked at his three nude friends stretched on the shore and was mesmerized by their naked bodies... The three young hunks were oblivious of Franz staring at them, as they were talking and making jokes... Of course, Franz didn't miss that chance, and he took his time to check them out really well... The three of them had semi-hard dicks, and Franz could see Lutz's dick was rather thick compared to the two others, but he guessed the two others had longer dicks... He was pretty sure of that since he had briefly seen them earlier, sporting hardons... Indeed, they were all well endowed, he thought... The fact that Paul and Will were hairless aroused him, and he began thinking about shaving his own dick and balls... He wondered what Lutz would think about that... then thought he wouldn't give a damn: All Lutz was interested in was sex! He wouldn't care whether his dick was shaved or not... Franz even woundered if Lutz would notice... Staring at his friend's well toned bodies made Franz's boner throb, and he had no choice but to stay in the water, since he didn't want his friends to see his hardon: He knew Lutz would laugh at him and make jokes at his expense...

„Come on Franz... come out of the water and join us... We're going to have lunch...", Paul shouted to him... „Yeah... yeah... in a minute...", Franz replied... Paul began to serve to the others the lunch he had brought along, and opened a bottle of wine. „Come on Franz... what the hell are you doing? Won't you join us?", Lutz asked him... „Yeah... I'm coming..." „Is it because you're still hard that you don't want to come out of the water?", Lutz sarcastically asked... „Come on Franz... we've seen hard dicks before... so don't be shy, and join us"... Will said, and turning to Lutz, Will told him: Now shut your big mouth, and no practical joke!" Lutz laughed, but kept his mouth shot as Franz started walking out of the water to join his friends. And indeed, he was sporting quite a big hardon! Lutz looked at him and cleared his throat, showing a big smile on his face... „You bastard... you'll pay for that...", Franz replied. Poor Franz: Although he wanted his dick to go down... his efforts were vain and, the more he looked at his three friends' gorgeous naked bodies, the more his hard shaft kept throbbing... „WOW!", Will said... „You know Franz, among the four of us here... you've got the biggest dick... You shouldn't be ashamed... If I were you, I'd be proud to show my dick around... Lutz here is just jealous... maybe he has a thick dick, but never as long as yours..." „I feel stupid... I mean... just looking at you guys makes me hard like a teenager... I can't believe what I'm seeing... I'm not used to see naked dudes like you... except in my dreams... But that doesn't mean I'm a sex maniac, you know...", Franz answered.

Sensing Lutz was about to make another insensitive comment, Paul didn't wait for it to come and quickly answered: „Of course you're not a sex maniac... It's perfectly normal to get a hardon... and sometimes, I get one at the most inconvenient times. I'm sure all of us here have experienced that... Haven't you guys?" „Yeah... and sometimes, it can be pretty embarrassing...", Will answered, grinning... Seeing Lutz was taking a bit too long to agree with what he had just said, and guessing he was about to crack one of his bad jokes... Paul looked at him and said: „... And if I remember well... you got a major hardon the other day at the restaurant when we met that waitress... you know... What's her name again?... Jeannine, I think, huh?... you were so hard, you had problems walking out of that restaurant... Don't you remember Lutz?" Now Lutz

178

was turning red and if he was thinking about making fun of Franz, Paul's remark cut short his malicious inspiration... „I don't..." Lutz started to say, but didn't have time to complete his answer, being interrupted by Will who said, laughing: „Oh yeah! I remember... not only you had a hardon Lutz... but you were oozing so much you had a wet spot on your pants! Do you think we didn't see you, trying to hide it with your napkin? I wonder if Jeannine noticed..." „Okay, okay... cut it out!", Lutz answered... „You've made your point." Then, looking at Franz, Lutz said to him: „I'm sorry Franz... it wasn't very nice of me making fun of you like that... Sorry!" „Yeah... Well, that may be all true... but it doesn't solve my problem here", Franz said, looking down at his big hard dick... Paul looked at Franz and, in English, he said to him: „I told you Franz... Go for a walk in the woods... and take Lutz along with you...I'm sure he won't mind giving you a hand with your problem... as long as there is something in it for him... If you see what I mean..." Paul was laughing as Franz said to his friends: „Maybe I should go for a walk over there... To cool down a bit, you know... But I'm not sure I want to go there alone... I don't like to be alone in the woods..." „Come on Lutz... go with him, and leave us two alone for a while...", Paul said, grinning... „You want me to go for a walk in the woods? Are you crazy or what? Why would I go for a walk?", Lutz replied... „Well...", Franz answered, grinning, looking at Lutz, then looking down at his throbbing dick... „Ohhhh... That's what you have in mind, isn't it?", Lutz answered, grinning too... „There's nothing like a good walk...", Franz replied... „Okay... but while we're gone, don't eat everything you two... save some food for us...", Lutz said, looking at Paul and Will, laughing... „Don't worry... We'll wait for you before we start eating...", Will answered... Lutz rose and took Franz by the hand and, before Franz could realize it, he was following Lutz into the woods nearby...

After they had walked for a few minutes, Lutz turned to Franz and said: „It's perfect here... don't you think?" „Perfect for what?", Franz asked, teasing Lutz... „You've asked for it, you're going to get it: You're going to fuck me dude! And you're going to fuck me hard! I want to feel your big dick deep inside me... If you thought you could just tease me and then do nothing... you're dead wrong mister...", Lutz answered, laughing... „Oh my God! I was only thinking about a quick blowjob, you know... What Will and Paul think if we take too long for our walk?"

179

„They'll think that we're having hot sex...and that you're my poor victim... They already think I'm a sex maniac, so... nothing's new here... that's the way they see me already, I guess... What the hell! I might as well confirm my reputation...", Lutz answered, laughing... „But really... we can't do it here, can we?", Franz said... „Why not? there's no one around... lay down on your back, right there... and let me do the rest..." Without saying another word, Franz laid down on the grass between two big trees! He was too horny by now to argue with Lutz and in fact... he really wanted to fuck Lutz, and was very arisen by Lutz's plan, which was one of his old time fantasies: Making love with a gorgeous hunk, out in the open, feeling a hot summer breeze all over his strong body... In his fantasy, he was forcing a very handsome guy to have sex with him, and that had always made his dream more exciting... Now, Franz thought, he was living his fantasy! Of course, he was not really forcing Lutz to have sex with him... but nevertheless... He could imagine he was... and that was too much...

As he laid on his back, Franz looked at Lutz's strong body and watched him, as Lutz spit into his right hand and then smeared his saliva all over his hardening cock, slowly wanking it to hardness... „Shit Lutz... it's so fucking hot to watch you jerk like that... I can't believe I'm here, watching you do that..." – „You're forcing me to do that you know... I'm the poor victim here...", Lutz answered, grinning... Hearing that, Franz started grinning... He loved that! It was as if Lutz could read his mind... Lutz was now standing over Franz with his strong-muscled legs spread on each side of him... wanking his now very hard dick... „Squeeze your balls for me... stretch them... Yeah! just like that...", Franz said... „Oh God! Lutz... you're so sexy..." – „You're about to fuck me Franz... and I want you to fuck me hard! But first, I need you to lub my rosebud..." – „And how am I going to do that?" „I'm going to sit over your face... and you're going to tongue-fuck my asshole... That's how you're going to do it... And you better do a good job!", Lutz answered, grinning... Lutz didn't wait for Franz to answer: He placed himself over Franz's head and lowered his strong body so his rosy spot was now hovering right above Franz's hot watery mouth. With his hands, Lutz parted his tight compact ass cheeks so Franz's could have easy access to his smooth asshole... Franz looked up at Lutz's big smooth balls dandling over his nose and with his hot tongue, he began licking them... giving them a good tongue bath... Lutz lowered himself a bit more, so Franz was now able to take his balls into his watery mouth... Franz tried to take both balls into his mouth but didn't succeed... They were just too big to enter his mouth at the same time! He started working on one ball, licking it... sucking on it... squeezing it with his hot lips... Then he did the same to the other ball... Lutz was moaning, loving the incredible sensation he was experiencing for the first time... Lutz moaned even more when Franz moved his head and began licking his miracle inch... „Fuck! You're good Franz... keep doing that... I love it!" Then Franz started nibbling on Lutz's asshole, playing all around it with the tip of his hot tongue... He teased Lutz for a while doing that... before forcing his tongue deep inside Lutz's asshole... Lutz cried out in ecstasy when he felt Franz's hot and slippery tongue enter his tight ass and he lowered his ass a tad so Franz's tongue could glide deeper inside his hole... „Oh shit Franz... it feels so good... I'm going to have to marry you", Lutz said, giggling... „Um-huh!", Franz replied... thinking how much he would love that to happen... having Lutz as his mate for the rest of his life... As Lutz began to slowly swivel his ass over Franz hot tongue, Franz started to tongue-fuck him good. With his right hand, Franz took hold of Lutz's dangling balls and squeezed them... then pulled them down, forcing Lutz to lower his ass a bit more, thus allowing Franz's tongue to go deeper into his love chute... Now Lutz was gasping and shouting; his very hard dick oozing so much, he couldn't believe it... With one finger, Lutz spread some precum all over his mushroom cap, caressing it lightly, then with more vigour...

„I need to take good care of your dick...", Lutz suddenly said to Franz... Lutz moved and turned his body around very quickly, knelt on all fours over Franz's chiseled body, straddling him, facing his friend's big throbbing dick while presenting his asshole to his friend's hot mouth. A second later, Lutz started licking Franz's oozing dick head, and Franz quivered when he felt his cock enter Lutz's hot mouth... „Ahhhhh... That feels so good...", Franz shouted, feeling his dick head enter Lutz's throat... At first, Lutz gagged a few times, but soon enough, his throat muscles relaxed and allowed Franz's big dick to penetrate deeper into his vibrating tight throat... Franz rammed his boner right in... As Lutz's throat muscles relaxed even more, Franz began to gently moved his dick in and out of it, giving Lutz enough time to breathe... „That's incredible Lutz..." „Um-huh", Lutz replied... Franz went back to work on Lutz's well lubed asshole, and pushed his hot tongue deep inside it... It didn't take long before the two young studs were groaning and moaning with lust... totally lost in the intense pleasure they were giving to one another... After a while, knowing he couldn't last very long, Franz cried out to Lutz: „If you continue with that... I swear, I'm going to cum..." Taking Franz's cock out of his mouth, Lutz replied: „Oh!... no dude... not just yet... you have to fuck me first..." Before Franz could realize it, Lutz had moved his body around, still straddling him, but with his rosebud now hovering right above Franz's well lubed shaft... Lutz took Franz's dick into his right hand and guided it to his asshole, offering Franz his hot pucker. Lutz slowly lowered his body, and he felt Franz's big hard dick enter his tight ass lips... „Ohhhhhhh... that feels good...", Lutz exclaimed! „Oh shit yeah!", Franz answered, gasping, feeling his mushroom cap enter Lutz's well lubed asshole... Lutz gripped the undersides of his strong thighs and backed down on Franz's hard shaft, driving it to the hilt within his tight sizzling butt... Franz sighed as he arched his back, trying to drive his cock even deeper inside Lutz's hot fuck hole... „That's it Franz... Keep doing it... I love it...", Lutz said, panting... At first, Franz began to fuck Lutz very slowly... not wanting to hurt his beautiful friend... But when he realized Lutz was begging for more, he began ramming his hot rod so hard into Lutz's slippery ass that his cock slammed into his friend's tight hot ass... „Fuck me Franz... Fuck me hard!" Franz increased his speed, ramming his dick in and out of Lutz's ass... Then Franz put some saliva into the palm of his right hand and went to find Lutz's oozing dick, wrappind his lubed hand around it... „Oh shit Franz... yeah... wank me... yeah!" With his other hand, Franz grabbed Lutz's balls and started squeezing and stretching them... „Yeah... squeeze my balls... harder... Oh yeah!" Lutz shouted, panting and sweating... Lutz squeezed his ass mucles, making sure Franz's hard dick was rubbing his love spot, stimulating it with each thrust... Ramming his dick in and out of his friend's very tight love chute, Franz shouted with pleasure... As his hand began to bob faster and faster on Lutz's oozing prick, Lutz cried out: „Ahhhhhhhh.... I'm going to cum.... I can't hold it anymore..." „Me neither...", Franz answered, as he felt his balls ready to burst... Lutz was the first to explode, shooting wave after wave of hot cum all over Franz's face... over his lips, chin... Franz opened his mouth and received a generous gob of hot jizz that he immediately and eagerly gobbled... „Keep it cuming Lutz... come on... shoot right into my mouth..." And before Lutz could shoot another cum squirt, Franz began shooting his hot young spunk deep inside Lutz's hot and tight ass... and he orgasmed for what seemed like hours... Lutz shot two more cum squirts right inside Franz mouth: Franz took his time tasting his lover's jizz before swallowing it... „Oh shit Franz... You're swallowing my cum!", Lutz said, a bit stunned... „YEAH!", Franz answered, grinning... „And you taste so good: I love it! Haven't you ever tasted your own cum?" – „...No!", Lutz replied. „You should... It's delicious..." Hearing that, Lutz lowered his body over Franz's chiseled chest and started licking his own cum all over Franz's hot lips and chin... Feeling Lutz's hot tongue all over his lips, Franz hoped Lutz would go a bit further and start to kissing him... He was longing for a deep kiss from his hot lover... He wanted so much to be kissed by him... But that didn't happen... After having licked his cum from Franz's lips, Lutz raised his body, totally oblivious of his friend's needs and, looking into Franz's sparkling blue eyes, he said: „... You're right... my cum does taste great..." – „... Told you so...", Franz answered, grinning... „... Guess I've learned something new today, thanks to you pal!", Lutz replied, grinning... „And that was a great fuck dude... Thanks!" „... When I think you were laughing at me cause I was hard..." „Yeah... well, I'll never do that again, I swear... I just love having your big dick deep inside me... You've done a fabulous job screwing me... You and I are meant to be fuck buddies..." „Yeah!", Franz replied... thinking that if only Lutz could be in love with him, things would be perfect... That thought caused Franz's dick to decate inside Lutz's ass and it slowly made it's way out of it...

„Look at me pal! I'm a real mess...", Franz said, looking at all the cum spread all over his abs and chest... „...Yeah... and I can feel your cum dripping out of my ass...", Lutz replied, laughing... „What are we going to do? We can't go back to Will and Paul like that..." „Do you think they don't know about what we were doing here... come on...", Lutz answered, grinning... „Maybe... but it's no reason to show our cum soaked bodies to them..." „Tell you what... We'll run to the lake... I'll go first, then you run into it and I'll catch you there... don't worry, I won't let go of you... You won't drown, I swear...", Lutz said. „You swear you'll catch me?", Franz asked, with a worried frown on his face... Lutz took Franz's face into his hand and, looking straight into his friend's eyes, he said: „... I swear Franz... I don't want you to be scared... ever!" Saying that, Lutz lightly kissed Franz on the tip of his nose, then added: „Are you coming?"

„Okay... Go first, and I'll be following you..." Lutz rose and, taking Franz's hand, he started running towards the lake, laughing like a kid... When they got near the lake, Lutz let go of Franz's hand and ran right into the lake... then dived into the water. Seconds later he emerged then turned and, looking at Franz, he shouted: „Come on... run into the water... I'm here... don't be scared..." Franz smiled and started to run into the lake... and as he started falling into the water, he felt Lutz's strong arms grabbing him... Feeling Lutz's arms tightly wrapped around his body, Franz quivered... He looked at Lutz and, with a big smile on his face, he said: „Thanks buddy... Now I know I can trust you..." „Hey! I told you... When I say something, I always do it..." „Thanks..."

That was when they heard Will's voice, shouting to them: „Hey dudes... Did you lose yourself in the woods or what?" Both Lutz and Franz could see Will was trying not to break into a fit of giggles... „Go to hell, bastard...", Lutz replied, laughing his heart out... „Come on guys... join us... We haven't started eating yet... we were waiting for you to... find your way... out of the woods...", Paul shouted, laughing... „Hey... not you too!", Franz answered, grinning... „...Oh, cut it off... I'm just teasing you... now come on and join us...", Paul replied, still laughing... After Lutz and Franz had joined Will and Paul on the shore, they all started to have lunch and drink some wine... It was a beautiful summer day, and they were all sunbathing nude, a nice warm breeze caressing their young bodies... „It's beautiful here... It's so peaceful... it feels good to be away from civilization", Will said, looking all around the lake... „Yeah... and it's so secluded", Franz added... „You know what Paul? You should have a small lodge built here...", Lutz said... „Yeah... That would be fun... but they would need to build a road to bring the building materials in here... and I wouldn't like that... It would be too easy to come to the lake after that, and the place would no longer be so secluded", Paul answered... „Why build a road? The horses could easily carry the material up here... as long as you don't built a palace and keep the lodge simple... no electricity... no radio... no phone... just nature at its best...", Lutz said... „Hey that would be a great idea... what do you think Paul? And we could come here to spend some time, and really relax... just like we're doing now...", Will asked. „You're right... that would be nice... Yeah! ...I'll do it...", Paul answered, smiling... „... and you could hire a few men from he village to do the job...", Lutz added... „No... I prefer to hire a few construction workers from Paris to do the job... even if it's more expensive to do so... I don't want too many people to know about it... That way, the lodge will remain our secret! Otherwise, before long, the whole village will know about it...", Paul answered... „But I'll have to tell my manager... He has to know what's going on on the estate... But I'll ask him to make sure the secret is well kept!" „Good idea...", Will answered, grinning, once more thinking about how his lover was a wise guy... They spent the day like that, swimming, sunbathing, having fun... feeling free... They loved the experience, walking around stark naked, in total communion with the nature all around them... As the sun began to go down over the woods, Paul looked at his friends and said: „Sorry to say that, guys... But we'll have to go back the the Chāteau before it's too dark to walk through the woods..." – „Shit... so soon?", Will asked... Paul tenderly kissed his lover and answered: „Yeah... but you'll see... I'll have the lodge built in no time, and perhaps next time we come here, we'll even be able to spend the night here..." „I hope you will invite us sometimes... I love the woods over there", Lutz said grinning, looking at Franz... „You really are a sex maniac", Franz answered, laughing... „Yeah! And you love it as much as I do...", Lutz answered, laughing too... „You'll always be welcome to join us here at the lodge... both of you", Paul said, looking at his two handsome friends. So they walked back to the Château, where Paul realized he had a sunburn all over his back and butt... And he was not the only one with that problem... Nevertheless, they all had fun for the rest of their stay at the Château and, eventually, they returned to Paris, where real life was waiting for them...

A few days later, Paul was in the drawing-room, reading his German textbook, when Will came in from the study, where he had been on the phone, talking to his family back in Berlin... Paul looked up at Will's worried face... „What's wrong?", he asked Will... „...Oh... not much... It's just that my Dad told me there was a big air battle over the Channel the other day... and it seems the Luftwaffe shot down many british planes... I wonder where all this is going to lead us..." „Don't worry Will... I'm sure it means nothing...", Paul answered, smiling... „Maybe...", Will answered. Later, on July 18th, Paul was listening to Radio Berlin when he heard Hitler, giving a speech to the Reichstag members... Of course, Paul didn't understand everything Hitler was saying, but he understood enough to know that Hitler was offering to make peace with England... Paul took notes, since he wanted Will to translate a few words to him... When Will arrived later, Paul told him about Hitler's speech and showed him the notes he had taken... Will read the notes, then smiled... „Why are you smiling like that?", Paul asked, a bit offended... „I know... I made some mistakes... but I'm doing my best..." „Quite the contrary Paul... I'm smiling because I can't believe how fast you're learning German... Do you have a trick or something?" „...Aaaaaa, well... I study hard you know...", Paul answered, grinning but avoiding contact with Will's eyes... since he didn't want to tell his secret about his private lessons... „I know you, Paul de Brion... Are you hiding something from me?", Will asked, grinning... „Okay, okay... I have hired a private teacher..." „Ha!", Will exclaimed, laughing... „Now the cat is out in the open... That explains why you've been progessing so fast..." „... Not only that... but each day, I listen to Radio Berlin... and when Lutz, Franz and you speak in German, I try to follow you the best I can... But I've got to admit, and I hate to say that... but sometimes, I have problems to understand Franz's accent... Will started to laugh again and, going back to Paul's notes, he said: „Who said that?" „Hitler", Paul answered. Will grinned, and said: „Well... the Führer says that, in all good faith, he appeals to England's good sense and wisdom... He says his actual position allows him to make such an appeal since he doesn't speak as a man who has sustained defeat, thus begging for mercy... but rather as the victor, talking in the name of good sense..." „Oh... and what's the exact meaning of that last sentence... there?" „The Führer says he doesn't see why this war should go on anymore..." „That's what I thought...", Paul answered... „You see Will... I'm sure the war will be over soon..." Will looked directly into Paul's green eyes and started to laugh... „...But my poor Paul! Do you think for one second Churchill will accept to make peace with the Reich as things now stand? England would be forced to accept anything the Führer wants... And even if Churchill accepts and makes peace with the Reich... he knows this damn war would start all over again in two, maybe three years... He knows Hitler can't be trusted..." „Well... I hope you're wrong Will... and I hope we can live in peace soon." „Oh... I would love that too, Paul... But I'm not much of a dreamer, after all I've seen..." A few days later, the matter was settled when Churchill gave his answer to Hitler, saying England would have no peace talks with the Reich before the Wehrmacht had totally evacuated Poland, the Netherlands, Belgium, Denmark, Norway and, most of all...

France! Again, Paul had to admit Will had been right all along... At least, if he had been wrong about peace, Paul was glad he had made the right decisions concerning the gas tanks and the food coming every week from Bagatelle... At least, they didn't have to put with the severe rationing imposed by the Germans and they were not limited to the ration-books that were distributed by the occupier... And Paul smiled about the surprise he would soon have for his lover as well as for Lutz and Franz: He had given a contract to a construction firm in Paris to build a „pavillon" near the lake at Bagatelle... It would be a rather small pavillon... two bedrooms... a kitchen and a large living-room (nothing was simple with Paul...) and a graceful balcony would surrond the pavillon on three of its four sides, covered by a roof supported by thin white columns... But he had been told by the construction firm they really had no choice but to build a small road to the lake, so all the building materials could be brought to the construction site by small trucks. It was impossible to use horses to do that! Paul had no choice but to agree, but he made sure the road would be designed so it would be totally hidden from view, very well camouflaged under the big trees: To find it, one would have to know it was there... Paul also had to make another concession: A cable had to be buried, leading from the Château to the pavillon, to bring some electricity in, just enough to power a small refrigerator and an electric stove... that's all! No lights... no radio and, of course, no phone... although a phone line had also been burried, but not connected... Knowing the construction of the pavillon would rise some interests among some village people, Paul took the opportunity to have a large greenhouse built near the Château... Due to the German occupation, some exotic fruits were no longer available on the market, and coffee would soon disappear from the shelfs... All of those could soon be grown on the estate, thanks to the new greenhouse, and so Paul would not have to drink chicory instead of coffee, and be forced to only eat apples all year long... Furthermore, the construction of the pavillon would go unnoticed since everybody would be talking about the new greenhouse... And it worked!

Only the estate manager knew about the pavillon, as the staff had paid no attention to the fact that a few trucks had been driving into the woods... In August, when Paul visited the site, he was most satisfied by the results. The construction of the pavillon would be over in a few days, and everything around it would be restored to it's previous condition... Paul looked at the pavillon and was happy to see it was well hidden under the large pine-trees surronding it... The only problem was that the pavillon had been painted in white all over... Before leaving Bagatelle, Paul ordered the contractor to have it re-painted in green... so it would disappear in the surronding wilderness... Before leaving the construction site, as the construction was over, the contractor moved in all the furniture Paul had chosen, and made sure the refrigerator was working... Paul had not said a word to Will about the construction of the pavillon, so when Will said he would soon have a three day leave, right after the weekend of August, 24 and 25, Paul suggested they go to Bagatelle, and have some fun over there... just the two of them... Will gladly accepted, and Paul gave to his chef, monsieur Michel, special orders so their favourite food could be prepared and sent in advance to Bagatelle, along with a few bottles of very good wine... Friday, August 23, was a very hot summer day in Paris, and when Will got back from work, Paul was impatiently waiting for him... „We're leaving tonight for Bagatelle...", Paul told him, with a big smile on his face... „What? ... Right now?" „I've packed everything... not that we'll need much...", Paul answered, giggling... „You must be crazy... We can't leave tonight..." „Give me one good reason why we shouldn't leave tonight... one reason...", Paul answered, grinning... „(...)" „So... as I said, we're leaving tonight", Paul said, laughing...

They had a quick lunch before leaving and soon after, they were driving out of Paris... The night was warm and beautiful... and they were almost all alone on the road... „Do you still believe I was crazy when I ordered monsieur Pierre to fill up the big gas tanks? Thanks to all the gas we now have, we can drive to Bagatelle as often as we like, while most people have to stay in Paris... unless they go to a place where a train goes...", Paul asked Will, grinning... „...No... You were right all along...", Will answered, laughing... „Yeah!... But you were right about Hitler's peace initiative... as you were right about so many other things you've said... Sometimes, I wonder if you are not reading the future..." „Oh no... If you know the facts, it's easy sometimes to guess what's going to happen...", Will answered, laughing... „Maybe... but you're good at it... I guess we complete each other, don't we? And now, can you believe we have five days ahead of us... five whole days to enjoy each other... all alone... you and me..." „Well... don't forget about the staff at Bagatelle...", Will replied... Paul smiled to himself but didn't answer... Later, they arrived at Bagatelle and Will stepped down from the car to open the gates to the estate... Paul drove the car past the gates, and Will locked them back, then walked back to the car. A few minutes later, Paul parked the car near the new greenhouse, and they saw the manager walking to them with two horses in tow... Will looked at the new greenhouse, stunned... but didn't have time to say anything since the manager started to say: „Bon soir monsieur Paul... and good night to you, too, monsieur Guillaume... Everything is ready, just as you asked me...", the manager said to Paul, smiling... „Fine... and thanks... I appreciate...", Paul answered. Looking at Will, Paul asked him: „Do you know how to ride a horse?" „Sure... I've learned..." Will was going to say he had learned to ride horses in the Wehrmacht... but he didn't say it, because the manager was still there with them... „Fine!", Paul answered, smiling... „Then, follow me..." „Hey... What about our luggage? Where are we going?" Will asked... „We won't need it..." Paul answered, smiling to Will... „Trust me..." So Will followed Paul, riding on his horse, and soon, they entered the deep woods... Will could see there was a small road there... In fact, it was more like a trail, he thought... and it wasn't easy to figure out where it was leading to... As they rode down the trail, from time to time, Will could see the full moon shining through the trees... It was so beautiful... Everything was so calm and quiet... The only sound they could hear was the sound made by the horses, going down the trail... After quite a while, Will started to see the lake through the trees... „Ah... that's where we're going, isn't it?" he asked Paul, smiling... „Sort of...", Paul answered... „Sort of..." Will had not seen the pavillon yet, since it was so well camouflaged under the big pine-trees all around it... „There we are...", Paul said, as he ordered his horse to stop... Will looked and then he saw the pavillon... „AH! LA VACHE!", he exclaimed... Paul started laughing so hard, he scared an old owl perched nearby... „Do you like it?", Paul asked Will... „It's my gift to you..." „I can't believe it... I just can't...", Will answered, completely stunned... „Ah! La vache, huh?" Paul replied... still laughing... „Do you know what Will? We'll call the pavillon... 'La Vacherie'... What do you think?" „Shit... It must have cost a fortune...", Will answered, laughing... „Not that much... Don't worry... And I know you like being here...", Paul answered, tenderly smiling at Will... They dismounted from their horses and tied their harness to a nearby tree... Paul took Will by the hand and they both walked to the pavillon. „Wait for me here... and close your eyes!", Paul asked Will... Will did as asked, as Paul went inside the pavillon where he lit a few candles... Then he came out, and walked over to a few torchs, lighting them... When he was finished, he walked back to Will and said: „Now... open your eyes!" Will opened his eyes, and couldn't believe it... He thought he was living in a dream... „Oh my God Paul... it's so beautiful..." „You like it?" Will didn't answer the question and instead, started to kiss Paul with his full mouth... „... Well... I guess you like it...", Paul later said... They walked to the balcony and then, Paul said: „There's only one rule here... No one gets inside if he's dressed... We've got to get naked if we want to go inside..." – „How wicked of you...", Will answered, laughing... „That's the rule!", Paul answered, grinning... It didn't take long before they were both totally naked and, as Paul was about to enter the pavillon, Will said: „Wait... I want to carry you inside..." So he took Paul into his strong arms, and carried him inside... Kissing him passionately..." – „Ohhhhhh... do I see a dick rising here?", Will asked Paul, looking at his lover... „The night will be long, I'm telling you...", Paul answered, laughing then giving Will a tender kiss... „Yeah!", Will simply answered, grinning...

THIRTEEN
«WE HAVE THE RIGHT TO DREAM»

„How do you like it?", Paul asked... Will had toured the pavillon and was stunned! „It's perfect... simple (sure, he thought to himself: Paul doesn't know the meaning of that word...) yet comfortable... and I love that balcony...", Will answered... „We should run to the lake and take a dip... it's such a beautiful night...", Paul suggested. „Good idea" Hand in hand, they ran to the lake, laughing... They were drinking in the calm and quiet of the night, the full moon casting its silver rays over the lake... They ran into the water and realized it was quite warm since over the last few days, the temperature had been very hot... The lake was not very deep so the water had quickly warmed up... Will wrapped his arms around Paul's waist and lightly kissed his beautiful lover. Paul's hands began caressing Will's face, then he ran them through his blond, thick hair as they started kissing more passionately. Will sighed when he felt his hard dick rubbing against Paul's smooth crotch... and he loved the feeling of having Paul's hard cock pressed against his strong stomach... Will put his hands on Paul's ass cheeks, caressing them, pulling Paul into a tight embrace. „I love you Will... You're so beautiful! I'm the most lucky guy in the world to have such a gorgeous hunk with me tonight..." „You're mine Paul... and I will never let go of you... never... I love you so much" They went down deeper into the lake, and kissed for what seemed like hours. Then Paul, throwing his arms around Will's strong shoulders, lifted himself and put his legs around Will's waist, placing his hot asshole right over Will's throbbing prick... Will placed his hands under Paul's ass cheeks, supporting his lover, and stretched his legs to gain greater stability. „I want you to take me Will... right here..." Paul lowered his body just a tad and started feeling Will's dick slowly enter his rosebud... „Oh shit Paul... I'm so horny... Your ass ring is so tight..." „Yeah... but we only have water

191

to lube your big dick... we're going to have to go slowly...", Paul replied, grinning. „If it hurts, you tell me right away, okay?" „No problem... It feels good! We'll just take our time..." Paul went back kissing Will with his full lips, his arms firmly wrapped around Will's upper back. The tip of Paul's tongue went all the way inside his lover's warm mouth. They sealed their lips simultaneously, and their tongues swirled before they dueled... It was such a hot kiss... They were sharing their love for each others, passionately kissing... Paul lowered his body a bit more, and Will's boner started to make its way deep inside Paul's love chute... They both moaned, feeling the intense pleasure they were giving to one another... When Will shoved his dick up to the hilt within Paul's tight sizzling but, Paul gasped and shouted: „Ahhhh... it feels so good, having you deep inside me like that..." Paul started so swivel his ass on Will's hard cock, and since Will's dick was oozing so much, it didn't take long before Paul's love chute was pretty well lubed-up... „Oh fuck me Will! Thrust that big dick of yours deep inside me... I'm enjoying it so much..." Will began to swing his hips back and forth, fucking Paul's tight ass, plowing his very hard cock deep inside his lover's hot ass... Paul shivered, begging to be fucked harder and harder... Will kept plowing Paul's tight ass harder and harder, and when Paul squeezed his ass muscle all around Will's prick, Will gasped and accelerated his pace, massaging Paul's love spot with each trust of his big hard cock... „Oh Will... Oh Will... I think you're going to make me cum without even touching my dick...", Paul shouted, gasping... Paul could feel his dick hard pressed against Will's rippling stomach, and he cried out in ecstasy when he started shooting his cum squirts... They both reached orgasm at the same time, both panting and gasping... „Oh my God Will... I can feel you cuming inside me... it's so warm... Keep shooting Will... keep shooting..." Will was groaning so much, moving his hips back and forth, feeling his last rope of cum oozing out of his dick deeply inside his lover's hot tight ass... „You're becoming an expert Will... you fucked my ass just the way I like it! You're so good Will... WOW! What a stud you are!" „It's your tight ass that did the trick... and since you weigh much less in the water, it was easy for me to fuck you like that... I loved it! We'll have to do it again, won't we?", Will asked, with a loving smile on his face... „Shit!... Any time...", Paul answered, laughing.

„But for now, I suggest we go back to the pavillon and have something to eat, what do you say?" „Yeah! I'm starving...", Will replied, grinning... Will and Paul went back to the pavillon, then moved a small table outside on the balcony where they savoured what Paul's chef had prepared for them. The wine kept dowing as the two young studs enjoyed the warmth of the night... Later, Paul hung up a hammock between two columns, and the two lovers laid back on it, their strong bodies hard pressed one against the other... „I tell you Paul: Life is good, thanks to you..." „NO... thanks to you Will! Without you, I wouldn't be here... I would be in New York with my family, and I'm sure I would be bored... like I used to be before you came into my life..." „Same for me...", Will replied, before he started to kiss Paul. Slowly, the candles burned down and died, while the two young hunks drifted into deep sleep, Will's arms holding his lover in a warm embrace... The following days were spent sunbathing, swimming and exploring the deep woods surrounding the lake... However, like all good things, their stay at La Vacherie eventually came to an end, and they had to drive back to Paris, having gained a very nice tan...

A few days later, news that the Luftwaffe had started to bomb military airfields and military installations all over the South of England reached Paris... Everybody was talking about the air campaign over England... and about an invasion of the british Isles which, no doubt, would soon occur... One evening, Paul was reading when Will came back to the drawing-room with a worried face... Paul knew he had been talking to his father in Berlin, so he asked Will: „Hey, what's new in Berlin... How's your family?" „.... They are just fine..." „You look worried..." „...It's just that my Dad told me a few bombs have been drop over Berlin by the RAF last Sunday night..." – „Oh?" „... Yeah... He said that earlier that same day, German planes were on their way over England to bomb an airfield not too far from London, when two of our planes lost contact with the others. Because of the clouds, they didn't know where they were... Then, they were spotted and attacked by some very heavy fire from the British antiaircraft defences... Only then did they realize they were flying right over London! As the two pilots were scared like hell, they decided to drop their bombs to gain speed, and they flew from there as fast as they could..." „They bombed London?", Paul asked, stunned... „...Well, just a few bombs... and it's obvious it was an error, you know. With aerial navigation, errors like that do happen sometimes... Even the BBC said it

193

was obvious the two planes were lost over London..." „And then, the RAF bombed Berlin?" „The same night! And that was done on purpose... And not only that: They went back to bomb Berlin again the night after, and again last night..." „Shit! Did your Dad tell you about the damages?" „...Oh... just a few... here and there... nothing serious, really... But the Führer must be mad as hell! My Dad told me he's going to make a speech tonight at the Sportspalast in Berlin... and I guess it's going to be ugly..." „We should listen to it, you know...", Paul answered. „Yeah... I guess so..." So later that night, they listened to Hitler's speech and, as Will had said... the Führer was not in a very good mood! Not at all! „...I wouldn't like to switch places with Göring tonight...", Will said, grinning... „...No! Neither would I... It must be hard to explain how the Luftwaffe could let those British planes fly all over Germany to bomb Berlin... three nights in a row...", Paul answered, laughing... They continued to listen to Hitler and after a long speech, the Führer said to the crowd assembled at the Sportspalast: „...The British say they will multiply their attacks over our cities? Well... We will erase theirs from the face of the earth!" „I don't like the way things are going...", Will said. „The British should never have started that... I've seen what the Luftwaffe did to Rotterdam last May, and I tell you: All they left behind were ruins! I wouldn't like to be living in London right now..." „And what about your family in Berlin? The RAF will certainly be back...", Paul asked, worried... „That's what I told my Dad. But he said there's no danger! He said he's sure the next time the British planes try to bomb Berlin, they will be shot down by the Luftwaffe before they even reach the Reich...", Will answered. „What do you think?" „Maybe... I don't know. But anyway, my Dad said he can't leave Berlin, because of his patients... I just couldn't convince him otherwise", Will answered... „Anyway... what are you reading?" „Oh... I received a message from my father the other day, and he suggests that I invest some of my Grandma's money in some of our overseas possessions... „...Where?" „Well, he said there are some good investments to be made in our colony of Indochina... it seems there's a lot of money to be made with some caoutchouc plantations over there... He also talked about Tahiti. There, he suggest I invest in some vanilla plantations..." „Shit Paul... That's so far away..." „Yeah! He also talked about investments in Martinique. Something about a sugar-cane plantation over there..." – „Have you decided?" „...No, not yet. I want to read about those places

194

before I make a move... But I'm not too keen about investing into a caoutchouc plantation..." „Well... what about sugar-cane? What can you do with sugar-cane?", Will asked... Paul started laughing and said: „Sugar of course, silly! But most of all, they make rum! My father said there's a nice plantation for sale near a small village named „Le François" in Martinique... He thinks that would be a good investment... „And how do you think you would be able to import sugar or rum from there: With the war and the blockade, that would be next to impossible...", Will answered... „Oh... but I'm not thinking about tomorrow either... I'm talking about a long term investment... This goddamn war will end one day, and then, things will go back to normal...", Paul replied, grinning... „Yeah... You're right!" „...And there's more to it...", Paul added... „What?" „Well, I'd like you to invest a small part of the money I gave you along with me in that business venture... It could be a joint venture... You and me! It could be fun..." „...Are you serious? Me? Investing money on a small Caribbean island? A few minutes ago, we were talking about London and Berlin being bombed... and now, you're talking to me about a dream island so far away I'm not even sure I know where it's really located..." „I'm talking about the future Will... There's nothing I can do about the war... but perhaps, we can do something about our future! At least, it's worth a try, don't you think? Besides, we have the right to dream, don't we?" Will started laughing, then said: „...You are crazy Paul de Brion! But since I would follow you to the end of the world, I'm game! And I like your idea about sugar-cane: I love rum!" „...Yeah! I guess you do, don't you? But as I said, before we make a decision, we'll have to read a bit about Martinique and obtain more details about that plantation over there... I'll ask my Dad..." „Good! And I prefer going to sleep tonight thinking about Martinique than about London being ereased from the face of the earth!", Will replied, grinning... „So now you like my idea, huh?" „I've never been against dreaming you know..." „It's not just a dream... Not just a dream! Dreams can become reality, believe me! But first, you have to believe you can realize them, because if you don't, they'll always remain just that: Dreams!", Paul answered, with a smile on his face. „I put you in charge of our dreams... because without you, no dream is impossible!", Will replied, giving Paul a sweet kiss...

So over the next few weeks, in September and October, while London was being bombed nights and days, Will and Paul were doing all kind of

195

research about Martinique... about the products grown over there, about it's population... From his father, Paul obtained all the details he needed concerning the plantation for sale over there... Will and Paul were dreaming, while others were trying to destroy the world around them! Early that December, they finally made their mind, and decided to buy that plantation in Martinique! All the financial arrangements were made by Maître Langlois, Paul's attorney, who thought Paul and Will were crazy! But before long, the two lovers were co-owners of a sugar-cane plantation located more than 7 000 km from Paris! „... I can't believe it...", Will said, laughing, while signing all the contracts... „You've realized our dream! Will you ever stop dreaming?" „The day I'll stop dreaming will be the day I die. Until then, I'll keep dreaming..." Paul answered, laughing... However, the week after, Paul was not laughing anymore... Starting in September, he had made some investments in Germany and the results were rather encouraging. He had made some good contacts in Berlin, and now had a few business partners over there. And of course, they were eager to meet with him to talk about other business opportunities... A few days after they had signed all the papers pertaining to their new plantation in Martinique, Paul received a letter from the German embassy in Paris... When Will got back home that night, Paul was sitting in the drawing-room. Will looked at his lover, and with a worried frown, he asked him: „What's wrong Paul? Are you sick? You're as white as a gost!" „Read this!", Paul answered, giving to Will the letter he had received from the German embassy... Will read the letter then looked at Paul and said: „At least, you didn't have problems reading the letter: You are pretty fluent in German now... What will you do?" „I don't want to go! That's out of the question!", Paul shouted. „...Ohhhhh my friend! I'm afraid you're going to have to accept... Otherwise, it would be considered an affront... Do you know how many people would sell everything they own just to receive such an invitation?" „I don't care! I'll tell them that I'm sick!" Will sat beside Paul and took his hands into his. He looked straight into his lover's beautiful green eyes, gave him a sweet kiss on the lips, then said: „You're not like that Paul! You're a fighter! You're not going to hide behind the curtains, are you?" – „(...) I've never been to Berlin! And quite frankly, I'm scared like hell!" „I know my love..." Will went through the letter for a second time: It was an official invitation to attend a Christmas party Herr Funk, the Reich Minister of Economic Affairs, was going to throw right before Christmas at the new Reichskanzlei in Berlin. And the invitation said the Minister had invited businessmen from all over Europe to gather in Berlin, to „celebrate" the 'New Europe' Hitler was building... „...Now calm down Paul! It's not as if you were going to be all alone with Herr Funk: Hundreds are invited..." „(...)" „Besides, you won't be all alone in Berlin: I'm going with you! And perhaps, Lutz could come..." „Huh?" „Look: Lutz and I will be on leave for ten days during the holidays. We could go to Berlin with you, and we could spend Christmas with my family... I haven't seen them for over a year, you know!" „(...)" „Come on Paul: Say yes! The damn party will only last for a few hours... Then we'll have fun in Berlin! We'll visit the capital... and you'll meet my parents and my sister and my baby brother. They've heard so much about you! Of course, they don't know... you know... And being a guest, my mother will certainly insist that you have your own bedroom... and I'll probably end up sharing another room with my brother! But what the hell! „...Maybe... It would be fun to spend sometimes with your family, I guess. I'm sure it would... I would like that. But that damn party! I'll probably end up being the youngest guest there!" „Maybe... maybe not. But you'll meet your business partners, and I'm sure it won't be so bad. And you know, you don't have to stay till the end of the party: As soon as it is polite to do so, just leave! And you know what? I'll drive you to the Neue Reichskanzlei with my father's car! There's a vast underground parking under the Chancellery and I'll park the car there, and wait for you... So as soon as you're ready to leave, I'll be right there for you! What do you think?" „Thank God you're here for me Will! (...) Okay! We'll go!"

The day after, Paul made all the arrangements: They would fly to Berlin on a private plane Paul had leased for the duration of their stay in Berlin. The pilot was a member of the Luftwaffe, and was very happy to be able to spend Christmas with his family in Berlin, instead of being all alone in Paris... Lutz would also come but regrettably, Franz couldn't make it this time, since he would be on duty at the Swiss embassy during the holidays... Of course, before leaving, Paul went on a shopping spree and bought Christmas presents for every member of Will's family, as well as for Lutz and Franz... He spent a lot of time shopping for Will's present and in the end, he found what he was looking for! In fact, he bought two presents for Will: One he would give to him in Berlin, with the rest of his

197

family, and the real one he would give to his lover before leaving for Christmas. Will called his family to let them know about their visit... and they were all ecstatic about seeing Will soon and meeting his new friend they had heard so much about... Will's mother was a bit nervous about having Paul as a guest, since she knew he was from a very rich family. Will had to calm her down, explaining Paul was a very simple guy that didn't care much about fancy celebrations... and that his French friend was so happy to be able to spend Christmas with them since otherwise, he would have been all alone in Paris, his family being in New York! Will's mother felt sorry for Paul, hearing about that, and she told her son that Paul would be most welcome amongst them... No need to say Lutz's family and his girlfriend were all ecstatic too, learning they would soon be able to spend some good time with „their" Lutz!

On Saturday, Demember 14, Will and Paul were having breakfast when Will asked his lover: „Where are we going to put the Christmas tree?" „What Christmas tree?... What do you mean?" „... Well, you know... The Christmas tree...", Will replied, looking at Paul... „Huh?" Seeing Paul didn't know what he was talking about, Will explained to him that in Germany, around Christmas time, people would put a fir-tree somewhere in their house and they would decorate it with lights and all kind of trimmings... No such tradition really existed in France at the time. „You mean you want us to put a fir-tree INSIDE the house? Are you kidding me or what?", Paul answered, laughing... „Yes yes... and we could invite Lutz and Franz and we could have a lot of fun decorating the tree...", Will answered all excited... Paul looked at his lover: Will's blue eyes were sparkling with joy and excitement! How could he resist his blond haired lover? Obviously, Will was excited as a child, thinking about decorating a Christmas tree! „That would make you happy, huh?", Paul asked, still laughing... „YUP!... It's not Christmas without a Christmas tree...", Will answered, grinning! „Okay okay! But where the hell are we going to get a fir-tree? And what about the trimmings? Have you thought about that, mister wise guy?", Paul asked, grinning... „...You have lots of fir-trees at Bagatelle... We could go there and cut a nice one! And I'm sure that, with all the German soldiers and officers in Paris... some stores must know about our tradition, and they must be selling all the trimmings we need..." Paul looked at the ceiling in discouragement! But he knew he couldn't refuse anything to the gorgeous hunk smiling at him, so he asked: „You, silly! So, what do we get first: The tree or the trimmings?" „The trimmings, of course: No trimmings, no Christmas tree!", Will answered, laughing... „Okay... Let's finish our breakfast, and then we go to Galeries Lafayette to see if we can find some Christmas trimmings there... If they don't sell that kind of ornaments over there, then no one else does!" Paul answered, smiling. „And call Lutz and Franz... to see if they want to come to Bagatelle tomorrow to get YOUR tree!" It didn't take long before Will had everything organized! At Galleries Lafayette, they found the Christmas lights and all the trimmings they needed... „When I think you want to put those lights on a tree! We're going to burn the mansion down!", Paul said, laughing... „Nah!", Will answered, laughing his heart out... The day after, very early in the morning, Lutz and Franz arrived and they all drove to Bagatelle to get the tree. Driving back to Paris with a very large fir-tree tied to the top of the car, Paul said to his friends: „You're crazy... all of you! When I think gas is as rare as gold... I can't believe we're spending some just to get a ... tree..." They all laughed, knowing perfectly well that indeed, they were privileged... Later, they were all back on Avenue Foch, and the tree was put in the drawing-room... far from the fireplace, as Paul had demanded! They had a lot of fun, putting the lights then the trimmings on the Christmas tree... When the job was finished, Will said: „Now, let's turn all the lights off... and let's light the tree!" Paul had to admit the result was stunning... „It's beautiful, Will" he said... „Really!" Madame Louise and her husband monsieur Pierre were invited to join the party and they were impressed.... „I've heard about such a tradition in Germany... But I didn't know you also had that same tradition in Alsace", monsieur Pierre said to Will and Lutz... „Oh yes... Christmas trees are very popular in Alsace too ...", Will convincingly answered. „I've never seen such a beautiful Christmas tree!", Lutz said... „Me neither...", Franz added. Paul had a very satisfied smile on his face: When Will had suggested they buy just a few lights and some trimmings, Paul had bought almost everything they had on sale at Galleries Lafayette! Like always, he had not spared money! „Do you like it, Will?", Paul asked his lover... „It's beautiful... I've never dreamed of such a beautiful Christmas tree..." Paul smiled, thinking that it was a bit ironical to see two big, strong German soldiers like Will and Lutz, being so excited by a simple Christmas tree! Later that night, after all the guests had left, Will kissed Paul very tenderly and they made love

199

passionnately... Later, Will said: „Thanks Paul... You don't know how much you made me happy..." „If it only takes a Christmas tree to make you happy... it doesn't take much!", Paul answered, with a tender smile. „Oh but it does! It reminds me of my family in Berlin... when I was a kid..." „Oh but you're going to be there soon...", Paul answered. „Yeah! And thanks to you again..."

That night, Paul gave Will the Christmas present he had bought for him: A very beautiful golden watch from Bulova! And here's my gift to you...", Will said, as in turn, he presented a small box to Paul. „What is it?", Paul asked, all excited. „Ah! You're going to have to unwrap it..." So Paul went through the wrapping paper like a madman, then opened the small box and found two identical golden rings in it. „I told you last summer I was marrying you, remember? Now, we have our wedding rings! In Germany, a married man wears his wedding ring on his right hand, while in France, you wear it on your left hand. So I suggest you wear yours on your right hand, like we do in Germany, so it will mean to me we are married... and I'll wear mine on my right hand, like you do in France, and so it will mean I'm married to you... What do you think?" Paul had tears in his eyes. He took a ring and placed it on Will's right hand. Then Will took the other ring, and placed it on Paul's left hand... „I marry you again my love!", Will said, kissing Paul. „And I marry you Will. I shall be true to you till the end of my life!" – „So will I", Will answered. After a long night, making love again, Will and Paul finally went to sleep. That night, Paul's sleep was a bit agitated though, as he was rather apprehensive about his coming trip to Berlin. How would he be greeted by Will's family? After all, he was a complete stranger to them! Would his „friendship" to Will looks suspicious to them? Would he be thrown out of their house, should they ever discoverer the truth? And what about that goddamn party at the Chancellery... Paul wished he wouldn't have to go! That made him sick, just thinking he had to go there...

Soon enough... too soon for Paul... the departure day arrived: Monsieur Pierre drove Paul, Will and Lutz to the Bourget airport, where their private airplane and their pilot were waiting for them... „What's that?", Will asked, looking at a few crates... „champagne and wine!", Paul answered, grinning... „Three crates? Are you crazy?" „Well, one crate will be delivered to Herr Funk, the Reich Minister... to thank him for his 'nice' invitation! The second crate is for Lutz's family... and the third one is for your family!" „They will be embarrassed, you know...", Will answered. „... At first, maybe... But believe me, after a few sips of champagne, they will no longer be...", Paul replied, laughing... The pilot from the Luftwaffe walked to them and introduced himself: „I'm leutnant Kurt Weiner, at your service, Sir!" „Good morning leutnant", Paul answered, smiling at him. Then leutnant Weiner saluted Will and Lutz, knowing by the uniforms they were wearing they were Wehrmacht officers... Of course, Will and Lutz had waited until monsieur Pierre had left the airport before changing into their uniforms... „Sir, this is going to be a direct flight to Tempelhof...", the pilot said to Paul. „That's the name of the airport in Berlin", Will said to Paul, grinning. „Oh!", Paul answered. „I didn't know that..." „We have a beautiful day today, so our trip should go very smoothly. Don't worry, Sir!" „We have total confidence in you!", Paul answered. „And please, call me Paul... I'm younger than you are, so... And those two clowns over there are Will and Lutz..." The pilot smiled at them, showing perfect white teeth, and answered: „Fine with me, as long as you call me Kurt..." „Fine!", the three friends answered. They boarded the plane, and Kurt went to the cockpit, where he started the engines. The three friends were a bit apprenhensive, since they were all flying for the first time! However, as soon as the plane had taken off, they all started to relax... and after a while, they were smiling from one ear to the other! „Get ready Berlin: Here we come!", Paul shouted, laughing! „Yup!", Will and Lutz answered, laughing too!

After an uneventful trip, they landed at Tempelhof, where they quickly went through the formalities... As his Ausweis was checked, Paul looked around the grand hall and saw a large Nazi eagle up upon the wall, holding a laurel wreath in its claws with a large Svastika in its midst. Of course, Nazi flags were everywhere... and Paul felt very uncomfortable... Looking at Paul and guessing what his lover was feeling, Will whispered to him: „...You'll get used to it. Remember: We're in Berlin now..." Paul smiled to Will and nodded... „Have a nice stay in Berlin, mein Herr! Heil Hitler!", the customs officer said to Paul. „Thank you...", Paul answered. Minutes later, Will saw his father waving to them... Will smiled and waved back to him... „My Dad is right over there...", Will said to Paul... Paul looked at the man still waving over there and smiled: Obviously, Will had inherit his good look from his father, for he was a carbon copy of the man waving to them, only younger... „Dad!", Will shouted, dropping his luggage to hug his father... „Wilhelm", his father answered, smiling... „You look fantastic my son!"... „Oh, and Hi Lutz..." „Good afternoon Herr von Rundstedt", Lutz replied, giving the man a firm handshake... „Dad... May I introduce you to my friend Paul de Brion..." „We're most honoured to welcome you, monsieur de Brion..." the man said, warmly shaking Paul's hand... „Thank you very much, Sir... And please, call me Paul..." „Of course son...", Will's father answered to Paul, with a warm smile on his face... „You have no idea how your mother is anxious to see you all...", Will's Dad said. „Where are the rest of your luggage?" „...We made arrangements so they will be delivered home later...", Will answered. „Fine..." his Dad answered. „So let's go... let's not keep your mother waiting... and Lutz, will you be surprised to learn that your family and Klara are anxiously waiting for you at our house?" „I'm not suprised to hear that, Sir! I'm anxious to see them too...", Lutz replied, laughing... „And we know this reunion is possible thanks to you Paul: Will told us about that... and we're all very grateful to you for that...", Will's Dad said... „I'm so happy to be here Sir: Otherwise, I would have spent Christmas all alone in Paris..." „Yes we know Paul... Will told us about that, too... We're truly sorry, you know...", Will's Dad answered, feeling a bit uncomfortable... „Listen Sir, you're not personally responsable for the invasion of France... And besides, if the Wehrmacht had not invaded France, I wouldn't have met Will and Lutz...", Paul said, laughing... „...Yes", Will's Dad answered. Then, looking at Will, he said: „And Paul is quite a good friend, isn't he?" – „Yeah! You've got it right...", Will answered, looking at Paul, grinning... While they were driving through Berlin on their way to Charlottenburg, Paul saw how beautiful the city was... „You have lots of trees in Berlin, it must be very beautiful during summer time...", he said... „Glad you like my city...", Will answered, smiling... „Tomorrow, I'll take you for a tour..." Later, Will's Dad parked the car in front of a nice house and Will said to Paul: „Welcome to our home!" Paul looked at the house and found it to be a very nice place... It had nothing to do with his mansion on Avenue Foch, of course... but it was very nice nevertheless... As they were walking to the house, the door opened and a nice lady appeared at the doorstep: „WILHELM!!!... MY BABY...", she shouted, with a big smile on her face. Will ran to his mother, smiling, then took her into his strong arms, lifting

202

her up... kissing her... „Mum!" Lutz and Paul walked to the door, followed by Will's Dad... and Will said to his Mum: „Mum, this is my friend Paul..." „Come to me son... let me kiss you!", she said, smiling... Paul walked to her, and she kissed him on both cheeks. „I'm so glad to finally meet you... Will told us so much about you...", she said... „And I'm so glad to meet you too... needless to say Will told me a lot about all of you too...", Paul answered, smiling... They walked into the house where Lutz saw his parents and his girlfriend Klara. They all kissed, and all started to talk at the same time... Lutz introduced Paul to his parents and to his girlfriend, and they all welcomed him... Then Will introduced Paul to his sister and his brother... „Paul... this is my sister Karin..." „Nice meeting you Karin...", Paul answered, smiling to the good-looking girl who was blushing in front of him... „...And this is my baby brother Ludwig..."

Seeing Ludwig, Paul started to laught and said: „...Hi! Ludwig... You look so much like Will... If you were not younger, I would think the both of you are twins..." „Hi, Paul... I was eager to meet you... Will told us so much about you...", Ludwig answered, smiling... Then, turning to Will, he said to his brother: „...And I'll have you know Wilhelm von Rundstedt that I'm not a baby anymore... I got fifteen last July, in case you forgot!" „Ohhhhh... That's right... And I didn't mean to insult you, Ludwig: I can see how much you've grown since the last time I saw you... You're almost as tall as I am now... Come here and give me a hug, bro... I've missed you...", Will answered, with a big smile on his face... „And I've missed you, too, Will... You don't know how it is to grow up with that girl over there...", Ludwig answered, laughing and looking at their sister Karin... As the two brothers hugged, Will looked at his sister and said to her: „...I've missed you, too, Karin... and I can see you're turning into a very beautiful woman. I don't know how that's possible... but I have to admit it's true! Tell me: Do you have a boyfriend now?", Will sarcastically asked... „OH YOU! STOP THAT!... Stop teasing your sister", Will's Mumsaid, laughing... „I can see war has not changed you one bit! Don't start a fight with your sister, please..." As they were all laughing they went to the living-room, where they started talking about so many things, it was as if they could go through all the events of the past year and a half in only five minutes... Lutz and Will told all about their last campaign through Belgium and France and when Paul realized the others felt rather

203

uneasy about that, due to his presence... he made sure they all understood he was not holding them responsable for what had happened... Both young dudes also spoke about their apartment on rue Lapérouse in Paris, and of course, Will never mentioned that in fact, he was living with Paul on Avenue Foch... On a few occasions, Paul gave Klara quick glances and, though the girl was good-looking, he thought she wasn't the kind of woman Lutz needed: She was rather cold and distant, and not once did Paul see her smile during the whole evening... Later, all the luggage were delivered, as well as the two crates, the third one having been delivered directly to Herr Funk, along with Paul's „Thank you" card...

„You know Paul, your German is excellent: Where did you learn?", Will's Mumasked... „Thank you... But I still make some mistakes, you know... I took private lessons and, of course, Will and Lutz help me a lot... as well as one of our friends who's from Switzerland...", Paul answered, smiling... „... But please: Don't take the Swiss accent...", Ludwig said, laughing... They all burst out laughing, hearing Ludwig's remark... „... I know... The two clowns over there have already warned me against that danger...", Paul answered, laughing... Then Paul gave the first crate to Will's parents, and the second to Lutz's. „What is that?", they all asked... „...Well, just open them...", Paul answered, grinning... They were all stunned to discover all the bottles inside the crates, and Paul said: „You'll all have a taste of France during our stay here... and I hope you will enjoy it..." „But Paul... You shouldn't have... I can only guess how expensive all those bottles are...", Will's Dad said... „You're a very generous man, Paul: We don't know what to say... It's too much...", Lutz's mother added... „It's my pleasure... I'm so glad to be here with all of you...", Paul answered. „Let's put a few bottles of champagne in the fridge dear, so we can celebrate the return of our two soldiers and their generous friend...", Will's Mumjoyfully said, talking to her husband... „Good idea dear!", he answered. „I see you have a nice Christmas tree over there...", Paul said, looking at the tree... „But of course: It wouldn't be Christmas without a Christmas tree, you know...", Will's Mumanswered, smiling... „I know: That's what your son told me...", Paul answered, laughing... „...And Lutz and I forced Paul to decorate a big Christmas tree at his house: You should see it: It's huge!, Will said with a big smile on his face... „...So Paul... I understand your family is in New York?", Lutz's father asked... „Yes Sir: For the first time in my life, I won't be spending Christmas with them... I miss them... But things being what they are, there's nothing I can do about that. And of course, I couldn't travel to America for Christmas... It's too dangerous, even for ships crossing the Atlantic under neutral flags... And since the accident with the Hindenburg, it's no longer possible to make the trip on airships..." „Yes... that accident was very unfortunate...", Will's Dad said... „Yes... But I now have access to a phone line to New York... and I can speak to my Dad from time to time. I've even spoke to my mother before we left Paris: She told me that on Christmas Eve, they will all attend a Christmas service at St. Patrick Cathedral... and I'm sure they'll all be praying for me..." Paul said, with tears in his eyes. „I'm sure they will son... I'm sure they will...", Lutz's Dad said, patting Paul on his shoulder... „And I'm sorry I brought up that subject..." „Oh... no harm done, Sir: It makes me feel good, talking about them...", Paul answered, smiling... „I understand you have been invited to attend a Christmas party at the New Chancellery: Is that true?", Lutz's Mumasked Paul... „MOTHER!!!", Lutz shouted... „What?", she answered, a bit surprised... „Well... I don't think Paul really wants to talk about it, Mum... How would you feel if you had been invited to attend a party thrown by Churchill?" „Oh...", she said... „No problem!", Paul answered, smiling... Then he went on, explaining the reasons why he had been invited... and said that, indeed, he was not too eager to go to that party..." „I understand... But since you have no choice but to attend that party, I hope that later on, you'll tell us how it is inside the New Chancellery... They say it's very beautiful... Did you know it only took eleven months to build it?", Lutz's mother said... „Really?", Paul asked, a bit suspicious... „Oh but it's true!", Will's father said... „Construction workers worked over there by the thousands... days and nights... for eleven months! And they succeded... I don't know how they did it, but they succeded!" „Is it far from here?", Paul asked... „It's located in 'Berlin Mitte', on Voßstraße... not too far from Potsdamer Platz...", Lutz's father answered... „Anyway, I'll show you tomorrow... and the day after tomorrow, I'll drive you there for the party. I'm sure Dad won't mind if I borrow his car while we're in town...", Will answered, looking at his Dad with a big smile on his face... „Ohhhh, I see my son is back in town: I guess during your stay, I won't see much of my car...", he said, laughing... „You got it!", Will answered, laughing... „Hey guys... Don't forget to give me a call tomorrow: I want to go with you on your tour... We'll have some great fun!", Lutz said to his two friends, with

205

a big smile on his face... not noticing Klara was looking at him with a very angry look on her face... Seeing what was going on, Will looked at Klara and said to her: „...And of course Klara, I take it you will come with us...“ „Oh... I was born in Berlin, you know... So no need for me to visit a city I know by heart... And I don't think Lutz needs to go on that tour either...“, Klara coldly answered... Lutz didn't reply... But Paul could see on his face he was not too happy with what Klara had just said and the way she had said it! Poor Lutz, Paul thought: Instead of going on a tour with his friends, he will have to spend the day with Klara, holding her hand, telling her how beautiful she is... how much he's in love with her... and how much he misses her... Klara must be that kind of girl, Paul thought! And now, Lutz was cought in her web!

„So... What about some champagne?“, Will's father asked, trying to change the subject... They all agreed, laughing, and champagne was served to everyone except Klara, who said she didn't drink „that kind of French thing...“, and who kept watching Lutz, to make sure he was not drinking too much of it. Obviously, Lutz was very irritated by Klara's attitude. They were all having fun, as Ludwig kept cracking jokes about someone Will and Lutz knew from childhood... Will's father began serving the guests a second glass of Chamgagne and, as he looked at Lutz's empty glass, he asked him: „A second glass, Lutz?“ „Sure, thank you, Sir...“ „He's had enough, Sir...“, Klara said, looking at Will's father... „Huh?“, Lutz exclaimed, a bit astonished... „Yes Lutz... One glass is enough, don't you think?“, Klara answered... Staring at Klara, Lutz kept silent for a few seconds then, with a smile on his face, he said: „...I don't think so, Klara. Hey! After all, it's our welcome back party...“ „Is that what you do in Paris? Spend your nights drinking with your drinking friends?“ Klara angrily said. Then, looking at Will and Paul she added: „... Evil company is not good for you!“ „What?“, Lutz shouted, stunned... „That's what I think!“, Klara replied. Lutz didn't answer her but instead, he turned to Will's Dad, who was still standing in front of him with the bottle of champagne in his hands, not knowing what to do... and, calmly and politely he said him: „Thank you, Sir: I'll have a second glass, thank you!“ Hearing that, Klara instantaneously rose and, without even saying good-bye to anyone, she left the house, slamming the door behind her! „...Aren't you going after her?“, Lutz's mother asked... „...No Mum... I will allow no one to take control over my life: Not today... not ever!“, Lutz

206

calmly answered... Then, looking at Will and Paul, he said: „And guys... don't forget to give me a call tomorrow morning: I'm going with you on that tour!"

Later that night, after all the guests had left and while they were alone for a minute, Will said to Paul: „Poor Lutz: He's in big troubles..." „I sure wouldn't like to have Klara as my girlfriend... and I don't think she likes me very much...", Paul answered, grinning... „She never liked me either... cause I'm Lutz's best friend. She has always tried to put troubles between the two of us, you know! Luckily, she doesn't know about Lutz and Franz...", Will replied, laughing... „OH MY GOD!!!", Paul answered, laughing is heart out... „Yeah"!, Will said, laughing too... Eventually, they all went to bed and, as Will had forseen, he was sharing a room with his brother Ludwig while Paul, being a „guest", had a bedroom all to himself... „Sorry!", Will said to Paul: „There's nothing I can do about that..." – „I know... But I'll miss you...", Paul answered, grinning...

The day after, Will called Lutz early in the morning and Lutz quickly walked the short distance over to Will's house, where the three friends left to visit Berlin, with the car Will had borrowed from his willing father! First, they went to visit the Charlottenburg Palace, then drove to downtown Berlin. On their way, they stopped to see the golden winged Siegessäule, the triumphal column built to commemorate the Prussian wars... then went to the Reichstag, where Will explained to Paul all about that historic building... They drove through the Brandenburg Gate, and parked the car not too far from Pariser Platz, so they could walk back to admire the Gate... „It's beautiful...", Paul said, looking at the Gate... „And I love those horses on top of it..." „Napoléon loved them, too, so he stole them and had them sent to Paris... But after Waterloo, they were returned to Berlin...", Lutz said, laughing... „You're kidding...", Paul exclaimed! „No no... I swear...", Lutz answered... „And you see the beautiful building over there?", Will asked Paul... „That's Hotel Adlon... It's one of the finest hotels in Berlin..." Paul looked at the very beautiful building, then turned and looked down on the large tree-lined Unter den Linden Avenue, which reminded him of the Champs-Élysées in Paris... „It's so beautiful...", he said. „Let's have a walking tour... We're in no hurry, are we?", Lutz asked, smiling... They started walking and turned on Wilhelmstraße... and when they reached a large building, Will said to Paul: „That's the Foreign Affairs building... That's where von Ribbentrop works... and you see that large building over there, on the oder side of the street?" „...Yes..." „Well, that's the Propaganda Ministry... That's where the rat works!" – „Who?", Paul asked, laughing... „Dr. Goebbels..." „Oh... The charming guy you told me about?", Paul answered, grinning... „Yeah! The despicable little rat! I suppose you don't want to pay him a visit, do you?", Will asked, laughing... „...Not really", Paul answered, still laughing... They continued walking down on Wilhelmstraße then reached a nice palace and, looking at the palace, Will explained to Paul: „That's the Reichskanzler Palace. That's where Bismarck used to live... and now, that's where the Führer lives..." „It's a nice palace... not too big... I'm surprised!", Paul answered. „Yeah...", Will answered. „Let's walk a bit further down the Avenue. Now... this building here is part of the Neue Reichskanzlei: You see that balcony over there?" „...Yes..." „Well, that's where Hitler stands to review the troops or salute the crowds...", Will explained. „... I'm glad he's not standing there right now...", Paul answered, grinning... „...That's only because he is not aware you're in town...", Will answered, laughing... „And you see those two big gates there? They lead to the open court of honour located inside the chancellery building... We'll drive through one of those gates tomorrow, when I'll drive you to your Christmas party..." „...How nice! I get sick, just thinking about it...", Paul answered.

They continued walking, then turned on Voßstraße, where Will showed Paul the very long and impressive building standing there, covered in sea shell lime. They walked down on Voßstraße for a while, and reached the building's Western grand Portico, with its tall columns, an armed guard wearing a black uniform and white gloves standing at the foot of each column... „That's it Paul! That's the New Chancellery building!", Will said. „WOW!, Paul exclaimed. (...) „It's quite different from what I had imagined... I was sure the New Chancellery was a grey, austere building... like Hitler is... But this building is not... Are you sure Hitler built it?" „... Well, yes... But it's Albert Speer, the well known architect, who created the building, not Hitler. The Führer only approved the plans...", Lutz said, grinning... „...You see those guards over there? They're from the „Leibstandarte SS Adolf Hitler", Hitler's bodyguard regiment... Don't even try to talk to them... They are not very friendly, if you see what I mean... I've never seen one of them smile...", Lutz said. „I don't think they even know how to smile...", Will added, laughing... „Hey guys... Let's walk a bit further down... Do you see that big truck over there?", Lutz asked... „Yes...", Will and Paul answered... „If it's what I think, we'll see something very surprising... „What?", Paul asked... „Let's watch for a few minutes...", Lutz answered... The three friends watched the truck for a while... and suddenly, they saw it disappear into the ground... „What's going on?", Paul asked, stunned... Lutz burst laughing, and answered: „Yup! There's an hydraulic lift to the Führer bunker there... and it's concealed from view by the pavement in the street... I've been told it's one of the most modern supply accesses of all of Europe... „Let's walk over there and have a look...", Will said... They walked to where the truck had parked, and saw nothing. Indeed, the truck had disappeared... and when they inspected the pavement, they saw nothing that would show there was a lift somewhere over there... „I've also been told that somewhere around here, there are five secret entrances to the Führer bunker, all concealed from view by the pavement around here... and that they can only be opened or closed from within the New Chancellery building...", Lutz further said... „I don't see them..." Paul said, looking at the pavement... „No... As you can see, they are very well concealed...", Lutz answered, grinning... „Where's the bunker? Under the New Chancellery?", Paul asked... „No no... There's a big garden on the other side of the building... and it's located deep under that garden...", Will explained. „Oh!", Paul said... He then looked down on Voßstraße and very far in the distance, he saw another Grand Portico, identical to the one near them. At the very far end of the building, he saw another large Avenue... „What about that Avenue over there?", he asked. „Ah... but that's the big swine Straße... I mean... the Herman-Göring-Straße", Will answered, laughing... Paul laughed, then turned to look back at the New Reichs Chancellery and said: „.... So... That's where I'm invited, huh?" „Yup!", Will answered, grinning. „Let's walk back to Wilhelmstraße... then let's go to the Gendarmenmarkt... You'll like it there... It's not too far from here..." Once they got there, Lutz said:

„I think Gendarmenmarkt is one of the most beautiful squares in Europe. Not as big as Place de la Concorde in Paris... but you've got to admit, Paul, that it's beautiful..." „Yes... It's very beautiful. Very impressive, too", Paul answered, with a very sincere smile on his face... „You see the magnificent building with the big columns at the certer over there?", Will asked Paul... „That's the Konzerthaus... and it's flanked by the French Cathedral on the north side over there... and the German Cathedral on the south side..." „Look at the domed towers that top the two Cathedrals...", Lutz said... „Yes... I must say I'm impressed...", Paul answered. „I think there's a staircase we can climb up to the domed tower of the French Cathedral... Want to give it a try?", Will asked his friends... „Let's go", Paul enthusiastically answered. The three friends climed the French Cathedral's circular staircase and reached a circular balcony that ran all around the big dome. From there, they had a spectacular view of the historic city center... „Berlin is a very beautiful city... I must admit... That's not what I was expecting. I love your city, guys! Except for all the Nazi flags everywhere, of course...", Paul said, laughing. „What's that big domed building over there?" „Oh... That's the Berlin Cathedral... It's the state Cathedral of the Prussian Kaisers", Will answered. „We'll go there later..." Paul took his time, looking at the beautiful city all around them. Little did he know that, in less than five years from now, this beautiful city would be reduced to rubbles, thanks to Hitler's madness.

They went down the stairs and then walked to Bebelplatz, where Will showed Paul the Old Palace and the ornate German State Opera house... „This is the site where the Nazis burned so many books back in 1933...", Lutz explained... „I've heard about that...", Paul answered. „And let me tell you: I think that was disgraceful..." „Yes... That was scandalous...", Will said. Of course, they visited the State Opera house, walked to the Neue Wache then to the Berlin Cathedral. Paul found it to be a very beautiful and impressive building... Later, they visited Altes Museum and after that, back on Unter den Linden Avenue, they walked to Pariser Platz and the Brandenburger Tor, where they recovered the car. They drove to Bahnhof Zoo and later, went to a nice restaurant, where they had a few beers, had lunch and just enjoyed the evening. Eventually, they drove back to Will's house, where his parents were happy to see them back! „Hey big brother", Ludwig said to Will „Next time, don't leave me behind! I'm no longer a kid, you know..." „Sorry Ludwig... Next time you'll come along with us, I swear!", Will replied, looking at his young brother who had grown a lot over the past year and a half... „I'm no longer a pest... You'll see!", Ludwig added, laughing... „Oh Lutz...", Will's mother said to him... „Klara called earlier... to see if you were here... I think she was looking for you, and I must say she was a bit rude with me..." „Oh I'm sorry to hear that Mrs. von Rundstedt: Please, excuse her...", Lutz answered, with a very sad look on his face... „You should dump her, that's what I think!", Ludwig said... „LUDWIG!!!", Will's mother shouted... „That's not nice to say..." „What? But that's the truth: She's just a pain in the ass...", Ludwig added... „LUDWIG!!! I told you: Stop that right now!", his mother said... „Okay okay..." Needless to say Will and Paul were trying their best not to break into a fit of giggles, while Lutz was looking at his shoes, blushing... „I will have to talk to her... She has changed!", Lutz said... „She has not changed one bit, Lutz. And that's the problem! It's just that now, you can see her for what she is: A bitch!", Ludwig said, laughing... „LUDWIG!!! I'll have to walk you to your room...", his mother shouted again... „...Yeah! Sure! And I'll be carrying you under my arm to my room, like a French bread...", Ludwig answered, laughing... They all started to laugh, hearing Ludwig's joke. Even his mother was laughing... „You know Mum: He's now much bigger and much taller than you are... so if I were you, I wouldn't try to walk him to his room...", Will said to his mum, still laughing... „Do you think I've not realized that, silly?", she replied, laughing too... „I just don't know what we're going to do with that big boy... Come here, you, and give me a kiss", she said to Ludwig, laughing... „Oh, and before I forget: I've called your mother Lutz, and I've invited your family for our Christmas Eve party, and your Mumgladly accepted! And I've also called Klara's mother to invite tem..." „And what did she say?", Lutz asked. „She said she must consult with Klara first, and that she's going to call me back later..." „She said that?", Lutz asked, a bit confused... „Yes", she answered. And when she sensed Ludwig was about to crack one of his jokes, she looked at him and said to him: „...Not a word, young man! It's not necessary..." Ludwig closed his mouth and looked at Will and Paul, with a devilish grin on his face... „Do you know what Paul: Can we exchange places?", Lutz very seriously asked him... „You could go and have a talk with Klara, and I would attend your party tomorrow: I would prefer to spend the evening with Hitler, even if I know that would be horrible... to having a discussion with Klara...". „That bad, huh?", Will asked... „Yeah! That bad!", Lutz seriously replied. „Anyway Lutz, I'm not going to see Hitler, you know. It's Herr Funk who's throwing that party, not the Führer...", Paul answered, smiling... Ludwig stared at Paul for a moment, then said to him: „...But my poor Paul! They're throwing a Christmas party at the New Chancellery, and you believe the Führer won't be there? You're in for a

211

big surprise my friend!" Paul suddenly turned white and, looking at Will, he asked: „Do you think he's going to be there?" „...Well... I don't know for sure... But it's true that since they've decided to throw the party there... there's a chance the Führer will show up, at least for a few minutes... I mean... It's as if the Americans were throwing a big party at the White House, and the President didn't show up!", Will cautiously answered, looking at the carpet... „OH MY GOD!!! I don't want to see him! I hate him!... Sorry Mrs. von Rundsteadt... I didn't mean to insult you...", Paul said. „Oh don't worry: I don't like him either. And I think I would prefer to go see my dentist, and have two or three teeth removed, than to have to spend an evening with the Führer!", she answered, smiling... „MOTHER!!!!", Will shouted... „That's not very cheering... We'll have to walk you to your room!" – „Better: I'll call the Gestapo!", Ludwig said, laughing... They all started to laugh, Paul included! „Well, thanks for telling me... I prefer to know in advance! But... yes Lutz... I would like to switch places with you: Just give me five minutes alone with Klara, and I'll settle her case... definitely!", Paul said... „PAUL!!!", Will shouted! „Oups! Sorry...", Paul answered, a bit embarrassed... And of course, again, Ludwig was laughing his heart out as he said to Paul: „I like you Paul! I do like you man!" „Anyway... I'll speak to her tomorrow! I just can't avoid it, can I?", Lutz stated... „Well Lutz... You and I are going to have a hell of a day tomorrow! A hell of a day!, Paul replied. „Shit, yeah!", Lutz answered.

FOURTEEN
«WHAT A DREADFUL DAY»

Lutz knew it was no longer possible to further delay the serious talk he had to have with Klara... So that morning, he walked over to her house and, as he rang the door-bell, he took a deep breath! Moments later, Klara's mother opened the door, and Lutz gave her a very nice smile... „Oh, Hi! Mrs Milch... How are you? Is Klara here?", he asked... „Good morning, Lutz... I'm so glad to see you. Please, do come in... How are you? You're more handsome than I remembered", she answered, smiling... „Thank you Mrs Milch... I'm doing fine!" „I'll call Klara: She's upstairs..." „Thank you..." Klara came downstairs and saw Lutz sitting in the living-room... „Did you come to present your excuses?", she asked him... „I beg you pardon?", Lutz calmly answered, although his heart was pounding... „...Yes! For the way you acted the other night, at Will's house... and yesterday... You preferred going with your friends to seeing me..." „Oh, I see Klara... (...) But please, do sit down... I would like to have a friendly chat with you..." As she sat she said: „Well now, I'm waiting for your excuses!" „...About the other night... the only problem is... I don't see what I did wrong...", Lutz said, carefuly choosing his words... „You were drinking like a beast!", she answered. „It's true I was going to have my second glass of champagne. Yes. If that's what you call drinking like a beast... But you know what Klara? I think that if you left like you did, without even thanking our hosts, it has nothing to do with the fact I was about to have a SECOND glass... (...) I think you were frustrated because I had refused to obey your command...", Lutz replied... „I told you not to accept that glass of champagne..." „...Yes..." Lutz answered, taking his time before saying: „You see Klara, I'm in the Wehrmacht, and I've been through a lot over the past year and a half... And I have no choice but to obey my superior's orders... But you're not one of my superiors, and I'm

213

not at your command. Now, you're a big part of my life, and I do love you... But you see Klara: My life doesn't stop with you. I love my family... I love my friends... As I said, you're a big part of it all... and I like that... But I will not drop all the other parts of my life because of you. And I will never yield to you control over my life!" As Lutz kept looking at Klara, he could see she was stunned! He didn't care about that, and continued saying: „Now yesterday... it's true... I've spent the day with my friends. But you were most welcome to come along with us, and have some fun. Instead, you chose not to come. Why? I think I know why! It's because you didn't want me to be with my friends! (...) You know Klara that I'm here for a few days... and that we'll have plenty of time to be together, you and me... But yesterday, it was Paul's very first day in Berlin, and we wanted to show him the city... Don't you understand that?" „...Oh, that Frenchman... with his champagne..." „I see you don't like him..." „No!" „But you don't even know him..." „I don't need to know him: I don't like him, that's all!" „And I know you don't like Will either..." „I've never liked that guy..." „And you've been rude with his mother yesterday, on the phone..." „She's stupid!" „I see. But whatever you think about her, she was kind enough to invite you and your family to join all of us for her Christmas Eve party..." „... Do you think for one second we're going to go? I've told my Mumthat was out of the question! We'll have our own small party here, and I expect you to be here with me..." „But my family has already accepted Mrs von Rundstedt's invitation...", Lutz said... „So what? Let them go, if that's what they want..." „(...) If I follow your thinking... I would be here with you... while my family, who I haven't seen for a year and a half, would be on the other side of the street, at Will's house, celebrating Christmas without me... Is that it?" „...Yes! If you love me like you said, I expect you to be here with me!" „I see..." Lutz kept silent for a few minutes, then he slowly rose, stared at Klara for a few seconds, then said to her: „I'm sorry to tell you that Klara, but I won't be here for your 'small' party! I'll be with my family and my friends over at Will's house. And if you really love me, you'll be there too, with your parents... Should you decide not to come, that will tell me a lot..." „We won't be there, Lutz! And that's final!", she shouted. „...I hear you. You don't have to scream at me, you know. I'm not deaf! (...) What else can I say Klara? I guess there's nothing else to say... and I'm sorry for that, really..." „Are you breaking up with me?", she defiantly asked... „No...",

214

Lutz gently answered... „I don't need to: You've already done that! (...) Now I think it's better for us to go our seperate ways... cause it won't work for the two of us. And I wish you all the luck in the world: I do hope you will find happiness, Klara, I really do!" Hearing that, Klara took one of her mother's china vase and threw it against the fireplace... „I've seen Scarlet O'Hara last year doing that in „Gone with the wind"... nice film... but sorry Klara: It doesn't work with me!", Lutz said, grinning... „Oh You! I hate you..." „...Have you ever loved me Klara?... Oh, and don't bother: I'll find my way out..." At that, Lutz left Klara and walked the short distance over to his home. He felt heavy-hearted, but also relieved... He gave Will a call... „At what time do you intend to leave to drive Paul to the New Chancellery?", Lutz asked his friend... „At around 1 p.m.... Why?" „I'm going with you... Will you be wearing your uniform?" „Of course... But... I thought you were supposed to have a talk with Klara today...", Will said... „...Yeah! I just did! And I'm a free man now..." „Oh?" „I'll tell you all about it later... And I'll be at your house on time!" „Fine..."

Of course, Will ran to the kitchen, where Paul was having a coffee with Ludwig and his mother, and he told them what Lutz had just told him... „I feel sorry for him..." Paul said... „But I think Klara was not the right... person... for Lutz!" „No, she wasn't...", Will's mother said. „Anyway... Lutz is old enough to know what's best for him...", Will replied... „I'm sure it won't take long before he meets someone else in Paris... I'm quite sure he never did anything with Klara: I'm sure she's frigid!", Ludwig said, laughing... „LUDWIG!", his mother shouted... „...What? Hey Mum... Lutz is young... he's very good-looking... I don't think he's going to be all alone for very long, if you see what I mean...", Ludwig answered, grinning... „Well... You're too young to talk about those things...", she answered. „Poor Mum! We're no longer in 1920 you know! I'm fifteen... Do you really believe I don't know about all those things?", Ludwig replied, laughing... „I'm going to have to wash your mouth with soap...", she said... „Yeah yeah...", Ludwig answered, laughing... „Just try to put your hands on me..." he added, while running out of the kitchen, laughing his heart out... Once Ludwig had left, she said: „I don't know what we're going to do with him! He's growing to fast... and I think your father and I have lost the touch. We're getting too old for that... I wish you were here Will, to talk some sense into him..." „Perhaps next summer, he could come to Paris and spend some time with me... You know Mum: It's

215

not easy for him to grow up with two women... you and Karin... I know you're doing your best, and I know Dad is doing his best too... but nevertheless, it's not easy for Ludwig... And most of the time, Dad is at his office... Oh, I don't blame him... but you know how it is..." „Ludwig? In Paris? But... Where would he stay? With Lutz and you? You work all day long... so most of the time, you're not at your flat... Ludwig would stay there all alone? All day long? I don't think so!", she stated. „Oh... But during his stay, Will could move to my house... and Ludwig could stay there with us. I have a good staff, and a good chef... And most of the time, when I have to, I work from my study at home... so Ludwig would never be left alone...", Paul answered, smiling at Will's Mum... „...Well... maybe... I'll have to talk to your father about that. And anyway, we have lots of time before us to think about it, don't we?", she answered... „Yes Mum...", Will answered, giving his Mum kiss... „You're a good son Will... You've always been!", she said, smiling at her handsome son. „Now if you will excuse me", Paul said... „I've got a shower to take, and I've got to get dress. Remember: I have a NICE party to attend at the Neue Reichskanzlei!"

Later, when Paul came down, wearing his black full dress with a nice bow-tie, they all looked at him and Will's mother said: „My God, Paul! You're so handsome... If I weren't married, I would marry you right now..." „No chance, Mum: I would marry him first!", Will said, laughing... They all laughed. Then Lutz got there and minutes later, the three friends left for the Neue Reichskanzlei... The traffic was heavy on Wilhelmstraße... but eventually, they reached the Neue Reichskanzlei, where guards checked Paul's invitation, as well as the identities of the other two in the car. Seeing all was in good order, the guards stood at attention and shouted: „Heil Hitler! Welcome to the Neue Reichskanzlei!" „Heil Hitler!", Will and Lutz answered, being German soldiers. Paul remained silent. „I can't believe I'm here!", Paul nervously said, as Will was driving the car through one of the big gates... „Oh... It's just for a few hours... You'll live to see the end of it, don't worry! And remember: We'll be waiting for you..." „Thanks guys... I really do appreciate..." Many cars were slowly making their way inside the Court of Honour, driving bumper to bumper... and when they neared the flight of stairs leading to the main entrance, Lutz said: „Shit guys: Look at the two big nude statues over there..." The three friends looked at the statues of two well muscled

Greek Gods, cast in bronze... „I wish my Mum could see that... she would be flabbergasted!", Lutz said, grinning... Minutes later, Paul got off the car... „Wish me good luck guys... I'll need it!" „I love you Paul... You're not alone here: I'm with you!", Will answered... Paul walked his way up the flight of stairs to the main entrance, over which stood a very large sculpted Nazi eagle...

„God bless me!", Paul thought to himself, before showing his invitation to another guard: „Heil Hitler!", the guard said to him, as he showed him where to go... First, Paul found himself in a small entrance hall, then was guided to the very large Mosaic Hall. Many guests were already there and Paul joined the crowd. He looked up at the very high ceiling and saw the huge stained-glass ceiling, lit up by artificial lights... The Hall was stunning, Paul thought. The walls were entirely clad in special reddish-grey Schnöll marble, and its fiery and smoky red color was most striking! Paul looked at a huge door at the end of the Mosaic Hall and admired its very large frame made of blue marble: The contrast was stunning, indeed! And of course, over that huge door stood the usual golden Nazi eagle, spreading its wings... What else! Paul thought. Looking around him, Paul noticed that at regular intervals, the marble walls were delicately inlaided with white birds... Again, the result was stunning! And what about the marble floor, Paul thought: It's beautiful! While Paul was admiring the Mosaic Hall, three mem walked over to him, and one of them said to him: „I am told you are Herr de Brion... our business partner from Paris? I'm Herr von Schultz... May I introduce you to the two gentlemen here..." „Oh nice to meet you, gentlemen... Nice to meet you, finally", Paul answered, smiling at his German business partners... „Nice meeting you, too, Herr de Brion... We know we will have a chance to meet with you later this week... so for now, I suggest we all enjoy the party... (...) I saw you were admiring the Mosaic Hall! Would you like to see more of the Neue Reichskanzlei? That can be easily arranged, you know..." The man didn't wait for Paul to answer, and made a sign to a guard standing not too far. Before Paul knew it, the guard had walked over to them and was saying: „Heil Hitler, Herr von Schultz... Can I be of any assistance to you?" Obviously, Paul thought, Herr von Schultz was well known at the chancellery... and no doubt this tour of the building had been planned well in advance! „Yes my friend", Herr von Schultz said to the guard..."We would like to have a little tour of the New

Chancellery, to show our friend from Paris the greatness of the Reich..."
„But of course, Herr von Schultz: I'll be your guide!", the guard answered,
beaming... Oh my God! Paul thought to himself: There we go... feeling
sick hearing about the „greatness" of the Reich. But of course, he had no
choice but to go on that goddamn tour! First, they went to a huge circular
Hall, then the guide opened two very large doors, and Paul saw the Great
Gallery right in front of them. He was stunned! „That's the Marble
Gallery", the guide explained. „It's bigger than the Gallery you have at
Versailles...", he added, looking at Paul. „It's only more modern in style...
and the tapestry you see here, as well as all the others down the Gallery
are from the Gobelin Manufacture, of course..." Paul looked at the
beautiful tapestry and asked himself if their guide would go as far as to
tell them how much the Führer had paid for it! Obviously, Hitler was a
newly rich, and wanted to make an impression on everyone visiting the
building! Paul wasn't impressed at all, but obviously, their guide was! He
looked at the guide and wished he could kill him on the spot, to put an
early end to the damn tour! „Now gentlemen, please, follow me...", the
guide said. They walked down the very long Marble Gallery for a while,
then the guide stopped in front of a very big door. Two guards were
standing there, on each side of the door... „Now gentlemen... These doors
lead to the Führer Study! And if you look up over the marble door frame,
you'll see a big crest, with the letters „A" and „H" intercrossed... They
mean „Adolf Hitler", of course!" "What else!", Paul thought. "How
imaginative!", he sarcastically said to himself. Now Paul was really
beginning to seriously hate their guide... Looking back at the closed doors
to the Führer Study, the guide said: „But don't worry: You'll get a chance
later to see the Führer Study! Now please, follow me..." They walked to
another very large Reception Hall, then to the Reichskabinettsaal... „This
is the room where the Cabinet members meet...", the guide said. „Oh...",
Paul said... „And do they meet on a regular basis?", he sarcastically
asked... „... This room has not been used, yet...", the guide answered, with
a stupid smile on his face. „I see", Paul answered, grinning, knowing
perfectly well Hitler was ruling the Reich by signing decrees, not
bothering

to consult his lackeys... The guide showed them a few other rooms,
then they went outside to see the gardens... „I've been told there's a
bunker somewhere over here", Paul asked the guide... „Oh yes, Sir. It's

the Führerbunker! It's over there... But of course, you can't see it, since it's 10 meters below the ground and protected by approximately 4 meters of concrete... but the small round concrete tower you see over there is one of its emergency exits...", the guide proudly said. Paul looked at the place. How could he have known that, five years from now, Hitler would commit suicide in that bunker, and that the garden where he was standing now would be the place where the Führer's body would be burned... Again, they followed the guide, went up a flight of stairs that lead to a large porch, where their guide said: „Behind those big French-doors is the Führer Study... Each door is 6 meters high and 2 meters large..." "What do I care!", Paul said to himself. „Now gentlemen, it's time to join the other guests inside the Führer Study..." The guide nodded to a soldier standing guard near one of the French-doors. The guard opened one of the doors and they all walked inside the Führer Study. Many guests were already standing there... making small talk... „Thank you very much for the tour, young man!", Herr von Schultz said to the guide... „Yes... Thank you...", Paul added, smiling at the guide.

Once inside the Führer Study, Paul realized it was a very large room. As they were walking to a large fireplace, his business partners told him: „Oh please, Herr de Brion, please... excuse us for just a moment... There's a gentleman over there we really need to pay our respect to..." „But of course gentlemen... Please do...", He answered to them, smiling... Paul was so relieved to be left alone for a few minutes... He started to look around and continued walking to the big fireplace. Once there, he looked up over its mantle, and gave a look to a large framed oil painting... „...That's Bismarck you're looking at...", Paul heard someone say behind him... He turned and saw the goddamn guide standing there, smiling at him! Paul was desperate: How could he get rid of that man, he tought for himself! „...I see...", he had no other choice but to answer... If only he could tell the guide he didn't give a damn about Bismarck and all the rest... „Did you know the Führer Study is 27 meters long and 15 meters large?" the guide stupidly said... „The ceiling over here is 10 meters high..." „You don't say... I see you've learned your lesson well..." Paul answered, not interested at all by all those stupid details... „Oh yes...", the guide answered, with a big smile on his face, too stupid to realize Paul was fed up, and just wanted to be left alone! „...Yes... And you see: All the walls here are clad in red Austrian marble... All the door frames are made

219

of solid brown ebony, while the ceiling is clad in very, very expensive Brazilian rose-wood!" This time, Paul didn't answer, and didn't even look up at the ceiling: Rather, he started looking around to see where he could go, to get rid of the damn guide once and for all! But before he could make a move, Paul saw Herr Funk walking over to him, with a broad smile on his face!!! Oh shit, Paul thought: After the guide, now the old goat himself! What else after that? he asked himself... „....Ahhhhhh, Monsieur de Brion... What a pleasure to see you again...", the old goat said... „And thank you so much for your nice gift to me: Thanks to you, at Christmas, I'll be drinking the best champagne in the world. Thank you!!!" „Think nothing of it, Sir: It's my pleasure!", Paul answered, smiling to the old goat! „....And I do hope you enjoy your stay here in Berlin... Did you bring your wife along?" "Ah! There he goes!", Paul thought. "He wants to know if I'm married! Or if he has a chance with me..." „...Well Sir, I'm not married yet... But yes, my fiancée came along with me...", Paul answered, grinning... „You know how things are in Paris... My flancée and I live together as if we were married... but I like to stay free... I'm young, and women are so beautiful..." "What a liar I make!", Paul thought to himself. "But if the old goat thinks he's going to put his hands into my pants, he's in for a big disappointment!" „... Yes, I understand... and you're such a good-looking young man, it must be easy for you to find beautiful women...", the old goat answered, trying not to show his disappointment... As Herr Funk said that, a chamberlain announced, with a very strong voice: „Ladies and gentlemen: Der Führer! As two big doors opened, Hitler came in, and was greeted by a loud „Heil Hitler", shouted by the crowd assembled in the Study... From where he was standing, Paul could hardly see the Führer... But seconds later, Paul heard Herr Funk say to him: „...Come my young friend... Let me introduce you to the Führer: I told him about you, and about the fact that you personify the future of the New Europe he wants to build..." „Oh Sir... I'm not worthy of such an honour, you know", Paul replied, not wanting to meet with Hitler! "What the hell am I going to do?", Paul asked himself. "This must be a bad dream: I'm going to wake up in a minute... and I'll laugh at it..." It was a bad dream alright, but he was not sleeping! And before he realized it, Herr Funk had him by the arm, and was walking him over to the Führer! "Oh shit!", Paul thought: "That can't be true! That just can't be true!" But it was all too true!

Taking Paul by the arm, Herr Funk walked him over to the Führer... and before Paul had time to realize it, he was standing right in front of Hitler... „Mein Führer", Herr Funk said... „This is the young man from Paris I've told you about the other day... Mein Führer, this is Herr de Brion!" Hitler looked at Paul then smiled to him and shook his hand, as photographers were taking pictures... „Herr Chancellor... It's an honour", Paul had no choice but to say... „I must say it's quite a surprise for me, meeting you today..." The Führer grinned, then said to Paul: „AH! Paris! What a beautiful city! (...) And you're such a young businessman... You represent the future... You're the reason why we're working so hard to built a New Europe, so young people like you can thrive! And France will be a big part of that dream!", Hitler said to Paul, holding his hand and looking at him straight in the eyes, with his steel- blue eyes... „Yes, Herr Chancellor...", Paul politely replied... „And that's why France must help us defeat England...", Hitler added... Paul didn't have time to answer that, since many other guests were waiting to be introduced to the Führer. Paul gladly ceded his place to others! Thank God, Paul thought: It's over! Later, Paul said good-bye to Herr Funk as well as to his business partners, then he walked so fast through the Mosaic Hall, you would have thought he was running for his life! He felt sick, and wanted to leave as soon as possible... He gave a guard the ticket he had received earlier, and the guard made a call... „Your car should be here soon, Sir", the guard told him a few seconds later... „Thank you!" „Heil Hitler", the guard shouted! Paul didn't answer. He walked to the doors, which were opened for him by two other guards. Paul passed them and went outside where, minutes later, he saw a familiar car enter the Court of Honour... „Thank God", Paul thought to himself... „Not too soon..." When the car stopped, Paul got inside and said to Will and Lutz: „Let's leave this goddamn place as fast as possible..." „That bad?", Will asked... „That bad!", Paul answered... While they were driving up on Hermann-Göring-Straße, Paul asked: „Do you know a place where we could go to have a strong drink? I need one right now!" „...I was thinking about the same...", Lutz answered, grinning... „I need a strong drink, too"... Will drove them to a pub he knew and where the three friends had a few drinks. After a while, Paul started to relax... „... You met the Führer?", Will asked, after Paul had told them about the party... „Yeah! And thank God, we only spoke for a few seconds..." „Shit! (...) And how is he in person?", Lutz asked... „... Not as

221

I had imagined", Paul answered. „For once, he was not screaming, like he always does when we hear him on the radio... He was calm and very polite! He warmly kept my hand into his... but what impressed me most are his cold ice-blue eyes... It's as if he could see through me..." „Yeah... I've heard about those cold eyes...", Will answered. „Anyway! Enough about that damn party! (...) Turning to Lutz, Paul said to him: „Now I want you to tell me about Klara... If you want to, that is..." „Hey, you're my friend: I've nothing to hide from you...", Lutz answered, grinning... Then Lutz went on to tell Paul what he had already told Will earlier... „So it's over?", Paul asked... „I guess so!", Lutz answered. „And how do you feel about it?" „... I don't know... I feel sorry, but at the same time, I'm glad it's over..." „I think you made the right decision, Lutz: That girl didn't deserve to have you!", Paul answered, smiling to his friend... „...Maybe...", Lutz replied. „Hey Lutz: You're a great guy... I'm sure that, soon, you'll find a nice girl you'll fall in love with... With a stunning look like yours, it won't take long...", Paul said, laughing... „Hope you're right! And in the meantime, at least... I have Franz for good sex...", Lutz said, grinning... „Yeah. But please Lutz: Take care of him... don't exploit him! And don't hurt him, please", Paul said. „I know you've been very honest with him...", Paul continued to say... „But nevertheless, I'm just afraid he's going to suffer... and I wouldn't like to see that..." „Hey: Don't worry Paul... Franz keeps telling me he's not in love with me... so..." Paul was not surprised to hear that. It was obvious to him that Franz didn't want to loose Lutz, and had decided to suffer in silence... „Yeah... Well, just be nice to him, will you?", Paul added... „But I am...", Lutz answered. „Good!", Paul said. Paul thought that, if Franz had chosen not to tell Lutz he was madly in love with him, he had to respect his decision, and so he didn't push the subject any further with Lutz... „... Now guys, I don't know about you..." Paul said... „But I'm exhausted! It's been a long day... What do you think we go back to Charlottenburg and hit the sack?" „Good idea", Will answered... „Let's go back...". „Hey: What are your plans for tomorrow?", Lutz asked... „... I was planning on showing Paul the Olympic Stadium...", Will answered. „Will you give me a call?", Lutz asked... „Sure!" True enough, the day after, the three friends as well as Ludwig went to visit the Olympic Stadium and Paul was very impressed by the huge and beautiful structure... They visited a few other places, then decided to go back to Will's house since it was getting cold, and snow had

222

started falling... „It's a lot colder here in Berlin than it is in Paris...", Paul observed... „Yeah! Winters are cold and windy in Berlin...", Will answered... „And it can get very damp too! That's the worst part, I think". Later, Will looked at Paul and said to him: „Hey! You're day-dreaming..." „Sorry! I was thinking about Paris...", Paul answered, smiling... Since Ludwig was sitting with them in the car, Paul couldn't say to Will he wished they were in Paris instead of Berlin, so they could kiss and make love! Here in Berlin, with all those people around, it was not possible to even think about kissing... Paul was badly missing the physical contact with his lover... That night was Christmas Eve... and they had a lot of fun. Will played some Christmas carols on the piano, and they exchanged their Christmas presents. And of course, they were all impressed by Paul's proverbial generosity... „I wish my brother Hans could be here with us tonight...", Lutz said, a bit sad... „He's older than you are, isn't he?", Paul asked... „Yes... He's twenty-five... and at the moment, his regiment is stationed in Norway...", Lutz answered... „In his last letter, he wrote that it's very cold up there... and that he wished his regiment could be transferred some place else to the South...", Lutz's mother said... „Poor Hans! He must think I'm lucky to be stationed in Paris...", Lutz said. „That's exactly what he wrote in his last letter...", Lutz's father replied, laughing... „Let's just hope this war ends soon, so our sons can come back home and have a normal life...", Lutz's mother added. „I don't see the end of it", Will said... „When we flew to Berlin the other day, our pilot told us that every day and every night, the Luftwaffe keeps bombing London and other major cities all over England... but that doesn't work, I guess... since the British are not begging for peace yet! (...) In fact, our pilot said the British are fighting back, and every day, many of our planes are shot down... „Well, let's not think about the war tonight... and let's celebrate...", Will's mother said. „You're so right, Mrs von Rundstedt... And let's thank God: Our sons are well, and are in no danger! Even Hans in Norway is safe, since it's very quiet on that front...", Lutz's father said. „Let's drink to peace...", Will's father said, rising his glass of champagne... „To peace!", they all answered...

Over the next few days, Paul had several meetings with his German business partners, and a few deals were made... The day before they few back to Paris, Paul was attending one of his meetings, and Will was all alone with his mother, having a coffee with her... „Son... Is there something you would like to tell me about you and Paul?", she asked, smiling... „Huh?", Will answered, a bit puzzled... Will's Mum took her son's hand and, looking at him straight in the eyes, she said: „I'm your mother, you know... I gave life to you and I've raised you! I can see through you Will... and there are things you just can't hide from a mother, however hard you try. I've seen the way you look at Paul... and the way he looks at you..." Will was blushing and it was obvious to his mother her son was very ill at ease... She tenderly smiled to him and said: „Whatever you do with your life Will, always remember that I love you, and I'll always support you, you understand? And whenever you want to talk about you and Paul, I'll always be here to listen to you. I will never ever condemn you... Besides: Paul is a very nice young man, and I know he's a good man. And I can see how happy you are when he's around you! All I want is for you to be happy in life! The rest is not important to me..." Will raised his eyes to his mother and smiled... „You know Mum... it's not easy to speak about those things... I can't even explain them! All I know is that I love Paul. And he loves me! What harm are we causing to others?" „...I know, Will... But you know most people are not as broad minded as I am! Your love for Paul is a very dangerous one... Please: Be very very careful... I fear for your life!", she answered. „Don't worry, Mum... We are very careful! We took all the necessary precautions to make sure no one will discover our secret. We act very cautiously, I swear. (...) Does Dad know?" Will's mother started laughing, then answered: „Do you think your father would see a thing like that? Of course not! He has no idea! And I'm sure it never reached his mind... Do you want me to talk to him about that?" „Not now, Mum! I'm not sure I could deal with that for the moment..." „When you're ready, tell me... But remember Will: Your father loves you very much... I'm sure he would understand and I have no doubt he will support you. Don't presume otherwise..." „You may be right Mum... but I'm just not ready yet to talk to him about that, that's all!" – „...First, you have to start feeling comfortable with yourself!" „Oh it's not that mum... I feel very comfortable with who I am... I can't explain why I'm in love with Paul, but that's the way things are, and I accept that! It just that... (...) I don't see why I have to explain my situation to others? If I were straight, I wouldn't have to explain anything, would I?" „...Well... I guess we all presume that everybody is 'straight', as you say... So there's no need to explain anything about that... But you're different Will, and

224

you know how people are: They tend to reject differences... Sometimes, differences have to be explained..." „...Yeah... anyway, don't tell Dad for now... And don't tell Karin nor Ludwig..." „Oh, don't worry about Karin finding out: Sometimes, I wonder if she's living on earth, or on some other planet! (...) With Ludwig, it's different! He's a very wise guy, you know... and he admires you so much. If there is one person I wish you could talk to, it's Ludwig... He needs you, Will... And I have no doubt he would understand! One day or another, he will find out about your secret... Do you think you will be able to hide the truth from him, if he goes to Paris to visit you next summer? If you don't tell him and he discovers the truth, he will be hurt to find out you didn't trust him enough to tell him the truth..." „(...) Okay Mum... I'll talk to him before we leave tomorrow..." „Thanks", she answered, smiling... „So, what about the rest of your day? What are you planning to do?" – „...I don't know yet... Paul won't be back until late this afternoon, and Lutz is gone to see one of his cousins..." – „Why don't you go skating with Ludwig at the Grünewald park?" „Where is Ludwig?" „He's going to be back for lunch, don't worry! I think that's all he does nowadays: Eat, eat, eat!!!", she answered laughing.

And later, when Ludwig got back home, they started laughing again when they heard him ask: „Ummmmm.... it smells good in here: What's for lunch?" Looking at his Mum and at Will, he asked:

„What? Why are you laughing like that?" „Nothing bro! It's just we had guessed you would be hungry...", Will answered, still laughing... „Hey... I'm still growing up, you know..." „Yes! Well, I hope you'll stop growing up soon, cause we'll go bankrupt, trying to feed you!", their Mum said laughing. „Now sit: lunch is about to be served!" – „Where's Paul?", Ludwig asked Will... „He's at a meeting with his business partners. (...) I was wondering... After lunch, you and I could go skating in Grünewald: What do you think?" „Just you and me?" „Yeah!" „Ah! Cool... I'd like that...", Ludwig answered, with an excited smile on his face. Right after lunch, both brothers left for Grünewald, where they had a lot of fun skating. It was a nice sunny day, and lots of people were there, enjoying the fresh air and the beautiful nature all around them... During the afternoon, Will and Ludwig took a break from skating and went to a small restaurant to have a nice cup of hot chocolate. They sat near a large window and were watching the skaters having fun when Ludwig asked Will: „You're leaving tomorrow, aren't you?" „Yes... Tomorrow morning..." „I wish you could stay longer! If only I could go to Paris with you... Karin is driving me crazy, you know..."mWill laughed, then said: „Don't tell anyone yet, but maybe next summer –and I stress MAYBE– you'll come to Paris and spend sometimes with us over there. I've spoken to Mum about that, and she said she will talk to Dad..." „Are you serious Will? I would travel to Paris and stay with you?" „...Yes... and about that... I have something I'd like to tell you... about Paul and me..." As silence fell, Ludwig could sense Will was ill at ease... „...I see you find it hard to spit it out! But don't worry Will, I think I already know what you want to tell me!" – „Huh?", Will exclaimed... „What do you already know?" „I think Paul is not just a good friend to you, like Lutz is (...) I may be wrong, but I think Paul and you are... well... more than just friends...", Ludwig answered grinning... „You're the devil himself!", Will said, laughing... „No... I'm just your 'baby' brother, like you say! And I love you Will. I got suspicious... and I kept observing you and Paul... Oh it's not obvious you know, it's just something I could feel, looking at you two..." „Does it..." „No Will... it doesn't bother me at all... I don't give a damn about that. But if I ask you a question, will you answer me?" „Yes..." „You're not really sharing that flat with Lutz, huh?" „....No... I live on Avenue Foch, with Paul..." „I knew it!", Ludwig shouted, laughing... „Now bro, I want you to keep that a secret between you and me..." – „Don't worry, Will: My lips are sealed!" „Mum knows I'm in love with Paul, but she doesn't know about the rest... and of course, Dad and Karin know nothing about that..." „...Don't say a word to Karin: She's such an hare-brained silly girl!", Ludwig said, grinning... „That's not nice saying that about our sister!" Will answered. „She's not that bad Ludwig! It's just that she's a girl, so she doesn't think the way we do... But that doesn't mean anything else. Girls are different, that's all!" „Yeah! Well, I'm going to send her to Paris, so you have a „chance" to spend a few days with her: It won't be long before they will have to put you into a madhouse...", Ludwig answered. Will laughed his heart out, then said: „Okay okay... I know it's not easy for you. But promise me you're going to stop teasing her all the time like you do! How do you think she feels when you're teasing her about her 'small breasts'... That's not very nice, you know..." „(...) Okay... I'll stop doing that...", Ludwig answered, with a sorry look on his face... „Thanks!", Will said, grinning... „Now, let's go home. It's getting dark and I guess Paul will be back soon..." – „You really love him, don't you?"

226

„Yes... With all my heart. I don't know what I would be doing without him..." „I'm happy for you Will... and Paul is such a nice guy..." „Thanks bro! (...) „And now, let's go home..."

When they got back home, they saw that Paul was already back and was having coffee with Will's mother... As Will and Ludwig entered the kitchen, Paul smiled at Will, and Will's mother looked at his eldest son as to ask if he had had a „talk" with Ludwig... Will looked at her and nodded, letting her know he had talked to Ludwig. She then said: „Fine! Now Ludwig, Will trusted you enough to tell you about a very important secret: Don't betray his trust..." – „I won't Mum! Don't worry! I love will... and I love you, too, Paul!" Paul looked at Ludwig, and with a big smile on his face, he told him: „Thanks Ludwig: You're a pal!" And turning to Will, Paul said: „And your mother and I had a pleasant talk while you were gone..." „I see... and I'm glad to see she didn't crucify you...", Will said laughing... „Hey you! I'm not Klara's mother, you know...", Will's mother said, laughing... „THANK GOD! I can't stand being in the same room with her and her nasty daughter..." Ludwig said... „I only wish they were not living on our street: I just keep bumping into them, and it makes me sick, just looking at them..."

„Did you know that when Klara's father bought their house, he paid almost nothing for it?" Will said to Paul... „After the Jewish family that used to live there had disappeared one night, he bought the house from a special agency at a ridiculously low price!" „Perhaps he didn't know about the real owners...", Paul said, looking at Will... „Oh no! He knew all too well... and it didn't bother him a bit...", Will's mother answered... „I wonder if they're Nazis?", Ludwig asked... „I don't know... and Lutz told me he doesn't know either! But one thing is certain: They do not disapprove of Hitler's politics...", Will said. „At least, they don't fly a Nazi flag in their front yard!", Paul said..."But that's only because they don't have a flagpole over there... and Klara's father is too cheap to buy one...", Ludwig answered laughing... After supper, they all enjoyed the evening, Ludwig being the funniest of all, as usual... For their last night in Berlin, Will's father opened a few bottles of champagne and as he walked to Lutz, who had joined the party with his parents, Herr von Rundstedt asked him, with a grin on his face: „I wonder if I should offer you another glass of champagne?" Quickly, and using his perfect imitation of Klara's voice, Ludwig said: „No no.... don't encourage that drunken scamp! One glass is already too many for him!" „Go to hell Klara!", Lutz answered, laughing is heart out... „Mind your language, young man...", Lutz's mother said, laughing... They were all laughing, and the fun continued into the night. But eventually, Lutz and his parents had to leave since the morning after, the three friends had to leave early for Tempelhof...

That morning, Lutz walked over to Will's house with his luggage and, as Will and Paul were about to leave, Will's mother kissed the three of them with tears in her eyes... „Take good care of one another... I love you! And Paul... you're always welcome here: Our door will always be opened for you..." „Thanks a lot. I've enjoyed my stay here so much, thanks to you all", Paul answered, smiling at Will's Mum. Will's father drove them to Tempelhof, along with Ludwig... At the terminal, they all hugged, and as Will and Paul were about to leave, Will's father said to Paul: „Take good care of Will: He's precious to me!" Will looked at his father with an interrogative face... „I was not born yesterday, son!", his Dad said, grinning. „Mum told you?" „... She knows?", Will's Dad asked, a bit surprised... „No. She didn't say anything to me..." „Oh!", Will answered... „If you ever want to talk with me about ... you know... You know where to find me, son! I love you..." „Thanks Dad... It means a lot to me! It's just that I didn't have the courage to tell you... I'm sorry!", Will answered. „...I understand son... But never forget that my love for my children is stronger than anything else. Never hesitate to come to me...", the man replied, smiling at his son. „Now go, and take good care of one another..." Will and Paul hugged the man, then walked over to where Ludwig and Lutz were standing. The hugged Ludwig, and Will told his brother, with a smile on his face: „Now remember: You stop teasing Karin, huh?" – „Yeah...", Ludwig answered, grinning... „And count on me bro: I'll do all I can to convince Dad to let you come to Paris next summer! And in the meantime, I suggest you take some French lessons..." „...That's what I intend to do...", Ludwig answered, with a big smile on his face... „Take good care bro! And you too, Paul..." Then, looking at Lutz, Ludwig said: „...And you... I hope you'll soon find yourself a good-looking girlfriend... And please, this time, don't choose a frigid one!" Lutz started laughing, then said: „Come here Ludwig, and give me a big hug!" They hugged, and minutes later, the three friends walked through the terminal, then over to their plane. As they were sitting aboard, waiting for take off, Lutz said to his friends, with a satisfied smile on his face: „Now guys... back to

228

Paris!" „...Can't wait to be home...", Paul replied, looking at Will, with a very sexy smile on his face... „Ohhhhh... I suspect you have something on your mind...", Will replied, laughing... „...Just wait: I don't think we'll go to sleep early tonight!" „... But I'll bet you'll want to be in bed early though...", Will replied, still laughing... „You got it!", Paul answered, laughing. „Lutz: Don't leave me all alone with this guy... He's dangerous... He's going to rape me...", Will said... „How lucky you are! I only hope Franz is not working tonight... I would gladly let him rape me...", Lutz answered, laughing too... „Yeah... But don't forget what I told you about Franz: Take good care of him...", Paul said, looking at Lutz... „I know... I know... Don't worry: I won't hurt him!", Lutz answered, smiling... Later, as the plane was about to land at the Bourget Airport, Paul said: „Ah! La douce France!" „Paris, we warn you: We're back", Lutz shouted, laughing... „...Yeah. Let's go home!" Will added... „Home?", Paul asked Will... „Yes: My home is where you are, and nowhere else...", he answered, smiling...

„... I love you Will, do you know that?" „I think I do..." „... Wait till we get home...", Paul said... „Just wait!!!" „Oh boy!", Will answered... It's going to be a long night..." „Un-huh!", Paul answered, grinning...

FIFTEEN
«IT HURTS SO MUCH...»

„Franz will be happy to learn it's over between Lutz and Klara...", Will said to Paul, grinning... „Yeah... But I'm not so sure it's a very good news though...", Paul answered. „Why's that?" „...As long as Lutz was going out with Klara, he wasn't fooling around, here in Paris... And since she was far away in Berlin, Franz didn't see her as a real threat... But now that Lutz is a free man, I'm sure it won't take long before he starts looking around and with his good look, he won't have troubles finding all the women he wants... You know how women keep looking at him, so..." „...You think that he..." „I don't know Will, I don't know! But I think Franz shouldn't celebrate too soon..." – „Shit! I din't see it that way..." „Yeah!"

The winter of 1941 went, and in April, everybody was happy to see spring coming back... During that winter, Will had received many letters from his brother Ludwig who had succeeded convincing their parents to let him go to Paris at the end of June, to spend the summer there with Will and Paul. Will had no doubt Ludwig had kept harassing their parents about that all winter long, and he smiled to himself, thinking that his parents had probably given up, being tired out by Ludwig's ceaseless demands... In the end, it had been agreed Ludwig would be staying with Will at Paul's mansion, and that from time to time, he would also come to Bagatelle. All Ludwig was now waiting for was for school to end in mid-June, and he was counting the days. Sometimes, Will would receive a letter from him where the only thing he had written would be like: „Plus que trente-trois jours..." And Will had to admit Ludwig had made lots of progress in French during the winter! Again, Will smiled to himself thinking that when Ludwig had something on his mind, nothing could stop him from realizing it...

During that winter, Lutz and Franz were together a lot, and it was obvious Franz was walking on clouds: He couldn't have been happier! „You were wrong about them...", Will had said to Paul, grinning... „I hope so, cause if the balloon bursts, Franz will fall from very high...", Paul had answered! „Oiseau de malheur!", Will had replied, laughing... „Nah! It's only that I know Lutz is straight. He's going to fall in love with some girl some day: That's bound to happen..." „...Have you ever considered he might be bi?" Will asked... „...Has he told you so?" „Are you kidding? I don't think he wants to talk about that...", Will answered. „...I'll believe it the day Franz tells me Lutz has kissed him! And as of this day, it just never happened! Franz told me..." „...Oh...", Will replied... „Yeah! Oh! Oh! Oh!" A few days later, the four friends were having supper at Paul's mansion when Lutz asked Paul: „... Are you two planning on going to Bagatelle next weekend?" „...We can't... We're going to the opéra next Saturday night...", Paul answered. „Oh..." Lutz replied, with a very disappointed look on his face... „Why do you ask?", Paul said... „Oh it's just that I thought it would have been fun to go... The weather forcast is very good for the weekend...", Lutz answered. „...You don't need us to be there, you know... If you want to go, just say so... I'll just call my manager at Bagatelle to let him know you'll be there for the weekend...", Paul replied, smiling... „Are you serious?", Lutz said, with a very big smile on his face... „Hey! How could I say no to such a good-looking dude like you?", Paul answered, laughing... „And I presume this guy here will go along with you?", Paul added, looking at Franz... „...Now that you ask...", Franz answered, laughing... „Okay then... I'll call my manager first thing tomorrow morning..." „Thanks a lot, pal!", Lutz answered beaming... „Sure", Paul replied, smiling...

That Friday, Lutz and Franz left Paris for Bagatelle and once there, they went to La Vacherie, where food and drinks had been kept in store for them by Paul's manager... When they got there, it was late at night but the night was quite warm for a May night... „Hey! You know the rule around here", Lutz said, grinning... „No clothing..." Franz gave a look to his curly blond friend and smiled when noticing Lutz already had a sizeable bulge in his pants... Without a word, Franz walked over to Lutz, knelt in front of him and moved over to his crotch. He unzipped his pants and slowly pulled his hard dick out through the slit in his underwear. With his hot tongue, he licked a drop of clear precum from the beautiful cock head,

232

then put the head into his mouth and started sucking and licking it... „I love it when you do that...", Lutz said, moaning... Then Franz undid Lutz's belt buckle and the top button on his pants and pulled them down to his ankles. He maneuvered Lutz's big hard dick out of his underwear then pushed them down as well. In a swift move, Lutz sent his pants, underwear and socks flying to the other side of the room... One at the time, Franz began kissing and licking Lutz's firm and muscled thighs, running his hot tongue all over them, then kissing and nibbling on Lutz's inner thighs. When Franz's right hand reached Lutz's balls, he gave them a tender squeeze and a light tug. Then he began to tongue bath them... „...Ohhhhh", Lutz whispered... Before long, Franz was working on Lutz's big oozing and pulsing prick again. With his tongue, he started to stroke up and down the full length of the thick cock and soon after, he began deep throating Lutz's dick in his mouth... Lutz moaned when he felt his dick enter Franz's hot velvety mouth... While deep throating Lutz's massive dick in his mouth, Franz reached around Lutz's body and cupped his firm ass cheeks. He started to slowly massage the firm ass globes with his strong hands, his right hand rapidly locating Lutz's moist hole. Lutz moaned lightly, wiggling his bum. Franz middle finger slid between Lutz's magnificently tight ass cheeks and began to caress his sweet moist asshole, as Lutz kept wiggling his ass. Soon the tip of Franz's middle finger entered Lutz's sweet hole. Lutz grunted, feeling Franz's finger wiggling around inside his bum. When Franz's finger located Lutz's tender prostate, Lutz cried out: „Oh shit man! Keep doing that... Yeah! You got it man..." Franz was still working on Lutz's oozing cock, taking it down his throat like he'd been doing this all of his life, while his finger kept massaging his walnut. „Ahhhh shit Franz! I want you to fuck me... pleaaaaaase, fuck me... I need it bad man..." Franz looked up at Lutz's beautiful face and, letting go of his dick, he smiled at his friend. He then rose and, in no time, he was out of his clothes...

Franz moved around behind Lutz, who was standing up, his legs largely spread apart... Franz walked to Lutz from behind, taking his friend's muscular body into his strong arms, pressing his chest on to Lutz's massive back that tapered to a small waist and perfectly sculpted ass. Franz felt his big dick squished between Lutz's firm ass cheeks: It felt so good there! Franz was oozing non-stop! With his arms wrapped around Lutz, Franz kissed his friend's muscular shoulder and, from

233

behind, he ran his hands down Lutz's well defined pecs where he started to rub and tweak his tender nipples. Lutz moaned loudly, feeling his erect nipples rubbed and pinched by Franz, who was also nibbling on his left ear lobe...

„Man... I've got to admit... you're getting good at it... Are you sure you're not getting some experience with some other guys without telling me?", Lutz said, grinning... „Nah. Besides... you wouldn't care even if I were fucking with other guys, huh? Remember dude what you told me: No strings attached...", Franz answered, grinning... „Well... yeah... but I mean... You would tell me if you were fucking with someone else, wouldn't you?" Lutz asked... „Why would I tell you? Would you tell me if you were fucking with another guy... or with a girl for that matter" Lutz had never thought about it that way... He had never thought about how Franz would feel if one day, he were to tell him that he was having sex with a girl... It had never crossed his mind before... „Well... that wouldn't be the same...", Lutz started to say... „Ah shut up Lutz, before you say some stupidity! Just enjoy what I'm doing to your sexy body... Don't you like what I'm doing?" „Oh shit yes... Don't stop!"

With his right hand, Franz reached down and felt Lutz's big cock throbbing and oozing lots of precum into his hand. Franz started wanking it, and Lutz began to moan again. And again, Franz was surprised that he could barely fit his large hand all the way around Lutz's thick cook... This reality kept surprising him... As his dick was being slowly fisted by Franz, Lutz wiggled his ass, feeling Franz oozing dick hard pressed against his arse crack... „It's so warm between your tight ass cheeks...", Franz said... Lutz sighed and looked back at Franz, saying: „Yeah... and now... I want to feel your hard prick deep inside me..." „Oh yeah? That's what you want, huh?", Franz answered grinning... „Stop teasing me: I know that's what you want, too...", Lutz replied laughing... „Big boy Lutz wants a dick up in his ass, huh?" „And you, is it my big fist you want to have on your face?", Lutz answered laughing... „I prefer my dick up in your ass... but under one condition though!" „Yeah... What's that?", Lutz answered grinning... „That right after, you'll fuck me..." „...Sure!" Lutz answered, still grinning...

„Okay pretty boy: Kneel on all fours...", Franz answered. Lutz went on all fours as Franz knelt behind him. He pushed his face into Lutz's ass crack, parted his tight, compact ass cheeks and started attacking his sweet asshole with his tongue and lips... „Ah! Shit! That feels good...", Lutz said moaning... „Do you think your next girlfriend will do that to you?", Franz asked, grinning... „Fuck! I'm not even sure she's going to be willing to give me head, so..." „Yeah..." Franz said, satisfied by Lutz's reaction... Lutz could feel Franz's hot tongue swirling all around his rosebud, licking it and kissing it... Then he felt Franz's hot slippery tongue darting at his ass... and it felt incredibly good... Franz gave Lutz a long, hot tongue bath. He took his middle finger to his mouth, lubed it well, then used it to caress Lutz's sweet moist asshole. It didn't take long before the tip of his finger was back into Lutz's asshole and again, Lutz grunted... Then Franz inserted a second finger, and when he started twisting around those two fingers deep inside his friend's bum, Lutz sighed... „Oh yeah! Put a third finger in there... come on...", Lutz cried out... Franz inserted a third finger and Lutz moaned again, wiggling his ass... „Now... go for it dude! Fuck me! Fuck me hard!" „Stand up... I want to fuck you while standing up...", Franz answered. They both rose to their feet and Lutz guided Franz's hard cock towards his asshole... Franz pushed his oozing dick forward into Lutz's beautiful round muscular ass: His cock slid into him easily, as he had done a superb job lubing it... It felt great! Lutz's asshole was hot and steamy, and it felt great, wrapped around Franz's hard prick. Franz couldn't believe how good it felt! He wrapped his arms around Lutz and started kissing his shoulder... „You smell so good Lutz... I love your smell..." He worked his tongue all around Lutz neck, then to his right ear, giving it a good tongue bath... He spit into his right hand, then went down to Lutz throbbing thick dick and started to slowly masturbate his friend... „Ohhhhh Yeah!", Lutz shouted out... Franz started to fuck Lutz's hot ass slow and steady with even strokes, sliding his big and slippery dick in and out of his hot tight ass. As he ran his left hand down Lutz's well defined pecs, Franz found his erect nipple, and started to rub and tweak it.... „Oh dude: I'm in heaven...", Lutz whispered... Hearing that, Franz started to fuck Lutz faster and harder, hitting his G-spot with each trust of his dick... Lutz was gasping and shouting: He loved the feeling... „You're a natural... You're so good... I can't believe it!", Lutz said, groaning and moaning... Franz grinned, still fisting Lutz's thick, throbbing dick... „Faster Franz... come on dude: Fuck me faster!" Franz went into overdrive, slamming his hips into Lutz's hot ass, driving his big dick in and out as fast as he could. „YEAH!", Lutz cried out, gasping with lust. „Y E A H! That's it!" Franz knew he had to get off soon... he had gotten so hot... „Keep wanking my dick, you bastard! I love it! I need it...", Lutz shouted... As Franz's big dick was stimulating his love spot, Lutz cried out: „...Oh shit Franz: I'm going to shoot... I can't hold it anymore. I can't" As Franz bucked his body up against Lutz's as hard as he could, Lutz started to shoot torrents of cum into his friend's slippery hand... „Ahhhhhhhhh Franz.... I'm cummmmmming... SHIT!" Franz was out of control now and he forced Lutz to lean a bit as he leaned over his back, grabbing at his friend's chest and squeezing him as tightly as possible... „Oh my God, Lutz: I'm cumming deep inside you..." „...Yeah! I want to feel your hot cum deep inside me. Cum, Franz! Cum..." Franz held on to Lutz as tightly as possible and when he felt Lutz's ass muscle squeeze his dick deep inside him, he shot volley after volley of his young hot cum inside him... He couldn't get enough of Lutz, and held on to him tightly as he pushed and shoved his dick into his friend until he was totally spent. And even then, his body continued to jerk involuntarily as he lay on Lutz's back... Seconds later, Franz let go of Lutz dick and brought his cum covered hand to his mouth, licking Lutz's hot cum from it... „Umm... you taste so good...", he said... „Good to the last drop!" „...That was soooooo good Franz!" Lutz answered, grinning... „You like my cum?" „Yeah... want a taste of it?"

Before Lutz had a chance to answerer, Franz took Lutz's beautiful face into his hands, turned it, and started cum-kissing him with his full lips... A bit later, as their lips parted, Lutz said: „Hey... I told you: No kissing!" „Oh but I wasn't kissing you... I was just sharing your cum with you... That's not the same...", Franz answered, grinning... „Yeah... well..." „Oh shut up, Lutz!", Franz replied laughing... „Well, sure... Just don't do that again...", Lutz answered grinning... „Yeah! Sure! You just can't admit you loved it..." „Go to hell!", Lutz answered, laughing... „Now, it's my turn to be fucked! Ready dude?", Franz asked... „Just a minute. I'm all sweaty... Let's take a shower first: What do you think?" „Okay. Let's do it together..." Lutz walked to the shower and when Franz joined him there, he was already standing under streaming water. Franz stepped in, but realized the shower was pretty small, and that there was just enough room for the two of them... Lutz began to soap and wash Franz's back when Franz turned around and put his muscular arms around Lutz's neck and pushed his tongue inside his friend's mouth. It didn't take long before Lutz pushed Franz away from him, then he said: „Hey! No kissing! I told you... I'm not gay, and you know it! That's the deal, remember?" „Yeah, yeah! I know... But you can't blame a guy for trying to steal a kiss from such a beautiful stud... I mean... you're so gorgeous Lutz..." „...I told you: Don't fall in love with me now..." – „I know, I know... I'm not!" Franz smiled to himself, thinking he was not „starting" to fall in love with Lutz: He was already madly in love with him! Lutz went back washing Franz's back, and Franz felt Lutz's hard dick pressed against his asshole. He sighed and looked back at Lutz, saying: „Take me, Lutz, please! I need your throbbing dick deep inside me..." „...I've got to take a piss first...", Lutz answered... „Ah come on Lutz... Can't you hold on?" „...Well... maybe..." „Just fuck me... Just do it! N O W!", Franz pleaded...

Lutz went down on his knees, behind Franz, who stretched his arms in front of him to rest against the shower wall... Lutz parted Franz's firm ass cheeks and with his hot tongue, he went right to his friend's asshole... When Lutz started to wiggle his hot tongue all around Franz sweet hole, Franz began moaning and started to swivel his bum... Lutz tongue entered Franz's hot tight hole and went inside it, as deep as he could... „That's so hot, Lutz... I wish I had known about that a lot sooner..." Lutz left hand let go of one of Franz's ass globes and went between his parted legs to find his big balls. As soon as he found them, Lutz gave them a tender squeeze and a light tug, while his tongue kept darting in and out of Franz's asshole... By now, Franz was panting and sweating so much, his muscled body started to glisten... He was so hot! He thought about turning the shower on again... but refrained from doing so, not wanting to ruin the good lube job Lutz was doing on his tender asshole... „Put your thick dick inside me Lutz: Go all the way in, please! I'm bracing myself..." Lutz rose to his feet and lined up his throbbing dick with Franz's asshole, then started to enter him... Franz gasped when he felt Lutz's thick shaft force its way through his tight ass ring... He did his best to relax his ass muscle and seconds later, Lutz was all the way in, up to the hilt! „I know Franz...", Lutz whispered into his ear... „I know... I won't move before you tell me to... relax... The pain won't last!" Without moving his dick, Lutz pressed his muscular body against Franz's back... wrapped him in a tight embrace and ran his hand down Franz's well defined pecs and started to rub and tweak his hard nipples... Franz moaned when he felt Lutz's hand work its way down on his torso to his cock, where he

237

started to play with his oozing dick... „Ohhhhhhh That feels sooooo good! I love it when you wank my dick...", Franz said, moaning... „How are you holding up pal?", Lutz tenderly asked... „...I'm doing great now... You can start fucking me... but go slowly at first!", Franz answered, with a grin on his face... „...I can see you're having a good time: Your cock is throbbing and dripping so much precum into my hand...", Lutz

replied, nibbling on Franz's ear-lobe... Franz sucked in a quick breath as he felt Lutz's dick slowly move in and out of his hot love chute. Then, Franz moaned and wiggled his hips as his lover's hard shaft started to slide in and out of his ass a little faster... Obviously, Franz was loving this, his muscular body being lifted with every thrust of Lutz's big dick up his ass... Lutz resumed jacking Franz's big cock as if he was working on his own dick... „Oh God, Lutz: I love feeling your slippery hand going up and down on my shaft... Go on! I love it..." Franz took the opportunity to contract his ass muscle from the outside in and back, causing Lutz to feel like his thick dick was being massaged... „Oh shit... Franz... You're good: Keep doing that...", Lutz whispered, slowly fisting Franz's cock... „I'm so close...", Franz whispered... „Let's not move for a while... Okay? I don't want us to cum too soon... I want the pleasure to last a little longer...", Lutz said... „Yeah!" A bit later, Franz felt Lutz's cock moving around inside his ass and he sighed... Then, Lutz went wild, slam fucking Franz's ass like a wild animal... slamming and thrusting his dick into his tight ass... Franz felt his cock throb uncontrollably into Lutz hand, who kept stroking it faster and faster... Franz'z dick began to get so hard, it took only a few more strokes before he started to cum... „Ahhhhhhh Y E A H!", Franz shouted! Lutz bucked his body up against Franz as hard as he could: He was out of control as he leaned over Franz's back, squeezing his friend's dick. Then Lutz felt his cum rise from his balls, and he started to shoot volley after volley of his hot cum deep inside Franz. He couldn't get enough of him. He held on to him tightly as he pushed and shoved his big dick into him. His body shook with the feeling of complete release and utter pleasure at the act... „You're so tight Franz... Your ass is so hot!" „... That was good...", Franz answered, still shaking.... „That was so good..." „I know", Lutz answered, grinning... „This has been one hell of a fuck!"

„... Are you still cumming inside me?", Franz asked, feeling something hot flowing deep inside his arse... „...No...", Lutz answered, giggling...

„I'm sorry, but I couldn't hold it anylonger..." „.... Are you pissing in me?", Franz asked in disbelief... „Y E A H... and it feels so good..." Franz could feel his back passage expanding to take the quantity of fluid being forced into it and he groaned, loving how it felt... Although he was giving it to Franz from behind, Lutz nonetheless caught a look of disbelieving glee on Franz's face as he experienced the feeling of being used as his piss dump! „That's gross"... Franz said, disconcerted... „Yeah! And you love it as much as I do...", Lutz answered, laughing... Lutz resumed fucking Franz, still pissing inside him: Once he'd started, he couldn't hold it back... The sensation of piss fucking was truly remarkable... Now that he'd finished pissing, Lutz began to fuck Franz forcefully, repeatedly and roughly, withdrawing and re- entering his arse, fucking him as deeply as he could... „Your chute is so wet and velvety... It feels incredible...", Lutz said, gasping...

Then Lutz decided he wanted Franz to ride him: He pulled out his cock, then lay on the shower floor. There was not much room, but just enough... „Come on Franz... Sit on me... sit over my dick!" – „Oh! What the hell!", Franz answered, grinning... He parted his ass cheeks and sat over Lutz's thick dick. It entered him again in one swift movement, but as it did so, the further loosening of his sphincter and the change of position led do the piss gushing out of his arse. They both started laughing... Before long, the wet warm piss was all over Lutz's blond pubes and groin area and as Franz began to ride up and down on him, his buttocks became wet with it too. As he was sitting over Lutz with his legs bent, Lutz was able to thrust up into his friend, as well as Franz to drive himself down onto him. „Oh shit... That's so hot...", Lutz shouted, panting and sweating... Lutz grabbed Franz's throbbing dick and started jacking it, faster and faster... Franz sucked in a quick breath, loving the feeling of having his cock wanked by such an expert hand... When Franz went into overdrive, slamming his ass on Lutz's shaft, Lutz could tell he was about to shoot... „Ahhhhhhh", Franz cried out, as he let his third orgasm of the night engulf his body. He shot his hot load into Lutz's hand and all over his friend's well defined pecs... As he was shooting his jizz, Franz squeezed Lutz's cock with his ass ring and Lutz barely managed to thrust two or three more times before spurting a wad of young spunk deep into Franz's hot and slippery arse: The feeling of orgasm went through him several times before he was done... „That was just incredible, wasn't it?", Lutz asked Franz, still panting... „...Sure was...", Franz answered, grinning... „I just can't believe you did what you did: To piss inside me... I mean..." – „Yeah!", a laughing Lutz replied... „How did it feel?" „(...) I'm ashamed to admit it... but I loved it! But don't you ever tell anyone about it... You swear to me?" – „...Okay, I swear!", Lutz answered, still laughing... Franz pulled off from Lutz and smiled to him, saying: „I guess a good shower is in order, what do you think?" „Not a bad idea", Lutz answered, grinning... „We are a bit messy, aren't we?" – „...To say the least...", Franz replied, laughing... After a long shower, the two friends went to bed as they were totally exhausted... Lutz wrapped Franz entirely in his strong arms and whispered to him: „...That was a hell of a night... Thanks pal! You are the best!" Franz was so happy, being held like that by Lutz. If it only meant Lutz was beginning to fall in love with him! But Franz knew better than that: He knew it only meant Lutz was a satisfied jock! Nevertheless, Franz felt happy and he sighed before saying: „...Night Lutz..." „...Night Franz..."

They didn't wake until late the next morning! The awaking was only more brutal for Franz when, back in Paris and only a few days later, he saw Lutz in a restaurant, sitting at a table with a girl, holding her hand and kissing her... Franz felt as if a train had hit him! He couldn't believe his eyes! A sharp pain invaded his whole body and he began to shake... „Monsieur désire t-il une table?", a young waitress asked him... „Huh? (...) NO... sorry... I've changed my mind, thank you", Franz politely answered, knowing Lutz had not seen him... He quietly walked out of the restaurant and once on the sidewalk, he leaned against a building. He felt sick, and didn't know what to do... Paul was sitting at his desk at the head office, reading some reports, when Mrs Mercier, his secretary called him: „... Sir... I have someone here who says he is your friend... and... well, Sir, I think you should come..." In a second, Paul was out of his office and as he walked over to his secretary, he saw Franz standing there, not looking well at all... „...Thank you madame Mercier... I'll take care of my friend here... Thank you!" – „.... Do you need...", madame Mercier started to say... „...Everything will be alright, don't worry...", Paul answered. Paul took Franz by the arm and walked him over to his office... Once the door was closed, Franz exploded and started to cry like a baby... Paul took him in his arms, and hold him tight against his strong body. „Go on Franz... Let it out..." „Thanks", Franz muttered, sobbing... „Now now! Nothing can

240

be so bad Franz. Come, and sit..." It didn't help saying that since Franz started to cry all over again... and kept crying until he had no tears left...

Paul took his phone and asked his secretary to call the Swiss embassy. Minutes later, he had the ambassador on the line, telling him Franz was here with him but was not feeling well. He reassured the ambassador, explained Franz only needed some rest... and told him he would certainly be back at work next Monday... Paul hung up the phone and, looking at Franz, he said: „Now, you come with me pal! We're going home!" Franz looked at his friend, with a dazed look on his face... „You're not going back to your place in that condition: You're going to spend the night on Avenue Foch... Come on: Let's go!" Franz followed Paul without saying a word. On their way to Avenue Foch, not a work was spoken. Once there, a strong coffee was served... and Paul finally said: „... Do you want to tell me what's wrong?" Between sobs, Franz explained to Paul what he had seen at the restaurant earlier that day... „I see... Sooner or later, it was bound to happen...", Paul said. „Did you know he was seeing that girl?", Franz asked... „No Franz... I don't even know who she is..." „He never said anything about her?" „(...)" „And thanks for not saying it..." „What?", Paul asked. „You know... the „I told you so..." remark... „Oh... I don't think it would be very useful to say that..." „Nevertheless, you did tell me I was playing a dangerous game... and now, it hurts so much... What should I do?" – „Are you really asking me?" „...Yes Paul... You're my best friend..." „You won't like my answer..." – „Go ahead..." „Okay. I think you should stop seeing, Lutz! Oh, I don't blame him, you know... He has been honest with you all along... But if you don't stop seeing him right now, it's going to destroy you... bit by bit..." „...But I love him so much..." „I know! And I'm sorry for saying it, but you're loosing your time... and what's worst is that while you keep seeing Lutz, you're not looking for anyone else... All you have in mind is Lutz! How can you fall in love with someone else if you see no one else but him?" „...There is nobody else I'm interested in..." „Precisely! Even if the most interesting guy was standing naked right in front of you, you wouldn't see him!" – „...If he had a nice dick... at least, I would look at it...", Franz replied, with a small smile on his face... „It makes me feel good to see you smile..." „Yeah! Thanks!"

„Can you take some vacation away from the embassy?" „...They owe me two weeks..." „Good! Now, if you intend to take your destiny into

241

your own hands and put a stop to your relation with Lutz, you're going to have to talk to him to explain why you're doing it. Lutz is a good fellow... and I'm sure he'll understand. After that, you'll have to go away for a while..." „...Huh?" „Yes. Do you intend to lock yourself up at your place and feel miserable and sorry for yourself?" „...But... Where would I go?" „Listen: I was planning a business trip to Geneva... and after that, I have to go to Berlin, to meet with my business partners over there... and then bring Ludwig to Paris for the summer... So, come with me!" „... As much as I'd like to... I can't afford that... Besides, when you're in Berlin, I know you stay at Will's place: I don't want to stay there... I wouldn't feel at ease there..." „...First, you'll be my guest: Will can't come with me this time, so if you come with me, I won't feel lonely... Second: I'll ask my secretary to book two rooms at Hotel Adlon in Berlin... You'll see... You'll love it there! And we'll have fun!" „...You must be kidding?" „Not at all... We could leave on Monday. I could call Kurt Weiner, our private pilot, to see if he's available... What do you say?" „We would go by plane?" „Of course..." „(...) But... I never took a plane before..." „Don't tell me it scares you..." „...I don't know..." „Anyway, you'll love the experience, and I'm not giving you much of a choice: We're not going by train, that's for sure!", Paul answered, laughing... „Okay, okay... Fine... I'm going with you! I'll talk to Lutz tomorrow..." „Let me give Kurt a call..." Minutes later, Paul was back, with a big smile on his face: „It's settled: We're leaving Monday morning! Now I suggest you call your family in Geneva, to let them know... Use the phone in my study: I have a direct line with Geneva..." „...How can I thank you Paul? And you will stay at my home while in Geneva, won't you?" „Thanks Franz... But if you don't mind, I prefer to stay at the hotel over there: I'll have some meetings while I'm there, and it will be easier if I stay at the hotel..." „...As you wish... But you're most welcome to stay with my family..." – „I know... but thanks. Now, go make your call..." While Franz was in the study, making his call, Will came back from work and Paul quickly explained everything to him... „Oh shit! I feel sorry for Franz...", Will said... „And I feel sorry for myself, knowing you'll be away from me for two long weeks..." „Yeah! I wish you could come... If only you could dump your damn army!" – „I wish I could...", Will answered, grinning... „...Before you know it, I'll be back... And while I'm gone, spend some time with Lutz: I'm sure he's going to need you... Unless he's very „busy" with that girl..." „...Yeah! He never said anything to me about her..." „Yeah... Well, she's in the picture now! And we'll have to make sure Lutz doesn't drop by when Franz is here..." – „Right! But it makes me sad, you know... We had so much fun, the four of us..." „Yeah... But I guess we'll have to get used to it..."

When Franz came back to the drawing-room, seeing Will there, Franz said: „...Oh!... I guess Paul told you..." „Yes... And I'm sorry Franz!", Will answered... „...Yeah...", Franz replied, with tears in his eyes.

„Now guys, let's have supper and after that, Will will play the piano for us, won't you Will?", Paul asked... „My pleasure..." Later that evening, Franz gave Lutz a call, telling him he wanted to see him next evening... „Sure!", Lutz said... not knowing what Franz wanted to tell him... „Come whenever you want... I'll be in the flat..." Needless to say that, that night, Franz didn't sleep well.. The dreaded day came too fast, and as much as Paul tried to entertain his friend during that day, his efforts were a big failure! When the time came for Franz to leave for his meeting with Lutz, Paul said to him: „Take my car..." „I'm too nervous to drive...", Franz answered... „...Okay then... I'll drive you there, and I'll be waiting for you in the car..." – „Would you do that?" „No problem pal!", Paul answered, smiling at his friend... „Let's go!" They drove to Lutz's flat and as Franz was about to get off the car, Paul told him: „I'll be waiting for you here... Take your time... and good luck my friend!" – „Thanks... If I had the choice, I'd go to the slaughter-house instead!" – „...Remember: Lutz is a nice guy..." „I know: I'm in love with that guy, remember?" „... Go now!..."

SIXTEEN
« I CAN'T GO ON ...»

„Hey! What's up?", Lutz asked, smiling, as he opened the door to Franz... „Hi Lutz!" „...Well... Don't stand there like that... come in...", Lutz said, taking Franz by the arm... „Thanks... but I won't stay long...", Franz replied. „What's wrong? You have the face of a man who's coming from a funeral...", Lutz jokingly said... „...I feel like that, too...", Franz answered. „Come here and sit Lutz... there's something very important I want to tell you. That's the reason why I came tonight..." „Oh?" „Yeah. (...)" „...Well?... Come on Franz, speak up, will you?" „(...) Well... you see... I think... I think it's best for us we stop seeing each other...", Franz finally said. „What? What do you mean? What did I do? (...) Is it because of that „piss" thing the other day?", a stunned Lutz asked. „...Oh no, no... It's not that at all... In fact, I really loved that...", Franz answered, grinning... „Then why?" „...You see Lutz... I've broken my promise to you... I lied to you..." „What do you mean you lied to me?" „...Remember... You made me promise I wouldn't fall in love with you?... and each time you brought the subject, I told you I wasn't in love with you? (...) Well, I lied! I'm really in love with you Lutz... So much so that it hurts! You can't believe how much I love you", Franz said with tears flowing out of his eyes... „...Oh come on Franz... Don't cry like that, please!", Lutz said, totally disorientated... „Don't worry... I won't bother you very long..." „Shit Franz... that's not what I meant... you're not bothering me at all...", Lutz answered, not knowing what to do. So he took Franz into his arms and said: „Come on now..." „...You see Lutz... for months now, I've been dreaming you would fall in love with me... That we would be kissing... that I would be able to tell you how much I love you... that I would finally hear you say you love me. But I realize now it's only a dream... and that dream is killing me bit by bit... I can't

245

take it any more... It's driving me mad! And I don't blame you: You've always been very honest with me! So I guess the only thing left for me to do is to stop seeing you... It's going to hurt like hell... I know... but there's no way out..." „But I don't want you to stop seeing me...", Lutz alarmingly said... Franz slowly released himself from Lutz's tight embrace then, with a very tender smile, he said: „...I'm sure you will survive Lutz... And I'm sure it won't take long before you meet a nice girl... if you haven't already, that is..." „...What do you mean?" „As I said... You've always been honest with me Lutz, so I'll be honest with you too: I saw you the other day in a restaurant with a beautiful girl... I saw you holding her hand and kissing her..." „...Oh, so that's why you come here tonight and tell me we have to stop seeing each other, isn't it? Would you be jealous?" Franz looked Lutz straight in the eyes and calmly answered: „Yes Lutz, I'm jealous... I'm jealous of her! I wish I were her... I wish you could kiss me like you kissed her... But I'm not her! And you will never kiss me the way you kissed her! That's what made me realize I'm chasing after an impossible dream! That dream will never come true! I can't spend my life going after such an impossible dream. Just like you Lutz, I have the right to know happiness, you know..." „...What can I say to make you change your mind? What, huh?" Franz tenderly smiled to his friend and answered: „Nothing! There's nothing you can say, because there's nothing you can do about how I feel... You can not change my feelings for you!" Franz slowly rose and gave a last look to Lutz, who was only wearing a tight T-shirt and a pair of cut-off pants. Franz looked at his strong shoulders and well defined pecs under his T-shirt... Then he looked at his curly blond hair and his beautiful blue eyes... as blue as the Mediterranean Sea... „God! You're so beautiful Lutz... I could lose myself into your gorgeous blue eyes... I'll never forget you Lutz! And I'll always love you: I don't think I'll ever stop loving you! But at least, I'll give it a try..." „...Don't leave me like that Franz... Please don't!", Lutz answered with tears in his eyes... „...Sorry Lutz! I've got to go now..." Franz left the flat as fast as he could and seconds later, he was sitting inside Paul's car... „Let's get the hell out of here before I change my mind...", he said to Paul. As planned, Franz spent that night at Paul's mansion, but he couldn't find sleep. From their bedroom, Will and Paul could hear him crying... After a while, Will said to Paul: „Go see him... We can't leave him alone like that, can we?" „...No..." Paul rose from bed, put his shorts on and said to Will: „Put your shorts on... I'll go get him..." Paul walked over to Franz's bedroom and, through the door he said: „Franz? Can I come in?" „Yeah", Franz sobered out... Paul went to his bed where he sat and looked at his blond haired friend... „I wish I could say something to help you... but I'm afraid there are no words to soothe such a pain... Come Franz: You'll spend the night with Will and me. At least, you won't be alone... That's the best we can do to help you..." They walked back to Paul's bedroom, and Franz went to bed, where he lay down between Will and Paul... „Now try to go to sleep Franz...", Paul said to him... „I'll try... And thanks guys: You're the best!" „Hey, we love you Franz: If you cry, we cry...", Will answered, smiling... „Thanks..." Later that night, as Will and Paul were sound asleep, Franz finally fell asleep, cuddled up close to his two friend's strong and warm bodies. He had stopped crying: He had no more tears left to shed. Before Franz had too much time to think, he was sitting next to Paul aboard a plane, ready to take off from the Bourget Airport... „How come it's so long before we take off?", Paul asked Kurt, their pilot... „I don't know, Paul... Air traffic it very very heavy... The Luftwaffe is moving out thousands of planes to the East..." „To Germany?", Paul asked... „No... farther East... To Poland I'd say... but even the pilots don't know for sure until they board their planes... and until they land at their final destination, radio communications are strictly forbidden...", Kurt answered. „What the hell is going on?", Paul asked...

„I swear I don't know...", the pilot sincerely answered... After a long wait... they were finally authorized to take off... Paul could sense Franz was all tensed up... „Your first time flying... that's why you're all tensed up like that, huh?" – „...Yeah!" „Scared?", Paul asked Franz... „A little..." „No reason to be... Here: Take my hand and hold it tight...", Paul answered, grinning... Soon after, they were flying to Geneva, and Franz started to relax. He even smiled! „That's better...", Paul said to him, smiling... When they landed at Geneva Airport, everything was quiet there... „...Quite a difference from Paris!", Paul said to Kurt... „Yeah!", the pilot answered, grinning... The week in Geneva went smoothly, as Franz stayed with his family, and Paul at the hotel with Kurt. Of course, they had seperate rooms, but at least, Paul was not alone all evenings long, as they had agreed to meet each evening for a drink at the bar, then for supper. Paul learned more about Kurt. He was a nice easy going guy. Since their trip to Berlin last December, Kurt had guessed Paul and Will were lovers. He told Paul so, but said he didn't give a damn about that, even though he was straight. Kurt was pretty well built, and very good-looking. He was a spirited man, and was always laughing. Paul liked that. „You know Paul? I think they roll back the sidewalks around here, after ten o'clock! I've never seen a place so dull in my life!", Kurt said to Paul one night, laughing... „It's not Paris, of course", Paul answered, laughing too... „But at least, we don't hear about that damn war around here!" „That's true... They are lucky not to be at war..." „Yeah. Same for Spain, Portugal and Sweden...", Paul added... „...You forgot to name Ireland...", Kurt answered, laughing... „True!", Paul answered, smiling... „I guess it's less dangerous when you live in small country..." „Oh, I'm not sure about that... Take Finland, Norway or Denmark! The fact they are small didn't save them, did it? And now, we've even invaded Yugoslavia and Greece... When I think the Nazi flag is now flying over the Acropolis..."

„Are you a Nazi Kurt?" „...Do I look like one?", Kurt answered, laughing... „Come on... I'm crazy, but not THAT crazy you know..." – „Sorry I asked...", Paul said, laughing... „...No problem! All I hope is that this damn war will end soon. After the war, I'd like to open a school, to teach clients how to fly..." „Hey... That's a great idea, you know..." „You think?" „Yes! And one day, I'm sure we'll be able to cross the Atlantic onboard commercial airplanes, you'll see...", Paul said. „I'm sure of that, too... But for now, let's go to bed: We're leaving tomorrow for Berlin, aren't we?" „Yeah!", Paul answered. „Franz will be here at ten o'clock, so we can be at the Airport on time..." „Fine...", Kurt answered, smiling... They left Geneva on schedule, but it took a lot of time before they were authorized to land at Tempelhof... „Why do we keep circling Berlin like that?", Paul asked Kurt... „...Lots of air traffic", Kurt answered... „And that's not normal... What the hell in going on here?", he added... „...Don't ask me!", Paul answered, grinning... And when they were finally authorized to land, Franz said: „Not too soon!" Paul and Franz went to Hotel Adlon, where they were expected. Everything was quite normal in Berlin... and nobody could explain to Paul why they had encountered so much air traffic at Tempelhof... Of course, as soon as he got to the Hotel, Paul gave a call to Will's family... Will's Mum told him she already knew he was in town, since Will had called to let them know... And they were expecting Paul and Franz for supper the night after: Ludwig was eager to see Paul, and needless to say he was more than ready to leave for Paris with his luggage... Will's Mum also said she had invited Lutz's older brother for supper, since he was back from Norway, on leave in Berlin for a few days... „Have you ever met Hans?", Will's Mum asked Paul... „No. But Lutz told me a lot about his older brother...", Paul answered her. „Ah! Hans said the same about you", Will's Mum answered, laughing... „He said Lutz wrote a lot about you in his letters to him..." After he had hung up the phone, Paul started to think whether or not it was a good idea to have Franz in the same room as Lutz's brother... but Franz said he didn't care... They went to Will's home, and had a lot of fun there, as Ludwig never stopped cracking jokes... „Did you know that since Lutz broke up with Klara last December, she hasn't said a word to me... When I bump into her, she acts as if she doesn't know me..." Ludwig said to Paul, laughing... „Not that I care: She's a bitch..." Paul looked at Franz... and was relieved to see he was laughing too... „So Hans... I understand you're back from Norway...", Paul asked him... „Yes... And I'm not going back there... My regiment is being transferred to Poland...", Hans answered... „What?", Paul exclaimed... „You, too? What's going on in Poland? The Luftwaffe is actually transferring thousands of planes over there..." „... I don't know", Hans pensively answered. „I don't know... They told us nothing about that... just that the day after tomorrow, we would be on our way to Poland: That's all!" „... Is there a rebellion or something going on over there?", Will's Dad asked Hans... „Not that I know of...", Hans answered.

During that evening, Paul had time to observe Hans... He didn't look like Lutz at all, Paul thought. Instead of blond hair like Lutz, Hans had short curly brown hair, beautiful brown eyes... square jaws, and was taller than Lutz: Probably 1.95 m, Paul thought. Hans was as masculine as Lutz though, and his masculinity was transpiring through each and every pore of his skin... He was strikingly good-looking, and acted as if he had never realized that... As they were leaving, Hans looked at Paul and Franz and said: „Hey guys: It's my last night in Berlin, tomorrow night... What are you doing tomorrow night?" „... Nothing is planned up...", Paul answered... „Good! We could go some place, and have some fun..." „...Sure... that would be fun!", Paul answered, smiling... „Hey: I want to go with you guys!", Ludwig said... „... I guess you're still a bit too young to enter night clubs my poor Ludwig...", Hans answered, with a sorrow smile on his face... „Shit!", Ludwig answered... „...Sorry...", Hans said.

249

Then, turning to Paul, he said: „I could be at Hotel Adlon at nine o'clock tomorrow night... and from there, we could go to a place I know, and have a drink..." „Fine!", Paul and Franz answered... As planned, the three friends met at nine o'clock the night after... and they all went to one of the last night clubs still opened in Berlin... „Hitler has ordered almost all of the others closed...", Hans said, as they walked into the night club he had choosen... „... Yeah! I know...", Paul answered, with a sad smile on his face. „I'm sure that in Paris, it's quite different... Lutz is very lucky to be stationed over there... and tell me: Since the time he broke up with Klara, has he made a new girlfriend in Paris?", Hans asked Paul... „Oh... He did!", Franz answered, smiling at Hans... „He's very popular with women, you know..." – „That's my baby brother!", Hans answered, laughing... „You're Swiss, aren't you Franz?", he asked... „... Don't tell me about my Swiss accent, PLEASE!", Franz answered, laughing... „No, no...", Hans answered, laughing... „It's just that Lutz never said anything about you in his letters to me..." Franz kept smiling, although deep inside him, he felt very hurt, hearing that... How come Lutz had not even said a word about him to his brother? How was that possible? After all they had been through... Not a word! He had been Lutz's lover for almost a year, and Lutz had not even mentioned his name to his brother! Shit! „... Well... I guess he's too busy with women...", Franz answered, laughing... „Yeah! That's Lutz alright!", Hans joyfully answered... After a few drinks, the three friends parted since Hans had to leave early for Poland the day after... „I wish you good luck Hans", Paul said, shaking his hand. „And I hope you'll be able some day to come to Paris... You'll always be welcome there..." „Thanks a lot, pal! And tell Lutz to take good care...", Hans answered, smiling... „I will...", Paul answered. „Take good care Hans: You'll always be welcome in Geneva too...", Franz said to him, shaking his hand... „And take care, too, pal... It's been fun meeting you...", Hans answered, smiling... The night after, Will's Dad drove Ludwig to Hotel Adlon, where he had to spend the night with Franz and Paul, since they all had to leave early for the Airport... „... You're going to have to share a bed with me Ludwig", Paul told him... „...I just couldn't get another room for you... I don't know what's going on here, but the Hotel is booked up!", Paul said to Ludwig, with a sad smile on his face... „Oh, no problem... except I have to tell you about that bladder problem I have...", Ludwig answered, laughing... „... If you piss on me, I'll kill you!", Paul answered, laughing... As they were ready to go to sleep, Paul looked at Ludwig... „What?", Ludwig asked... „It's just that the more you're getting older, the more you look like Will...", Paul answered, smiling... „Yeah! But just don't try to fuck me during the night, cause I'm not into that...", Ludwig answered, laughing his heart out... „... It's going to be hard to keep my dick away from your arse crack, you know...", Paul answered, as he burst out laughing... „...Keep trying, cause otherwise you'll lose your precious dick..." „I'll try... I'll try" Paul answered, still laughing... „And Ludwig?" „What?" „If you wank tonight, please don't shoot on me...", Paul said, still laughing... „Oh... No problem about that Paul: I've already wanked three times today... So... I should be okay for the night..." – „... Are you serious?", Paul answered... „Sure! Hey: I'll be sixteen next month... So...", Ludwig answered, laughing... „Okay, okay... But as I said, if you wank tonight, remember: Don't shoot on me!" „...I'll try to remember that... I guess Will wouldn't be happy if I did..." „Nope!", Paul answered, grinning... „Paul... Can I ask you a question?", Ludwig asked... „Sure!" „Do you and Will... well... do you really fuck?" „That's not a question to ask young man", Paul answered, a bit stunned by Ludwig's openness... „Why?", Ludwig answered... „I'm just curious... And if I don't ask you, who will tell me... Will won't tell me, I'm pretty

sure..." „...Well... Yes... We fuck!...", Paul cautiously answered... „And do you eat my brother's cum?"

„L U D W I G!", Paul shouted... „What?... I eat my own, so why not?" „You do that?", Paul asked... „Sure! And I like it...", Ludwig answered, grinning... „It tastes good you know..." „Oh stop that Ludwig: I feel horny now, because of you...", Paul answered. „You haven't answered my question..." „... Yes. I eat Will's cum, and he eats mine. Are you happy now? (...) Now, let's go to bed, and shut up: No more questions, you hear!", Paul answered. „Oh Paul?" „W H A T?" „If you wank during the night... please... don't cum on me... Please?" Ludwig said, laughing his heart out... „I can't believe we're having this discussion...", Paul answered, laughing... „Hey... I like you Paul. And do you know why? Cause you're honest with me! You're not a hypocrite! And do you know what? Although I'm not a homosexual, I'm not afraid going to bed with you tonight. Why? Cause I know you love my brother! I know you would never touch me..." „... You're so right Ludwig. I love you as I love my own brother! Now, give me a big hug, and let's go to bed... They hugged for a few seconds, then Ludwig said: „Hey: Unless I'm wrong... Since you're in love with Will... that makes you my brother-in-law, doesn't it?" „... Yup! I guess so...", Paul answered, laughing... „Good! So you're part of the family now..." „I hope so!", Paul answered... „Yes you are!" „Now, let's go to sleep, you silly..." „That's only because you want to abuse my young and very sexy body, huh?", Ludwig asked, laughing... „... It's true you've got a sexy body... but sorry: Will is sexier than you... and I just can't wait to hold him into my arms..." „You really love him, don't you?" „...You wouldn't believe how much, even if I was telling you..." „I'm happy for you two, Paul. Really! And thanks for letting me come to Paris! Without you, I know it wouldn't be possible..." „You're most welcome Ludwig. I'm so happy you're coming. And you don't know how much Will is... He loves you Ludwig!" „I know Paul... and I love him, too..." „... Now: INTO BED! F A S T!!!", Paul answered, trying to look stern... „... Yes mother!", Ludwig replied, laughing...

Early the morning after, they were raised by a call from Will's father: „Do you have a radio in your room?", the man asked... „... Yes", Paul answered. „Well... listen to Radio Berlin right now: Goebbels will be making a very important announcement in a few minutes... Call us back later, will you?" Will's Dad asked... „Yes", Paul intriguingly answered... „Get up", Paul said to Ludwig... „That was your father on the phone... He said we must listen to the radio... Goebbels is about to make a speach..." „Are you kidding? You want me to get out of the bed to listen to that rat? Why should we be listening to him anyway?", Ludwig answered, yawning... Paul ran to the radio and found Radio Berlin. At first, they heard a military band playing „Horst Wessel Lied"... „Oh shit! Not that song again... I can't stand it...", Paul said. But then, they heard Goebbels saying that, at three o'clock last night, the Reich had decided to invade russia, to stop in advance an invasion of Germany from that country... „... They are CRAZY!", Ludwig shouted... Paul immediatly called back Will's father... „Have you heard?", the man asked... „Yes!" „Please, Paul.... Take Ludwig out of the Reich as soon as you can. We trust you with his life..." – „You can count on me Sir: We'll be leaving soon..." „They say Tempelhof is closed now..." „Don't worry, Sir: I'll find a way out. Don't worry!", Paul answered... „...I know you will, Paul: I trust you! God bless you son!" „Thanks, Sir! God bless you, too... And as soon as we reach

Paris, we'll give you a call..." – „... All the phone lines with the outside world have been cut...", the man answered...

„... You trust me, Sir?" „Yes!" „So don't worry... We'll be out of here... And Ludwig will be safe with me, I swear to you... „... We love you son... And tell Ludwig we love him..." „...I will, Sir!" „Good luck!" „Thanks. I love you, too..." As soon as he hung up, Paul called Kurt, their pilot, who confirmed Tempelhof was closed to civilian air traffic... „... Okay", Paul answered... „Then, we'll leave by train... Are you coming with us?" „... I wish I could, but I can't. I have to stay here in Berlin, and wait for my orders..." „Is there something I can do for you?", Paul asked... „No Paul... but thanks! Take care...", Kurt answered. „You, too... take good care!", Paul replied. Paul, Franz and Ludwig ran to the railway station, where Paul bought first class tickets to Paris... „I hope you're not in a hurry, Sir: The military trains have high priority now..." „No problem", Paul answered, smiling at the clerk... „As long as we get there..." „Oh you will... you will... But it's going to take much longer than usual..." „...We don't care...", Paul answered. On their way to Paris, on many occasions, their train was diverted to railway sidings, and they watched many military convoys pass at full speed on the main line, loaded with hundreds of tanks and other armoured fighting vehicles... „...There're moving them to Russia...", Ludwig said, as such a convoy was passing by..." „... Yeah! At least, we know now why the Luftwaffe was moving out all those planes to Poland... and why Hans's regiment was sent there too..." „...Do you think he's fighting in Russia?", Ludwig asked, with a terrified look on his face... „... I don't think his regiment was part of the first wave that went into Russia, though he's probably in Poland by now... Maybe he'll be part of a second or a third wave...", Paul answered... „... I'm glad I'm not old enough to be in the army...", Ludwig answered. „Yeah! And I'm glad they're moving all those planes and tanks out of France... and I guess many regiments will also be moved from France and sent to Russia...", Paul said. „... Do you think Will and Lutz could be sent over there?", Ludwig asked... Paul smiled and answered: „Nah! They are translators... not fighting soldiers..." „...But they are soldiers nonetheless...", Ludwig said.

Paul had never looked at it that way. To him, Will and Lutz were non-combatant soldiers... so why would they be sent to the Russian front? The more he tought about it, the more he convinced himself that that didn't make sense... Things would have to take a very bad turn on that front, before soldiers like Will and Lutz would have to be sent to fight over there... The Wehrmacht is so powerful, Paul thought, the Russians are no match: Before long, this campaign will be over... and Hans will be back! Paul was sure about that! „... What are you thinking about?" Ludwig asked Paul... „...Oh... I was thinking about that campaign... I'm pretty sure it won't last long...", Paul answered, smiling at Ludwig... „Yeah... But Russia is a vast country you know... I wonder what the military objectives are...", Franz asked... „I don't know. Russia is such a backward country... I suppose the Wehrmacht will want to take Moscow though...", Paul answered. „..."Moscow" It's so far away...(...) Didn't Napoléon take Moscow back then?", Ludwig asked Paul... „...Yeah..." Paul answered, thinking about how catastrophic the Russian campaign had been for Napoléon's armies... Yes!, Paul thought, Napoléon had taken Moscow, but only to see the city burned to the ground by the Russians... Then winter had come, and hundred of thousands of French soldiers had starved to death... „...Wasn't Napoléon defeated by the Russians?", Franz asked... „No!" Paul answered... „He was beaten by „le général hiver!" „Who was that?", Ludwig asked... „... Winter... He was beaten by a General called „Winter"! All the Russians had to do was to wait and let winter do its job...", Paul answered. „...Well, that was then... Nowadays, things are different, aren't they?", Ludwig asked... „I suppose they are...", Paul slowly answered... „I suppose so..." „Hey! Let's play cards...", Franz joyfully said... „Good idea", Ludwig answered, smiling... After a long trip, but before they had reached Paris, Paul said to Ludwig:

„...Now, I've got to tell you about a few rules... and we expect you to go by those rules obediently..." – „...What are they?", Ludwig asked... „First, remember you're from Strasbourg. I've already explained that to you..." „Yes!" „Second rule: You'll speak German only with Will, Lutz and me... If someone else is present, never ever say a word in German... Now, your French is good, but not that good. So for now, keep your big mouth shut as much as you can... It's better for people to think you're shy than to discover you're German..." „...Me?... Shy?", Ludwig answered, laughing... Paul looked at Ludwig with very threatening eyes, but before he could say anything, Ludwig said: „...Okay, okay... I understand..." „Third rule: I've told you about „La Vacherie" at Bagatelle... This place is secret... and it's the only place where Will and me feel free and totally at ease. It's our place, and unless we invite you, we don't want you to go there... When we go to Bagatelle, you'll be staying at the Château, understand?" „...Yes... No problem...", Ludwig answered, grinning... „Fourth and last rule: You don't make fun of Franz's Swiss accent..." Hearing that, Ludwig burst out laughing and said: „...Ah shit Paul: That's not fair!" „Yes it is", Franz answered, grinning... „And if you don't obey that rule, I'll call the Gestapo, and have you arrested!" – „... And I'll tell them you're a spy...", Ludwig answered, laughing... „Bad luck, my friend! I'm covered by diplomatic immunity: There's nothing they can do against me, except send me back to Switzerland!", Franz answered, laughing... „...Too bad!", Ludwig answered, grinning... „So those are the rules...", Paul concluded... „And as long as you go by those rules, there will be no problem, and we'll have fun all summer long..." „Fine with me!", Ludwig answered... When their train stopped at the Gare de l'Est in Paris, Paul said to Ludwig: „Bienvenue à Paris Louis!" „Louis?", Ludwig asked... „Yup! We left „Ludwig" in Germany, when we crossed over to France..." „...Oh...", Ludwig answered... „Get used to it...", Paul said, laughing... When they walked out of the railway-station, Will was waiting for them. Ludwig was very happy to see his big brother, and as they hugged, Will looked at Paul and asked: „...How was your trip?" „Not so bad, under the circumstances...", Paul answered. „...Of course, we heard about Russia... We were all stunned here...", Will said... As they were driving through Paris on their way to Avenue Foch, they dropped Franz at his place, and as he left his friends, Franz said to Paul: „Thanks a lot Paul... Thanks to you, I feel much better now... You were right: That trip really helped me. Thanks again!". And, looking at Ludwig, Franz said to him: „... Have fun Ludwig during your stay... and don't forget the rules..." „See you soon, Franz! And don't worry: I swear I won't make fun of you because of your accent... Oh!... But Franz?" – „Yes?" „Do you have a French dictionary?" „Yes..." „Well... If I were you, I'd check the meaning of the word „suisse"... „Swiss? ... Well... it's someone from Switzerland..." „Yeah... But in some other French-speaking countries, it also means something else...", Ludwig answered, laughing... „What?" „I wonder if you have stripes on your back?" „... Stripes? What do you mean?" „Ahhhhh... it's for you to discover pal! If I can't make fun about your accent, at least, I'll make fun about your

255

stripes!" „Go to hell!", Franz answered, laughing... „...I'll give you a call...", Paul said to his friend... „Okay... and thanks again...", Franz answered. And as soon as he got home, Franz checked his French dictionary and realized the word „suisse" was also the name used in some parts of the world to describe a squirrel-like rodent called chipmunk... and that indeed, a chipmunk does have large white stripes on his back! „The little devil!", Franz thought to himself... „He'll pay for that joke..." Needless to say Will and Paul were laughing, too, when Ludwig told them what a „suisse" meant... „He's going to kill you...", Paul told Ludwig, laughing... „...But before he kills me, I'll have a lot of fun teasing him about his stripes...", Ludwig answered, laughing too... „Oh boy! Summer will be long...", Will sighed... When they got to Paul's mansion, Ludwig said: „...Shit, Paul! Shit! I knew you were rich... but I never thought you were THAT rich... This is not a mansion: It's a palace!" „... Don't exaggerate...", Paul answered, smiling... „...And that's where I'll be staying all summer long? I can't believe that..." „... You'll get used to it... I did!", Will answered, laughing... „...And don't forget: We'll go to Bagatelle, too...", Paul added... „I can't wait to see that place...", Ludwig answered. That night, after Ludwig had gone to his room for the night, Will and Paul found each other again in their bedroom... „...I've longed for you so much...", Will tenderly whispered into Paul's ear... „...Me too! And what's that, that I feel down here?", Paul asked, as he put his hand on the impressive bulge Will had in his pants...

„...Ohhhhhh, it feels soooo good! Keep rubbing it...", Will sighed...

SEVENTEEN
«AN UNFORSEEN EVENT»

„Ohhhh... It feels sooooo good: Keep rubbing it...", Will sighed... Will started loosening his pants, but Paul stopped him: „Let me help you with that...", he said, grinning... He went behind Will, his arms grabbing his lover from behind and holding him tightly against him. Will leaned back against Paul and felt his lover's hard cock through his pants, pressing against his butt... Paul began to unbutton Will's shirt, and when it was all unbuttoned, he slowly took the shirt off. Then, he began to kiss the back of Will's neck, while his hands ran across his lover's full round pecs, where they found his big and puffy nipples. Paul gently squeezed them, and Will began to moan softly... Paul's right hand went a bit further down, and he started to lovingly caress Will's six pack stomach... „You have such a nice, smooth chest... It's perfect!", Paul whispered in Will's ear... „I've been thinking about you since the day I left for Geneva... I love you so much... I want you, and I want you now!" „Thank God you're back! I wanked each night while you were gone, thinking about you... Now, I want you for real...", Will answered. „Yeah... I know what you mean...", Paul replied, grinning... He then slid his hands down Will's pants and unzipped it. He slid his right hand under Will's underpants and found his hard throbbing dick... When he felt the precum wetting Will's underpants, he grinned and began rubbing his hand over the wet dickhead... „Ohhhh... You're going to make me cum!", Will sighed, as he turned his head to look back at Paul... „... Oh no, you don't... Not yet! I've just started with you...", Paul answered, before he began to tenderly kiss his lover... His right hand started to feel Will's low hanging balls... so soft... so perfectly round... Will lifted his arms and reached back to stroke Paul's blond hair... Paul was still kissing Will's neck and of course, he had a raging hardon, too... „I love you Paul", Will whispered... Paul turned

257

around to face Will: He couldn't wait any longer, so he quickly removed Will's pants and underpants, then rose again and took Will into his strong arms. For a moment, he stared at his lover's beautiful face, then leaned in to him and began to kiss him passionately.

Will felt his throbbing dick hard pressed against Paul, and through his pants, he felt his lover's hard cock: Obviously, Paul was as hard as rocks... Paul's hands found their way down Will's strong back, and his right hand went to his crack. It didn't take long before he found Will's tight hole, and Will's whole body tensed then relax when Paul started to tease it with the tip of his finger... „Oh Paul... I want you to fuck me... I want you so bad...“ Paul quickly stripped off his clothes and took Will back into his arms, holding him tightly... Paul leaned in to his lover to resume kissing him, and their oozing dicks collided... Then Paul became aware of Will's hand on his cock, and as Will started to stroke their hard oozing cocks together, Paul moaned into his mouth... They stood there, kissing and touching for a few minutes, then Will said: „...I can't wait any longer... I need to feel your dick deep inside me...“ Paul grinned then he threw Will on their bed. He stared for a while at his gorgeous lover, lying on his back... Then he joined him, and kneeled between Will's big muscled legs. He then slid his hands over them, and he felt Will's muscles twitching. When he reached Will's beautiful smooth balls, he leaned into them and began kissing them then licking them. As he started to suck in Will's balls one by one Will began moaning, loving the incredible pleasure Paul was giving him... Paul moved on to suck Will's cock... But first, he began teasing it with his tongue, and after a while, he suddenly took all of it deep inside his warm mouth. Will started to breath heavily and it didn't take long before he began to make loud moans... Sensing Will was about to cum, Paul suddenly let go of his dick, and the next thing he felt was Paul kissing and licking his way to his miracle inch... „Oh Paul: You're torturing me...“, Will cried out, as he tossed back his head... Quickly, Paul stood on his knees and then put Will's smooth legs over his strong shoulders. As Will's ass was nicely elevated, Paul looked at his rosy pink and hairless hole... „Ohhhhh That's beautiful... What a nice hole you have...“, he said to Will, with a tender smile on his face... „...Yeah!... And it's all yours to take...“, Will answered, grinning... Paul lubed one of his fingers with his saliva, then slowly inserted it into Will's hole... „Ohhh... That feels so good...“, Will moaned as he lay there with his eyes closed, masturbating

258

slowly... When Paul inserted a second, then a third finger, Will shouted: „Aah, yes man! That's it... But if you keep stimulating my love spot like that, I'm warning you: I'm going to cum!" Paul grinned then removed his fingers from his lover's tight hole. He went down on him, and kissed him gently. Will opened his eyes and he whispered to Paul: „Pleassssssse! Fuck me now... give it to me...." Paul gently pushed his huge oozing dick against Will's asshole, then asked him: „Are you ready, my love?" „Shit Paul: I want you so bad... I've been ready for days now... Please..." Very gently, Paul moved forward his dick on Will's hot hole and soon, it started to slide in... „Ahhhhh... That's good Paul...", Will cried out, as he was finally getting what he wanted... Once Paul was in, he slowly started moving forward and backwards, looking straight into his lover's beautiful blue eyes... As Will resumed masturbating, Paul said: „You're so tight... It feels so good to be inside you like that..." Paul leaned down a bit, and began kissing Will while making thrusting movements with his hips, driving his hard dick deep inside his lover's chute... Then he began to move harder and faster, in and out of Will's love chute, and his breathing increased... „Yesssssss!", Will shouted out! He was now writhing on the bed with delight... and he was loving the feel of Paul's warm hard dick pushing in and out of his, Paul's big smooth balls banging against him... Paul leaned onto his lover again. Still fucking him as fast and as hard as he could, he began to kiss him ardently. As Will was wanking his cock faster and faster, he felt he was very close to cumming... He squeezed Paul's cock with his ass muscle, and his whole body started shaking and tensing up. Then he came! „....Oh... Ohhhhhhh... Paul! I'm cumming..." As Paul felt Will squeezing his cock, he shouted: „.... I'm cumming too.... I can't hold it any more..." As he climaxed, Paul became louder and louder and shouted out when his cum burst deep inside Will's love chute. And as Will ejaculated, his tight ass muscle squeezed Paul's cock even harder...

Will was gasping and shuddering as he kept shouting his young cum all over his six pack and on his chest. Some of it even flew over his head, and landed on the bed... „... I can't believe how good it feels Paul..." „... I know my love... I swear I know... That must be our best fuck!" „Yeah!", Will answered, laughing... Paul collapsed onto his beautiful lover, their strong bodies sticking together with Will's warm cum. They started kissing and laid like that for a long time. Their breathing returned to

259

normal and eventually, they fell asleep like that. The morning after, Ludwig was still sleeping and Will and Paul were having breakfast when Paul asked his lover: „....Hey... Did you see Lutz while we were away?" „Yeah... Several times..." „And... How is he doing?" „He's seing that girl... you know..." „What's her name?" „Marie...", Will answered, grinning... „Have you met her?" „Yes... at the flat, on rue Lapérouse..." „She was there?" „... She had spent the night over there...", Will answered, still grinning... „Oh! Lutz isn't losing time, is he?... Have you talked to him about her?" „...Not really... He just told me she's a „friend", that's all!" „...But he's having sex with her..." „That's obvious to me...", Will answered. „Thank God, Franz doesn't see Lutz anymore..." „Yeah! But I guess that soon, we'll have to invite Lutz for supper cause I know Ludwig wants to see him... What do we do if he wants to bring along his new girlfriend?" „Well... First: It's obvious we won't invite Lutz and Franz the same night. Second: If Lutz wants to bring her over here, I have no problem with that... do you?" „No... not at all. It's just that... you know... having Lutz over here, and not Franz..." „We'll have to get used to it...", Paul answered, with a sorrow smile on his face. „Why don't you ask him today if is free tomorrow night... He could come for supper... and tell him his girlfriend is welcome, too... That way, he won't feel uncomfortable..." „...I will", Will answered... „And what are you planning to do today?" „...I'll let Ludwig decide... but I was thinking about taking him on a sightseeing tour..." „...First, I want to see the Eiffel Tower..." a beaming Ludwig shouted, as he walked onto the veranda where Will and Paul were having breakfast... „Ah! There you are...", Paul said to him, smiling... „Did you sleep well, bro?", Will asked, smiling at his brother... „...Like a bear!... But I had problems going to sleep last night... I heard very suspicious „noises" coming from your room... if you see what I mean! I had a hardon, just thinking about what was going on there...", Ludwig answered, laughing... „L U D W I G", Will shouted, as he started blushing scarlet red... „...Oh come on, Will: Don't start acting like Mum. Do you think I don't know what you were doing? You were fucking, weren't you?", Ludwig asked, still laughing... „...I can't believe I hear my baby brother say things like that...", Will answered, showing a discomposed face... „Hey, bro: Don't be shy with me... I know you two fuck... Paul told me so... and I couldn't care less about that, if you want to know!" „PAUL!", Will shouted, looking at his lover... „What?", Paul answered, laughing... „He asked me... what was I suppose to do? Lie?" – „...You didn't have to answer his question...", Will replied! „Oh yeah? You know how your brother is! He would have harassed me non-stop, up until the moment he was satisfied with an answer...", Paul replied, laughing... „You bet!", Ludwig said, beaming... „...Oh! Shit! It's going to be a very long summer...", Will answered, discouraged... „Oh come on, bro", Ludwig cheerfully said... „I told you I don't care about what you two are doing together... and I respect both of you. I love you... and I swear, I don't want to embarrass you, Will. It's just that I'm curious, and I want to know... If I don't ask you those questions, where am I going to get the answers? From a gay prostitute? No thanks! He would think I'm interested and would offer me his services..." „...I can see from here the face you would make...", Paul said to Ludwig, laughing... „It wouldn't be nice!", Ludwig answered. „...Yeah, well... okay... ask all the questions you want, but I want you to respect our decision, if we choose not to answer some of them... And that doesn't mean you can barge into our sex life at will...", Will said to his brother... „Of course not... I told you: I respect you too much for that, bro...", Ludwig answered, with a sincere smile on his face... „...So: You want to see the Eiffel Tower?", Paul asked Ludwig, grinning... „...Yeah", Ludwig answered, beaming... „That's the first thing I want to visit... But there are so many other things I want to see..." „...Well, we'll take it one day at the time, won't we?", Paul answered, laughing... „Well, I've got to leave you two: Have fun!", Will said... „... And don't forget to ask Lutz if he's free tomorrow night for supper, huh?" „I won't...", Will answered grinning, then giving his lover a wet kiss on the mouth... right in front of Ludwig! „...What a way to start a day!", Ludwig said, laughing, watching Will kissing Paul... Will looked at his brother with a grin on his face then said:

„...I'm glad you're here, bro! And have fun today!" „Thanks Will...", Ludwig answered.

Of course that day, Paul and Ludwig went to visit the Eiffel Tower... Then many other sites... They had a lot of fun, and the fact that Paul's wallet was full of money did help, and as usual... he didn't spare it... The night after, Lutz and his new girlfriend Marie came for supper, and Ludwig was glad to see him... Marie was a nice girl... Very good-looking... and quite friendly. Will and Paul did their best to make her feel at ease... and they all enjoyed the evening... After their guests had left, and as Will and Paul were walking into their bedroom, Will closed the door behind them, then looked at the door and at the wall all around the door... „... I can't believe what I see...", Will exclaimed, laughing... „Yup!", Paul answered, grinning... The door as well as the wall had been padded, and the whole thing had been upholstered in nice blue silk, the colour of Will's eyes... „...Now I swear Ludwig won't be able to hear a thing from in here... If he gets a hardon, it won't be because of us...", Paul said, laughing... „...Can't believe it...", Will answered, grinning... Two weeks later, Paul got a call from Lutz, who wanted to know if he was free for lunch... „Sure...", Paul answered... „Will is free today, and he's taking Ludwig to Versailles for a tour of the palace, but I'm not going... Where do we meet?" They agreed on a restaurant, where they met later... „Hey", Paul said to Lutz... „You have a worried face..." „Yeah... I've just learned my brother Hans has been sent to the Russian front..." „Oh... Do you know where he is?" „No... He's not allowed to tell. All I know is that he's serving under the command of none other than Generalfeldmarschall von Rundstedt, Will's uncle... „Does Will know about that?" „... No... Not yet... I just learned about that this morning... von Rundstedt was promoted to Field Marshal last year, and I learned he's now the commander of army group South... All I know is that army Group South is now fighting deep inside Ukraine, and I've been told their next objective is to take Kyiv. So necessarily, that's where Hans is fighting..." „I hope he's fine... He's a nice guy.. and I hope he'll be alright..." „Thanks Paul! I hope so, too. (...) But if I wanted to see you, it's not cause I wanted to talk about that..." – „Oh?" „...No... You see... (...)" „...What?" „(.......)" „...Come on, Lutz: Speak your mind..." „(...) Well... I wanted to know... how Franz is doing..." „Ah!", Paul answered. „... I miss him... a lot..." „Oh?" „...Oh, cut that out Paul, and tell me..." „...Well... I know he met a guy who works at the Swedish embassy... Recently, there was a party over there, and that's where he met that guy..." „... Is he in love with him?" „I don't know Lutz... I swear... All I know is that he's seeing that guy, and he seems to be happy... That's all I can tell..." „Have you met that Swedish guy?" „(...)" „Oh come on Paul... you can tell me that..." „... Well... Yes..." „How is he?" „He's a very nice guy..." „That's not what I meant... Is he good-looking?" „Oh come on, Lutz: Why do you care? You're in love with Marie now, and she's perfect for you... So please, leave Franz alone, will you?" „No, and no again!" „What do you mean „No, and no again" ?" „No, I'm not in love with

262

Marie... And no, I won't let Franz alone..." „Okay! Fine with me! Now, will you please excuse me: I've got to go...", Paul bluntly said as he rose... „...Don't leave Paul! Please! I need you...", Lutz said, sounding desperate... Hearing that, and seeing Lutz really looked very miserable, Paul slowly sat down and said: „You need me? What for?" „You didn't answer my question: Is he good-looking?" „... Why do you ask Lutz? Why?" „... To know if I still have a chance with Franz. That's why! Are you happy now?" „(...) Yes he's good-looking...", Paul answered. „... How good-looking is he?" „...Um... He's twenty-four years old... He's tall... blue eyes and has golden blond hair... You know: The Viking type... If I wasn't so much in love with Will, I would not hesitate to put my slippers under his bed...", Paul answered, grinning... „Oh Paul, please: Don't rub it in..." „...Well, you wanted to know, so... And besides: What do you mean when you say you want to know if you still have a chance with Franz? „... Do you think he's still in love with me?" „(...)" „Please, Paul!" „...I'm sure he's still in love with you, yes! But he's trying to forget you... And I don't want you to hurt him, you hear me ‚Lutz?", Paul severely said... „...I will never hurt him, Paul", Lutz replied, looking at Paul with tears in his eyes... „What's going on with you Lutz? One day, you're with Marie... and I know that, from time to time, she has spent a few nights with you and please, don't tell me you're only playing cards with her... and now, you tell me you want a second chance with Franz. Sorry! But I'm all mixed up, pal!" „...So am I..." – „What do you mean?" „I don't know, that's the problem... And you're right about Marie: Yes, we've made love... And yes, I loved it! But I'm not in love with her! When I'm with her, it's not like when I'm with Franz... I miss him... a lot... I swear Paul!" „Now calm down... Are you okay?" „...Yes..." „... Are you telling me you're in love with Franz? Is that what you're telling me?" – „(...)" „Is it too hard for you to admit it?" „...But I'm not gay..." „That's not what I'm asking you! I'm asking you if you're in love with Franz..." – „...To be in love with Franz would mean I'm gay..." „...Not necessarily... You might be bi..." „Be what?" „Bi!... as in „bisexual", you silly..." „Oh! Do you think that's possible?" „Why not?" „...All I know is that I want to see him... But I know he won't take my call, if I call him... Can you help me?" „You're my friend, Lutz, and I love you. But Franz is my friend, and I love him, too. If I help you... do you swear to me you won't hurt him? Cause if you do, I swear, I'll break your neck!" „I swear Paul! I swear to you..." „Okay. Now, next weekend, we're going to Bagatelle with Ludwig. We'll stay at La Vacherie, and Franz will be there, too... I won't say a word to Franz... but on Saturday, why don't you come... Will and I will take Ludwig for a tour of the estate, so you'll have a chance to be alone with Franz..." „...Would you do that for me?", Lutz asked, with a big smile on his face... „I've already told you in the past: I can't resist a gorgeous hunk like you..." Paul answered, laughing... „But don't make me regret it!" „I won't, Paul. And I owe you big for what you're doing..." „You owe me nothing, pal! If only you could find enough love in your heart to kiss Franz... I know he would be the happiest man in the world. So I'm crossing my fingers, and I pray that it just might happen... That's the reason why I'm doing it..." „Thanks!", Lutz answered, beaming... That night, Paul told Will everything Lutz had said... and he also told him about his plan for the next weekend at La Vacherie... „...I hope you're right... because otherwise, it's going to be a catastrophy..." „...I know. But I had to follow my gut instinct, and let it all happen...", Paul answered. „Well... I'm right there with you, so if it doesn't turn the way you hope, we'll be together to face the result..." – „...Which might be catastrophic...", Paul answered, grinning... „Yup!" „...I'll take that chance!" „Hey: I'm taking it with you!", Will answered. „Thanks!" „...When have you decided to become a procurer?", Will asked, laughing... „Go to hell!", Paul answered, laughing too...

On Friday night, Franz went to sleep over at Paul's mansion, since they had planned on leaving early for Bagatelle the morning after... As they were all having a beer, and as ludwig kept looking at Franz, grinning all the time, Franz looked at him and asked: „...What?" „Oh... I wonder how the stripes on your back are doing...", Ludwig answered, laughing... „Oh you, little rat!", Franz answered, laughing... „But you'll have a chance to check them out, since at La Vacherie, we always go around naked... „Huh?", Ludwig exclaimed, with a suspicious look on his face... „Well, we'll make an exception this time, since Ludwig will be there with us, and we'll wear shorts...", Paul answered... „But... is it true that when you're there, you're all stark naked?", Ludwig curiously asked... „...Yes it's true", Will answered, laughing... „But as Paul said, we'll wear shorts while you're there with us, don't worry..." „Oh, but I don't care... and don't change your habits on my account. As long as there is no girl around, I don't care running around naked. But if girls are allowed there... no way

I'll be naked in front of them: I would be sporting a permanent hardon... and after a while, that would hurt!" They all burst out laughing, and Will said: „As you wish... but if you want to wear shorts, feel free to do so..." „Don't tell him that, Will! I want to see him naked, so I can laugh about his small equipment-", Franz said, laughing... „Yeah?" Ludwig answered... „Well... we'll see tomorrow who's laughing last?" „Ohhhhhhh", Franz answered, laughing... Well... Franz wasn't laughing anymore the day after, when they got to La Vacherie, and he saw Ludwig naked... „...I've notice you're not laughing, Franz? What's wrong?", Ludwig asked him, laughing, showing around his equipment... „...Yeah, yeah... You win! You're pretty well endowed... Are you happy now?", Franz answered, grinning... „...You're pretty well endowed too, as I can see... And it's a pity you're gay, cause you would make a woman very happy, with the toy you have...", Ludwig answered, laughing... „...Well... I don't know about women... but I know about men though... and from what they told me, I make them pretty happy! Want to give a try?", Franz asked, laughing... „Go to hell Franz... I'll never give you a chance to touch my gorgeous body! Only women can touch me that way...", Ludwig answered, laughing... „Oh, what a pity! But anyway... you're too young for me...", Franz replied, still laughing... „Glad to hear that! But you know... If you know a nice girl at your embassy... just let me know...", Ludwig said... „Sorry Ludwig: All the girls working at the embassy are as frigid as nuns..." „Too bad!" As Will was walking over to them, Ludwig heard him say: „Hey, bro! Put your shorts on... Paul and I want to take you on a tour of the estate...". Then, looking at Franz, Will said: „I guess you'll prefer to stay here, sunbathing... you've already visited the estate..." „Yeah! I'll stay here... No problem! And have fun... Oh, and Ludwig?" „What?" „... Don't try to fuck a cow: She might not like it!" „Fuck you, man!", Ludwig answered, laughing...

Once Will, Paul and Ludwig had left, Franz lied down on a transat, and he was sunbathing when he heard someone walking in his direction. He opened his eyes, then saw Lutz... „...(...) What are you doing here? They didn't tell me you were going to come...", Franz said to Lutz, sounding quite alarmed... „Take it easy, Franz... I didn't want to scare you... I just want to talk to you, that's all...", Lutz answered, with his most charming smile... Franz felt his stomach stir... He looked up at Lutz... and took time to admire his perfect features... his beautiful curly blond hair...

265

his gorgeous blue eyes... his strong shoulders. God! This guy is just perfect, Franz thought! „... Can I sit?", Lutz asked... „...Yeah, I guess..." Franz answered, feeling a bit uneasy about the fact he was laying there, naked, with an all dressed Lutz sitting right next to him... They stood like that for a while... not saying a word... just looking at the lake... „...You said you wanted to talk to me?", Franz asked after a while, looking at Lutz... „Yeah... I mean..." „...(...)... Well: I'm here!", Franz said. „(......)" „...Come on Lutz: It can't be that bad... what is it you want to tell me that is so hard for you to say?" Lutz kept looking at his feet... not saying a word... Franz could sense he was very nervous... „Okay Lutz... Look: I'm going for a swim now... and when I'm back, you better tell me what you want to say to me cause otherwise, I'm leaving you here, and I'll walk over to the Chāteau..." Franz slowly rose, then started to walk to the lake... The water was warm, and Franz started to relax. And since he didn't know how to swim, he didn't go too far into the water: He made sure he had water up to his shoulders, but never more than that... He was moving around in the water when suddenly, he fell into a large hole... He started to panic, and tried his best to keep his head out of the water... but the more he was panicking, the more he was going down into the deep water... and he was not able to cry for help or anything like that: Because of fear, he had just lost his voice! All the while, Lutz was sitting on his transat, looking at Franz... He smiled, when he saw Franz agitate his arms up over his head... Then he remembered Franz didn't know how to swim... He rose, walked nearer to the lake and shouted: „Are you alright Franz?" He got no answer... and he couldn't see Franz anymore... Realizing what was going on, he quickly took his shoes off, than ran into the water... „Oh my God", he shouted..."NO!"

266

EIGHTEEN
«DON'T DIE ON ME NOW!»

Realizing what was going on, Lutz quickly took his shoes off, then ran into the lake... „Oh my God!", he shouted... „No"! In no time, he reached the exact spot where he had last seen Franz and dived under the water, where he found him seconds later... Franz had simply foundered and had slipped into unconsciousness. Now, he was slowly drowning. Lutz grabbed him by the waist and pulled him out of the water as fast as he could. Then he took him into his arms, and ran out of the water to the shore, where he laid him down. As tears appeared on Lutz's face, he looked at Franz and shouted:

„Are you alright? Please... say something..." Franz didn't answerer: In fact, he was no longer breathing! Tears were running down Lutz's eyes as he looked at the unresponsive Franz... „NO.... Don't leave me! Come back..." Then Lutz leaned on Franz, tilted his head backward, closed his nose with one hand and pushed his chin downward with his other hand to open his mouth. In no time, he had his mouth over his friend's mouth, and started to blow air into his lungs... For once, Lutz was glad he was in the Wehrmacht, where he had learned how to give artificial respiration... After two or three resuscitations, Lutz checked Franz's pulse... It was weak... but it was there... „Don't give up on me, you bastard! I love you... Fight for your life Franz... PLEASE... fight..." Lutz went back to give Franz artificial respiration and, suddenly, Franz recovered respiration and began coughing... Lutz turned Franz's head to one side and shouted: „Come on Franz: Spit it out... all of it... spit it all out..." Tears were still running down Lutz's eyes and as he watched Franz regain full consciousness, he started to cry like a baby. „Don't you ever, ever do that again to me... you scared the hell out of me... you bastard... I love you so much! I don't want to lose you! Do you hear me, damn you?" „.... I... I didn't do that on purpose you know...", Franz finally replied... „SHIT! ... I know you didn't...", Lutz answered... Franz looked up at Lutz, who was still kneeling close to him, and he whipped out a few tears from Lutz's face... With a grin on his face, Franz said: „... I guess you were really scared... To go as far as to tell me you love me, I mean... But thanks anyway... And thanks, Lutz, for saving my life..." „...If I told you I love you, it's cause I do, Franz... That's the reason why I came here today: To tell you that..." Lutz leaned again over Franz, and their lips lightly touched. „... I do love you, Franz! It took me a long time to realize it... or to admit it to myself... but I love you... and I don't want to lose you... ever... you hear me? I guess it's time for me to accept me for who I am..." An awkward moment of silence followed, but then Franz decided to break it, as he said: „...But you're not gay..." Lutz grinned, then looked Franz straight in the eyes and answered: „...I know... I guess that makes me bi, doesn't it?" Franz got up from where he was lying and sat next to Lutz. For a moment they just looked at each other. Franz couldn't believe what he was hearing... Then he said: „...Am I dreaming, or what?" Lutz smiled at him and answered: „...I'm not afraid any more to tell you I love you, Franz... cause that's the truth!" Then Lutz moved to Franz, and their lips touched, then froze for a moment. Lutz's lips were so soft and warm... Their touch made Franz shiver... It was amazing, Franz thought! So he decided to let Lutz do his magic... Lutz gently pushed Franz down, and lay on top of him. When he started to kiss Franz passionately, Franz felt his cock hardning, hard pressed against Lutz's wet pants... „I love you, man...", Lutz later whispered into Franz's hear... „Do you still love me?" – „...More than you can ever imagine...", Franz answered, with tears in his eyes... „... Don't cry Franz... I'm here with you... I'm here now... I'm not going anywhere..."Franz's hands slid down over Lutz's back. As Lutz raised his strong body a bit, Franz moved his hands in front of Lutz and began to feel his chest through his wet shirt. He started to unbutton the shirt and pulled it over Lutz's head. Lutz's skin was soft and smooth as a baby's. Franz looked at his full round pecs and at his beautiful nipples... He gently squeezed them and smiled when he heard Lutz moan softly... Franz licked them carefuly and then lightly sucked each one of them... Franz slid his hands over Lutz's six pack stomach and, looking Lutz straight in the eyes, he said: „... You're so beautiful, Lutz... You're gorgeous! I can't believe you're here with me..." „I'm all yours, Franz...

Will you take me back? Please..." „... I'm all yours, too, you know that! I'm so in love with you Lutz... This is too good to be true..." „No, it's not..." Lutz quickly raised, took off his wet pants and underpants, and went back to lay on top of Franz... Lutz ground his crotch into Franz's, and within seconds, he felt his dick stiffen... Franz's arms were firmly wrapped around Lutz's upper back... Lutz moved his head towards Franz's, and his full lips touched Franz's. „...Please, Lutz: Kiss me!" Franz whispered, his lips pressing firmly against Lutz's... The tip of Lutz's tongue poked Franz's lips until he parted them. Franz lowered his arms on Lutz's back, and he encompassed his ass globes. Lutz continued grinding his crotch into Franz's, and stuck his tongue inside his lover's mouth. Franz shuddered when he felt the tip of Lutz's tongue touch the roof of his mouth. Then, Franz's tongue touched Lutz's, and they sealed their lips simultaneously... Their tongues swirled before they dueled, and their kiss intensified. Their cocks throbbed. Franz locked his arms around Lutz's strong shoulders, and hold him tight... not wanting their kiss to come to a close... Lutz and Franz were gasping, and by now, their dicks were oozing like hell... Like all great things, their kiss finally came to an end and, as Franz opened his eyes, he said: „...Fuck me, Lutz... please... I want to feel you deep inside me... please..." Lutz looked into Franz's deep blue eyes, and tenderly smiled to him... „This time Franz, I won't have sex with you: I'll make love to you..." Franz smiled back to his lover, and answered: „...Please, make love to me..."

Lutz kneeled down and shoved Franz's legs apart, then stood on his knees in the middle of them. As he was admiring Franz's big oozing dick, Lutz said, with a grin on his face: „... When have you decided to shave your dick?" „...Oh! A while ago... I just love the feeling of being hairless... I got the idea when I saw Will and Paul... I think it's sexy. What do you think?" „I think you look fantastic! And you sure are sexy!" While saying that, Lutz took Franz dick in his right hand, and gently jacked it... „...Ohhhhh! That feels so good...", Franz moaned... Lutz completely squatted in front of Franz, and pressed his lips into his navel, before he kissed his crotch, lowering his head. He then began to slowly lick all around Franz's hairless dick, and Franz cried out in sheer ecstasy when Lutz took his swollen knob into his warm mouth... Franz's precum was flowing generously, and Lutz softly moaned, slowly tasting his lover's sweet nectar... Then, Lutz went to kiss Franz's smooth balls, and Franz

269

groaned when Lutz began sucking his nut sacs... „...Oh! Lutz... Ohhhhh!" „...Please, Franz: Kneel on all fours, will you?" „...With pleasure", Franz answered, grinning... As Franz did as asked, Lutz kneeled down behind him and pushed his face into his lover's ass crack. He just loved that big round muscular ass, and Franz moaned when he felt Lutz's slippery tongue and hot lips attacking his asshole. Lutz began to tongue bath Franz's asshole and, with his hands, he parted his lover's tight compact ass cheeks, to have better access to his warm hole. As he started to tongue fuck his lover, Lutz grinned, hearing him moan... With his right hand, Lutz went around Franz's waist, and found his oozing dick. He wrapped his fist around his hard prick, and Franz cried out when Lutz squeezed his oozing knob. Then Lutz began to slowly masturbate his lover, still fucking him with his hot tongue... „I'm in heaven!", Franz cried out... „I won't last long... I warn you... I'm going to cum..." – „Un-Huh!", Lutz answered... Lutz squeezed Franz's cock a few times with his slippery hand, and Franz became louder and louder, then shouted out, when his cum burst onto Lutz's hand... „Ahhhh! Shit!... I love you, Lutz... I love you!" Franz had never felt so good in his life... and this was his best orgasm... and it lasted for what seemed like hours... When his orgasm started to subside, Lutz let go of his dick and used his lover's cum to lub his own dick as well as his Franz's pink and hairless asshole... „Yeah!... Fuck me! Fuck me now...", Franz shouted out. „God!... I love that feeling...", he cried out..."Push your dick all the way in, Lutz... Please! Don't keep me waiting...". Lutz's big dick went in slowly, and once he had fully penetrated his lover, he laid down on top of him, and started thrusting, rhythmically... „Aah! YES!" Lutz cried out... Franz felt so warm and fitted Lutz so perfectly... „I love you Franz! I love you, do you hear me? I LOVE YOU"... Before long, Lutz's hands were all over his lover's body... his nipples... his firm pecs... Then, Lutz took Franz's big cock in his hand and grinned, realizing Franz's dick was still as hard as rock, even though he had ejaculated only moments before... Lutz started jacking him while thrusting his dick harder and faster in and out of his tight ass chute, stimulating his lover's walnut with each thrust of his dick... „...That's it, Lutz! Ohhhhhh.... Keep doing that..." Lutz could feel Franz squeezing his cock from time to time, using his ass muscle, and he kept moaning as he worked his hips back and forth... „More, Lutz... more! Don't stop! I think you're going to make me cum... are you about to cum, Lutz?" „I've been

270

so close three times Franz... are you ready to cum?", Lutz asked, gasping... „Yesssssss... I'm going to cum right now..." "Me too, Franz... Ohhhhhh Franz! Oh! My God!...", Lutz cried out... „God! I can feel you cumming inside me... It feels so good..."... Franz rocketed the fastest trio cum squirts right past Lutz's hand... and he watched them splashed on the grass... Lutz was groaning, slowly moving his hips back and forth, feeling his last rope of cum oozing out of his dick deeply inside Franz's hot ass... „...Shit, Franz! Thas was sooooo good!" „Hell yeah!"

Will you be surprised to learn it was the moment Will, Paul and Ludwig choose to come back to La Vacherie and, as they were walking towards the lake, they saw Lutz fucking Franz as hard and as fast as he could... When they saw what was going on on the shore, Paul told the other two: „...Keep quiet... and let's get the hell out of here..." „Hey!", Ludwig said... „Isn't that Lutz with Franz?" „Yeah!... come on guys...", Will answered... „No way: I want to see what's going on...", Ludwig replied... „Don't tell me I have a voyeur as a brother! Move your ass, bro! And let's go...", Will said, grinning... „...party pooper!", Ludwig answered... „Yeah!", Will answered, as the three of them began to silently walk away from the lake... Lutz and Franz never realized they had spectators... and as their orgasm subsided, Lutz's dick slowly made it's way out of Franz's hot asshole... Franz turned and laid down on his back on the grass, as Lutz laid down on him. Franz firmly wrapped his arms around Lutz's upper back... For a moment, they just looked at each other. Then, Lutz said: „It feels so good, telling you how much I love you! I've missed you so much, Franz... I was no longer able to go on without you..." „It's the happiest day of my life: I swear!", Franz answered, with a big smile on his face. „I believe you... It's the same for me..." Lutz leaned onto Franz, and started kissing his lover passionately for what seemed like hours... After their lips had parted, Franz looked at his blue-eyed lover and said: „May I ask you a question, Lutz? You don't have to answer me if you don't feel like it..." – „Sure: Go ahead..." „Did you make love with her?" „No, Franz! I had sex with her... that's all! I've never been in love with her..." „Oh!... and... did you do it ... more than once?" „Yes..." „Oh!... and did you like it?" „Yes... Yes I did! But it's not like making love with you, Franz... Not at all..." „(...)" „But yes... I liked having sex with her..." „What will happen now?" „Nothing, Franz. Last night, I talked to her, and told her I wasn't in love with her... and so I broke up with her..." –

271

„What did she say?" „Oh... I guess she was sad... but in the end, she thanked me for being honest with her..." „You were!" „Yes. And my turn now: Did you make love with that Swedish guy?" „...How come you know about him?" „...I'll tell you later. Please, answer my question..." „...Same as you: No, I didn't make love with him... But we had sex... a few times..." „...Was he good?" „Oh come on, Lutz! Why do you want to know?", Franz answered, laughing... „...Because I'm jealous... and I want to know...", Lutz answered, grinning... „Poor Lutz... You've got no reason to be jealous... I've never been in love with him. But he's a nice guy, and yes: He was good! But not as good as you. Are you happy now, silly..." „What are you going to tell him?" „What?" „...Well, now that you're moving in with me on rue Lapérouse..." „...I'm moving where?" „Oh! Did I forget to tell you? As soon as we're back in Paris, you're moving in with me...", Lutz answered, laughing... „...Shit! You're moving fast..." „Yeah! I've waited too long already..." „We'll have to ask Paul, to see if it's okay with him..." „Oh... I don't think he'll mind, quite the contrary... If I'm here today, it's thanks to him..." „Huh?" „Yeah... I met him the other day, and we had dinner... I asked him about you, but he did not want to tell me much... Obviously, he was trying to protect you, and he seriously warned me not to hurt you..." „...That's Paul...", Franz said, grinning... „Yeah! Anyway... I had to tell him I was in love with you and that I wanted to make up with you before he finally accepted to tell me a few things... That's when I learned about your Swedish friend... and I was so jealous, hearing about him..." „...Poor Lutz!" „...Don't laugh! (...) Anyway, I told Paul I needed his help so I could meet with you. At first, he refused... But in the end, when he realized I was sincere, he accepted to help, warning me that if I did anything to hurt you in any way, he would smash my face..." „He's my best friend, you know... And I know he loves you, too..." „...I know... And that's what he told me... That he would smash my face, even though he loves me, and even if it would hurt him doing so...", Lutz answered, laughing... „He's one of a kind, you know... I will do anything to help him, if he ever needs me...", Franz replied. „...Me too... I swear..." „Now... If I move in with you..." „What do you mean „IF"..." „...Okay... I'm going to move in with you, but you know... I make a good salary, working at the embassy... And I intend to pay the rent to Paul... I don't want him to pay for us..." „... I can't pay my fair share... Not with the meagre allowance I receive from the army...", Lutz sadly answered... „...I know... But I'll pay Paul my half of the rent... I know Paul wants to help you... and that's alright with me... But I don't want him to pay for me when I can pay my fair share..." „Okay! Fine with me...But... ah...Will you talk to your Swedish friend?" „As soon as we get back to Paris, I will", Franz answered, grinning... „Give me a kiss, my love..." They tenderly kissed, then Lutz said: „Let's go into the lake, and wash ourselves..." „...Are you crazy or what? I'm not going back into... that... thing..." „...Oh yes, you are! Otherwise, you'll be scared of water for the rest of your life! Now, I'll be holding your hand all the time... and I swear we won't go deep... We'll stay in shallow water... Don't you trust me?" „...You've already saved my life: Of course, I trust you...", Franz answered, grinning...

They walked into the lake together, Franz holding tight to Lutz firm hand. After they had washed and cleaned, they walked back to the pavillon. Seconds later, Will, Paul and Ludwig got there too... Franz told his friends what had happened... and that he had nearly drowned. He explained everything, then he told them he Lutz had had a good... talk... and that they were back together... „A good talk?", Ludwig said, laughing... „I'd rather say a good fuck, yeah!" „... OH! YOU!..." Will said, looking at his brother with a menacing face... Then, turning to Franz and Lutz, he said: „Sorry guys... We were coming back to La Vacherie when we saw you on the shore... you know... and when we saw you were... kind of busy... we quickly walked away... and this clown over here didn't see much of what was going on..." „Yeah! Because of you! I wanted to watch... but those two refused...", Ludwig said, grinning... „Am I the only one who's straight around here, or what?", he asked, laughing... „Hey pal... I'm bi, if you care to know..." Lutz answered, laughing... „And I couldn't care less about that... does it bother you?" „No... I don't give a shit about that...", Ludwig answered. „Nevertheless... I'm curious... and I want to know... well... How it feels like... you know... to fuck like that..." „...Yeah... I can see that you're curious...", Lutz answered, laughing and looking at Ludwig's half-hard dick... „And if you keep talking about that... you'll get a very impressive hardon, from what I can see..." Ludwig was now going red in the face... „...Oh come on bro... Don't worry about that: We all understand. And no, it doesn't mean you're gay cause you're having a hardon in front of us! And if you ever want to wank, go inside and wank: We don't care. We all love to wank, so... But that doesn't give you the right to barge into our sex life, do you understand? I've already told you that... Wank all you want... eat your cum... play with your love spot all you want... ask all the questions you want... but don't spy on us...", Will said to his brother... „Okay Will... I won't! (...) But... what's that, my „Love spot"...? „Oh... don't worry... Franz will tell you!", Lutz answered, laughing his heart out... „I guess it's his turn to pass on the knowledge..." „Yup!", Will answered, laughing, looking at a stunned Franz! „...Now guys, I don't know about you, but I'm starving... Why don't we bring the table outside on the veranda, and have lunch? What do you think?", Paul asked... „... Great idea...", they all answered... „... And with all the physical activities you had... I guess that must work out quite an appetite...", Ludwig said, laughing... looking at Franz and Lutz... „Hey bastard! Why don't you go over there and jerk-off for a while... That will cool down your hormones a bit...", Franz replied, laughing, looking back at Ludwig... „...Yeah! And I bet you would like to give me a hand with that, wouldn't you? I know you long for my hot, gorgeous and sexy body...", Ludwig answered, laughing his heart out... „Sorry kiddo!", Franz answered... „You may have a very nice body and a big dick... but I prefer grown and experienced men like Lutz here... Besides, if you keep teasing me about that, or about the „stripes" on my back... you can forget about me telling you about your „love spot"..." „Okay, okay... But if I stop, do you swear you'll tell me?" „...Yes, I do!", Franz answered, grinning, savouring his victory over Ludwig... „Okay then. I'll stop teasing you..." „Fine!" „Now, guys... let's have lunch... and give me a hand with the table...", Paul said. And looking at Ludwig, Paul then said: „And you... go wank... so after we can have lunch in peace!" They all started laughing, even Ludwig... who took his big dick in his hand and began to act as if he was going to jerk-off right then and there... „...Oh come on Ludwig: If you cum... please, don't come on me!", Franz said, laughing... Then, seeing Ludwig was about to tease him again, Franz asked him: „Were you about to tease me again by any chance?" Ludwig burst out laughing and answered: „...I didn't do it, though..." „And what the hell were you about to say?" „...That if I was to cum all over you, you would probably love it... and eat my cum... But I didn't say it. I didn't!" – „Better you didn't"... Franz answered, laughing. „Now, let go of your dick, go wash your hands and let's have lunch... And no Ludwig: I don't

274

want to lick your hands!" „Gosh! Too bad I didn't think of that one before you did!", Ludwig answered, laughing...

Later that day, Franz was laying down on his transat, sunbathing, reading a book, when Ludwig moved a chair right next to him, and started to stare at him, with an innocent smile on his face... „Why the fuck are you staring at me like that?", Franz asked him... „I'm waiting for my lesson...", Ludwig answered, laughing... „Ah, shit! I knew you would keep bugging me about that..." – „Hey! It's not my fault... I'm just a curious guy..." – „Yeah... Well, the curious guy will have to wait..." „As you wish... but I'll keep staring at you until you tell me..." „Okay, okay... Your love spot is a gland you have... that all men have... It's your prostate. And it starts working when you're arisen.... and then, if you start playing with it, if it's stimulated by something... like a finger or a dick... well... it gives you a lot of pleasure! Now, are you happy?" „No...", Ludwig answered... „What do you mean by NO...?" „... Where the hell am I going to find it?", Ludwig replied... „...In your ass! Now, bug off..." „You're kidding me... Where in my ass?" „It's for you to find out...", Franz answered, grinning... „Show me!" „Oh no! That's not part of the deal!" „Come on, Franz... be a pal!", Ludwig said, pleading... „NO! If I were to do that, I know you... you wouldn't stop teasing me about that... and about your „HOT", „GORGEOUS", „FANTASTIC" and „SUPERB" body... No way!" „...You forgot to mention „SEXY"...", Ludwig said, laughing... „... YOU SEE!!! You just can't stop teasing me..." „Okay, okay... I SWEAR I'll stop teasing you for good, and I'll get off your back for good, if you show me!" – „Oh come on, Ludwig... Leave me alone!" „PLEASE, Franz..." „(...) Okay... but later... and in the meantime, ask Will for some lube..." „For what?" „Some lube, stupid! I'm sure he has some..." When Ludwig left, Franz was glad to be left alone, and went back to the book he had been reading... But his peace was short lived... „...Here!" Ludwig said to him, minutes later... „Look at what I have" Franz looked up and saw Ludwig smiling at him, holding a bottle of lotion in his right hand... „Ah Shit! How come you're back so soon?" „...The sooner you'll show me... The sooner I'll get off your back", Ludwig answered, laughing... „You swear you'll keep your promise?" „I SWEAR!!!" „Okay... Let's go inside the pavillon. I'm certainly not doing it here in the open!" „Fine with me!", Ludwig answered, with a satisfied smile on his face. As they were walking to the pavillon and came across Will, Paul and Lutz, a beaming

275

Ludwig said to them: „Franz is going to show me..." The three friends started laughing and looked at Franz, who was showing a very discouraged face... „...At least, I'll have him off my back after that...", Franz said to his friends, with a resigned smile on his face... „...Come on Franz... Move your fany...", Ludwig shouted... „Yeah! You'll see in a minute what I'll do to yours...", Franz answered, grinning...

NINETEEN
«AN EXTRAORDINARY SUMMER»

„What do we do now?", Ludwig asked Franz, as soon as they had walked inside the pavillon... „... Get on all fours..." „Huh?" „... Do you want me to show you or not?", Franz impatiently asked... „Okay, okay... but you won't put your dick up my ass, huh?" „...No! Don't worry... I won't give you that pleasure!", Franz answered, grinning... „Now, spread your legs a bit, so I have easy access to your asshole..." – „Will it hurt?" „At first, it will... just a bit... but you'll get used to it, and then you'll love it. Just relax, will you? (...) Now, start wanking..." „Huh?" „...Look ,Ludwig: As soon as I'll find your love spot, you'll get a hardon, whether you want it or not... so better make the best out of it..." „...You swear you won't tell the others you saw me wank?" „...As long as you keep your promise and you get off my back, I swear to you that I won't tell anyone..." „Okay!" „...Here: Put some lotion on your dick... You're going to love the feeling...", Franz said, grinning... As Ludwig did as he had been told, Franz kneeled down behind him and parted his young friend's compact ass cheeks... „...Nice ass you have... Too bad you're not gay: Lots of guys would love to have fun with you...", Franz said, grinning... „Yeah! Well, you're the only guy who will ever have the chance to look at it...", Ludwig answered. „...Ready?" „Yeah!" Franz lubed his fingers well, then started to smear some lotion all over Ludwig's hairless asshole... „Okay now: Start wanking your dick...", Franz said to him. With his right hand, Ludwig started to slowly bob on his prick and seconds later, he felt Franz push against his

rosebud with his index finger... „...Oh! It hurts...", Ludwig shouted... „I know... It's your ass ring... We'll give it a chance to get used to my finger... Just relax, will you?" „Okay" (...) „Now... How does it feel?" „It doesn't hurt anymore..." „Okay" Franz slowly pushed his index finger

277

deeper inside Ludwig's chute and he heard his young friend moan when he first hit his love spot with the tip of his finger... „Ah shit!...", Ludwig shouted... „That feels good... What did you do?" I hit your love spot, that's all! Now you know where it is... So that's it: I'm done!" „...Are you kidding? You're going to finish what you've started, won't you?" Ludwig asked... „Huh?" „...Hell! I'm oozing so much... I can't believe it... Don't leave me like that... Let's finish the job... and you can wank, too, if you want... I don't care..." Franz grinned, hearing that... He had been Ludwig's age, and knew how important your first sexual experience is... „...Okay Ludwig... but only this time..." „Yeah! And keep your mouth shut about it..." Franz smeared some lotion on his big hard dick, and started jerking it off, while playing with his finger deep inside Ludwig's asshole... As Ludwig started groaning and moaning, Franz inserted a second finger, then a third... „Shit Franz... That's incredible...", Ludwig shouted... „I know", Franz answered, laughing... Franz decided to stop wanking his dick, and with his free hand, he took hold of Ludwig's dangling smooth balls, squeezing and twitching them... „Oh my God! Oh my God!", Ludwig cried out... „Yeah!", Franz replied... „I take it you like that..." „...I love it...", Ludwig groaned... „I'm going to cum... Oh shit! It feels so good... I'm going to cum..." Franz suddenly felt Ludwig's ass muscle squeez his fingers, and he pushed them deep inside his young friend's love chute... „Ahhhhhh", Ludwig cried out, before he began to fire torrents of cum... He orgasmed for what seemed like hours... Franz let go of Ludwig's balls and went back to wank his own oozing dick: With his well lubbed hand, he bobbed faster and faster on it, and it didn't take long before he began to shoot his jizz all over the floor...After a few seconds, he slowly removed his fingers from Ludwig's asshole, and he smiled when he heard his young friend moan... „...Thanks, Franz: You're a real pal! I've never cum like that before, I swear..." „...Yeah! Now, will you get off my back?" „I'll never tease you again, Franz: I swear... And I'll never forget what you did for me today..." „My pleasure!", Franz answered, laughing... „...Now look at us: We're all sweaty! Let's dive into the lake, and wash ourselves...", Ludwig said... When he turned to look at Franz, he saw fear on his friend's face... „Hey, Franz: Don't be scared! I'll hold your hand, and I'll stay with you in the water all the time. Trust me, will you?" – „...Should I?" „...You're my friend Franz: I swear you can trust me..." „Okay..." So they walked over to the lake and, as Ludwig had said,

278

he never let go of Franz, and stayed close to him all the time... As they were walking out of the lake, they saw Will, Paul and Lutz walk in their direction, smiling... „...So... Tell me: Did Franz show you?", Lutz asked Ludwig, grinning... „...Yeah! Now I know...", Ludwig answered, laughing... „Good! Now, you'll stop teasing him?" „Yup!", Ludwig answered, laughing... „And thanks again, Franz... I owe you one!" „...Just stay off my back and I'll be very happy!", Franz answered, laughing...

At the end of the weekend, as Will, Franz and Lutz had to go back to Paris, it was decided Paul and Ludwig would stay at Bagatelle for a while, since Ludwig was having a lot of fun, working on the farm with the employees and their children... A few were his own age... It was also agreed Will, Lutz and Franz would be back next weekend. One day, as Paul was at the Château, sitting at his desk, reading a report, the staff governess came in, to tell him: „Monsieur le Curé est ici pour la visite paroissiale..." „Merde! Il ne manquait plus que le Curé!", Paul replied. „Show him in...", he said. „Ah! Monsieur de Brion... How nice to see you...", the Vicar said, walking into Paul's study... „Nice to see you, too", Paul answered, with a resigned smile on his face... „Please, do sit down... I wasn't expecting

you, I'm sorry..." „Oh, but my parochial visit was announced last Sunday, at the end of the mass... but then, it's true I didn't see you there...", the Vicar answered, with a grin on his face... Paul burst out laughing and said: „... Well, Father, I'm a good Catholic and I do believe in God... but let's just say I don't like to take my bath in Holy water!" The Vicar burst out laughing, hearing that, and answered: „... You're not the only one... As long as you don't forget God loves you... The rest is not important..." – „...And I thought you were going to be mad at me cause I don't attend mass..." „Oh no! I'm not that kind of a man... If you want to come to Church, that's fine. If you don't, I respect your choice, and once in a while, I'll come to you..." Hearing that, Paul started to relax... and they began talking about the village, the estate... all kinds of things... „I went to see your new greenhouse before I came to the Château: I'm impressed...", the Vicar said... „Yes... but it's a lot of work, you know... We're growing all kind of plants in there, including coffee..." – „Yes, that's what I saw... Very clever of you..." „Well, if it works, I'll have some sent to you...", Paul answered, smiling... „I think it's your young cousin I saw working there..." „Louis? Yes... He's from Strasbourg..." „... Keep an eye

279

on him... I saw him working with Marie-Hélène over there... and I know that girl well. She's from the village... and she's... well... let's say she's precociously dangerous, if you see what I mean... She already has quite a reputation... And her father is not an easy man...“ „Who is he?“ „Charles Lagardère... He works for you on the estate...“ „Oh yes! But I'm afraid I don't know him very well...“, Paul answered. „...Yes... Well, as I said, just keep an eye on your young cousin...“ „Oh I will, Father, I will...“, Paul answered, laughing... And as the visit was coming to a close, Paul said: „... I was going through some of my grandma's financial reports the other day... and I saw that each year, she used to give your church a donation...“ „... Yes: Your grandmother was a very generous parishioner...“ „Then, I must keep up with that tradition...“, Paul said, as he took his check-book, and began to write a check... „...That's not the reason why I came to visit you, son... I didn't come to ask for your money... I came to make sure your at peace with your soul...“ „I know you didn't come to ask for money. You didn't bring the subject: I did! And don't worry about my soul... Here: Take this check... and I hope I'll have the pleasure of having you for supper one night... It's been a pleasure talking with you... and I'm glad to see you're not telling me I'll go the hell, just because I'm not too much of a church-goer...“ „...You don't have to stand in a church to talk to God: He's always with you, he created you... and he loves you!“ – „Thanks Father... I'll give you a call... so you come for supper one night...“, Paul answered, smiling... „... I would love that. And don't worry, son: I won't lecture you...“ „I know you won't...“, Paul answered, laughing...

After the Vicar had left, Paul decided to walk over to the greenhouse, and give a look to what was going on over there, with that Marie-Hélène girl... just in case... Ludwig and the girl were nowhere to be found, and no one seemed to know where they were... Paul looked around the farm, but he couldn't find them... Where the hell are they? he asked to himself... After a while, he stopped searching for them, went back to the Château and finished reading the reports he had to read. Then, he left the Château, and slowly walked over to La Vacherie, since it was a very hot day, and he wanted to take a dip into the lake... You won't be surprised to learn that when he got near the pavillon, he heard moans coming from the shore... He silently kept walking and then saw Ludwig making love to a blond girl.... right there... on the grass... Paul didn't say anything and walked back to the pavillon, where he waited for Ludwig to finish his

„job"... Later, when Paul saw Ludwig walking alone on the shore, he walked to the veranda and cleared his throat, to make his presence known... Ludwig raised his head, and was stunned to see Paul standing on the veranda, staring at him... „...Oh!...", Ludwig exclaimed... „How long have you been there?" „...Long enough to see what you were doing... Where is she?" „...She went back to the green house...", Ludwig piteously answered... „I see (...). Now, come here, and sit with me pal: We have to talk..." Ludwig slowly walked over to the veranda, knowing he was in big troubles... „...You're going to send be back to Berlin, aren't you?", he asked Paul, looking down at his feet, like a child who had been cought doing something very bad... „...Come and sit, please!", Paul calmly answered. A nude Ludwig walked to the nerest chair and sat, still looking at his bare feet... „...Look at me young man...", Paul said. Ludwig slowly raised his head and looked at Paul... „...I'm mad at you! Really MAD !!! But no, I won't send you back to Berlin... But do you know why I'm mad at you?", Paul asked... „... Cause I fucked that girl?" „...No! You're dead wrong, mister! Cause you brought her here, at La Vacherie! You broke one of our most sacred rules..." „... I made her promise she wouldn't tell..." „Yeah! Sure! You have no idea how girls are, do you? Can you imagine your sister Karin keeping such a secret to herself? Can you?" „(...)" „That's what I thought! Stop thinking with your dick once and a while... and start thinking with your head! Can you do that Ludwig?" „... I'm sorry Paul... so sorry...", Ludwig answered, with tears in his eyes... „You won't send me back to Berlin? You sure?" „... Come here, you devil, and give me a big hug!" Ludwig ran to Paul and hugged him as hard as he could... „Now, go inside and fetch us some beers...", Paul said, laughing... When Ludwig came back with two beers, he sat, gave Paul his beer, then said: „...So, you're not mad at me cause I fucked her?" „...No!", Paul answered, grinning... „But there's another thing you probably didn't think about: What's going to happen if she falls pregnant?" „Huh?" „That's what I thought! (...) If she fall's pregnant, are you ready to marry her?" „...But... I just got sixteen last month...", Ludwig answered, going pale in the face... „...I suppose your dick didn't think about that, did it? (...) Now, if you're going to fuck like an adult, and if you want to be treated as an adult, you're going to have to act and think like one! You're no longer a kid, you know..." „...What's going to happen, if she falls pregnant", a very scared Ludwig asked... „...For the moment, there's

281

nothing we can do... We'll have to wait and see... and pray! Now, I'm going to give Will a call tonight, and ask him to bring you a few rubbers..." „...Rubbers?" „...Yeah!", Paul answered, laughing... „You put them over your dick when you fuck, so you don't make the girl pregnant... I'll show you how it works... But in the meantime, PLEASE, don't fuck her! Have fun with her all you want, but don't fuck her!" „... Thanks Paul... I don't know what to say..." „Well... you can tell me now: Did you like it?" „Well... I loved it! I can't believe how good it is..." „...First time?" „For me, it was. Not for her! She told me..." „Yeah, I heard she's rather „popular"... if you see what I mean..." „I didn't know about that...", Ludwig answered, a bit annoyed... „But she's great with blow jobs..." „I'm happy for you, dude!" „I'm so glad you're not mad at me, cause I had sex with her..." „Hey pal: I love sex just as much as you do... it's just different..." „Not so different, you know: She was thrilled when I asked her to finger-fuck me...", Ludwig answered, laughing... „... You did not!", a stunned Paul answered... „You bet I did!", a beaming Ludwig answered... „Franz had taught me, remember?" „And she did it?" „Yeah! I told her how to do it, and she dit it like a pro!", Ludwig answered, laughing... „... I can see that it makes you hard, just talking about that...", Paul replied, laughing and looking down at Ludwig's hardon... „...Oups! Sorry!" „No problem, pal... go inside, have a wank, then bring us back two more beers, will you...", Paul answered, laughing... Of course, Paul later called Will and told him everything. Will was stunned... „My baby-brother...", he said. „Yeah, well he's not a baby anymore...", Paul answered. „And don't forget to bring the rubbers..." When Will, Lutz and Franz got to La Vacherie for the weekend, they all laughed, hearing from Paul what Ludwig had done... and they congratulated Ludwig for his „exploits", as they said... „Thank God, Mum and Dad can't hear me telling you I'm proud of you, cause you fucked that girl...", Will said, grinning... „...You won't tell them, will you?", a nervous Ludwig asked... „Are you crazy? They would kill me... They would think it's all my fault... that I didn't look after you...", Will answered, laughing... „Just use the rubbers, and I'll keep my mouth shut, bro..." „I will... I swear to you...", Ludwig answered, with a big smile on his face... A few days later, he wasn't smiling anymore when Paul told him Marie-Hélène's father had paid him a visit... „Oh shit! What happened?", Ludwig asked, scared like hell... „He came to see me... I was at the Château, sitting at my desk, when he came and said to me: „Your goddamn cousin raped my girl!" „What did you say?", Ludwig nervously asked... „I'll tell you how it happened: When he said that, I looked at him, and I told him to sit, and calm down..." – „... I'm telling you your cousin raped my girl, and that's all it does to you?", the man asked me... „... As far as I know, she was a very willing participant...", I answered. „... How can you say that? My poor girl... she's so upset..." „... I very much doubt that...", I said. „They must get married! Her good reputation must be saved!", the man said. „Stop that, will you! No one is getting married... and certainly not my young cousin! Now, it's a bit late for you to worry about your daughter's reputation! She already has quite a reputation around town, you know... So don't play that game with me... I'm warning you..." „What did he say?", Ludwig asked... „... He was stunned that I already knew about his daughter's reputation..." – „... Who told you?", the man asked me... „...I have my sources", I told him... „And don't think you can fool me just because I'm young: I've seen the rain fall before today! ... Now: I'm sure we can settle this „thing" like gentlemen, can't we? Maybe a check would help you to digest better?" „...I'm not that kind of a man, you know", he answered... „I'm sure you're not", I told him, grinning, while writing a check. (...) „Would this amount be sufficient?", I asked the man... „... What did he do?", Ludwig asked... „Oh", Paul answered to him... „He took the check and walked right out of my study, that's all... but before he left, I had time to tell him something... „What?", Ludwig asked... „... Don't you ever come back to me with that story, monsieur Lagardère... for not only will you be out of a job, but I'll see to it you'll never find another one around here. Do we understand each other?" „Shit", Ludwig said... „What did he say?" „He just said he would not cause us anymore troubles... That's all!" „(...) And how much did you give him?", Ludwig asked, again looking at his feet... „Stop looking at your feet like that, will you? Even if you keep looking at them like that, you won't see them grow...", Paul answered, laughing... „...How much?" „That's my business... not yours...", Paul answered. „... I want to pay you back... Not now, cause I can't. But I will, I swear..." „... That's nice, telling me that. But you'll never know how much I paid that scamp! And you owe me nothing. That will remain between you and me. And I don't want to hear about it anymore. The book is closed. Definitely closed!" When Ludwig raised his head, Paul could see tears were running out of his eyes... Ludwig then walked over to Paul, and gave him a big

283

hug... „Okay, okay... It's all over now. Dry your tears, and put a smile on your face, will you?", Paul asked him... „Thanks! That's all I can say, but I say it to you from the bottom of my heart...", Ludwig answered. „I know...", Paul answered, grinning... The rest of the summer went well and, of course, from time to time, Will had to bring back from Paris new rubbers, cause Ludwig seemed to need them in „großen Mengen", as he said... „Mein Brüderlein ist immer am Rammeln! Ein Hase! Das ist ja unglaublich!" , Will said to Paul, laughing... „Er ist ein Teenie...", Paul answered, laughing... „Yeah... Maybe... But he will find it hard to go back to Berlin...", Will stated... „... About that... I wonder..." „What?", Will asked. „... I don't know... He's going to be seventeen next year... Could he be forced to join the Hitler Jugend? Or the Wehrmacht?" – „(...)" „I think we should start thinking about that, don't you think, Will? If the Russian campaign isn't over by then, and if your parents are willing... he could come to Paris, and be registered at a private school here... I would gladly pay the tutition for him... Hans is already fighting on the Russian front, I wouldn't like to see Ludwig sent there too..." „... I never thought about that...", Will answered. „I guess we could talk to my parents about that idea..." „Yeah... And his French is pretty good now..." „Yeah... But don't tell him a word about the idea... because he will keep bugging us all year long about that...", Will said, grinning... „I know!", Paul answered, laughing...

At the end of August, Paul, Will and Ludwig flew to Berlin, since school was about to start, and Ludwig had to be back... Will told his parents about Paul's idea, and they said they would think about it, since they didn't want to see Ludwig being incorporated into the Hitler Jugend nor the Wehrmacht... and be sent to the Russian front... „... I'm sure I could ask Herr Funk for a military deferment in favour of Ludwig. He loves me, I think... He won't say no...", Paul said to Will's parents, laughing... „... And you know, the campaign in Russia is far from being over... They are trying to take Kiev, and it's almost September... Moscow is so far away, I don't think they will be able to take the place before winter comes...", Will's father said... „...That's what I think, too...", Will replied. „We'll let you know concerning our decision...", Will's Mum said, smiling. „Thanks." Of course, Ludwig couldn't stop thanking Will and Paul for the extraordinary summer he had spent in France, thanks to them... „I'll never forget what you did for me, guys: You're the best!", He said to Will

284

and Paul, as he hugged them... „I love you, guys... Take good care..."
„You, too, Ludwig... And don't forget: You're a grown man now, so act
accordingly...", Will said to him, grinning... „I swear I will, bro..." On their
way back to Paris, Will said to Paul: „.... I'm convinced this whole thing in
Russia will turn sour... So don't wait Paul, and start asking Herr Funk for
a military deferment in Ludwig's favour... Let's not wait until it's too
late..." „Count on me!", Paul answered, smiling... It didn't take long for
Paul to send Herr Funk his „special" request for a deferment, along with
a generous „donation" to help „the cause" and a big crate full of Dom
Pérignon bottles... The reply came at the end of November: Starting July
1942, a three years military deferment would be granted to Ludwig, as
long as he could prove he was studying in France the whole time... As
soon as Will and Paul got the reply, Paul made a few calls, and in no time,
but without him knowing it, Ludwig was registered with one of the best
private colleges in Paris, starting September first, 1942! The proof of
registration was sent to the Wehrmacht, and the official deferment papers
were received soon after... „Thank God!", Will said... „And thanks to you,
Paul... You didn't have to, but once again, you've proved your love to
me..." „Hey... I know my baby brother is safe in New York! So now, we'll
make sure Ludwig is safe here, in Paris..." „... And from what I've heard,
life is far from being easy at the moment on the Russian front. I've been
told they're freezing over there... and Moscow hasn't been taken yet..."
„...At least, we know Hans is in the South... Let's hope they are not
freezing there, too..." – „Yeah!", Will answered. A few days later, on
Sunday December 7th, Paul ran upstairs to wake Will... Telling him to get
his ass off the bed and get downstairs, to listen to the radio: „You won't
believe me, even if I tell you... So come, and listen for yourself...", Paul
said to him. „What's going on?", Will answered, annoyed... „There was
an announcement minutes ago... The Americans were attacked at Pearl
Arbour..." – „WHAT? (...) Where the hell is that? And attacked by
whom?", Will asked, stunned... „... Come downstairs, and listen to the
radio..." „... This is not possible! I mean... Who would be crazy enough to
attack America? (...) You must be wrong!", Will answered. They ran
downstairs and started listening to the radio... Then, there was an
announcement... They didn't know it yet, but their lives were about to
change... Again!

TO BE CONTINUED

As Paul's life intertwines with the enigmatic Will in the heart of occupied Paris, tensions rise and secrets unfold. The second book marks a turning point where loyalty, love, and survival are tested like never before. Paul faces an impossible choice that could change everything he knows about friendship and betrayal. Meanwhile, Will's mask of duty begins to crack, revealing a vulnerability that could jeopardize both their futures. As whispers of resistance grow louder and danger closes in from all sides, the stakes are higher than ever. Will the lovers defy the odds and find solace in their connection, or will the unforgiving world around them tear them apart?

Dive into the second part where forbidden passion meets peril, and trust becomes the ultimate weapon in a city on the brink of collapse. The continuation promises heart-stopping moments, daring escapes, and a bond that challenges the boundaries of loyalty and desire:

Olivier Bernard

Crossing Fates
Gay Love in Freedom Beyond Loss and Grief

In the last part of the trilogy, Jack, the first-person narrator, invites readers to join him on an emotional journey in Martinique. At 15 years old, Jack is grappling with the complexities of self-discovery, especially as he begins to understand and explore his identity as a young gay man. His growing realization and acceptance of his sexuality are central to this part of the story, and his friendship with Paul becomes a crucial source of support in navigating these challenges.

This part of the series delves into the emotional intricacies of friendship, identity, and love, highlighting the transformative power of connection and mutual support. It offers readers a deep, emotional exploration of coming-of-age in a complex, often uncertain world.

Let yourself be taken on an exciting journey filled with unexpected encounters, lived history, and personal discoveries and follow Jack to the island of Martinique:

Olivier Bernard

Crossing Shores
A Journey of Gay Love and Self-Discovery